The End of the Line

Heroes of the Line

Book 5

By

J. A. Carlton

Table of Contents

1 1

2 52

3 79

4 123

5 1299

6 23232

7 24949

8 320

9 356

10 385

11 403

12 425

13 472

14 497

15 519

16 558

17 575

18 601

19 619

GRATITUDE 635

1

---

*B*right yellow walls, glossy painted cinderblocks of the type found in most

American elementary schools and some dormitories of higher learning institutions, surrounded him. He was in a hallway and at the far end of it the wall was made of slick, marble-like cement, also coated with something glossy, but for some reason, not painted that crazy, buttercup yellow. 'God, I love that color…' the crisp green scent of Wee's aftershave filled his senses, bringing with it a warm, summer-sunny glow of tranquility.

What was important was every meaning the scent brought to him, it brought him back to this past summer, one particular, and particularly perfect day. The fine-spun polyester of the red and black plaid football blanket was soft beneath his calloused hand. The way it laid so light atop the strong springy thick leaved grass at the little rise just behind the "Welcome to Highland Park" sign; (recently re-painted on those weathered old wooden boards), was a surprising detail he suddenly knew he'd never forget. He lay back on the blanket watching the clouds go by, filled with something he was afraid to name. He and Howie Emerson, the youngest of three brothers who'd all gone to the same college, had spent the early hours of the afternoon just chilling, sucking down Zima's until their heads were spinning and their guts were ready to chuck it all back up. But finally, they were together, and they'd just moved forward in their 'friendship' to a place neither of them could, nor wanted to retreat from. He was in love, and it was the kind of love he knew would only grow stronger over the course of his life, it would nourish his soul, help him understand his place in the world and give him the strength to be the best man he could be. It would give him permission to be whole in ways he'd never thought another human being, besides his little brother Cal, (who'd known he was gay before he did), would.

In the memory of that day, even as he headed toward the third door from the last at the end of the hall, he envisioned the bright, wondrous smile on the young man's face as he came bounding out of the graffiti clad, public bathrooms, looking very much like he wanted to skip up the hill. The sight tickled Ryan, making his belly flutter and his heart skip to its own beat.

He reached the door; his hand on the knob as the Howie of his memory wafted to his knees onto the blanket beside him, then leaned over, trapping him between his arms and under the bridge of his body. His warm, faintly salty scent filled his nose as the college freshman leaned in, a grin of epic proportions stretching his mouth before he swept it tantalizingly over Ryan's upturned lips.

The lights were off, but the room smelled of sweat and something faintly metallic.

"Wee?" he whispered, not wanting to wake the younger man if he was sleeping.

The telltale sniff that usually accompanied tears moved through the darkness an instant before Ryan's hand swept on the light switch.

"No…" was all the freshman had time to choke out, but it was too late. The light was on and the man he loved stood staring at him from the door, his expression moving from open curiosity to a curiosity borne of a quickly blossoming anger.

"Jesus…" he breathed moving into the room, shutting the door behind himself, and throwing the lock. His gaze roamed over the bruised, bloodied, and broken flesh visible beneath Wee's long brown curls.

"Lemme guess, that closet fucker Mattheson…" Ryan whispered sitting beside him on the bed, reaching to the desk for a bottle of water and the box of tissues.

"Promise..." Howie's whisper trembled despite a deep strength that wrapped around him, quelling the fire right out of Ryan's need for revenge.

"No," he shook his head, taking a soggy washcloth out of Wee's hand and using it to gently start cleaning away the streaks of blood from his nose and split lip.

"Please..." Wee asked again, his arctic blue Emerson eyes, one of them looking purple due to a burst blood vessel, fixed on Ryan's gold green's, and held them captive.

"For now," the older man capitulated, cradling his best friend's jaw before Howie angled his cheek into that warm, work roughened hand then kissed it even as the first of several tears slipped from the corner of his eye. "Tell me you gave as good as you got."

"Thanks," Wee nodded, squeezing his eyes shut, pressing his face into Ryan's warmth, trying to hide his shame from the only person he knew could or would actually understand it. A second later his smile filled Ry's palm, "I dislocated his shoulder and a couple fingers."

"Good man," Ry smiled. "Nick'd be proud. I know, I know, he doesn't need to know... but he would be proud."

Wee nodded letting him sweep away another line of blood. Just because he could fight, didn't mean he took any joy in it.

"Hey," he whispered raising Howie's face up, sweeping their lips together, tasting the tear-filled gasp beneath him before a molten wave of love surged through him. "I'll take care of you," he assured just before Wee grasped him behind the head unleashing a fierce passion that told Ryan all he'd ever need to know.

He closed his eyes ready to relish the soft sensuality of the younger man's lips

3

on his, but in the darkness, the sensation never came.

Instead, there was a sound, huge, and woody and full of thunderous cracking like something giant falling over in an ancient forest. The scent that filled him was different now, earthy, musty, and burdened with the heat of something torn asunder. He tried to see, there was something important, something monumental he needed to remember, or wake up to, but he didn't want to.

Unfortunately, what he wanted didn't seem to matter as he strained to open his eyes, wondering what kind of world he'd encounter when he finally managed.

There was darkness at first, then fuzzy outlines and the vague sound of timbre weaving itself through layered susurrations too rhythmic to be elemental.

Voices? Then slowly came awareness of self, *weight, ow, fuck…ache, what… tree, can't breathe… bright, heavy, can't breathe!* Then there was a 'pop' and an ungodly, galactically catastrophic supernova of burning down his belly, *uh nuh...* Then what he was sure would be his last thought, *"Wee…".*

The sudden set of extra beats from his heart lit his chest on fire all over again. But life wasn't done with him just yet, so with a grimace on his face he moved his head toward the voices, the memory of it all coming back in a flash he wished he could ignore.

He turned his head back the other way when he realized the voices were echoing off the wall at his side.

No knowledge of where he was or who these beings might be, he spared a thought toward the demon who'd been a part of him for so long, *you still kickin' in there y'little bastard?* But there was no answer, it never answered, it didn't want anything to do with the human it'd bargained with, it only wanted the life experience and didn't care what it had to do to get it. If it had to kill, it would kill, if it had to keep the vessel alive it would keep the vessel alive. It didn't care what the vessel did; it killed, it took revenge, it loved, it ate, it eliminated, it raged, and it was soothed and the Aeshema enjoyed every moment of it all.

All around him were bodies, some laying down, some seated, but most of them being ministered to.

Those who were bustling seemed to be working to set up or settle in, he couldn't tell which for the moment.

From across the expanse, which was lit by a combination of those crazy luminous stones as well as some strategically placed light holes in the upper walls of the cave, a young Sidhe male, with his bronze hair in a single braid down his back, and matching bronze eyes, strode to him. He was favored with a warm smile before he crouched down and rested his hand on Ryan's forehead.

"Welcome back. I am grateful to say you have cost me quite a bit of my stockpile of herbals."

Ryan's smile was reflexive, his sandpaper dry tongue swept over equally dry lips, "…bet against me?" he mouthed more than actually spoke.

The Sidhe's brows furrowed, and his lips pursed, "Oh most definitely, in spite of your…unique advantage," he winked reaching out of Ryan's line of sight for a bag.

"Name?" Ryan croaked as the Elder Healer's first acolyte lifted his head and eased several drops of water into his mouth.

"I have heard them call you Ry or Ryan," he smirked without missing a beat.

A faint huff followed by a slightly more pained smile this time tilted his lips. If there was life in his body anywhere, he'd find a way to appreciate a good smart-ass comeback.

"Ahh you mean mine," the acolyte nodded understanding the human wasn't quite up to his sense of humor yet, "I am Dunkun, First Acolyte to the Elder Healer of the Fierowen." He watched Ryan's expression go blank and knew the human hadn't understood a thing he'd just said, "I am a friend. You've had a long journey back, but you must continue to rest."

"Wee?" He craned his head around looking for the man he'd pledged his life to.

Dunkun cocked his head to the side, "Your love?"

"'es," Ry nodded working hard to try and shift his position while worry creased his brows, "wh, ere?"

"He has joined the others in battle against the firdur, the Oemir bade him stand with the king."

"Uh," his voice grated again as his fingers reached toward the water skin, "..'mir?"

"Yes," Dunkun smiled, an unmistakable air of excitement behind his conspiratorial whisper, "he has returned, as he swore before his death."

It was overwhelming. Ryan rolled his head back and forth, his lips pursed, brows furrowed and pain turning his eyes down, "wh... what?"

"Much has happened since the aine haud fell, I know only that you were the most grievously wounded, apart from the boy who died."

"Died?" the word squeaked from his throat as he pushed his head into the cushion beneath it, trying to remember who was there, *were they there? No... they were... Nick went to catch Frank... boy? What boy...uh nuh... not Tommy...* breath stumbled its way out his chest.

"You must rest human, you are extraordinary but still mortal, you will be needed when the time is right..."

"Who knows?" he grunted.

"The She of the All has been with you since the aine haud..."

"Please," he grabbed the healer's arm.

"But she has left. You rest, I will bring Heru Areen."

"Deal," Ryan sighed as consciousness gave way to exhaustion leaving Dunkun to keep his word and find the queen of all Sidhe.

He drifted between times and worlds of his past for a short time before a Sidhe woman even more stunning than her daughter, seemed to glide to him.

When she sat cross-legged beside him, as if she was just another person, Ryan couldn't help but be surprised. From the moment they met their first of these people, he'd noticed they all seemed to have this 'other-worldly' aura, each of them exuding a sense they were somehow untouchable in spite of the fact they were just as corporeal as everyone else. Ilirya's wounds from the firdureen were proof enough.

"Welcome back. I am Areen, queen of the Fierowen, wife of Khazeer and mother to the She of the All. Your mate has been beside himself."

"So you sent him to war? He's a lover not a fighter," he wheezed not caring that she didn't get the reference.

"Harma meleth," she smiled with a duck of the head, before clarifying, "Frank bade him stay at the tower, we were waiting for the other rulers to arrive for a summit, he was to act as the Oemir's proxy. Semet and Tur's attack was both unanticipated and fierce.

7

How they managed to have so many vestiges so close, and so many schades as well as Nahroehn at the ready," she shook her head, "they must have had…"

"Someone…inside," he hissed while pushing himself to his side, a first step before trying to sit up. He had a feeling getting to his hands and knees was going to be a whole world of hell he couldn't fathom just yet.

Recognizing his intent, Areen rose to her knees, positioning herself at his side, ready to help steady him, or help him back down, depending on what his wounds and will would allow.

"It is possible." She acknowledged, something dark and far away in her expression gave him the shivers.

He knew it wasn't just an off-the-cuff supposition, but there was something more to it that felt like it belonged to the ages.

"Tell me… 'bout my kids. Frank alright?" he asked, his breath panting and wheezing, "Nic…atch him?"

"You must focus on your own healing right now. Harma Meleth has come to his destiny, even my daughter cannot see where that will lead."

His hand collapsed onto her shoulder, his grip, five steely talons while the other reached for and pulled on her offered arm, he rocked back, forward, then back again and finally gained the momentum to pitch forward enough, leaning almost all of his weight on her while righting his legs.

"Mmmnick?" He grunted as sweat poured down his face and over him, soaking the robe they'd dressed him in. His fingers tightened on her arm as his eyes drove into hers, "What," he pulled forward, sweat streaming now, "'bout Nick?"

THE END OF THE LINE

"He is alive," she assured, her carefully calculated response obvious in spite of the distraction caused by his physical state, "he has returned to the realm of man."

Ryan's strength seemed to drop right out of him in the span of a breath as he crashed to his hands and knees, heedless of his own pains as relief coursed through him, "...thank god." He breathed.

"Yes," she mused, distracted by whatever she was hiding from him, "better he is there." She shook her head, "I believe."

In his current position Ryan was already almost uncomfortably close to the regal female, but with her strange musing he pitched forward a handful of centimeters which brought his face within a hairs breadth of hers, their eyes painfully close, "What's wrong?"

"There will be time later..." she tried to re-direct him, but the hunter wasn't having it as a half-grunt, half-growl rolled out of his throat before he leaned back to pierce her with his gaze.

Areen sighed, cocked her head, and pursed her lips, "in Frank, the soul has found its home, Nick is... without."

Fighting a wave of foggy, fuzzy darkness, Ryan wasn't sure what he heard. The noises, voices, and assorted sounds around them ebbed and flowed, making his head pound and his heart race while his stomach tried to resist the urge to turn itself inside out. It was the first of many battles he was going to have to face.

"Without what?" he grunted, his comprehension failing.

"Without a soul," she clarified.

With her quiet declaration his arms buckled and he fell face to the floor, where he took a couple shuddering breaths and slid into darkness.

--

Nick led the way into the house, stopping short just inside the living room, his gaze moving over everything.

The blood had been cleaned up to the point he couldn't even tell where it'd been. Everything not broken had been righted, and the coffee table was crowded with food and surrounded with chairs enough for all of them.

Vahl emerged from the kitchen with a pitcher and a stack of plastic cups, "Will your friend live?" he asked as the five of them shuffled in, each one plopping into a chair, exhausted.

Frank locked the door, closed the blinds and finally the drapes, ensuring complete privacy.

"They said it looks good, but they're not sure," Nick sighed watching the others dig in as if they hadn't eaten in days. "They said if he doesn't get an infection he has a good chance."

Leaning across the chair he saved for Nick, Charles entwined his fingers in the teens, wobbling despite being seated. They'd stitched him up and sent him home with instructions to not let him sleep for at least 24 hours.

Nick draped his arm around the boys' shoulders.

Charles squeezed his hand and craned his neck up, looking into the younger boy's eyes with more than just gratitude. He knew there'd be time later to figure out what exactly this kid was, but for the moment all he knew was that his life would never be the same, because of Nick.

Dropping a brush of the lips to the boy's temple Nick asked,

"What about the body?" as he moved into the kitchen to set a pot of coffee brewing.

"The bones are burning though I fear my spell work is... less than up to the task, They will most likely require a second burning." Vahl followed him into the kitchen and stood, leaning against the door jamb, "You are the eldest, it is you who should be the keeper of the soul."

"Yeah well, I guess it didn't like the neighborhood anymore," he muttered with his back to the Sidhe, his hands pushing down on the counter and his head lowered as the coffee started brewing, filling the air with its warm, earthy scent. "Where do we go... from here?" he seemed to sing before shaking his head, "I can't think straight. I don't know what to do."

"You must rest, we all must rest while we can, otherwise we can be of no use to either world."

"You've sworn your fealty to Frank, you've kept him safe, stood by him, thanks."

From behind Vahl, who inclined his head in acknowledgment of the praise, Mickey slipped into the kitchen then turned to the Sidhe warrior.

"Hey turncoat, give us a minute willya?"

But the Sidhe looked askance at Nick before budging. If the eldest son didn't want to be alone with this half-breed child, Vahl knew it was in his best interest to defend this boy as well.

Meeting the warrior's eyes he inclined his head.

"So, what's up with the kid?" Mickey asked, a cutting edge to her voice.

"He was with us in the first line, he's got an eye for detail that'll be helpful."

Mickey nodded, "Yeah I know that, but what was *that*? You ballin' him?"

"Yes."

His blunt reply took her by surprise. That she'd tried to shock him or shame him with her own crass bluntness didn't matter.

"Really? Since when do you want someone touching you?"

"He loves me for who I am, not for who I was somewhen else."

"Love!?" she scoffed, "He's a kid! What the hell does he know about love? You and me, we have a history of ages! You can't tell me you're willing to throw that away!"

Exhausted, Nick turned his face up and met her eyes, his hand motioning her closer.

The energy of suspicion radiated from her, filling the space between them even as he opened his arms, beckoning her into them.

"I told you before, you can have anything you want from me, but you don't get to use your insecurities to bully me *or* Charles."

"Bully!?" she demanded, "I don't give two shits who you want to fuck or get fucked by…" she shook her head, steadied her breathing, and pressed her forehead to his chest for a long moment before turning her face back up and looking deep into his enigmatic expression. "Just don't throw away what we have, we've had…" she shook her head, "what we CAN have."

She swallowed hard then asked, "Do you love him?"

His brows furrowed as his finger stroked her cheek, "I'm not capable of love, not for you, not for him, not for anyone. I know he says he loves me as I am, can you say the same?"

In his arms she gasped, her mouth falling open and tears glazing her eyes as she cupped his stubbly cheek, "How can you ask me that?"

"Because I don't know."

Mickey pushed herself out of his arms then leaned in, her hands on his chest as she rose to tip toe touching their lips together. The tears slid over the rims of her eyes as she nodded and turned away, leaving him alone, slumped against the counter, his head spinning with too much to make sense of.

Several seconds, or maybe it was a multitude of minutes, later, Frank's new-ish face craned into the kitchen from the dining area doorway, followed by his body, "Nicky, c'mon eat."

But the older boy shook his head, "kinda nauseous."

"That's 'cause your gut's empty man," Harry Jr. poked his head around the entryway and tossed a green apple to Nick, "put some gas in the tank you'll feel better in no time."

However reluctantly he ripped a chunk from the apple, when its sweet tartness hit his tongue, it set his stomach roaring instantly.

"Jesus, when's the last time you ate?" Harry asked.

Nick turned and poured a cup of coffee then handed it to the younger version of his best friend, "I don't know. Would you bring this to Charles, he can't fall asleep till tomorrow night."

"Yeah sure, so what's with you and the kid anyway? Not that it's my business mind 'ya, but you know Mickey's been kinda pining for ya right?"

"He's a friend, and my lover, she and I have… things to work out before we go there," Nick answered without thinking twice as he pulled Ry's bottle of scotch from the cabinet and poured himself 3 fingers in a water glass. He slugged back a good strong mouthful of the stuff and shook his head, "and since when is any of this anybody's business?"

"Your lover?" Frank whispered, his wide surprised eyes looking deep into his big brothers' before he echoed Mickey's own question, "since when do you actually want someone touching you?"

The corner of his mouth tilted up as he rested a hand on his visibly worried little brother's shoulder, now almost level with his own, "apparently, sometimes it can be nice."

Harry's hands came up and a slightly comical look crossed his face, "I already said it wasn't my business, or anyone else's man, just sayin' the girl loves you, might not wanna count her all the way out y'know?"

"I'll take it under advisement," Nick nodded then swilled the second half of the scotch, belched, and gagged just before Frank handed over his soda.

"Thanks," Nick swigged on the can, belched again, and shook his head, "god that stuff's rank."

"Soda or scotch?" Frank asked.

"Both," he shuddered.

"Can we talk Nicky? Just you'n me?"

"Den," he nodded following as his little brother led the way, "You guys look after Charles, don't let him fall asleep alright?"

From the couch Mickey shuffled a deck of cards with Vahl

14

shifting the food to the dining table, "we're on it."

He stopped, made a point to meet her eyes and smiled, "thanks."

The faint flush and smile told him she read his gratitude correctly, he meant it, and whatever else could come between them, he openly appreciated what she was doing, the role she was playing for them, whether it be with watching over Frank, or Charles. It was also true that since coming back he hadn't given any indication he felt any other way toward her than accepting.

Still in the running, she told herself. If she had to share him with someone else, well, it certainly wasn't the first time. Whatever this future held was beyond her ability to see. In fact, since actually meeting Frank and Nick in this time line, there was almost nothing about their futures she could fathom, which was partly responsible for fueling her insecurities. *This is* not *going to be easy,* she sighed dealing the cards.

"Are you going to be able to do this?" Frank asked closing the door.

"What? Gather anyone and everyone who fights monsters and organize them to save our world? I don't know." Nick admitted then asked, "Are you going to be able to gain the confidence of and lead at least 3 Sidhe kingdoms against the living dark to keep them from breaking through over here?"

Frank plopped next to his big brother, his hands clasped between his knees as he shrugged.

Nick found both the posture and gesture reassuring in a way he hadn't realized he needed. Both of them looked so different in every physical aspect other than the eyes they were so familiar with, it was getting easier and easier by the moment to lose track of who they'd always been, to who they were each becoming.

"I don't know, I think the kingdoms are the last thing we need to worry about, there's something… deeper that's more important." Frank sighed, "did you learn anything?"

"I wasn't back long enough, we sent Mickey and Harry to get you and Vahl not long after Charles and I got here," he leaned back, "I left early this morning to dump the car and burn…" he stopped, lurching straight back up with the realization, Frank didn't know he'd killed a man, other than the pastor.

At the same time he wondered if he should tell Frank, the younger boy asked, "Burn what?"

Nick nodded, "Evidence. After you threw me out of the realm I landed in Austin."

"Texas?"

"Yeah, got into a little trouble."

"What kind of trouble?"

Nick huffed a humorless chuckle, "the, 'I killed a human piece of shit' kind of trouble, I can't tell you this Frank, if something goes sideways… the more you know, the more trouble it'd mean for you too."

"You killed someone?… else?" Frank whispered, his eyes widening as his heart tripped and his belly flipped. They both knew their destinies were about as far from a game as could be. Eventually they'd be called on to take lives to save lives, but he hadn't expected it to happen so soon.

"He was a piece of shit Frank, a guy who kidnaped, tortured, and sold kids and babies to the highest bidder… I'd do it again in a heartbeat," Nick offered.

"Did he try to kidnap you?" the littlest Emerson asked, though it was obvious in the timbre of his voice he didn't think he should've, and probably didn't really want to know.

"He tased me, thought he was gonna torture me… I shouldn't be telling you this."

Frank's belly squirmed, "Like Pigg?" he whispered.

"Worse. Pigg was a sick-o perv, but this guy was a whole other class of scum."

"Was Charles there?"

"That's where I found him, I remembered him from the vision we got from Harry."

Frank nodded, "I remember."

"Yeah, so I asked him to come here with me."

"If Charles is your lover that makes you gay now right?"

Nick's emergent smile was bright and soft with good humor as he reached over and squeezed Frank's shoulder gently, "I like being with him…"

"You mean like sex?"

"uh huh."

"But you never liked it before, anyone touching you, I know how you felt when Leanna did… what she did, and what… what… else people…" Frank's voice trembled. His breathing was shaky, and the same rose color that always tinged his cheeks when he was on the verge of crying started to blossom as he tried to make sense of the vile nature of the memories he now carried. He couldn't really understand how the person whose memories they were had changed so much he now liked something that once hurt him.

Nick took a deep breath catching his little brother's eyes, "I'm sorry you know those things, and I'm sorry you're stuck carrying all that shit around…"

"But if it hurts…"

Nick quickly shook his head, suddenly understanding Frank's confusion, "It's not like that… lemme see if I can explain this right… you know how when you have something someone else wants, and it's someone who's your friend so you don't mind sharing it?"

Frank nodded.

"But if someone stole it from you, or threatened you in order to get what you have you'd feel hurt right?"

"I got a word when Ne'Min had me,"

Nick nodded.

"'violated'. Is that the right one?" Frank asked watching his brother's expression carefully.

"Yeah," he nodded, "when someone goes through your stuff, or steals your stuff, or takes something you don't want to give them, yeah that's a violation. Remember when you were little, your first Scooby lunchbox?"

"Uh huh," Frank nodded, "when Bruce stomped on him?"

"Yeah," Nick breathed, "But it wasn't the lunch he took that hurt."

Frank nodded, "he took *Scooby* from me."

Nick nodded, "Exactly. But it's different when you *want* to share, when you want to show someone your room instead of them just going in and looking through your stuff right?"

"Yeah of course."

"Sex is the same, it's sharing something with someone who means something to you, well, that's how it's supposed to be anyway. Point is when it's with someone who's your friend, sharing feels good," Nick sighed, "does that make sense?"

Frank nodded, "I guess…but what about Amy Archer? You were all warm and soft when she kissed you goodbye…"

A glowing grin grew over the teen's face as he nodded, "yeah, I really liked that a looohhhhht too…"

"and Mickey… she wants…" Frank stopped, his face bright red, wondering if he should be talking with Nick about this, but he was curious.

While with Ilirya, he'd got a large combination of experiences from Nick which were now coupled with things he'd felt for himself, and the Oemirs. There was so much it had him so confused he couldn't figure out what was normal and what wasn't.

"Yeah," Nick nodded again, "I remember, and I hate to say it but… I get a little twitchy in my belly when I think about her, so, yeah, I'll take her up on her offer… I'm actually pretty sure I'm bi…"

"but you don't know?"

"I'm… pretty sure."

"But not for sure, for sure? How can you not know?"

19

Nick shrugged as his smile tilted to the side and turned sly, "I never even thought about dating, didn't want any part of it you know that, let alone wanting to have sex."

"But you said it was nice," Frank frowned turning his eyes from his big brother, "was it that you didn't want to cause you had all the hurt and now since I got it, the idea doesn't scare you anymore?"

If he could take all his baggage back, Nick knew he'd do it in a heartbeat. After all, he didn't spend the last four and a half years keeping his history to himself for nothing, but it was all wasted, leaving the one person who mattered most to him bogged down in a swamp of emotional gunk not his own.

On a positive note, since the memories *weren't* Frank's, and if Nick understood his little brother's gifts at all, he knew the boy simply knew facts and how *Nick* felt about them, but gratefully had none of the effects of firsthand experience.

"Sounds probably right," Nick admitted, "without my half of the soul, I don't have the feelings that went with all the garbage, so nothing to ruin anything new y'know?"

"So now you wanna have sex with Mickey too? If I have your half of the soul too, does that mean you can't feel anything?"

"I thought it would, but now I'm not sure. I know I feel some things, anger, content, physical pain, and pleasure."

"Love?"

Nick tried to probe the hollowness inside, like a tongue probing a new empty tooth socket, he didn't want to lie but he didn't want Frank to worry about so much, so he went with the one truth he knew simply had not changed, "Well," he began, "don't tell anyone," he urged.

Frank's eyes bulged and he nodded, miming locking his lips and throwing away a key.

"You're still the most important person in my life, so that *must* mean I still love *you*, so there you go…"

Frank's expression fell a little and he looked puzzled.

"What?" Nick asked.

"Why don't you want me to tell anyone? Everybody already knows you love me best, it's not like it's a secret," Frank challenged.

"I know," the older brother teased.

"So then how can you not know if you're gay or bi?"

Nick closed his eyes, a faint smile turning up the corners of his mouth as he recalled what few positive experiences he had this far, then after a minute shrugged, "Let's just say I'm sure. Does it matter to you? Does it make you ashamed or angry with me?"

Frank leaned back, a dark surprised look twisting his face, "Don't be dumb. Long as you're not liking getting hurt or being afraid, is all I care about."

Nick sighed leaning back, relieved. "You're a pretty awesome little brother y'know that?"

"I know," Frank nodded leaning back next to him. "We need a plan, we need to get the right people organized in this world in case they break through. I don't think there's enough Sidhe anymore to fight back Tur, Semet and the firdur but I think I found a starting place."

He dashed to the door, slipping into the hall, "stay here, I'll be right back."

Dizziness played with Nick's senses while he downed the last bite of his apple, then leaned back with his eyes closed. The juices mingling with the taste of scotch while the world swam in a light haze all around him.

Frank dashed to the front door where he left the pack with the book and canvas he and Vahl stole from the stronghold.

As he passed the others, all engaged in a hand of poker, a faint stream of dark gray slithered through his vision making him start upright.

He took a curiosity filled look around the room and at each of the faces there, none of whom were paying any attention to him. Mickey was explaining why four of a kind beat a full house to Vahl, while Harry and Charles had their heads together over Harry's phone, apparently watching something of interest, most likely on TikTok or YouTube. With furrowed brows he shook his head and reached down for the bag one more time, only this time when his gaze crossed the white painted wall, it seemed to disappear, as if he was looking out of a window onto a battlefield in front of him.

There were bodies strewn in numbers he could barely reconcile, many of them being swarmed by sooty streaks of dark wrapping itself around them and finding various ways to slither inside, infiltrating them.

What the hell? He wondered as cold started deep in the pit of his guts. It spread quickly outward when he realized the bodies being taken over were suddenly starting to move again. *No way…*he tried to look away, to see Vahl, Mickey, anyone, or anything other than the travesty filling his mind.

Nicky? He thought as a particular column of smoky darkness caught his attention, turning with its blunt end pointing at him, as if it knew he was there, as if it knew he was watching it, and very much as if it could see him back.

His heart leaped as it lurched off the ground, a glimpse of an almost familiar shape in the background, peering out from behind a shallow hill as it shot itself at him. Taken off guard, he stepped back and knew nothing else as his body fell to the floor.

In the den, a swatch of dark flowed through Nick's mind, so abruptly, so pervasively he bolted upright, immediately recognizing the sudden absence of his little brother's presence.

He lurched across the room and into the hall just as someone's back moved toward the front door.

"What the hell happened!" he barked pushing through the assembled group to Frank who lay on his back on the floor, obviously unconscious.

--

A tiny puff of electric green fire forced the pervasive subterranean darkness into another miniscule retreat, at the same time it emblazoned the rag tag and jagged features of the tunnels into his mind as he inched forward on a quest he wished could have been anyone else's.

The stench of death grew thicker the deeper into the Bedowen heart he ventured, it was fresher, and heavier now and no longer held the sweetness offered by the passage of ages. His heartbeat sped, thudding harder in the enormous barrel of his chest, enough so, as the pads of his paws hovered over the earthen floor he could almost feel its bits vibrate beneath them.

An instinct twitched the feather-like scales at the base of his neck just before his gaze penetrated further into the decayed heart of the corrupted land catching sight of a long, spear-like triangle laying on the floor. A tail, and it still had flesh and scales on it, but was its owner still alive?

He raised his snout, taking a sampling of the acrid air. His forked tongue poked out toward the tail, seeking evidence of life and in a flash, the faint glow of living heat took form in his brain.

In spite of his eagerness, his step slowed, unsure, in fact quivering with fear of what he would find, or how his kin would react to his presence. He even almost entertained the idea of turning around and pretending he didn't see it, but the fragment of an instant of hesitance was quickly lost as the tail rose and shifted. It swept just a hint more than a paw's worth of the silt-like granules into an eruption that shook his bones with the force of an earthquake before falling suddenly still. In another split second, the sound of a large body, straining against its woody captors came into the cups of his ears.

"Who's there?" came a dry, almost sinister whisper from the darkness up ahead.

"I've come to save the living," he whispered in return, pushing himself forward into the dark, dreading the sight he'd feared having to face for millennia.

Upon entering the area completely, Diagas stopped. He couldn't help noting the size of the body before him, encased by angry and once ferocious tree roots that had dug their way into its very flesh to feast upon its life essence.

His gaze moved up and over the entrapped body, toward the long, sagging, emaciated neck, and finally came to rest on the weary, aged face. Where once full flesh, covered in brilliant opalescent scales large as platters had hugged the bones beneath, the flesh now hung like crepe paper; empty, on the verge of lifeless. A rapid fluttering pulse was visible beneath that droopy and dry skin as wasted vessels carried whatever was left of the creature's lifeblood through it.

"Then move quickly," the voice rasped as the body pulled and twitched against its malevolent prison, as if to prove there was something inside worth saving.

Diagas, still at the rear of the ancient one looked the once great creature over, analyzing how the roots of the forests' trees had it bound, searching for a place to begin setting it free.

"How many others live?" he asked before angling his long rectangle shaped head and lifting one of his lips, exposing the first of his two-foot-long fangs and angling it with astounding precision under one of the most slender tendrils of root.

A swift twitch of his head severed the woody vein.

"None have so much as groaned in years...or maybe ages, if there is a difference," the ancient one whispered an instant before those life-draining roots around and within its body began to move, suddenly desperate to cling to its eternal free meal.

A slow rumble grew from the chest of the captive dragon as they dug deeper, slithering further into its veins while the larger ones, wrapped around its torso began to squeeze, as if to wring every possible morsel of nourishment from the once grand beast rather than let it escape.

"Buuuurrnn it!" the ancient one ground before the sounds similar to dry wood cracking under pressure presaged its torment.

A blaze of enraged helplessness burst to life in the heart of the

Green Flame Clutch's last surviving descendant as he drew breath, heedless of the questing tendrils now seeking purchase within him. He exhaled a brilliant, almost electrical arc of green over the senior dragon.

Above them the ground shook and earth fell, covering them in dust as the larger roots withdrew leaving dark empty holes in the scales and skin of the captive dragon.

That almost no blood flowed from those now vacant openings was a sign Diagas knew could not bode well for the being's survival.

--

Far to the North-west, where the green of the Bedowen gave way to a spindle of Fierowen desert betrothed to a delta at the mouth of the Akirowen, the joint in the planet shook. The only giveaway was a trickle of sand between the marsh reeds that thrived on whatever the land or sea chose to offer. When the few grains of sand settled to new positions, a marsh beetle pushed itself out of its silica burrow racing toward the green as behind it, a thread of black overtook the space it once called home, and began to grow.

--

On the western-most edge of the spine of the Dragonbow mountains the heat of the sun; all too precious with what they both now knew for certain was coming, pressed them into the last bit of stony wall keeping them from the Eastern slope. That was where they'd find the entryway to the lands of the Gargol, the Fae and so many they'd once called friends.

It's been far too long, we never should have left them to themselves after it was done, we should have done something, we should have been... more. Ilirya thought, as shame burned hot in her cheeks.

26

--

Frank! His nephew's name was stamped into his consciousness as it came back. Along with the name, came the knowledge of something seriously wrong. When awareness made its full return, he realized his weight was being pulled through his shoulders.

"Mmm?"

"Easy tiger, you passed out again, if you can go back, you might wanna," came a voice he was familiar with but somehow didn't recognize as one of his own. *Lou.*

"Don't listen to him kid, you gotta come back, best to face it all as it comes… whatever it might be," urged another he actually knew well. *Shep.*

Sensation made its way down his body and into his legs as he started pedaling them, trying to get some control. It only took a few heartbeats though it fell like an eternity, but he finally managed to hold his own weight. Now all he had to do was manage to match the speed they were moving lest one of their guards decide to prod him along with the point of his spear.

Trying to shake the wide variety of horrors swirling in his mind the eldest Emerson asked, "Where they takin' us?"

"Y'know, I plumb forgot to ask."

"Wherever they want," Shep and Lou answered together.

"Why'd you guys stay behind, you shoulda gone with the others," he grumbled.

Shep huffed, "S'not like they gave us a choice kid, they're a shit ton faster than we are, and much as we might've wanted to, it's not like we'd really leave ya to the wolves… or whatever's out there."

"Quiet!" one of their guards practically barked, poking Dylan in the shoulder with the tip of his spear, just deep enough to get the literal point across, this was no companionable outing.

"Still on the path…" He muttered almost imperceptibly then glanced at Lou, "nothing ever changes."

If there hadn't been a spear-point at his own back Lou would've stopped and stared dumbfounded at the eldest Emerson, "Tell me you didn't see this and didn't say a fucking thing!" he demanded in the angriest of tiny whispers.

Dylan's head gave an equally tiny twitch, as if trying to deny what Lou was saying. What he'd seen wasn't this exact circumstance, but now, with them both literally and figuratively on this path, he could see how it could well lead to what he'd feared from the moment he got his first vision in this world.

In his mind's eye he watched it all unfold again, his brother consumed by a swirling mass of darkness as it ruptured the flesh from him bit by bit, a dark, heavy presence just beyond his perception somehow seeming to direct it. Every particle of him flung into the air, a fine mist of color that had once been a living man, hurling itself out from inside him, literally un-making him, his still living screams reverberated with the mist out into the world to be carried on the shoulders of those who continued to live.

--

Worry far too intense for his tender years left crevasses in Nick's forehead and a deep bowing frown pulling the corners of his lips down. His eyes stayed fixed on Frank's inert form laying on the couch in the den. He was still unconscious, technically, but Nick sensed something moving deep inside him and was weighing the pros and cons of trying to find out what it was.

It wouldn't be the first time either of us has been in each other's head, but what if what's going on in there is as bad as I think it is? What if I get drawn in too? What if we both die in there and there's no one left to save the worlds? Should I or shouldn't I? C'mon shrimp, wake up! Shake off whatever's got you… it's my job to be there for him, it's what I do… I can't let him be there alone. And like throwing a light switch, the decision was made. He scooted the chair forward, arranging himself so if he fell, he'd hit the floor and not wind up smothering his shrimp-o. Next, he took a deep breath and set his fingertips onto either side of Frank's skull letting them sink in as he closed his eyes.

Bracing himself for whatever vile carnage his little brother might be struggling with, Nick's awareness sort of 'popped' into existence right next to Frank's psychic self. The two of them stood side by side. Frank's focus on a swirling, raging torrent of darkness futilely yet tirelessly throwing itself at the young man, stymied by some unseen barrier.

"Firdur," Nick *noted, recognizing it for the way it'd attacked him and Harry in the car.*

"Yep."

"It sees us?"

"Yep."

"S'this real?"

"Yep." Then Frank sighed, "Look back there, behind it."

Nick shifted his gaze and realized they were standing on the edge of the nexus of the kingdoms of the other realm. They were shrouded by greenery looking toward the Fierowen, where even from this distance they could see the tower had been under siege and sustained heavy damage. The giant crystal that capped the tower and was the strongest weapon they had against the dark had been rocked

29

from its moorings. It hung at a precarious angle over the edge of the observation platform, ready to fall at the slightest provocation.

After a moment, his eyes slid down toward the land itself, where freckles peppered the otherwise sunburnt sand. He knew they were bodies, dead soldiers from both sides whose numbers grew the closer his gaze traveled to the tower.

"Jesus Christ what the fuck?" he breathed barely able to believe what he was seeing.

Frank's answer was soft and distracted, "the summit was attacked."

"Yeah, I can see that… is this real-time?"

"I think so."

"Why can't it get you?"

Frank's gaze flitted back to the vestige, which had taken to rearing back and pummeling itself toward the youngest Emerson only to flatten out as if hitting glass; flecks of its own being casting off into the ether with each unsuccessful attempt. "No clue." He shrugged.

He turned to face Nick, "we should go back, this isn't good, but there's stuff we need to talk about, and I can't do anything about this right now."

"Dude, you're not gonna be able to do anything about this at all, it's done, all either of us can do is get enough folks together to hold the line in our world, or seal the way or something… and find some way to help this place fight it back. If this place falls it's not gonna matter what we do for our universe, how hard we seal it, it'll still wind up gone one day."

But he realized he'd lost Frank's attention. The younger boy's gaze had moved off to the left, peering deep into a finger of woods reminding Nick of where he'd had the vision of meeting Ilirya for the first time in another line; a line where she'd hidden them under a blanket of grass as the daylight hours passed. A shiver ran through him alongside a certainty of something over there meaning more to them than either he or Frank could know right now.

"You see that?" Frank whispered, flicking his head toward the same spot.

Nick leaned forward just a bit, cocking his head to the side to match Frank's posture. The change in perspective showed what his little brother was looking at. There seemed to be a tallish, pale, almost ghostly figure with long black hair clinging to a shadow. It was facing the tower, but somehow Nick knew whoever or whatever it was, knew he and Frank were there watching.

"Schade?"

Frank shook his head, "Nuh uh."

"You sure?"

The youngest Emerson turned and met his eyes, "how can you not be?" then turned back to the tower and the bodies littering the ground beneath it.

"Whaddya mean? You know what it is?"

"Yep."

Another chill ran over Nick's skin and his mouth ran dry with sudden certainty, "Oemir's ghost?"

A slow smile canted the corner of Frank's lips, but his head gave a tiny shake, and he huffed a chuckle, "no."

He drew a quick deep breath and met Nick's eyes again, this time, wholly present in the moment and the tasks awaiting each of them. "C'mon, we got a lot to do."

Both young men gave a quick jerk like snapping awake from a light doze. Their eyes met, and in a way only brothers understand, they smiled.

"What or who was that?" Nick asked.

Frank smiled shaking his head. His eyes fell to his pack and the belongings he'd left the den to get. "Good you brought 'em in!"

"Yeah so what's the big hoo hah?"

Frank handed the tome to Nick and unrolled the canvas, propping it up against the back the sofa using pillows to help keep it in place.

"When's the last time we built a fort and camped out in the living room on a Saturday and just watched cartoons?" Nick asked with a smile in his voice.

"Been a long time, maybe what… six or seven months ago? Right?"

Nick nodded, "wanna shove all this shit in the closet and just build us a fort for the night? Screw the rest of the worlds?" He was only half-serious and the look Frank threw him said he knew it. Even so, for a single instant, both boys were tempted.

"First thing after we win," Frank smiled.

"Deal, maybe make a day of it, go see a movie, grab some burgers then come back and marathon the Harry Potter's…it'll be like old times. Whaddya say?"

Nodding and smiling Frank spread the book open on the floor in front of the canvas flipping its pages until he'd opened to the center and the full double page spread of the oak, "Awesome, c'mere, take a look at this…."

"Holy shit," Nick sighed sliding down onto the floor next to him, both of them propped up on their elbows, their feet in the air.

"That's what I said!" Frank ran his hand over the picture, leading Nick's gaze toward the end closest to him, "Lookit, it looks kinda like a Chinese finger puzzle right?" he asked tracing the tree spread horizontally between the two pages, a pinup only a physics nerd could love.

"Yeah, but did you see this?" Nick asked, peering closely at one of the strands of fibers that made up the roots of the tree.

"You see it too? The DNA?"

"Kinda hard to miss when you really look at it."

"Yeah, well step back and look again," Frank suggested, watching his big brother's expression as he sat up and got a different perspective on the artwork.

"That's weird, it looks like one of those trees from Madagascar, you know, the kinda upside down ones."

Frank nodded, "Yeah but look different at it," he said angling the book in a different way.

"I dunno what you want me to see."

"Remember that show we watched that one time about how maybe wormholes to other universes might look?"

"You mean the one with the Muppet that floated around the ship?"

"Nuh uh, not that one, the science show on PBS."

An image came immediately to Nick and to his surprise it matched the drawing of the tree, he saw it now as clearly as Frank had in the fortress.

"Huh…" Nick felt his scalp begin to tingle just before he got a shiver, "why does that give me the shivers?"

"Me too but Nick, I think it's 'cause look," his fingers spread out on one end of the trunk/tube, then on the other, "count how many roots and branches…"

Nick did and felt his brows furrow and lips purse, "thirteen, just like the dots in the pendant."

Frank nodded; his young face wide open with a seriousness he shouldn't have known for at least another decade. "Do you know what it means?"

Nick gave a curt nod, "We know the roots represent each of the lines of heroes so it makes sense the dots would too… they move on the page in the pendant…"

"Lemme see." Frank leaned over, hooking his finger into the collar of Nick's shirt, and pulling it aside, "Holy crud! What happened?" he asked, fingering the divot of melted skin on the side of his big brother's neck.

"It happened when I made him put the soul from me into the pendant."

"Where is it? Is it with Cathbad?"

Nick dropped his head forward, his shaggy dirty hair obscuring his face, "Mmm."

"It's okay Nicky, we're both just doing the best we can, we're not ready, but we gotta at least pretend to be, at least in front of the others."

"Fake it till we make it?" Nick sighed while Frank nodded.

"Does that go all the way around?" he asked.

Nick sat up and leaned forward as Frank rose to his knees following the scar around the back of his neck, "Yeah."

He continued his inspection around to Nick's opposite side then pulled the shirt away and peered down the collar. "Wow," he breathed then leaned back, "you reek."

"Sorry," the elder Emerson muttered with a faint smile before pulling his shirt all the way off so Frank could see.

"It's not the first time. Duuuude…" Frank grinned poking at a splotch just above the burnt pocket of flesh in the middle of Nick's chest, "You got hair on your chest" he giggled, then poked the hole, "jeez, did it hurt?"

"Like a motherfucker."

"Does it still?"

Nick shrugged, "sometimes, depends on how I move or what I do."

"I think you're wrong Nick."

"Hmm I'm pretty sure I still know when something hurts or not."

"I don't mean that," Frank said wincing as he traced the edges of the pit then felt the depth of it. "I mean about the soul, about why it didn't go back to you."

"Yeah, you said there wasn't room anymore."

"Yeah," Frank nodded leaning back on his heels, taking in the rest of the bruises, scratches, and scars on his big brother's body as the door opened and Mickey poked her head in.

"Me and Harry and the turncoat are gonna take shifts watching over Charles, you guys should get a full night, we can figure shit out in the morning."

"Sounds good," Nick nodded pretending to be oblivious to her almost tangible, meandering gaze, "thanks Mickey."

Her mouth opened, then closed as pink stained her cheeks. She gave a nod and took a breath, "the turncoat's got the first shift with Harry keeping half an eye on him."

Nick gave another nod.

"His name's Vahl," Frank corrected without really paying her much attention, "for now he's an ally."

"A guy turns from his own once, he'll do it again, remember that kid," she admonished glad to have a clean reason to leave the room without looking like a lovesick puppy.

Once the door was closed Nick pushed himself to his feet using Frank's shoulder for stability, to say he was exhausted was like saying the oceans were wet, and he was pretty sure the scotch he'd swilled was just making it worse.

"I'm gonna get a shower and some sleep Frank."

"Why'd you let them hurt you? I never seen you beat up like this, you can even take Ryan sometimes without using your power. You didn't have to let it happen."

Again, Nick's head fell forward even as he shook it, "yeah I did."

"Fetik?"

Surprised more than he should have been, Nick nodded. Tilting his head and needing to make sure it was still his little brother talking, he had to ask, "what do you know about him?"

"… and then Leanna…" Frank nodded without answering, "did it at least work?"

A shrug tilted the corner of Nick's mouth.

Harry held back by Fetik's men to keep him from interfering, the horrible amount of self-control it took to let the corrupted Sidhe keep landing blow after blow, was almost embarrassing. Then there was the restraint required to keep himself from grabbing the envious and bitter soldier into the crux of his elbow to lift and twist, decapitating the enemy he could only remember despising because his guts told him to, he didn't even want to think about it.

His mind turned to a heartbeat or two before he lost consciousness, the sight of a tall, dark-haired Sidhe making bats flap in his stomach, while his team entered the clearing… now HE was worth thinking about.

He skipped over the interactions with Leanna and her waiting women, focusing instead on the Captain of the Guard's face. He'd called himself Julius and the name rang a bell deep in his chest. He was beautiful with long brown hair and eyes that didn't hide the pain inside when he looked on Nicks' injuries.

There was something he'd been holding back though, and if he got a chance to speak with the soldier again, he'd ask about it. The thought of meeting him again brought a full smile out onto the elder brother's lips.

"Did it?" Frank asked again, snapping Nick from his reverie.

The small rise and fall of Nick's shoulders betrayed his own uncertainty, "not tonight shrimp."

The youngest Emerson nodded, fully able to sense not just his big brother's fatigue but a slowly growing weight inside him, the same weight keeping the soul from going back to him. With luck, there'd be time to talk about it later, when Nick was rested and able to handle the truth of what Frank was sensing.

"Yeah okay, we'll figure it out in the morning. Sleep good Nicky," he bolted to his feet wrapping his arms around the elder boy, taking whatever comfort he could while they were together, just like he'd always knew they were supposed to be.

"You too," Nick slurred swiping his hand over Frank's head with a sleepy smile softening the hard edges of the day.

He left the den pulling himself up the stairs without so much as a word or look into the living room.

In the bathroom he sat on the toilet while the shower warmed up. His filthy shirts slid out of his hand, whispering to the floor while from somewhere deep inside he found the necessary energy to strip out of his jeans and maneuver himself under the steamy spray.

There was no vigor as he rubbed soap from head to toe, just the robotic act of going through the motions.

Feeling his head bob then jerk back up he flipped off the hot water and let the cold rinse the soap away, giving him just a few more minutes of energy to wrap himself in a towel, and shamble into his room leaving his clothes where he'd dropped them. Eventually they'd get picked up.

At the side of his bed he shook his head, "really?" he grunted but realized she was snoring. "Whatever," he sighed sliding between the sheets and turning so they were back-to-back. When he woke, he wouldn't remember so much as his head hitting the pillow.

--

"You are certain you know the way?" Ilirya asked as the road diverged.

"It has been many an age my lady, but I could not forget if I desired to. It is two days run each way without a mount."

"I expect the same to the Fae and the others, if you return before I do, tell my mother what you learn."

"Yes my lady. Fortune be with us both."

"With us all." The She of the All nodded, embracing the younger woman firmly before securing her pack and taking off on a path so overgrown it might as well not have existed at all.

"By Danu..." she groaned after a few steps, "we've been so, neglectful," she fought back heartbreak and tears, "please, don't let it be the end..." then took off again, hoping the run could wear out the thousands of years of guilt.

--

"You should not try to rise, you are far from healed," Dunkun advised even as Ryan pulled himself onto both his knees yet again.

"No one can tell me where Wee or our kids are. I felt something wrong with Frank, it was kind of an echo, but I know it was the kid; but not alone, it might've been Wee too, but..." he explained while catching his breath, then lifted his left leg to plant his foot on the floor as his grip climbed higher on the Sidhe's arms. "Jesus motherfucker that hurts," he groaned hardly able to believe trying to stand could be such a tribulation.

"You suffered grievous injuries, pain is the price you pay for surviving them, even your...guest cannot change that," Dunkun smiled.

"...don't know what you're talkin' 'bout," the agonized man grumbled trying to push down through the left leg while pulling himself up with both arms.

Reflexively the First Acolyte to the Healer tried to lift him up, but stopped as he growled, "don't help me!" and with his teeth gritted, nearly howled with the pain of drawing his right leg up to plant that foot as well.

With whatever was left of his energy, he lurched and pulled at the same time, landing himself firmly in Dunkun's embrace, afraid to bend his knees for fear they would buckle, and he'd wind up face down on the floor again.

"I did it," he grinned gasping and holding tight to the man as sweat made him slick inside his gown, "I did it, h'okay, I did it…"

"Indeed you did," Dunkun smiled patting him on the back before sweeping an arm around him and turning him toward a large rock serving as a bench about three feet away, "care to sit?"

Ryan's eyes locked on the rock, his heart skipping a beat, "shit, it's a mile away."

"Every journey begins with but a step, yours will be longer than most," the bronze haired Sidhe offered.

Pulling on his new friend, he dragged that damnable left foot forward, and, making sure it was set flat on the stony ground, did the same with the right, "You must be great at parties," he grunted.

Dunkun smiled as his charge took up the challenge one agonized step at a time, "I am."

--

Alone in the den, Frank sat at the desk with a notebook and pencil, his gaze flicking back and forth from the canvas to the tree in the center of the tome. A deep level of his mind swam with undercurrents he couldn't grasp yet, while the upper levels wondered how he could make use of the information in front of him.

There was also another level wondering why none of the others were tormenting him, or trying to dissuade him. In fact he wondered if they were even there, or if they'd somehow decided to be somewhere else.

"Maybe they don't have much power in this universe like ours are less…" he mused quietly, tapping the eraser against his lips then gingerly placed the lead against the paper. He began his list with the same fastidious number 1 he would've used for any homework assignment, separated by a parenthesis instead of the period his big brother used.

Who can we trust? He wondered, *Nicky of course, Mickey, Harry, Lou, Wee and Ryan if they're still alive.* Instead of writing out the question, he listed those he was certain would stand with them by first initial. Once he'd gone through the humans they knew, his mind turned to the Sidhe he'd met; there were so many in so little time, but Frank Emerson was well accustomed to listening to his instincts.

He knew he trusted Julius and through him, Errmot and Boaz, but still wasn't sure about Vahl. *But he stood by me the whole time…me.* It was then his blood ran cold as a horrible thought came to him, *what if I'm the one that can't be trusted? They're all in me, quiet for now, but they sent Nicky away and I couldn't stop 'em…* a tiny whisper filled with shame reminded him next, *I wanted him gone too, even if it was just a little, I wanted it too, oh god. I could get him killed, I could get them all killed!*

He drew a tremulous breath, his eyes filling with water he swiped away on his sleeve, *no, I'll never let it happen.* Then another thought hot on the heels of that one, *what if I can't stop them?* The unexpected sinister response he received didn't give him the slightest bit of comfort, *there's always at least ONE way…* followed by an image of Ryan's gun. He shook his head, *NO! Gotta be a different way.*

Boiling over with sudden frustration he threw the notepad and pencil across the room, then got out of the chair and whipped it on its wheels across the floor where it bounced into the closet and toppled onto its side. Shaking his head he leaped to the corner of the sofa and curled into it with his knees in his chest and his chin on his knees just as a knock sounded on the door.

"Frank, you alright dude?" It was Harry's voice on the other side.

"Fine!" he spat, then not wanting to take his frustration out on Harry, changed his tone, "just knocked the chair over."

The teen's face appeared in a crack between the door and the jamb, "You sure?"

"Yeah," Frank fingered his hair off his face, "how's Charles and Vahl?"

Harry shrugged, "alright. You should get some sleep kid, when's the last time you got a solid eight?"

"Does being unconscious count?" he asked in a half-hearted snarl before shaking his head, "Nicky in his room?"

"Yeah, pretty sure Mickey is too."

"You can sleep in mine when it's your turn. I'll just bunk here," Frank offered lurching off the couch to right the chair. "Since you're here, can you grab me down a pillow…" he stopped short, his hands resting on the back of the desk chair, which was at a comfortable height just above his belly button, "huh, wait," he said as the boy took a step toward the closet.

"What?"

Frank shook his head, bypassed Harry, and reached into the closet, not on tip toe, not jumping and trying to grab the corner of the pillow or blanket, just simply reached up and slid them off the top shelf.

"I'm tall," he muttered with a small smirk.

"Not that tall," Harry stepped forward to show they were almost the same height, the boy had however, passed him up by about 2 inches, and was about two shy of the six-foot mark.

"Still bigger than you,"

"But still just a kid, don't forget that, whatever else is going on in there, you're just a kid."

Before his eyes, the youngest Emerson seemed to shrink a little as his expression showed relief at the reminder.

"Thanks."

Wordless, Harry shrugged, delved deep into Frank's eyes, and closed the door, "you sure you're okay? Anything you wanna talk about? I mean we're supposed to be these great friends and all right?"

Frank nodded turning his gaze on the young but still familiar face, "thanks Harry. It's just good to know you're here."

The teen blushed and shrugged, his hand on the knob, "any time kid, you need anything you holler."

Frank shot him a half smile and a nod, "night Harry."

"Night Frank," then closed the door unsure of so much a part of him wanted to run away, while the other part of him really wanted to turn out to be the kind of man his older self was.

Still frustrated, and more than a little worried he may very well wind up being the reason two whole universes could fall, Frank stretched out on the couch, his eyes locked on the ceiling but seeing only darkness.

--

Night fell quick in the woods, an altogether different kind of dark than which arrived with the enemy. This dark was restful, and comforting, promising peace whereas living dark only promised void at best, oblivion level destruction at worst.

The years he'd been trapped on this plane, in this world, left him with a yearning to find release. He'd almost had it not too long ago, thanks to the hands of a little boy who trespassed here and listened to the advice of his heart; the same little boy he'd only moments ago had a vision of, watching from the edge of the Bedowen with his big brother at his side.

Understanding he'd been released by the child for a reason neither of them could have foreseen, he turned his attention away from the peace he wanted. Instead, he focused his vision on Ilirya's back retreating into the woods on the other side of the continent. There was another woman too, though she was headed south and east from the split in the trails at the tail's tip.

"Gargol, Fae, what's left of any of them?" he wondered aloud before turning in the direction the other woman had, and stepping through time and distance, toward the land of the stony warriors called the Gargol; those who'd been the first to learn the secrets of light held by the great dragon and her first children.

--

Day broke cool and cloying through a heavy cloak of gray mist, soaking the prisoners through to their skins.

Their guards had been driving them through the night with spear-points prickling at their backs which, in the fog, and coupled with their dripping sweat, began to itch with teeth griding intensity.

"I feel like a fuckin' bear with a burr in its fur," Lou hissed.

"Smell like a fuckin' bear," Dylan threw back.

"Whine like a fuckin' bitch," Lou accused.

"Fuck off," Dylan ground.

"You wish, why the fuck d'ju come here anyway? No one needs you, and it's not like those kids want you… fuckin' useless," the son of Conchobar muttered shaking his head.

"Shut your piehole," Shep breathed, "neither o'ya would be worth your weight."

"Go to hell!" The eldest Emerson brother stopped in his tracks, wheeling around at his old family friend, and grabbing him by the shirt-front, despite his tied hands.

"Get off him!" Lou growled low, also turning, shoving Dylan away from Shep.

The three of them stood, bound, staring at each other, panting, and surrounded by enemy soldiers who seemed quite content to wait for, and watch whatever may yet happen.

As if a shot straight from the universe struck the spot, the three humans moved in unison. Bound hands struck like hammers, and grabbed at clothes while legs whipped out, knees and feet striking as the poison of the diseased forest eroded whatever sense of camaraderie there might have been between them.

--

A whiff of something amiss stopped Ilirya in her tracks. The tiniest of her hairs stood upright while a chill coursed through her bones deep enough to make her step falter. Her stomach churned in a way she hadn't felt since the last time Oemir's soul transitioned out of her knowing. Such an event, though infrequent throughout the ages, never sat well. But now, this instant, there was a deeper foreboding burrowing through her soul, one she'd never felt before, not even through the war she lost her love to.

The sound of blood rushing in her ears, the strong beat of her heart and the pulse surging through her body were the first things she dismissed as she stopped running. A thought toward her beloved Raziel flew through her mind, taking wishes of wellness and healing to the devoted equine as it went. In its wake, a warm breeze prickled the sweat on her skin as it danced its way between the leaves on the trees.

She craned her neck, her eyes scanning what of the sky she could see. All was blue and punctuated with the fluffy kind of clouds that favored forested and water laden areas, but somehow it was wrong.

"Silly," she chided herself, though her expression hardened, and her head tilted to the side, listening for everything unnatural while playing at insecurity for whatever evil may be hoping to pounce.

Feigning fear, she wheeled left then right, slipping a short sword into her hand from within her fitted outer cloak, ensuring her readiness when whatever it was, decided to stop playing with her and spring to action.

--

"Get the wounded inside!" Wee ordered, "Secure the gates, post guards on the wall and start sealing the breaches! Anyone who can walk or move stone should be working in shifts. Two hours then rotate out for rest!" He was commanding by the seat of his pants, and he knew it.

There were none of Khazeer's generals or commanders to be found. Wherever they might be, and whatever they might be doing, it wasn't here.

If it hadn't been for the young warriors he'd heard called fledglings, who immediately took to his command, he wasn't sure anyone would've bothered listening to him, let alone doing as he instructed.

Spotting one of those fledglings, a serious youth who seemed to be scanning the area for a place to be, Wee dashed to her side, "what's your name?"

"Fern sir." She gave a faint nod.

"Go inside, find Khazeer and Wellyn then report their status to me."

Again, a quick nod came just before she started to dash into the badly damaged structure, but Wee's casted hand grasped her upper arm, "and find an officer who can relay the state of our defenses to me, in fact send them to me, I'll be working on the wall with the others."

"Sir." She nodded then dashed before he could grab her again.

Another young warrior slipped into her place as he stood, numb, his good hand on his hip, and the thumbnail of the bad one wedged between his teeth while he looked out into the surrounding landscape.

"Sir."

"Yeah?"

"You're Oemirkin?"

"Wee Emerson," he introduced himself.

"Ahh son of…"

"Just Wee."

The youth nodded, "Wee, I am Torn."

"Between what?" he asked absently.

"Pardon?"

A quick jolt went through Wee's consciousness as the boy's statement registered, "that's your name…" he noted, too exhausted to be anything but on the edge of befuddled.

The young man nodded.

"Good to meet you," he offered taking and shaking the blood crusted hand, "what do you need?"

"What of the bodies?"

Taken by surprise, his stomach roiled, and a small squirt of bile shot into the back of his throat, he couldn't get the image out of his mind if he scrubbed it with steel wool, dead bodies, infiltrated by living dark, used…

"Burn whatever's left."

"And those who… were… taken?" the youth stammered, making Wee look at him a little more closely. He couldn't have been more than 20, maybe 25 years old, and he too was trying to reconcile what he'd seen.

"Do we have any trackers?"

"Surely some."

"Gather as many as you can who're able, send them out in all directions for three hours or until they come on the enemy, whichever happens first. If they can, they should kill any they come on, if not, they need to get back here as fast as possible and report to whoever's in charge."

"That would be you sir, I've not seen a captain or commander since before sun rise, and many were seen…usurped."

The young Emerson shook his head frowning, "there was a king, in green, Tropus, he was joined by riders…"

Torn nodded, "Yes, they're of the Bedowen, those of his guards who stayed behind would be the ones who joined him."

"Yeah, where'd he go?"

The fledgling shrugged, "I cannot be certain, but if they stay their course, they may be heading for the bridge."

"Bridge?"

"Between lands?" Torn frowned wondering just how much this human knew of their world as Wee shook his head.

The young warrior let out a deep sigh, "there is a place of mysteries between the forests of the Bedowen and the Dragonbow mountains where strange and ancient beings and happenings are said to be."

"Any ideas what he'd be looking for there?"

"None sir… or too many to list depending."

"Give me your top three?"

Visibly frustrated and wanting to move forward Torn did as asked, "Given what the firdur have done," he shrugged, "first children."

With Wee's confused look he breathed deep, "The first children of the great mother. Vetala, Gloamare, Heliosons."

Wee's unknowing expression deepend and inflamed Torn's sense of frustration and urgency, "Oemirkin, there are things you MUST learn."

"Then teach me."

The fledgling huffed and shook his head. "They were allies once, whether they still exist or not has long been a point of uncertainty. The last war brought destruction and losses greater than could be counted, all parties had wounds to tend and before long, too much time passed."

"Wait, so you all fell out of touch and never bothered to re-establish communication? For *millennia*?" Wee half stormed.

Torn gave a nod.

"You're as bad as humans," Wee muttered.

The youth bristled, "At least we do not kill our own."

Wee's mouth fell open, and his good hand gestured to the bodies littering the ground, "really?"

"Schades are no longer Sidhe," the fledgling defended his kind.

"Riiiiiiight, 'cause that's not splitting hairs…" Wee snarled then shook his head, antagonizing the youth would serve no one. "Never name the well from which you will not drink," he warned then let out a long, bereft sigh, "shit." Shaking it off, he met eyes with the young man and nodded.

"Alright," he patted the youth on the shoulder, "Remember, three hours, no more, no less, we need you back before nightfall. And make sure the trackers have plenty of rations and water."

"Sir." He affirmed already trotting off to a lower part of the inner wall where many young soldiers and what appeared to be a couple dozen farmers were mingling with rakes, hoes, bows, and swords over their shoulders or strapped to their hips. They gathered around Torn for several long moments before sharing whatever they each had in satchels and splitting up, heading out into the lands surrounding the Tower of the Sun.

Taking another look around, Wee moved toward a small group working on reinforcing what looked to be the beginning of a large hole in the wall. Stopping to grasp a stone he whispered, "shit," as he put it onto the slow growing pile, then "shit," again as he moved the next one, then "shit," as he continued, while slowly others who were working the same portion of wall, took up the whispered chant.

2

Sarah Farrell, 45, single, mother of one adopted child stopped at

yet another light pole, the raft of flyers in her hand growing steadily smaller as she taped another one to the steel tube. She'd spent a lot of good money at the copy place to have the thousand flyers printed in color, mostly because of her daughter's striking and somehow alien brilliant blue eyes. She'd fallen in love with the little girl the instant they met. She was smart, sensitive, kind and iron willed. She was everything Sarah admired in a person, and somehow, she'd lost her.

When they met, no one had known the little girls' name, and if she'd had one, she certainly hadn't been inclined to tell anyone. She was just four years old when Sarah, walking down the street, toward the local bakery for her morning bagel and schmear, saw a little black-haired head pressed up against the window glass.

At first, she couldn't help but smile at the image as she entered the bakery, fishing a five out of her pocket. Any thought of the kid passed quickly out of mind though as she greeted Wendy, the doughy morning cashier with the wild nest of burgundy hair and had a quick chat about the weather.

Then Raphael came out from the kitchen, his eyes fixed on the front window as a pity filled scowl turned down his mouth.

52

She couldn't help it, her eyes flicked to the mirror behind the counter and locked onto the brightest blue eyes she'd ever seen. It was an accident really, she hadn't wanted to look into the child's eyes, but it just happened, and just like staring into the eyes of one of those Precious Moments figurines, she was suddenly helpless.

"Who's the kid?" she asked, unable to yank her gaze away.

Raphael shrugged, "no clue, been hangin' 'round since last Friday... not too long after you left, so... about 8ish?" he mused. "I got a mind to chase her off but..."

"He can't," Wendy drawled and shrugged helplessly, "I can't either."

Sarah handed back the change from her breakfast and pointed to a blueberry muffin, "I'll take one of those too."

And as if she'd somehow heard the exchange or knew the muffin was for her, the child pushed her way through the door. She strode with a strange certainty to Sarah's side, and slipped her hand into the woman's as she looked up, a smile the size of the Grand Canyon on her face.

"Looks like you made a new friend," Wendy shrugged with her mouth and reached forward, presenting the child with the muffin.

"I guess so," Sarah chuckled looking down at the little girl who stood beside her, peeling off layers of the muffin and unceremoniously stuffing them into her mouth while looking up into her eyes. "Now, young lady, just who do you belong to?"

Once again, she slipped her hand into Sarah's and made her point perfectly, though wordlessly clear.

The legalities began almost immediately. Sarah did everything right and now, twelve years later, her daughter was missing, and her heart was breaking.

"Where are you mouse?" she stroked a finger down the picture and blinked back the mist rolling over her eyes.

The little girl who became her daughter, never told anyone her name, it was as if she hadn't had one at all, and though they'd put out word nationwide to find her parents, she knew, sooner rather than later, she'd be a mother.

She called her mouse, not because there was anything shy or demure about the child, but because of the pure abandon with which she'd literally clutched her belly, rolling on the floor laughing and kicking her feet the first time she saw him.

It was as if she'd never heard of Mickey Mouse before, or seen any kind of cartoon at all, let alone a Disney, but when Sarah pointed him out, telling the as-yet-nameless little girl his name, she beamed, stuck her thumb into her chest and proudly declared herself, "Mickey!"

"No sweetheart, Mickey's the boy mouse, Minnie's his girlfriend," she'd tried to explain but the child wouldn't have it. And so, after what seemed an eternity of cajoling, and with the explanation that a girls' proper name could be shortened quite comfortably, the young girl nodded her reluctant assent and became, via "Michelle", Mickey.

Just a few hundred miles away the girl she called 'mouse' rolled over, the scent of the one person she'd know anywhere filling her nose and bringing a smile to her face. *"don't worry mom, I'm fine and I love you."*

She pushed the sentiment toward the woman she'd needed to raise her, who she knew was being crushed with grief and fear. Still, it was better than the fate she'd face if Mickey gave in to the need to make contact to assure her she was exactly where dozens of lifetimes told her she was supposed to be. If she did, Sarah would be drawn inexorably into events with an undetermined end, leaving her own almost certain.

Resigned, she shuddered a deep breath through a pained smile as she leaned up on her elbow and looked down onto Nick's sleeping face. His hair was a bed-y mess half plastered to his cheek and forehead. The other half of his head looked like something had been nesting in it.

"If you only knew," she whispered before sliding down and snuggling beside him, her arm draping soft across his abdomen.

"Mmm?" he hummed rolling toward her, his arm wrapping around her, pulling her close, his lips seeking hers as his eyes fluttered open meeting hers with good humor. "Good morning."

"Good morning," she grinned back. They met halfway, lips warmed and soft with sleep brushing as if they'd known each other all their lives.

"S'not fair," he whispered so softly she felt the motion of his lips rather than heard the statement.

Her own pursed with a curious tilt, "what?"

"I'm in a towel, basically naked."

"Yep."

"You should be too," he purred, puckering lightly around the angle of her jawbone.

"Make me," she smiled stroking the soft stubble over his chin.

He swallowed hard as light shone bright in his face.

She could feel his muscles trembling and see his pulse thumping fast and hard in his throat. The marked difference between how he'd been before and how he was now, in this moment, did not escape her notice, or her relief.

He pulled back, looking deep into her eyes, "are you sure? Have you ever?"

The corner of her mouth tilted as the essence of timelines crossed one another and she remembered him asking her almost the same thing the first time they made love in the first line.

"I'm sure," she sighed, "and not in this life."

His sleep-soft smile was all she needed to warm her from head to toe as he brushed their noses then rolled off the bed, the towel falling to the floor as he lunged toward the desk and the large box of condoms Harry Sr. left there. He made to grab the towel but missed, so let it lay where it landed.

When he turned back toward the bed with his arousal bold between them, she chuckled, her cheeks turning pink in a way that sent fuzzy heat unfurling from his toes on up.

He was vaguely aware the idea of a girl chuckling at the sight of him naked and hard should have made him crazily self-conscious, especially at fourteen, but something deep inside knew it wasn't a judgment. Her reaction was nothing more than her own nervousness, and acceptance of all he was, which actually made him feel much more awkward.

"What?" she asked, making him aware of just how attuned to him she was.

He closed his eyes for a deep breath, allowing warmth to come back, to trade places with the awkwardness. When it did, he shook his head and put the box on the nightstand then returned to his side, next to her.

His hand hovered above her abdomen while his eyes fell to hers, so similar it was almost like looking into a mirror. When her lips pursed, then pulled into a smile, his fingers danced over the fabric of her shirt, sliding it up in centimeters, to expose her midriff and belly button.

He frowned at the sight of a fresh patch of bright pink, shiny scar tissue just above the front of her hip, "what's this?"

She shook her head, "nothing to worry about," but the skeptical lift of his eyebrow warmed her heart just a bit. It showed he had some concern for her. "When the light spear killed the vestige on the first night, I took a piece of tree."

He shook his head, "I didn't know."

"No reason you should have," she pressed her palms to his cheeks and brushed his lips, watching as his eyes flicked over her otherwise pristine skin.

"That's some pretty fast healing," he mused.

She nodded, "mostly the resin, and what we are."

"You're an inny," he smiled bending forward, perching his lips below the little concavity, "I think I knew that." He admitted before lashing a teasing circle around it with his tongue, making her gasp while her belly trembled.

"It's not supposed to be used inside," he frowned.

She drew his face up to hers, "you're more removed than I am."

His body grew to its mature size as his fingertips, followed by his hands slipped beneath her t-shirt, exploring upwards to the elastic of her bra. She writhed under his touch, arching her back, as he rucked the shirt up and finally off then sought out the back of the undergarment.

"Here, let me," she offered sitting up.

"Lemme get it, I might wanna get used to it," he smiled now on his knees and moving behind her.

"What about Charles?" she asked swallowing hard as he leaned down, quickly analyzing the hook and eye closures and making short work of them.

"He doesn't wear a bra," Nick grinned spreading his legs, and easing her between them, her back to his front. His hands glided around her, tossing the tiny bit of underwear to the floor. His fingers slid slow and light up her arms to her shoulders, then down across her chest, forcing her to arch backward against him until she grasped his hands and put them where she wanted them, filling his palms with her.

Beneath his palms her nipples sprang to hardness, sending a jolt down to his groin, his still hard member twitched against her back as his lips came to her neck and puckered their way up to her ear.

"Don't tease me Nick," she whispered feeling him smile as his fingers went from brushing across her swollen nipples to giving them a quick pinch, pulling a chirp from the depths of her throat.

"Too much?" he asked.

"Huh, uh," she panted rolling head back and forth against his neck. Her hair was soft and smelled like the mountain waters shampoo he was used to. A drop of warmth spilled from the tip of his penis and his hips thrust forward of their own accord as his arms crossed in front of her pulling her firm against him.

"Shit," he grunted, "sorry," unable to let her go for the moment. He was stuck, his muscles so tight he couldn't open his arms, though he wasn't yet relegated to the point of humping her like a dog. The image flushed his cheeks and forced a barking laugh out of him as he squeezed her once and finally felt himself let her go.

"What?" she asked leaning forward while pushing her sweats down over her rump revealing a purple thong riding the cleft of her buttocks.

His grin was sheepish, "thought I was gonna start humping ya like a dog for a second."

She looked over her shoulder at him, unsure if he was joking or not, until she realized he wasn't, then there was nothing she could say. Her mouth opened and closed a couple times before she shook her head and smiled.

"You better put one of those on," she finally said motioning to the condoms. "That's a lot of rubbers, you're making kind of a big assumption, aren't you?" she smirked.

"It's Wee and Ry's, but Harry made me promise to use 'em."

"Senior?"

Nick nodded.

"Smart man, especially if you're gonna be having sex with both me and Charles."

Nick's brows furrowed as he opened one of the silver dollar sized pouches, "together?" he muttered, paying more attention to the device than to the girl who'd shed the last of her clothes and now sat on her knees facing him.

"Let's just get comfortable with each other before we start

59

talking about that."

Her statement took him by complete surprise, his head snapped up, his lips twisting strangely. Of all the times in his young life he'd been handled, violated, used, or abused, at first it was 'secret' and then with Leanna it was a business transaction, but it was one person at a time, Pigg never shared, and for that he was grateful. Then when he and Charles started having sex it was just the two of them. The idea she might be open to more than just him, made his stomach roll a little uneasily.

Reading his look, she reached through the distance between them and stroked his cheek, "I'm not interested in anyone but you. I don't want anyone else inside me, you're mine and I'm yours, no one else's, but if you wanna fuck with him too that's your business."

He was dumbstruck, unable to do more at the moment than just look at her, the condom pinched between his fingers.

Mickey shook her head, took the device, figured out which way it went on, then slipped his hypersensitive rod into her hand and slid the thing onto his head, slowly rolling it over him.

"Holy…. fuck…" he grunted shocked by the sensation as she stroked him with one hand. She took his hand into her other one and rose up onto her knees.

Pressing his fingers between her legs she thrust her hips forward until his middle finger slid along her cleft before slipping into her suddenly very slick void. "…huh…" he grunted edging forward as she lay back, guiding him toward her.

When she was on her back he rose over her, his mouth capturing hers, one hand kneading a breast while one or two fingers of the other moved in and out of her, exploring her landscape, learning what kind of touch, where, did what to her.

Every time her breath quickened, or hips bucked, he noticed his own doing the same, his body flexing in time with hers as she began to pant and emit tight little squeaks from the back of her throat.

"Jesus Nick, do it! Get in me already," she urged grasping him and pressing the blunt tip of his head to her center with one hand while the other grasped his hip, pulling him close.

He ducked his head, his mouth clamping on a breast as her legs wrapped around his lower back pulling herself up, and him into her.

His mind seemed to explode even as he heard her squeak and felt her pause just before she gave another hard pull and a grunt as his head pushed through her resistance, and she took the full length of him inside.

He felt a slight pang at the instantaneous twist of a frown on her face, but in the next instant it was gone, and he was riding a cresting wave he found he'd grown comfortable with.

"I'm gonna come," he whispered before putting his mouth back around her nipple at the same time his hips angled down then back up starting what for him was a delicious friction he hoped she would eventually enjoy.

An off-color swatch caught his attention, making him bolt upright, searching from his hand to Mickey and down to the sheets, "holy shit, you're bleeding! Is it your… you know…" he swallowed, "thing?"

"My *thing?*" she smirked.

He took a quick breath and forced himself to say it, "period. Your period, or did I hurt you?" he stammered, a look of uncertainty and fear on his face.

61

"It's what happens when you pop a girl's cherry, sometimes we bleed, and no it's not my period, I would've told you."

Relief coursed through him, "thank god, Jesus you scared the shit out of me."

"I thought you would've known."

He shook his head as she lay back down against his chest, "I never had sex with a virgin before, I'm sorry if I hurt you."

Beneath her ear his chest gave a quick quiver as he took a tremulous breath.

"A little pain, a lot of pleasure," she lied, "how about you?"

"No pain, a lot of pleasure," he dropped a kiss to the top of her head.

His eyes flicked to the clock as the morning rays finally pierced the curtains, "we have so much to do, and I don't have a single idea where to start."

She rose up, kissed him softly and wrapped herself in the towel he'd dropped earlier, "We'll figure it out after we get cleaned up. Wanna join me?"

He shook his head and watched her leave the room then sat back against the headboard, the blood-stained sheet between his legs. His chest trembled with another deep breath and a wave of despair flew through him ripping a small choking sound from his throat.

He drew his knees up, his eyes on the streaks of blood on his hand, but his mind focused on a huge pool pouring out onto a linoleum floor. He remembered the fading pulse visible in the divot of his victim's neck, a glimmer of surprise and curiosity slipping from the depths of the man's eyes, as if he couldn't fathom why anyone would want to kill him. Words seemed to carve themselves into the sadistic child trafficker's forehead, made by a detached hand he still knew was his own.

Just as it had in the moment of cold necessity, fire shot up the veins of his forearms in the form of rivulets of dark.

Squeezing his eyes closed, he took comfort in the emptiness behind his lids, hiding the image from him. "I had to, it was the right thing…" he whispered feeling his biceps and forearms starting to cramp, his arms curling upward, reaching toward his face. Still squeezing, sparklers went off in his mind like fireworks, but refused to wink out.

"I had to…" he insisted only to be forced to re-live the repercussions of his action, the unforeseen consequence of taking Charles with him, resulting in Harry being stabbed by the pastor. "I didn't mean for it… he should've let us go… he wasn't supposed to…" he muttered.

In his mind, the sparklers finally stopped, leaving behind more smoky darkness until that too dissipated, leaving him with the sight of the blade sticking out of Harry's body, "he's *supposed* to be with us, Pastor should've, he just…" *'a life for a life'* soared through his mind but he shook his head.

"I had to!" he whispered only to be reminded by his subconscious, *'you WANTED to'*, "shut up, stop…" he pleaded before pressing his face into his hands, catching hot puffs and the moisture of several unexpected droplets from his eyes whose origin he didn't understand.

He struggled to unfold his arms, eyeing the underside of them, noting the darkness in his veins, hoping to see it recede only to find it growing bolder, darker, and forcing its way through the elbow joint into his biceps.

"No, no, no, come on…." He grabbed the wood of the headboard, hoping to try to force the darkness down and out into it like he'd done the night he returned from the schade stronghold, but it wouldn't budge.

He shook his head, a faint wriggling in his tummy made itself known then went away.

"Damn," he whispered, then once again caught sight of the blood on his hand before lifting the sheet and looking down, grateful to find his now flaccid member clean of the stuff, glad he'd worn the condom.

He knew it was natural, he knew where it came from, but his stomach clenched as the memory of Ezra's blood flowing out came rolling back again, this time keeping company with other images, one in particular he thought he'd put to rest years ago. It was as if a dam burst, setting memories free along with their emotional charges.

He heard the stifled crying of a child, sitting in the bathroom, needing to relieve himself but unable to for the pain and blood when he pushed.

"Nicky? You okay?" he remembered Frank's thin, high voice muted by the bathroom door.

He could even still, feel himself nod and sniffle up his tears, *"just bakin' some brownies…"*

"You sure?" Frank had asked, his young voice heavy with doubt.

"Hey, do me a favor, go put on one of those dinosaur vids…"

"OOooh which one?" Frank's voice lit with excitement.

'don't care… just go away shrimp, leave me alone,' he thought, *"Your choice,*

just tell me which one it is and what's happening."

"Cool!"

The next part of the memory still made his low belly feel hot and heavy, Frank went to do what he said, and he'd given up on trying to go.

There'd been 'plink's' in the toilet, the sound of them made him nauseous, and the paper was soaked red just like he knew it would be. The water in the bowl was also red, not just pink, but red. His knees had knocked, and his stomach rebelled after he filled his underwear with paper. He'd pushed the handle and sent the evidence of his torment into the sewer just in time as his stomach squeezed and emptied itself into the swirl.

And still there was more, so much more running through his head, hitting him all at once, memories like that one, some others were even worse. There was laughter when he bit back squeals of pain made by careless fingers, or instruments or threats against his mother or brother.

What he didn't understand was why it was all coming now. He lurched out of bed wrapping himself in the sheet and scrambling for the bathroom. He slipped past Mickey just as she was coming out with the clothes he dropped last night.

He slammed the door and plowed across the floor on his knees, leaning over the toilet, his stomach clenching, dry heaving into the bowl.

"Son of a bitch…" he gasped between heaves only to notice the sensation of wetness sliding out of his nose

He pinched what he figured was a glut of snot away and grimaced when he saw blackness covering the stubs of his fingers.

What's that mean? Is it good? Please let it be good! He retched again, *I'll puke my insides out if I have to…please…*

"Hey, you alright?" Mickey asked quietly, peeping through a crack in the door.

With his forehead on his forearm, across the bowl Nick nodded, "Fine. Check on the others…'kay?"

Caught between the desire to give him comfort and the desire to continue to prove herself to him, Mickey nodded, "sure… if you need anything just shout."

"…yeah," he coughed.

He sat on his knees for a few more moments, waiting for another wave to come, or for it all to pass. "I gotta go see Harry," he sighed. Like a thrown switch, the nausea vanished, Nick got to his feet and hit the shower, prepared to do at least one good thing today.

--

In the bowels of the earth below the Bedowen, with the ancient one's neck twined about his, Diagas leaned back, his mighty claws tearing through the rock beneath as he strained to pull the ancient dragon free from the last, deepest root still holding him captive.

"Pull hatchling!" he growled, his own claws also rending the earth with strength the younger dragon never would have imagined it could still have.

As they pulled together, something changed, a slip from deep inside forced an involuntary groan followed by a gurgling sigh as the tree root gave up its hold and the elder dragon slid free. The two stumbled, entangled by the neck, but filled with satisfaction, began to laugh.

After the moments of relief spent themselves the elder eyed the younger Diagas, "Green flame clutch by the look of you, are you all that's left?"

Rolling to his feet Diagas bent his neck, "I believe, though whether there are others here or not…"

"There are, we must free them, it is time."

"You are of the firsts. I am Diagas," the comparative youth introduced himself.

"Zu of Siris," he greeted, his wizened eyes squinting close as his long-scarred face scowled, turning toward Diagas, breathing him in, "humans have returned."

"Yes."

"I smell them on you."

"They passed me by days ago."

"Their stench lingers, the world of the great mother is in danger, if the apes have returned it is time to rise once more," he swung his head toward another corridor and puffed hard, a small shower of sparks falling limp from his snout.

Diagas stepped forward, angling his own snout toward the opening, and showering it with a small emerald flame.

Behind him, the elder's lungs worked like a bellows, a dry, rasping earthy sound reminding him of detritus being crushed, and in another moment, the sound reversed itself with a great blast of heat followed by a short-lived lance of yellow flame.

The corner of his mouth turned up as he cast a glance back at the old one, wondering if perhaps he wasn't nearly so infirm now that he was no longer being fed upon.

--

When they started laughing at the brawling humans was when things took an unexpected turn. None of the men, who'd been occupied with pummeling each other would've paid an iota of attention to their guards, until the laughter started.

"Lovin' it now ya'pisser!" Shep scowled as his fist broke through the facial bones of one of their guards, "didn't cut my teeth on killing demons for nothing ya'shit!"

Lou and Dylan on the other hand, were happily wearing themselves out just trying to keep the others from getting to him.

His knuckles were bruised and bloody, but the boiling rage inside wouldn't let him stop, couldn't let him stop until the last 'crack' of facial bones gave way and whatever lay behind the nose caved into the front most part of the brain. Finally the being's eyes glazed over and whatever he'd been, was no more.

Through the fight, such as it'd been, Shep remained completely unaware of all the others around him, nothing could distract him from destroying this representative of the enemy. Now, leaning back, sitting on his heels, gasping for breath, reason tip-toed back to the forefront of his mind just in time for a skull splitting pain to erupt at the back of his head, and for the dim recesses of the forest to go completely dark.

With all three of the human men unconscious, a wall of undulating darkness came forward. It spun out three tendrils, each one wrapping a human into itself, each man impaled on thousands of needles of multi-dimensional existence as it picked them up and continued moving in the direction the princess indicated. Her guards, no longer so eager to underestimate the humans, stepped over or around their dead.

--

Dressed and washed, but looking like he hadn't eaten, slept or been sane... ever, Nick stopped at the bottom of the stairs. Harry junior was asleep on the living room couch, Charles was trying not to fall asleep in one of the wing-backed chairs, and Vahl was in the kitchen with Mickey, making heavenly fragrances fill the downstairs.

"Frank's in the den." She motioned buttering another two pieces of toast then dropping them on a plate.

Nick nodded, turning down the hall and slipping into the den to sit on the side of the couch where Frank lay sleeping, looking somewhere between the nine-year-old he was, and an adolescent Sidhe.

"Hey shrimp," Nick dropped a hand onto his little one's chest, "gonna go see Harry, wanna come?"

"Mmm'arry?" Frank groaned stretching as far as he could, and at the moment able to touch both ends of the couch with his fingertips and his toes.

"Yeah."

"Mmm'kay," he rolled onto his side, squeezed his knees into his chest and hugged the pillow under his head, "mmm'kay."

"Just you and me, we'll leave the others here."

"Mmm hmm." Frank nodded though his eyes never opened.

"Y'got 10 minutes."

He got another nod and smiled then ruffed the kids' hair, and headed to the kitchen for some coffee and whatever else had been cooked up.

"How'd it go last night?" he asked heading directly to the coffee pot only to be confronted with Mickey turning from the counter, surprising him with a ready mug.

"Well enough, we were able to keep the boy awake," Vahl answered over his shoulder, adding a pinch of something to the skillet.

"Thanks," he nodded before turning a soft, pleasant smile to the young woman.

Her cheeks turned slightly pink, and she stood a little straighter, happy with the burgeoning change in their relationship.

"Mornin'," Charles smiled pouring a glass of orange juice and snagging a piece of toast before the plate touched the table.

"How're you doin'?" Nick asked sitting down across from him.

"Tired, really wantin' to take a nap."

Nick shook his head, "not yet."

"I know."

Nick reached across the table taking the boy's hand into his, "we need you to be healthy."

Again Charles nodded, his smile wan, and his eyes glassy, though Nick noted his pupils were even and looked quite normal.

"Can I talk to you for a minute?" Charles asked, his voice soft while his eyes glanced around from Mickey to Vahl who'd gone back to pushing a bunch of eggs, vegetables, and assorted stuff around in the big skillet; then to Frank who shambled in still rubbing his eyes but dressed and ready to head out.

Rising, Nick nodded then looked at his little brother who stood once again, about a head shorter than him, "you brush your teeth?"

Frank's head tilted up as he opened his mouth, letting Nick cradle his chin.

Nick smelled the strong peppermint of their natural toothpaste but there was little evidence the younger Emerson had actually brushed.

"Grab a piece of toast then go do it for real this time."

With a smirk and frustrated sigh Frank nodded, "don't leave without me."

"Hey!" Nick called as an afterthought.

Frank turned.

"Get a roll of double-sided tape and a pouch of calcite and a small blacklight."

The little one squinted at him with his head tilted to the side, "I thought we were gonna go see Harry?" he asked wondering what else his big brother might have in mind.

"We are."

Frank shrugged, "'kay," detouring back through the kitchen and into the garage, snatching a piece of toast on the way.

With a soft smile Nick led Charles out of the kitchen and into the freshly vacated den.

"Nick, the pastor's dead, we can't hide this," Charles' eyes started brimming over with water, "it's my fault, if I hadn't left he'd've never..." he shook his head.

"It's not your fault. He attacked Harry."

"He wasn't himself, there was something, something wrong with him, when he came by yesterday morning... it was like there was something eating him from the inside out... I should've just gone with him, but I couldn't, I was so scared... he had pics of Ezra, he knew we did it..."

Nick shook his head, holding the boy's hands. "He didn't *know* anything, no way he could've, but you can bet your ass a guy like that would've done anything to get you back into his fold... there's a bazillion guys like Ezra out there, and you can bet that same ass he would've pimped you out to any of them to get what he wanted."

The horror creeping through Charles' face sent a strange twinge through Nick's belly.

"No."

"Yeah, Charles, a guy like that couldn't care less what he's gotta do to keep up his lifestyle... I'm sorry man but you weren't much more than something he could rent out for a few bucks."

"Fuck you," Charles spat, his horrified expression turning to one of reluctant belief, "you don't know anything!"

Nick understood the boy's anger, as well as his need to deny the truth but there wasn't time to coddle him. There was, however, the distinct possibility if he pushed too hard too fast, he might spook Charles and he'd wind up going to the cops. *I need to go look at the fire pit, clean it out, make a bonfire or two...* he mused.

"You believe what you need to about the pastor, but think about this; what he was doing to you was abuse, it was also illegal, it's called prostitution. If he's been doing it to you since you were 13, at that time it was called child trafficking," he watched the older boys' eyes start to glass over with tears as the truth was spelled out for him.

"You need to wonder why he'd travel halfway across the U.S. to get you back... was it because he couldn't go on without you, or is it more likely he wanted to make damned sure you'd never tell anyone what he'd been doing to you? How many times did he make you feel worthless by telling you you're broken? That something's wrong with you, you're an abomination because you like guys, before sending you out to get tortured and raped by a sick fuck like Ezra..." he stopped and took a shuddering breath while wiping away the cascade of tears spilling out of his own eyes in time with the ones coursing down Charles' cheeks.

"I'm sorry," Nick whispered sweeping away one of the shimmering tracks before sliding his hand behind the boy's neck, "whether you decide to stay or go, remember, we take care of our own."

Charles sat there, heat of anger boring into Nick's eyes, battling with both hurt and exhaustion.

Nick frowned, "Look, Frank, and me, we're going to see Harry. Why don't you think about what *you want* to do, I wouldn't make you do anything you don't want, but just... take some time okay?"

Slowly Charles nodded, "Yeah, I'll think about it."

"Good, try and maybe... I dunno, stay on your feet, make sure you don't fall asleep."

The older boy gave another nod then drew a deep breath and withdrew from Nick's gentle grip, "Did you have sex with her?"

"I told you I would," Nick answered without missing a beat.

Wordless, Charles took another shaky breath.

"We'll talk later," Nick assured at the same time Frank's knock sounded.

Again, the older boy nodded, this time his eyes fixed hard on the floor in front of him, the healthy glow he'd had at the outset of this adventure was gone now, at least for a while, and his skin seemed to be hanging a little more lax. The change gave a subtle tug to something inside Nick. He crouched in front of Charles, moving between his legs, gently lifting his chin with a finger.

Behind them the door came open, admitting Frank who watched as his big brother leaned in, pressing the newcomer's lips to his own for a tender moment before relinquishing him.

"I mean it."

Charles met his eyes, hope reignited in them. He allowed himself to crack a smile, "okay."

"Good," Nick smiled back, stealing another kiss before rising to his feet and turning to Frank. "You brush 'em for real this time?"

In answer, Frank let the plastic bag with the supplies slide down to his elbow, then stuck his fingers into the corners of his mouth, lifting and lowering his lips to show Nick he'd done as asked.

"Good, let's go." He turned the younger boy ushering him out the door.

"See you later Charles," Frank smiled and waved, happy when the newcomer raised his hand and smiled back.

"So what was he so sad about?" he asked leading the way out the front door only to have their plans dashed at the sight of the boys' stolen car. It was half-crashed on the front lawn, its rear passenger tire flat off the rim, which was definitely dented "Son of a bitch!" Nick cursed.

A set of keys came dangling forward over his right shoulder, "You can take mine, but so help me…" Harry Jr. whispered with a smile in his voice. "Can I come, or you want me to wait till later?"

"You mind waiting a bit?" Nick asked trading keys with him.

"S'cool, I figured you might wanna talk with him on your own. You tell that old codger he better not fuckin' die on us!"

Frank stepped forward wrapping his arms around the teen, "We will! Thanks Harry!"

"Yeah man, thanks," Nick smiled shaking the teen's hand before reeling him in for a quick bro-hug.

"No prob," the young man smiled.

"Oh hey," Nick turned suddenly, "can you do us a massive favor?"

"How massive?" Harry spocked an eyebrow at him.

"Can you clean the firepit down to the dirt then start a big ass bonfire in there? Replenish the ashes?"

"Are you shittin' me, what the hell...ahhh fuck... the guy," he nodded.

"Yeah. Make sure there are no bone fragments or traces of the body in the pit, then maybe... I dunno... what the hell do we do with the ashes and stuff," he groaned, no sense of the slightest clue of how to hide whatever remnants might be left.

Frank looked between the two, shrugged and took the keys, climbing into the passenger seat to wait.

"I'll figure something out, I got some friends in...places," Harry assured heading back inside with a wave of the hand.

Slipping behind the wheel Nick sighed, "thanks Harry," and just as he was about to put the car in gear, the front door opened again,

Mickey rushing out with something in each hand.

"Egg sandwiches…eat," she handed both of them to Frank, who passed one to Nick, then pulled two bottles of water from her pockets and handed them over too.

"Thanks Mickey,"

"Thanks Mickey," they chimed leaving her smiling and waving as they hit the road.

"How close to big trouble are we?" Frank asked unwrapping his sandwich once Nick turned them onto the main road.

Nick ripped into his, his stomach quivering in anticipation of something delicious, "Probably pretty close, gonna depend on Charles, a lot."

"Damn, this is awesome!" he gasped as Frank took his first bite.

"Vahl knows how to cook… real good!"

"He sure does." Nick grinned.

"Twenty-five cents," Frank smiled chomping into another bite.

"Hm?"

"Twenty-five cents to the swear jar. You said 'damn', and I think the 'f' word too, and probably a lot of times, so maybe a dollar or two."

Busted, Nick chuckled, "yeah you're probably right. Twenty-five cents for you too."

"Damn," Frank huffed then asked, "Why was he so sad?"

"Charles? Twenty-five cents."

"Dang! Yeah, why was he sad?"

"He's stressed, concussion, exhausted, had to face a bad truth about the pastor, and before you ask, don't," he warned.

"'kay," Frank frowned around another bite.

"…and he took a chance to go halfway across the country with a total stranger and leave his whole life behind for something he never coulda figured could exist."

Frank turned to face his big brother, his mouth in a tight pucker, "What did you tell him?"

Nick smiled down a gargantuan bite of the breakfast; there was corn, bacon, cheese, spinach, and from what he could tell some French fries all cooked into the egg, all of which was then wrapped into two pieces of Super Seed toast made heavy with butter. "Mmm, dang man… awesome!" he raved, "I wonder if I could un-eat this like they do in the cartoons, just so I could eat it again…" he mused.

"That would be nasty gross." Frank grimaced.

"Yeah…" Nick grimaced thinking about it, "it would. Anyway, I told him everything he needs to know, he saw a schade while we were on the road. Then at one of their subways, he saw them and a vestige come through, and he saw me hold them back, and he's seen me snap back, then go forward again, it makes sense he'd be wierded out right?"

"Totally. Sheesh, talk about dropping him in the deep end."

"Yeah well, we survived it, he will too."

"What if he's not the same as the Charles we knew before?" Frank asked.

"I don't know."

"We could be really screwed."

"Yeah."

"We'll ask Harry, see what he says, he'll know," Frank smiled, his certainty helping Nick feel just a little more comfortable too.

3

"You must also rest, you ordered us to rotate in a timely fashion, you must lead by example," a robust though tired woman he'd been working alongside admonished handing over a flask of water.

Wee was soaked to the skin and his broken arm was throbbing almost to the point of being intolerable, he wanted to scream, he wanted to shake it, pound it, smash it! He wanted to cry and melt the world with his despair as his mind played dozens of horrible scenarios like a catalog of doomsday movies, none of which ended well.

He wanted Ryan, his easy smile, his grandiose if sometimes false bravado that everything would work out, he wanted to hear his heartbeat and know whatever else happened, they'd survive, and so would their boys. But what he wanted didn't matter to the universes.

He'd pushed it all too far, too hard, not just through the attack, but by working consistently through the last three shifts, and he was going to pay merry hell for it in more ways than he was prepared for.

At some point, Fern came back to tell him neither Wellyn nor Khazeer was conscious, so he sent her back to wait until one of them awoke.

There'd been no news yet from Torn or the villagers he'd rounded up, but he knew they should be returning almost any minute. Six hours he'd been at it, and he was so exhausted he could sleep for a week, but at the same time so full of fear and uncertainty he knew if he tried there'd be only nightmares of what he'd seen and fought against, to fill his mind.

"What's your name?" he panted, sliding down the wall till his knees were in his chest and his wheezing turned to breathing again.

"Janell," she sighed sliding down the wall beside him and offering her hand.

"Wee, nice to meet you," he smiled.

She nodded, "same."

They sat in awkward but companionable silence for several long moments.

"There is a great deal of damage to the tower," she eventually said.

"Yep."

Another several moments seemed to crawl by before she looked up at the team working to get the giant crystal at the top of the tower mounted onto a mobile platform, and noted, "work on the light spear seems to be going well… largely."

"Yep."

"Sun will be setting far too soon, we may not withstand another attack."

"Yeah," he sighed.

"The infirm and the children should be well situated in the

mountain."

"The injured will be joining them soon enough I s'pose."

"Any word on the King and his Captain?"

"They're alive, just not conscious yet."

"Then you are our defense?"

"Nope," he shook his head motioning to the end of the balcony and down, "they are, down there."

She rose peering over the wall, noting for the first time, a long line of Sidhe stretching in each direction far enough to encircle the tower, though not the village.

They were down so far she couldn't see exactly what they were doing but it was more than just marching and holding a line, of that she was certain.

Wee joined her in looking onto the artisans, crafters, and mages below, "They're warding the tower... it's powerful enough spell-work in my realm, should be... incredible here," he smiled resting a hand on her shoulder, "if they can buy us the night we may stand a chance until reinforcements get here."

Janell turned, her face a mask of pain and anger, "And exactly who would you expect? The Gargol are gone, none have seen so much as a flash of their life light in more than a millennium, for all we are aware...." her lips trembled, "The dragons? They abandoned us before the battles were half fought let alone 'won'," she scoffed, "dwarves? Our allies are gone... either abandoning us for our abandonment of them or extinct! Not a voice has been heard, not for millennia. There is nowhere for us but the mountain itself." She sniffed motioning to the East and the Dragonbow mountains where Areen and Ilirya had taken those who could not fight.

"What about the bridge? The ones that live there?"

"Hah!" she scoffed a sound so filled with pain it seemed to stab him, "just another place for ours to meet a fitting end, just like the mountain itself!"

"Who are the ones that live there? Torn told me names but they don't mean anything."

She cocked her head to the side, her face crumpling with disbelief in his ignorance, "how are you a son of he who should've been king of all without knowing these things?!"

Wee shrugged, "mortal time runs different, a lot got lost along the way… please?"

Shaking her head, she huffed, "they were the first ones, beside the dragons themselves they are the most ancient of all creations, first even to the Gargol. The Heliosons were born first, some say they were born from other worlds even before ours, but they danced and capered bringing light, life, and joy everywhere they went, but they could be fierce and deadly as well, especially to the dark. It ran from them!"

"We could definitely use some of them around," Wee nodded his head, "go on."

"We were still the rose of worlds," she folded her hands into the shape of a flower, "our worlds back then in the first times, when the dark first prodded, testing our petals, seeking our weaknesses… none were ever sure where they came from, which world birthed them, but then came the Gloamare…"

"Gloamare?"

A sinister smile twisted her mouth and darkened her eyes, "they are the warriors of light, with the Heliosons they pushed back the dark and wrapped our worlds in the energy of light, it was millennia until it tried to breech our defenses again."

"and the third ones… the vvvvv something?"

"Vetala, do not speak lightly of them. If any still exist those whom the firdur have stolen will soon be free of their captivity and finally able to die."

"What do you mean?" Wee asked.

"They devour the dark. For those on the cusp that firdur has overtaken, they will finally be allowed peace. The Vetala will drive the firdur out…"

"What do you mean finally? I thought the dark animated the dead?"

"Some certainly had passed, but by no means all. Those who hadn't the good sense to die before firdur got to them, now must suffer possession until it lets them go."

Wee ran his hands through his hair, his stomach roiling at the prospect of possession 'til death.

"You did ask," she reminded him.

"Fuck me…are you absolutely certain none of them remain?"

"As certain as one can be for not having seen, hide, hair, or ember of one since the war in which your first died. Without any of them at our sides we, like your ancestor will likely not survive this assault, our universe stands alone, the rose has blown apart in the winds of time, we are alone, and we will end the same."

The youngest of the elder Emerson's couldn't have said why the idea of this strong woman trying to sniff back tears of hopelessness made him angry but it did.

With her state a fan to the flame in his heart he fixed his gaze to hers, "we've got a saying where I'm from, 'it ain't over till it's over', and lady, it's nowhere near over." He turned toward the tower, suddenly determined to go see Khazeer and Wellyn for himself.

Meandering his way from the outer corridor, inward toward the pinnacle spire at the center of the tower, in the same direction as Khazeer's office, where they'd had their gathering earlier, he stopped at what looked like a door.

"I'll be damned," he breathed stepping closer to the thing which opened when he was within a couple feet of it. "sensors, but what kind?" he shook his head noting it was definitely more of an elevator than anything else, "unless I step in and the other side opens up..." so he stepped inside, the beautiful semi opaque crystal on the other side illuminating just as the door started to close.

"Hold!" came a female voice followed by the sound of running bare feet while he held the door open.

"This is just really freaky," he muttered, the idea of something like this, here, and so similar to technology on the other side of the veil more jarring than anything else he'd come across so far.

"Ula," he nodded as she joined him.

"Son of Oemir," she nodded passing her hand over the crystal, "good...you're still well," she smiled and swept another page aside.

"It's like a friggin' cell... pages... how the hell..." he wondered then catching her confused expression nodded, "yeah, m'okay, you too... where are you going?"

"I must see Khazeer, Lachlan is with the others watching the grotto. A pod of basilocetes has been found slaughtered near the Accursed Fault."

"From what I've heard he's still unconscious."

"Not to mention there are villagers performing intricate spells best left to the Senior Mage," she shook her head, her mouth turning down with concern.

"The wards should hold until reinforcements come… with luck they'll get us through the night. What're basilocetes?"

"YOU?! YOU orchestrated this?!" she demanded as the lift opened without so much as a jiggle.

"Yeah, we need the protection…and what's the 'accursed fault'?"

"YOU knew such a spell? How?" she shook her head, clearly dumbfounded and more than a little flustered as they exited onto the floor. Her seaweed plaits shaking as she sought an answer.

He smiled and shrugged, "It's ancient, our forefathers didn't forget everything. Besides, it's the same one we use to protect the house, and at least four of those folks performing them are mages, well they said they were."

"Beyond belief…" she hissed leading the way to the King and Queen's primary throne room and entering as if she had every right to be there.

"Why?" he asked following her to find himself standing right in front of the Elder Healer.

From a bench in the shadows of the room, Tierus rose, moving to the son of Oemir and the queen of the Akirowen, the dried blood of their king flaking from his arms and armor as he joined them.

"I took watch for Fern sir Oemirkin, the healer sent her to rest."

Wee gave a curt nod clapping the boy on the shoulder as the

senior Healer shuffled to them.

"They're both alive… barely…" she huffed, a tuft of orange colored hair dangling down from the side of her cap, "stubborn fools, each as bad as the other… tell them to stay put, what do they do? They get UP! They *ripped* themselves wide open all over again! We don't have any venom left!" she hissed at them.

"I'll send for some of our stores to be brought, the leviathans have been generous this cycle," Ula assured, then turned to Wee, "Basilocetes are deep sea mammalians, and the accursed fault lies beneath a sea of sargassum weed, warming the waters to grow the feed required by those who spawn their young there."

"I'm sorry." Wee nodded.

Ula tapped the crystalline tail hanging out of her ear, "Lachlan, from my satchel bring the leviathan venom then send whoever is available, in a skiff to retrieve more, and have my sail ship prepared to leave immediately."

The Elder Healer's relief was tangible throughout the room, "Thank Danu, no more mending!… as if the body was a garment! Hideous!" she stormed.

"We need to see Khazeer," Wee asked, his voice soft but firm.

The ancient woman's mouth popped open as if to deny them their wish, but quickly thought better of it.

"He is… recovering… slowly so do not tax him," she ordered, punctuating her words with a fingertip to his chest before pointing into the heart of the room and stepping aside for them.

Wee's breath caught in his throat, the sitting King of All Sidhe lay looking a wasted wisp of his earlier self, in spite of the strength still shining in the depths of his eyes.

Together Ula and Wee pulled up chairs beside the bed, the queen of the Akirowen motioning the elder Emerson to the one closest to Khazeer.

"Go on, tell him what you've done!" she hissed, her disapproval deeply etched in the lines on her face.

--

From the elevator Nick couldn't help but notice the silhouettes of two police men entering Harry's room.

"Holy shit, please let them have just got here, that would be some real good luck!" he thought to Frank, unable to keep from remembering the first time he ran into cops here, it was the day he'd nearly lost Frank to Ne'Min. It was just over a week ago on this plane, and he was still, in actual years, just a teenager, but in terms of experience, despite all the training they'd been through, he'd only been a child. He shook his head wondering how both he and Frank managed to survive those first few events, then figured it must've been dumb luck more than anything else.

Swallowing hard, he leaned against the wall, Frank's hand in his, hoping the story he'd planted in Harry's head actually got through to the older man. There'd been a precious few moments between the ER team getting him stabilized, an operating room opening up, and the police arriving that Nick had taken advantage of by slipping his fingers into the older man's head and planting images of the story they were going to have to stick with, in there.

His biggest concern was whether or not the cops talked with the orderly who'd helped them get Harry and Charles into the hospital, the one he'd told the truth to. He took several deep breaths and shook his head, angry he'd said anything to the orderly at all, he should've just kept his mouth shut. *Live and learn... never again* he thought before allowing himself to be adult enough for the task at hand. *"You think Harry got it?"* Frank asked, as attuned to his big brother as always.

"I sure hope so…"

"What if they talked to that guy? You said it happened at the house…"

"I know…I wasn't thinking… But…"

"But you told Officer Stern we were all out."

Nick nodded, *"We stick with what we told the cops. We've got numbers on our side."*

"Okay," Frank confirmed watching his brother grow taller and broader, till he filled out his clothes. He grinned as the older boys' chin became peppered with dark stubble, exactly as he'd looked the previous evening when they brought Harry and Charles in. *"You look like dad…"* the thought was soft, warm, and just a little sad as it flowed from Frank to Nick, striking the older boy right in the heart.

For a second he thought about how much he missed their father and what his murder had done to their family. A moment later he pushed the melancholy away, there wasn't time to think about it right now.

With a silent meeting of the eyes, Frank gave a nod, then a squeeze to Nick's hand before letting go and following him into the room.

"Hey, we interrupting?" Nick gave a faint smile.

"Mr. Emerson, good morning," one of the officers who'd taken his statement last night greeted.

"Officer Stern," Nick nodded extending his hand.

"Hiya Frank," the officer took it smiling at the youngest Emerson.

"Hi," Frank smiled moving around the adults to sit on the bed at Harry's side, setting the plastic bag on the bed table, "how are you?"

A dark burning squeeze made itself known in Frank's chest at the sight of their best friend. His skin was ashy, and seemed to hang from his skull, his eyes were dark inside whites that'd gone yellow and red, and they looked kinda rheumy and slick. *He's old,* Frank's eyes flicked to Nick's, *"he's a old man!"*

"So much better now you're both here," Harry smiled, a little glow coming back beneath the gray of his skin as he reached forward, wrapping his arms around the younger boy, "what'cha got in the bag kiddo?"

Frank shrugged, "just some stuff for an art project."

"Cool, maybe I can help you with it."

"I was hoping you'd wanna," Frank grinned and sat back in his friend's embrace listening to the others talk.

"Nick, this is Detective Harleson, he's going to be helping us track down Mr. Armstrong, and Mr. Brown's attackers, would you tell him what you told Officer Jackson and myself last night?"

"Sure," Nick nodded, "we'd been out, doing a fall run,"

"We? Who's 'we'?" Detective Harleson, tall, lean, and citified asked.

"Me, Frank, Harry, Jr., Mickey, Charles..."

"I've got all the names, they're all staying at your place right?" Officer Stern confirmed.

"Yeah, we all kinda work together, doing community outreach and stuff, we just shifted the base to my... our house," he explained motioning between Frank and himself.

The Detective nodded, a pen scratching in a palm sized spiral bound notebook most of his co-workers saw as a quaint affect of his persona, "So... you were all out... together?" he asked.

"No, Frank and I were together, Harry was in his car, and the others were with junior," Nick clarified.

"So, what all were you doing?" he glanced up from the notebook, a skeptical gleam in his eyes. Frank felt a general sense of suspicion from Harleson, but no indication that at this moment there was a trail this particular dog was sniffing with any real zeal.

"Dropping off some clothes and jackets at the warehouses, there are a few different buildings where homeless flop…"

"S'one of the areas we do rounds at once every couple months, depending of course," Harry confirmed.

"So, I finished my rounds and went to meet up with Harry, see if he needed help with whatever was left of his load and found him on the ground with the knife in him."

"You told Officer Stern you didn't see anyone else on the street is that right?"

Nick nodded, "yeah, whoever got him was gone."

"How about you Frank, you see anyone?" he asked.

Frank dropped his chin to his chest, shame on his face, "I was asleep in the back seat. It was a good day till I woke up," Frank sighed.

"Which was when?"

"Nicky shouted for help."

Nick nodded his agreement, "By that time the others had got to where we were, so we grabbed Harry, wrapped up the blade as best we could and hauled ass here. I was afraid we'd lose him if we waited for an ambulance."

"Remind me to have someone swipe a set of Oregon plates, put 'em on the bastards' car and move it," Nick thought to Frank who nodded.

The detective nodded then turned his attention to Harry, "you said earlier it was a guy, did he say anything? Was he trying to rob you or anything?"

In his bed, Harry shook his head, "man I don't know... he was mumbling all over the place, you know how some of those lifers get, can't make heads or tails out of half the crap they spew."

"Lifers?" Harleson asked.

Harry huffed, "lifelong users..." he explained.

"Ah," the detective nodded "so you said he was a white guy, about five-ten, salt and pepper hair, kinda dadbod but not really fat, wearing jeans and a dark jacket..."

"Yeah... probably one I brought down there..." Harry frowned, "other than that I got nuthin' man, I'm sorry."

"Okay," Harleson nodded then turned back to Nick, "and what about the other one? The young man with the concussion?"

Nick nodded.

"What?" Harry asked, his brows furrowing.

"Charles," Nick informed him, "yeah, apparently while he was on his part of the rounds, someone clocked him, knocked him out, robbed him," he sighed, "it was bad night all around."

"That's Charles Brown right?" Harleson asked, something a little off-putting in the tone of his voice until Stern jumped in.

"He stays with you all?"

"Yep."

"How long have you all been together?" the detective asked.

"Harry and us have been together for years, the others just a few weeks or so," Nick answered.

After a quick glance at each other, Harleson flipped back a couple pages in his notebook and showed it to Nick, "that your address and phone number?"

"Yep," Nick nodded, "house phone's the best number to reach me at, we still have a machine."

"No cell?" the detective asked with an odd sort of frown to his face.

"Oh yeah," Nick nodded, "but it's a few years old and doesn't hold its charge real well, you still want it?"

"Yeah, I do."

Nick rattled it off then confirmed it on the paper, "even if you think you're leaving a message, call the house too, that way I'm sure to get it."

And just like in the t.v. shows, the detective handed Nick a card with the admonishment to call if any of them found out or remembered anything new.

Adequately somber Nick nodded shaking hands with the man, "will do, thanks."

"We'll let you know if we find him."

"Good," Nick growled, his eyes turning dark, "maybe you could leave me in a room with him for a few minutes when you do?"

"Bit of a scrapper eh kid?" Harleson asked motioning to his face.

Nick flicked a corner of his mouth up, still painfully aware of the cuts and bruises he bore, "not by nature, no," he admitted then added, "unless someone goes after one of mine."

There was a twitch of dark curiosity from the detective at Nick's own bit of sinister humor, but at the same time it seemed to set the detective at a little more ease as he and Stern walked out, promising to keep in touch.

With the surprise formalities finished Nick pulled up the one chair in the room and sat facing their old friend, breathing hard as a greasy sweat rolled out over him.

"What'd you tell 'em?" he asked, shaking as Harry patted the back of his hand.

"Nothing different from what we just said. You put something in my head… that's what popped out my mouth…" the old man cocked an eyebrow along with a faint smile.

Nick fell back in the chair, his heart still hammering though his breathing returned quickly to normal, "I'm so sorry Harry…" he whispered as Frank dashed to the threshold, peered out into the hallway to make sure both the cops were gone, then closed the door.

"They know something, probably about Charles, maybe he got ambered," Frank whispered.

Nick nodded while chewing on a thumb nail and mumbled, "ambered? He's sixteen, and emancipated…"

"S'not your fault kiddo," he sighed struggling to push himself still a little more upright, until Nick reached over and hit the 'up' button, "thanks."

"If I hadn't…"

"Shut up!" Harry snarled, "don't you say a word!" he warned, "no way you could know goin' out would'a caused a problem, whatever that bastard's issues are, they're not anyone's but his own, you get me?!" he demanded before pressing back against the mattress, breathing hard and putting a finger over his lips. "You stick with what you KNOW!"

"Alright," Nick nodded squeezing the old man's hand, "alright, I get ya. I just wish…"

"Me too," Frank nodded, resting his head on Harry's shoulder.

"Me three," he agreed, "so tell me… how's the family doing?"

Nick turned to his little brother, "give us a minute alone and go make that call willya? Ask either junior or Mickey to handle it."

Frank frowned but nodded dashing into the bathroom, figuring it was alone enough.

Harry's brows furrowed, "what's up?" he asked.

"This could go very bad very fast. How'd I meet Charles in Austin? How'd I get there? Okay I ran away, stole a car from the dealership even. It crapped out, I met Charles, convinced him to come back with me, pastor puts out an amber, we stole cars, and forget about the whole… you know what thing…If those guys show up at the house with him there we might lose him, he's completely freaked, there's no telling what he'll spill. If that happens we're likely gonna need a place that's NOT in this universe."

"'Hold it! Hold it… I got a few other places," he rasped grabbing a pencil and paper from the bed-table. "What else?"

"The tower of the sun fell last night, me'n Frank had a vision. They attacked the summit, the vestiges were… they were… shit Harry," he swiped a mitt down his face, feeling the soft layer of whiskers there, "this is too damned big… and I don't know what to do, let alone how to do it!"

A chuckle huffed out of their best friend just before he winced with the vibration and reached up to ruffle the boys' hair, "kid I got just a little advice for ya."

Nick's eyebrows shot up and he nodded sniffing back his fear.

"One step at a time. Just do one thing at a time. This, this is your home. Defend it."

"Frank's got the soul, they were screwing with him over there, but here they don't seem to be as strong…"

"I don't care where it was born the first time, I just care where it belongs now…and you boys… this is where you belong."

The corner of Nick's mouth tilted up but there was more worry than humor in his eyes. "The dark took the dead, it's using them," he took a shaky breath, "…they put it in me," he whispered so faintly Harry wasn't sure he heard it, "…when they had me…" he gasped then glanced back at the still-closed door to the bathroom, "…I can feel it…"

"Say again?" Harry whispered, the furrows in his aged face deepening.

"It's like it's crowding, inside my skin, inside…ME… and even Frank knows… he knows that's why the soul didn't come back, why it went to him… because there wasn't room inside me anymore…

what if it takes over? What if it's trying to... I dunno... *change* me, or... something? *Use* me, like it's using them, take me over or something, I don't know but I can't let it... but I don't know if I can..." he couldn't have stopped the confession if he'd wanted to, and though he knew he shouldn't be laying this on Harry, there was no one else he trusted more.

Frank had his own issues to deal with right now and the last thing he needed was to worry about whether or not his big brother was going to turn into a detriment to the mission.

Harry's frown was fearsome, but he hid it quickly as his hand twined in the front of Nick's t-shirt, pulling him close, "Hey, hey! You listen to me Nick, whatever's going on inside, you're stronger, you remember that! YOU are stronger than anything anyone can do or put in you..." He stopped and nodded, "is that why Frank asked if you got any tats?"

A strange, fuzzy weight seemed to squeeze all around the elder Emerson, as if he was neither here, nor there, but somehow stuck between moments just waiting to suffocate him. He nodded his suddenly far too heavy head, his voice barely a whisper, wondering if he should show his best friend, and wanting to, almost driven to see his horrified expression. *wonder what it'd do t'him.* "It runs through my veins..."

The bathroom door cracked open, "are you done yet?"

Nick snapped back to the moment, the fuzz dispelled as he half-choked on a gulp, "yeah." Looking down at his and Harry's linked hands the darker than normal outline of his veins caught his gaze, still, for the moment, he let his hand, and the subject drop.

"Good..." Frank returned to Harry's bedside. "First thing is I think we gotta make sure to protect this universe... but I can't figure out how just yet... but there's more... we figured it out when we were in the schade stronghold the other night, me'n Vahl found some stuff..."

"No, first thing we gotta do is get that art project underway," Nick corrected, "we can fill him in while we're working."

"Just what kind of art project are we talking about here Nicky?" Harry asked, sweeping the bag into his lap, and peering into it before smiling, "two-sided tape... a bag of calcite... and a blacklight, boy you are just something else aren'cha?" he sighed contentedly.

"Yeah but where are we gonna put it that they're not gonna sweep it away?" Frank asked realizing they had the makings of a binding ring to keep their friend safe from schades if not the dark itself.

With a slow smile Nick tilted his head up.

"Aaaahhhhh!" Frank grinned wondering if he'd ever be as smart as his big brother, "dude that's awesome!"

"It's more protection than he had last night," Nick shrugged, "speaking of which, any idea when they're gonna let you come home?"

"I'd guess another day or so," Harry sighed, "the surgeon said there were only a couple nicks on the liver. Thanks to the old spare tire. If it'd hit the large intestine like they thought, man it coulda been a lot worse that's for sure..." he shuddered.

"Poo bag?" Nick asked.

"*Poo* bag?" Frank grimaced.

"They thought they might hafta," Harry nodded with his own grimace.

"It's when they make your guts come out your stomach, so you poo in a bag," Nick explained.

"Eeeeewwwww!" Franks face squeezed in a twist of disgust.

"Now how'd you know something like that?" Harry asked.

Nick shrugged, "YouTube rabbit hole, colon...scope...I think?"

"Colostomy," Harry corrected.

"Gross!" Frank shook his head as Nick opened the sack of calcite and Harry started to unspool the tape a couple feet at a time.

While they worked, Frank explained what he and Vahl found, and what he and Nick thought it might mean. They shared ideas and theories and by the time they were done coating one side of several sections of the tape they'd moved on to filling the older man in on what was going on at the house.

Kneeling on Nick's shoulders to press another small section of tape to the cross beams between the ceiling tiles Nick nearly dropped Frank.

They'd returned to the subject of Charles and the emotional issues he was having dealing with everything, when Frank explained, "If Charles goes it'll be easier for Mickey to get Nick, but he won't 'cause he gets wood every time he sees Nick, so he won't go anywhere."

"Jesus Christ Frank!" Nick hissed as Harry chuckled then winced.

"Well he does! It's not like he can hide it... and we're all guys 'cept for Mickey anyway but she doesn't care."

"Shut it!" Nick scowled blushing madly while handing the young one another piece of coated tape. Standing at the foot of the bed

Nick had no choice but to look at Harry.

"It's just us Nick, it's no big deal, and if the boy's in love with you it'll be easier for him to open his eyes to the truth, I know he's gotta be thinking this is his fault. When that son of a bitch came over yesterday morning, while you were out… he was half-tempted to go back with him. Fucker did a great job brainwashing the kid, maybe you can help him straighten out."

"Can't straight gay Harry you know that," Nick quipped with half a smile.

"You know what I mean boy, straighten out his upstairs head, there's obviously nothing wrong with his downstairs one. Speaking of which, you're using them rubbers yes?"

Nick paused a second, looking from the wall to Frank's curious expression as it craned down in front of him, then down to Harry's expectant one, "Yeah."

"Good, maybe you'll be more careful in this line than you were in the first," Harry mused.

"Whaddya mean?" Frank asked.

"Sex cooties," Harry smirked, "that's why you gotta wear a rubber."

"Sex cooties? You had sex cooties! So gross!" Frank scowled and placed the last piece of tape across the area of the head of Harry's bed, "does that count for Sidhe too?"

"Counts for everyone," Nick answered, lowering the boy down to the floor before craning his head back to inspect their handiwork, "why, you already making moves on Ilirya?"

"NOOO!" Frank answered a little too quickly, his face turning scarlet as he flopped into the chair with his arms crossed over his chest and his chin tucked, "one of the Oemirs kissed her… and, and,…" he stammered looking back and forth between Harry and Nick's expectant expressions, "…and it was nice," he 'harumph'ed'. "And I think I remembered… things…"

"And you liked it," Nick finished with a huge grin even as Frank nodded while a couple tears slipped from his eyes, "what're you crying for? You didn't do anything wrong, it's natural, and it's part of you."

"But you gotta remember kiddo… you're only nine," Harry interjected, "she's thousands of years old and she lost the love of her life and there's gotta be some part of her thinking YOU ARE that love… but you don't have to be if you don't feel that way."

"Really?" Frank sniffed.

"Really."

"Really." They answered together.

"But… what if…" he started then stopped and shook his head again, still beet red.

Nick slipped into the chair next to Frank wrapping his arm around the younger boy, "Frank, she's waited thousands of their years, you sure as hell don't have to rush into anything you're not ready for."

"But you did!" Frank pouted, "you did lots before you were ever ready, and you're only okay now 'cause I got the soul…"

Nick sighed wrapping the kid into a tight embrace, "I told you before, it's different when you *want* to share than when someone just… takes…"

Frank nodded, "but I think I want to share but I don't know, and I don't know *how* to know or not."

"Then you're not ready yet," Harry smiled gently.

"Exactly," Nick agreed, "and when you are, you *will* know it."

"You think so?"

"Yeah," both elders nodded.

"Will I like boys or girls?" he asked.

Nick shrugged, "I don't know… does it matter?"

"I dunno."

"Well, when it's the right time, you'll know."

"But what if I like both."

Nick shrugged again, "so what?"

"Isn't that kinda copying?"

"If it's love would it matter?" Nick asked.

Frank gave a quick shake of his head then pointed at Harry whose eyes had slipped closed, and even breathing was punctuated with light snores.

"Just let your heart tell you who it loves, and you'll be fine," Nick whispered, "but for now, just remember it's okay to be a kid."

"You sure?"

"One hundred percent," the older boy smiled.

Shoulder to shoulder they leaned back, each lost in their own thoughts as they too slipped into a light sleep unaware a milky white eye, in the sliver of bathroom darkness had watched and heard it all.

--

On the driveway Mickey frowned, her hands on her hips, "and you're going to explain to your mom you're on the state border for what? You decided to go to Redding for shits and giggles?"

Harry Jr. shook his head, "I'll figure something out it's not like we can leave this thing here, if those dicks come 'round it's gonna be effed up enough if they don't decide to run plates…Frank said they knew something, just couldn't say what…he also said don't say anything to Charles about that."

"Gotcha, and you really wanna get your mom involved in this?"

"No, I don't *wanna*…" he bit.

"So look, she doesn't expect to hear from you till the weekend right?"

Harry nodded as he strained to mount the new tire one of his contacts brought over, "Yeah."

"So we have the pastors' keys and shit. Thankfully, his phone got smashed… I made sure to crush all the bits inside so it can't be traced. We need to get rid of all that crap anyway, so since you got new plates on it, why don't I go with, follow behind till you think it's good to ditch the car. Then we ride back together, or maybe go to Umatilla and ditch his car there, then just hop a bus back?"

On his back, pushing the tire all the rest of the way onto the stems with his feet, Harry pursed his lips, "s'a good idea, I think we should take Charles with us… he's jumpy as a bug on a hotplate, get him away from the house. Vahl can run interference if they do actually come by."

"They're cops," she sighed holding out the handful of lug nuts to him, "of course they're gonna come by. Leave it to adults to screw

102

everything up. Ass holes don't even understand we're the ones gonna be saving the world they're so set on destroying anyway, I mean what's that about?!" she ranted.

"What about those old guys from the other night?" he smirked glancing out the side of his eye at the girl.

"At least they're hunters, they're not trying to screw things up... just fix 'em."

"That older brother sure wanted to screw someone...not like you were lil miss..."

"Keep talkin' buddy," she drawled with a smile, "I can't help it, it's in my blood..."

"Momma always warned me girls were trouble."

"She say anything about boys?" Charles asked joining them with a light arm over Mickey's shoulder while a yawn of epic proportions stretched his mouth wide and he said, "You probably should let me come with."

Huge half-circles lay under his bloodshot eyes, while he watched Harry leaning heavily on the four way, tightening every other lug before going back around again.

"We were just talking about that," Harry grunted, giving each lug one last lean before letting the car down.

"I could be another set of eyes, and I really don't want to deal with cops."

Mickey and Harry both nodded.

"What I really wanna know is how Vahl got all the blood cleaned up so perfectly," Charles muttered, "I mean I can't see even a spot..."

Harry shrugged but Mickey piped up, "It's a glamour. He just hid it."

"What?" both boys asked.

She nodded, "Yeah, it's still there…"

"And we been walking through it all night? Sheeeeit that's sick."

Mickey shook her head and sighed, "it's a little more complicated than that but… don't worry we're not tracking it."

"What's a glamour?" Harry asked.

"An image spell. Usually, folks use 'em to cover up zits and stuff, most of the time it's pretty lightweight magic."

"Magic? For real? C'mon…" Charles scoffed, drawing a strange but deep smile from the girl.

"Really? Other universes, other species, living dark… and you can't buy the prospect of a little spell?" she shook her head, "kid, do you know anything about what you've gotten into?"

Charles nodded, "Nick told me… it's just… spells? Really?"

"Yeah," she nodded, "really… wow do you have a lot to learn."

"Spells and magic and all that stuff… that's all the devil's work."

"There is no devil, there's no god, that's lesson number one," Mickey stood eye to eye with the boy, "everything, magic, spells, wards, all of it, it's just harmonics and physics, it's just the ways of energy and nature, there's no good or evil inherent in any of it, it's all about the intention."

"That's pretty Zen," Harry smiled wiping his hands on his jeans.

She grinned, raised her right foot to the inner part of her left leg, turned her arms out to the side, palms up, closed her eyes, and hummed, "Oommmmmm," making both boys chuckle.

"Doesn't change the fact that it's the truth," she nodded, returning to normal and motioning toward the house, "let's go fill in the turncoat and hit the road."

--

He watched her disappear behind a tree and smirked wondering if she was lying in wait for him or if she was tending to something else. She'd been aware of him from the moment he stepped through to follow her instead of Ilirya, but until evening began to descend she hadn't been overly concerned.

"I'm waiting," his voice was soft with a warm, wry bent.

With a questioning raise of an eyebrow she turned from the safety of the ancient wood and stood before him, taking measure of him from his mid-back length, raven hair, over his simple gray garments, to his deeply worn short-boots. He had no cloak, and only a simple belt and sheath with its dagger at his hip. He was so ill-equipped for any kind of journey it set off bells in the pit of her. Her eyes flicked behind him, looking for anyone else who might be waiting to ambush her.

There was benefit in the overgrowth of the path they'd been traveling, the sounds of others would be easily given away by the knee-high grasses. Far too long ago the way had been clear but now, it was only recognizable to those who'd once known it.

"Why have you been following me?"

"It's been long ages since my last visit to the Gargol and since then, these woods have grown foreign with time," he shrugged, "there is safety in numbers."

"And skulking should have me feel safe in your presence?" she challenged with a step toward him, her short sword at her side, ready for defense or attack depending on him.

"You have a mission, a time for meeting would come eventually."

"And it has," she nodded, "give me your name."

Another damnable smile turned his lips in a way she found suddenly very pleasing as he ducked his head, his finger scratching absently at a long-faded scar down the left side of his face, "I have been known by many."

"Then pick one."

With a deep breath he raised his midnight eyes to hers, "You may call me Minya."

"Minya?" she asked, a sneer dying before it could take hold of her lips.

"Minya."

He took a step closer to her, as she did to him, all her senses keen, taking in every detail she could, but still, there was something off. She sensed no malice from him, in fact no purpose in him at all save to continue moving.

"You have a mission, we should continue," he nodded down the path, "before night falls and we will need to hide."

"Hide?"

He nodded, "Do *you* know what now lives in these woods?"

The quick shake of her head was reluctant.

"Neither do I, hence hiding."

"There were once shelters not far from here," she offered pointing in the general direction of the Gargol territories, "I had not planned to stop but if you need to..."

"Then we'll not stop," he shrugged, "but time is precious."

"What do you know?" she asked leading the way through the underbrush, clearing a path for him with her knee-high boots.

"The Nahroehn fortress is on the move, grinding through the land toward the Bedowen. Living dark, schade, and their allies have attacked the tower, they move together openly in the night. We have no way to know if our allies still exist. This war may well destroy all life on Aderyn, and that is only the beginning."

"The tower is moving? And the beginning of what? What you know or what may come?"

"Yes," he answered simply and motioned her forward when she stopped and turned, an angry scowl on her face.

Eventually he would explain what he knew, once they reached the Gargol he would have to. He could keep his silence for now, and she would keep her eyes on him and tabs on the sense of uncertainty riding her spine. In enough time the reason for it would come to her.

—

"Wakey wakey, eggs 'n bakey..." Frank whispered into his big brother's ear, his eyes pinned on the older boy's hand as it returned with Nick's awakening.

"Sorry," he muttered pushing himself up a bit.

"S'okay, but you better be careful about your dreams, your hand went to the other side."

"Really?" Nick asked looking for confirmation from Harry, but he was still out. "How do you know it was the other side?"

"I could feel it. What were you dreaming about?" Frank asked lowering himself to sit cross-legged on the floor.

Nick shook his head, "I don't really know, It felt like being in Buck's bunker with all the lights off. Pitch black, but then you think you're seeing something but it's just the swirls in your eyes trying to see something different y'know? But it wasn't scary it was... cool, like comfortable, kind of temperature cool not *cool*, cool y'know?"

Frank nodded.

"When did you wake up?" Nick asked looking at his watch, noting he'd been out about an hour himself.

"About ten minutes ago," the younger Emerson sighed, "Nick, how do we get a message through a wormhole? I mean, we don't have the tech to shoot any kind of message into space and even if we did we wouldn't have any way to tell if we were shooting it in the right direction... I mean this is beyond anything..."

The deep distress on his little brother's face wrenched Nick's heart as he leaned forward to fluff Frank's hair, "You're thinking like we're earth-bound. With the energies on Aderyn there's no reason we couldn't reach them, especially if I can get Cathbad to help."

"Aderyn? How do you know that's what it's called?"

Frowning, Nick shook his head, "I don't know, it just came to me, like a dream, or maybe a memory from a long time ago."

"The first line maybe?"

"Maybe," he nodded.

"Like how you knew you had to 'out' Fetik?"

Nick shrugged, "It doesn't matter. What matters is getting to Cathbad or finding some kind of spell that'll reach through to the others. Thing is we're stronger over there than here so I'm going to have to go back."

"We..." Frank corrected.

"No, me. One of us has to stay here and help organize whoever we can find to keep their eyes on any of the subways."

"How do I do that?" Frank asked.

Nick cocked his head and spocked his eyebrow, "Really?"

Chewing on his lip Frank nodded and shrugged, "Like always?"

"Yeah man, but this time just start fishing for stories."

Frank's nod became more certain as did his expression, "Right, find people who've been affected by the dark, look for weird stories, supernatural, wiccan, wizarding chat rooms and stuff, have junior talk to his people and put out feelers."

"Exactly," Nick smiled feeling something inside kinda nibble on the back of his brain, but then shrugged it off. They'd both been subject to too many things in too short a time for either of them not to brain fart once in a while, "I bet Mickey could do a location spell to maybe show where there might be active subways or ones forming," he added.

"It's a good start," Frank nodded, "do you know where Wee keeps his spare bank card? We're gonna need money and I don't think my piggy bank's gonna cut it."

Nick nodded, "yeah, go in his desk, there's a hiding place between the top and bottom drawers on the left, it's where they keep our passports, there might be some cash in there too, but the extra card should be there."

"M'kay," Frank nodded.

"Don't let anyone know! Not even junior."

Frank's face squinched up, "don't you trust him?"

"'Course I do, but if he knows it's there someone could hurt him to get to it."

Nick smiled as his little brothers' eyes went wide with sudden understanding.

"One of us?" Frank breathed quietly.

"I don't think so... but why risk it?"

"Yeah," Frank nodded, "right. Why's anyone gonna listen to me Nick? You should be the one to stay, you look like a grown up, they'll know you're serious, I'm just a kid."

"Because I'm the one who made Cathbad take the soul out, I'm the one who made him promise if anything happened to me he'd give it to you... but... if he changes his mind, or if he tried to do something to it..."

"You're trying to keep me safe."

"Safe as possible. One of us has to look after this world."

"What about the other people in the painting? Do you think they're from Aderyn or do you think they're from the other planets?"

Nick shrugged, "I don't know, but Cathbad probably will."

"When are you going?" Frank asked.

"Soon as we tell the others the plan."

"Sounds like a good plan..." Harry grumbled softly from the bed, "what did I miss?"

"When did you wake up?" the corner of Nick's mouth turned up, relieved he'd come around so fast.

"Minute ago, you don't whisper as quiet as you think you do," he smiled back. "Sounds like you boys got a lot of work to do."

Frank nodded but Nick only smiled and shrugged with his mouth.

"Go do it," Harry nodded, "only place I could be safer, would be jail. Frank, you give me a call tonight and let me know how things are rolling along, or if there's anything I can help you with. I've got some contacts junior ain't got a clue about, but work with his first, 'kay?"

"Okay," Frank nodded hopping to his feet to wrap his arm around the old man for a hug.

Nick plugged Harry's charger into the wall behind the bed table and plugged it into his cell, leaving it within reach of a twist of the wrist before carefully taking his own hug, "it's already charged."

"Thanks kiddo," he tussled the boy's hair as his eyes started to drift closed again, "be careful."

—

"I gotta pack anyway so it's no big deal," Nick shrugged, "and it'll give me a chance to test out something I've been thinking about."

"What?"

"Where is everybody?" Nick asked moving quickly through the kitchen and living room while Frank checked the den.

"Vahl's in the backyard," he called then ran upstairs to check the bedrooms while Nick returned to the front door and looked out into the street and the driveway.

"Of course," he nodded to himself.

"What?" Frank asked joining him then noting immediately, "They must've gone to get rid of the cars."

"Yeah. What's Vahl doing?"

"Just sitting there, looks like he's maybe meditating or something."

"Alright, go get the stuff you brought back," Nick asked as he bounded up the stairs to his room where someone had brought his pack.

He grabbed it and the laptop and headed to Wee and Ryan's room.

His lips pursed thinking about the two men who'd been raising him and Frank for the last four years. Both of whom may well be dead as far as he knew. *I'd feel it* he thought with a shake of his head.

In the back of the walk-in closet stood their "gun closet", such as it was. It was actually an old supply cabinet Wee brought home from the office, after replacing it, the lock on the handle made it good enough. Reaching up to the top, Nick slid the magnetic key holder down and opened it up, grabbing a box of .9mm shells. Once he reloaded the magazine in the gun and a spare, he stuck the box into his pack and returned to the cabinet, wondering what else could serve his needs.

"Everything," he sighed shaking his head. There were half a dozen knives of varying sizes in there. Ryan even had two swords, a long sword and a Katana gifted to him by a collector he'd saved from a murderous thief. It wasn't particularly priceless, but it was supposedly made by one of Masamune's apprentices. Its origin didn't matter much to Ryan, just that it could kill. As far as Nick knew, he'd never used it, but he did like sharpening it.

Pulling Oemir's short sword from his pack Nick inspected the blade. It gleamed even in the low yellow light of the closet bulb, its edges sharp and unblemished. *Yeah,* he nodded knowing he was far more comfortable with a short sword than a long sword, even in his new adult body. *Stick with what you know. It's not like I'd even get a chance to pull it if Cathbad decided to attack me,* he realized but knew he had to risk it.

Closing and locking the cabinet, he sat on the bed, checking his supplies.

His collapsible baton was there, as was his lock back, and first aid kit and compass. He slipped his phone into a side pocket glad the energies over there kept their electronics charged.

It wasn't like they could call anyone since there were no cell towers, but there was another possible way he was curious about, *Walkie-talkie, c'mon gimme a free one.* He scrolled through the app store, then installed one that fit his needs.

His stomach gave an uncomfortable twist. He didn't want to go and leave Frank. In spite of Vahl keeping his 'shrimp' safe; as Mickey said, his easy change of sides didn't sit very comfortably.

Even the brief thought of her brought an instant of the taste of her lips on his and gave him a warm, pleasant, flush followed by the memory of hard muscled planes shimmering in dim light as he pulled Charles onto his knees, driving himself deep into the boy.

"Together?" he'd asked earlier, but now allowed himself to wonder for a moment what it might be like to be having sex with Mickey

while Charles had him. He was taken by surprise when he felt himself leap to life in the confines of his jeans. "Wow," he breathed turning his mind away from the idea. There was too much to do right now.

It took a couple minutes, and the gross idea of Wee and Ryan having sex to return himself to normal, allowing him to go into the dining room where Frank was just finishing spreading out the map, book, and painting he and Vahl stole.

"Vahl still out back?" he asked.

"Yeah," Frank nodded, "well he hasn't come back in yet."

"Good."

"You don't trust him?"

"Just because he's been helpful so far doesn't mean he's one of us."

"Okay," Frank nodded in spite of the fact he'd started considering the Sidhe almost a friend, after all, Frank held a knife to his throat and even cut him, but he'd helped anyway.

Pulling his phone Nick took pictures of everything then hit the record button while he and Frank went over everything they'd hypothesized, whether it might be accurate or not.

"You think the phone'll work over there?" Frank asked.

The elder Emerson gave a curt nod, "long as I'm not trying to call anyone I don't see why not. The energies over there are everywhere, it's like it's ambient."

"Isn't that Wee's sleeping pills?"

"Close, but no, and after he drove to the store and back while sleeping, Ry won't let him take 'em anymore, he switched to something called melatonin."

"Wait, he drove to the store asleep?"

"Yeah, scared the shit outta Ry, he wakes up in the middle of the night, finds Wee and his car gone..."

"When the hell was this?" Frank demanded, "You're dragged to another fuckin' universe…"

"Dude, language!"

"Screw language!" the little one barked taking his brother aback, "you get dragged to another universe, held captive a month, tortured, and been almost always out of my sight since you got back,"

"Hey, the exiling me thing was your idea, not mine." Nick pointed out, "Besides, it was a few months ago, while you were at camp. It's no big deal."

"But nobody told me!" Frank argued, his brows furrowing deep while his rosebud mouth pursed tight.

"You need to know when we take a dump or cut the cheese?"

Frank's face twisted with a look of disgust hitting Nick square in his curiosity, this kind of reaction wasn't like his little brother at all, "I can smell that thanks... this is bad though, it coulda got him killed."

"Which is why Ry put a stop to it," Nick brought the sudden argument back to a close, "are you done?"

"Still shoulda told me," Frank groused then shook his head and took a deep breath, "okay so... ambient..."

"Yeah, just means it's everywhere, just part of the atmosphere y'know. And in the palace, there's a kind of tech…"

"Yeah, like the elevator, it had kind of a touch screen, almost like swiping on a cell…"

"Right, and with the energy of sunlight collected through the light spear, there's not much'd surprise me about what they can do, so…" Nick shrugged. "And if it doesn't work, and I have to describe all this, what do you wanna bet he'll know exactly what I'm talking about?"

"Yeah," Frank chewed his lip, "do you think he's a bad guy?"

"No, just angry."

"Enough to maybe kill you?"

"Maybe. We did destroy his home, but if he didn't when he took the soul out, I don't think he will now."

"It wasn't us that destroyed his house," Frank protested.

"Doesn't matter. Anyway, we have to try. And if he won't help, then Julius and his men probably will. We're not entirely without allies."

"One guy and a handful of friends? Ry would call that kinda slim pickin's."

"Why are you being such a jerk all of a sudden?" Nick asked.

"You're a jerk! S'not my fault you don't wanna hear the truth."

"The truth that you're mad about not being told about Wee sleep-driving?"

"No! Yes! I mean…" the young one crossed his arms over his chest, "how can I do what needs to be done when nobody tells me anything?!"

"Wow," Nick shook his head, "really, this from you? You get multiple millennia of Oemirs passing through your brain at any given time, not to mention the odd 'normal' person, and you think we keep things from you... that's a lot of bullshit."

"You're bullshit!" Frank spat.

"Oh yeah? You tell me everything that passes through your mind...and everyone?"

Frank stopped short, "No. How'm I supposed to know what's important, until it's important."

"Exactly."

It took a minute for Frank to see how his own argument had once again been brought full circle, and as he did, his dark blue eyes turned glassy while his teeth worried his lower lip, and his head nodded without conscious direction.

Warmth rushed through Nick before he wrapped his arm around Frank's shoulders giving him a gentle squeeze, mindful of his still healing injuries.

"Look shrimp, we're all just doing the best we can with what we got."

Squeegeeing the glaze from his eyes with his fingers Frank turned, almost pleading with his big brother, "Take someone with you?"

The idea struck Nick like a tickle, and he actually giggled while tousling Frank's hair, "Oh yeah, Charles is on the verge of a nervous breakdown, junior's never been to another world, and he's needed here anyway. Mickey'd be fine over there, and maybe even be able to fight both physically and with magic if I could keep her mind on something besides my dick…"

"It was just an idea," Frank sorta pouted.

A hint of shame pinched Nick's chest, "It's a good one, but there's just no one I can take with, everyone's needed here, with you. Mickey and junior are going to be the ones you need to count on. Charles could balk, and if he does, if chooses to go, you have to let him."

"What if he goes to the cops?"

Nick sighed, "that's going to be his choice."

"He could get you put in jail!"

"Yeah," Nick nodded. "I killed a guy Frank, two guys, you think I shouldn't pay some kind of price?"

"You said you'd do it again…"

"Damn right I would!" he held Frank's chin between his fingers, "but taking a life isn't without consequences, it's just a matter of whether you're willing to accept them or not."

"So you're gonna go confess now?" Frank's expression morphed into something Nick had never seen before. It was something between a kind of rage and something else, he could swear, almost bordered on hatred, "never mind it was self-defense, and Harry defense! They let people go for that unless you lied. Do you wanna get put in jail?!" he shouted.

Nick frowned, "Listen, it *was* defense, but if Officer Stern and Detective Harleson do somehow figure out it was me, I don't think I can lie about it. If I was going to confess I'd've already done it. And for them to figure it out they're gonna hafta make room for possibilities adults don't usually allow themselves to believe in, so I think we're in pretty good shape, BUT, if they do come around and start asking questions, the only thing you can tell them is that I went out on some errands and said I'd be back later."

The littlest Emerson seemed to deflate, "What about Charles? We just… let him go?"

"No," Nick shook his head, "we *help* him get wherever he wants to go, have junior or Harry use their contacts. If he chooses to leave, we have to help him if we can, and if he knows we're on his side he'll be less likely to want to spill any beans."

"I'm not dumb y'know," Frank mumbled.

Nick grasped him by the shoulders, careful to avoid the pirini wounds, "What the hell's eatin' you shrimp? I'm the emo-freak, you're supposed to be the sensible one."

Frank shook his head, how could he tell his big brother; the one who'd already sacrificed so much, literally giving away not just the soul he'd had all his life, but letting himself be used in so many other ways that Frank wasn't sure he could keep control of everything inside himself. How could he explain costing them their world didn't matter if he wound up doing something, or letting someone else do something to hurt Nick or anyone else in their little family?

In his mind, the welfare of the universe just didn't seem as important as the handful of people they were both relying on to get them through this. The whole idea felt like a betrayal that could burn Nick alive if he let it out.

He sighed, "I just… you're… shit… I got a headache bigger than the whole house… and there's so much can go wrong!"

Nick nodded, "I know, but hey, you're one of the smartest

people I know, just do the best you can and use the people around you, use their smarts, their opinions, their ideas."

I'm just a kid Nicky... so are you but you're... like you're ready and I'm not... why can't I be like you? He wondered even as he nodded.

"As long as you do what you truly believe is best, no one can ask anything else of you. I believe in you man but that don't mean a hill 'o beans if *you* don't believe in you. All you gotta do is listen to your guts, trust 'em like I trust you."

An explosion of twin tracks raced down Frank's cheeks, his mind screaming in spite of his understanding nod.

How could he tell his big brother he couldn't tell what things running through his mind belonged to whom, or from when? How could he tell Nick that without being able to reach out to his mind, Frank wasn't even sure he was himself anymore? Fact was, he couldn't, he either couldn't find, or didn't know the words and the worst part of it was he didn't know if it was something wrong with him, or something maybe one or more of the others was doing to him.

"I don't want you to... I know..." Frank's lips trembled, "...but you have to...", *don't leave me...I don't know if I can stop them, I'm so scared.*

Nick felt his own eyes water up as he wrapped his arms tight around the other boy, the pinch in his chest had become a burning sensation, "You're gonna need to be as strong as I know you are and stick to the plan, trust Mickey and junior, they'll help you until Harry's up on his feet."

Frank wiped his eyes dry and sucked up his insecurities, "Nick, I love Harry like brother, but he's *old* now. I don't know when it happened but... it did and maybe he shouldn't..."

He knew what Frank was going to say, he'd had the same idea rolling around in the back of his mind since seeing their friend standing there with the pastor's knife sticking out of his body, but he dismissed it.

Not only would Harry not stand for it, he'd be crushed if the boys tried to keep him out of the mission, especially after he'd done so much to bring them here. They'd been together far too long, they all knew what was on the line. There was no way the man who'd spent a lifetime trying to create the circumstances to save two boys, who could then help save two universes would let those boys risk their lives without him.

"He'd never…"

"No, he'd never forgive us," Frank agreed.

"But his presence will reinforce your leadership, he'll hold you up whenever you need it."

"Like a General?"

Nick smiled, "Exactly."

The idea instantly calmed him, and he nodded, "Yeeeah, okay."

With their plans laid out as best as possible, the energy between them became charged with anticipation of positive action once Nick woke up his laptop, and Frank hopped online with Wee's.

They worked diligently, scouring news headlines, stories about strange storms, doppelgangers, and ominous dark shadows on paranormal websites and chat rooms. They even went so far as to put out some basic information about the living dark, things to look for, and some simple wards to help fortify homes against it. If hunters frequented some of these sites and boards, they'd hopefully help spread the word, and maybe even seek out some kind of connection.

"Harry can be the contact for them, they'll take him serious," Frank smiled after about the tenth site.

"And it'll keep him out of harms' way," Nick agreed.

4

W hen all was said and done, nine living dragons slipped free of

the bowels of the earth beneath the Bedowen forest, how many dead they were leaving behind, none of them wanted to contemplate.

In spite of Diagas being the one to free them, out of deference to Zu; the last of the Green Flame Clutch allowed the eldest to lead them all out into the light, grinding through the now, rapidly decaying forest of the once lush lands.

The ruby colored reptile raised his snout to the sky, his tongue sampling the air all around them until his attention fixed on a dark heavy scent to the north east. "There are pirini nearby my kindred!" he grumbled low, his voice a thrumming stimulation through their very bones, "A feast beyond imagining… they foul our world with their carrion stench! Find them! Feed until you can feed no more! And when you have taken your fill we will meet at the tip of the great mothers' tail to awaken our kin and take back what was stolen from us!"

The others shuddered, their heads bobbed in agreement, fluffing their frills, and filling themselves with the memory of their origins. Their snouts curled back as they too caught stealthy scent of the nearest of their ancient prey. Those who had wings stretched and fanned them, wondering if they still had the wherewithal to take flight, and those without wings faded from vision, camouflaged by their surroundings as they crept, slithered, or slunk toward what was certain to be a feast unlike any in the history of dragon kind.

"Beware the firdur!" Diagas hissed just loudly enough for all them to hear, but still a susurration natural enough to keep from alerting any of the ancient enemies that dragons were once more, loosed upon the lands.

--

"Silence them!" Leanna snarled as the soldiers she'd left behind returned with their prisoners wrapped in fragments of living dark, joining them in a small, wooded grove. A sinister smile stretched her mouth as the vestiges filled theirs.

Pinned motionless within the spiny tendrils, the kin of heroes each suffered more than they'd known possible. When the dark wrapped its bits around each of them, it gripped them with extensions of itself, thousands of needles whose bores it could manipulate at will to keep them under control.

Those needles could be either solid or hollow, dripping their blood from thousands of holes at any part of their body. The only bits spared so far as they could feel, were their eyes, but not one of them had any doubt the dark knew enough about human anatomy to torment them any way it wished.

For each of them, it was the first encounter with the enemy their forefathers fought to save at least two universes from.

Until the moment it'd been called forth by Leanna's soldiers, not a single one of them had the slightest understanding of the true depth and breadth of the gravity of what they were supposed to fight, and what had already once, been turned back.

None of them could have explained how the idea of a universe in peril hadn't left them shaken to their very atoms, until now. So for the first time in a long time, aside from the screams, moans, and groans of agony with every movement, they behaved.

--

Torn knew he should've turned back a long time ago, but he'd found a cadre of firdur and schades moving through shadows, toward where the Bedowen met the Western hind-claw of the mountains, and decided to follow.

It wasn't long after when his heart leaped in his chest and a smile greater than any he'd ever felt before lit up his face.

At first he couldn't believe what he was seeing as he hid beneath a thick prickleberry bush, taking cover from a flock of pirini. He remembered being a young Sidhe, watching models of various dragon species in the crystals. He'd never seen the peripheral shift with his own eyes, but it was exactly as it'd been imaged in the archive. So when he saw one indicating a ground dragon moving close by, he thought he must certainly be hallucinating.

Watching in disbelief he grinned, and followed the creature, (though it certainly knew he was there), as it stalked toward its favorite prey. The air held the buzz of tension as the beast coiled, bearing back on its hind legs, reeling its long neck tight to its body. The beauty and depth of its green scales had him hypnotized, and the creatures' gold, platter sized eyes shone like small suns in the deep of the forest.

He fell back on his behind as the being's neck, and almost its entire body shot forward, its glistening ivory fangs snatching a pirini off its branch in complete silence.

Snapping its prey in half with its powerful jaws, it turned its gaze to him, winked and sought out another of the carrion eating fowl.

Even with Torn watching, Diagas scored three more of the creatures before the flock finally sensed something and flew off.

"Do they see you?" Torn whispered as the creatures became ever smaller dots in the sky.

"If they had, their retreat would have been far more entertaining," the dragon smiled. Often enough had he been the beneficiary of a flock throwing the slower of their own out of the sky or off their perches to be fed upon in order to save themselves.

Gladly reminded of the old times, he swung his head around till his face was so close Torn could see the blood, bone and gristle between its teeth, and the frills in its nose.

Frozen in part terror and part wonder, the fledgling warrior stood up but remained rooted to the ground as the ancient being's tongue flicked out, sampling the air around him before dragging back, cleaning those muck filled spaces.

"Are you really real?" the young Sidhe asked.

Diagas' upper lip tilted in a strange but somehow comforting smile, "Are you?"

Torn nodded and swallowed hard, "As anyone else."

"We are returned to the world, it is time to bring balance back."

"The firdur has returned too, it attacked the tower of the sun through the night. It infiltrated the dead..." the youth panted, remembering what he'd seen and trying to keep a lid on his desire to vomit.

Diagas nodded his head, able to feel the depth of the boy's disturbance, "Humans have also returned, two passed me by only days ago. It is time to prepare for war once more."

Torn nodded, "A son of Oemir himself is leading at the tower though how he'll manage I cannot fathom. He bade us spread out and follow the schades and dark, to learn where they were congregating."

The dragon's eyebrow arched, "and what have you learned?"

"I saw..." he gulped, "Bedowen soldiers with man prisoners wrapped in firdur, there were too many for me to do anything but track them."

"Reeeeeaaaalllly?" Diagas mused even as Torn nodded, "Show me."

"Yes," the fledgling breathed, his mouth widening into a tentative smile.

Even after introductions had been made and the incredible fact of the dragon's existence had equally been made certain, Torn's heart skipped several beats when Diagas gave the youth a claw up to its shoulder and told him to, "hold tight."

It was as if the very nature of time and space was different in the presence of this wondrous being. The cumbersome trek toward the dark glade which seemed to take hours on his own, now took mere minutes.

He would swear he'd only taken a handful of breaths before Diagas came to a quick stop raising his snout to the sky. When he crouched, the fledgling instinctively clung low behind a row of his neck frills.

"Are they still there?" he breathed knowing so long as air passed his lips in any way, the dragon would hear him. Though they were still too far away for the soldiers and their prisoners to be much more than dots; there was no telling where the living dark may be or how many of their possessed kin may be patrolling the forest.

"Weapons?" Diagas asked out the corner of his mouth.

From his belt Torn slid a short-sword, holding it with a surprisingly steady hand before his golden eye, which he would suddenly swear was crinkling in a deep effort to contain laughter. Mildly embarrassed, the fledgling shrugged.

"Be still then, and see whatever you are able," he instructed while hunkering down, laying his long neck and oddly comforting, if fearsome face down on the ground. Every now and again his strangely beguiling, forked tongue would slip out and taste part of the world around them, but for the time being, Diagas was content to wait.

5

A sly smile stretched Vahl's lips as he once more, appreciated the strategic placement of reflective surfaces allowing him to see the two men on the front stoop, without his own position, or even existence within the house being betrayed. There was something in their bearing that told him these were the men Nick had warned him about, and Frank had prepared him for. They were this worlds' equivalent of law keepers. He drew a deep breath, steeled himself and opened the door.

"Hello," he greeted, peering closely at the badges they held up as he leaned against the jamb.

"Mr. Emerson?" the taller one with the more serious demeanor asked.

"No."

"Mr. Stevenson?" the other tried, as if he didn't know they were both well aware of what the Oemir and his mate looked like.

"No," he smiled but stuck his hand out as he'd seen Frank do with Sherry, "I am Vahl. The messers are away."

"Ah, well Vahl, I'm Officer Stern, and this is Detective Harleson, we're here to talk to Charles Brown."

"Apologies, he has gone with the others, they feared him falling asleep."

"Can you tell us where they went?"

Vahl shook his head, "No."

"No?" Stern asked.

"No, I cannot tell you what I do not know."

"They didn't tell you where they were going?" he asked.

"No," Vahl reiterated.

"Do you know when they'll be back?" Detective Harleson asked.

"I do not."

Both of the officers frowned, "Were you with them last night when the attacks happened?"

"No."

"Where were you?"

"Here."

"Doing what?" Harleson asked tapping his lower lip with his pen.

"Cleaning."

"Cleaning? Cleaning what?" Harleson asked.

"That which needed to be cleaned," he shrugged, "the kitchen, the dishes... managing the household."

"Managing the household?" Harleson asked, "You have an interesting accent, where are you from?"

Vahl sighed inside, their questions were going to make him do the one thing he really had no desire to. Keeping his disdain to himself, he cocked his head to the side and opened himself up, listening for whatever answers he could glean from the information and assumptions circling the officer's mind

"Ontario, Ryan is an old family friend." He offered after hearing one of them think it.

"Mr. Stevenson?"

Vahl gave a curt nod, "he asked me to watch over the family while they are away," he sighed, "they were distressed over last night's events. They'll not spread themselves so thin next time."

"Mister..."

"Vahl..." the Sidhe responded.

"You got a last name?"

Vahl's head tilted to the side, "Nahroehn."

"Nahroehn?" he questioned.

"Yes."

"That's an interesting last name... what is it... French?"

Vahl's head twitched to the side, "Tuath De."

Harleson shook his head, "What?"

"Celt," Stern tried to hide his smile, "he's Celtic."

"Ah," the more gruff detective nodded, "So, Mr. Nahroehn, do you know whose vehicles those are out on the street?" he asked.

"Two of them, yes," he answered, watching as both officers tilted their heads, waiting for elaboration.

It wasn't that Vahl didn't understand what they were asking, or what they expected of him, but he found he didn't care much at all for the arrogance and sense of righteousness seeming to ooze from them. He'd told Frank he would behave as close to humanly as possible, but with this most recent exception, it'd been thousands of years since he'd had anything to do with humans other than killing them. Now he remembered why.

"Well?" Officer Stern prompted.

"Ah... The dark one belongs to the eldest living Emerson, he too is away with Mr. Stevenson and... Wee. The large one belongs to the Steward, a family friend."

"Is he around?"

"No, though one could hope he has gone with his love," the Sidhe smirked. Just because he'd sworn his sword to the cause because of Ilirya didn't mean he had to wish the son of Conchobar well. After all, if they'd done away with him when they had him, firdur would've won the war millennia ago.

Officer Stern nodded, "so no one's here but you?"

"Correct, you are more than welcome to wait, though I do not know when any of them will return."

"Can you give 'em a call and find out?" Harleson asked, then frowned at the perplexed look that crossed the Sidhe's delicate but vaguely feral features.

He sighed, "come in," and led them into the living room, grabbing what Frank had called a 'cell' off the coffee table. He pushed on it just the way Frank had instructed and found it wasn't too different from the communication crystals their kind had been using for centuries. It was intriguing to see how the humans managed to develop technology independently. After several tense seconds he found the contacts and called Harry Jr.

Just a few minutes later, and being sure to press the red boat at the bottom of the screen, Vahl ended the call, "so, tomorrow then," he confirmed escorting the two officers to the door.

"It's hard to believe they didn't tell you they were going away for the day," Harleson frowned not liking the squirrely way his stomach was acting at the moment. Still, he got what he wanted, a statement from Charles who'd seemed out of it, though after being awake for close to 36 hours, it was understandable; he didn't feel right about it, but it was understandable.

"Nick and Frank are my responsibility, the others are... independent."

"Hey, speaking of Nick and Frank, you don't happen to know their ages do you?"

Again, and in spite of his now thundering head, Vahl opened himself up to the officer and whatever information might be floating around in his mind, "Frank, I believe has nine, maybe ten annuals and Nick..." he squinted his eyes getting two different ages from the man and considering Nicks appearance, chose to answer indirectly, "... I am not certain. He does appear older than he is," he smirked adding, "he is an old soul."

A quick phrase, 'said he was 14,' came to the fore, the information stabbing him right between the eyes. When he'd told Frank he had gifts too, he hadn't told the boy how much he detested using them. Not even Semet was aware of them, if he had been, Vahl had no doubt he'd have been forced to use them or suffer consequences he would rather not contemplate, like all the others his heru used and discarded.

Officer Stern stuck out his hand, "thank you."

The three exchanged handshakes, then as the two officers settled into their vehicle, Vahl closed the door but remained behind it, listening with his exceptional Sidhe hearing.

"Tuath De?" Harlseon asked.

"Formally it's Tuatha De Danann, children of Danu, a Celtic goddess, usually Irish, but Scots too... maybe even some Welsh and other Britons." Stern smiled.

"Why the hell would you know something like that?"

Stern smirked then raised his eyebrow, "and here I was wondering why you *don't* know something like that."

"You were a freak as a kid weren't you? Dungeons and Dragons, Alastair Crowley, The Cure... all that shit... tell me you weren't." Harleson charged thinking he had his new partner by the short and curlies, and visibly thrilled he'd have something to torment the older man with.

Officer Stern however shot his new partner's clay-pigeon hopes right out of the air, "Damn right I was, at least I didn't have to drug and date rape girls to get a little action like some of those muscle heads did."

"S'cause freaks never got any,"

A slow smile crept out over Stern's face as his eyebrows raised up, "you must not know any freaker chicks man... s'a shame. No clue what you missed."

"Bullshit," Harleson huffed.

"Such a shame."

"Someday you're gonna hafta tell some stories."

"Nah man, I'm a gentleman, my folks raised me right."

"Dude… decades ago."

Stern shook his head, "Code of honor duuuuude. You're just gonna hafta use your imagination."

After a moment of companionable silence Stern continued, "So, mister Nahroehn, what'd you think?"

"Something don't feel right, what've you got on the kid again?" Harleson sighed before securing his seatbelt.

Turning the computer toward himself, Stern searched "Emerson, Nick" then turned the screen toward his partner.

"Two Nick Emerson's, the father, murdered six years ago during a home invasion, and a junior, age… turned 14 this year, got a state ID with PL for the family business. He's home-schooled, so's Frank…" he accessed the DMV pictures of both Nicks and stacked them side by side. "Remember when home-schooled kids were the freaks?"

Harleson nodded, "These days seems like those're the only ones with any sense anymore. What's the business again? Damn if that kid doesn't look like his dad."

"The family owns the Like New Used Cars chain, kid just got the PL for moving cars between locations during non-peak hours."

"Shit man, how old's that pic?"

"Issued last year," Stern shook his head, "looks like a baby here,"

"Says he's 5'4"… he ain't 5'4" anymore…" Harleson pulled his phone and opened a picture taken at the ER entrance the previous night, then expanded it to get a better look at Nick, "Shit, kid looks like he's in his 20's, man, the changes in a year," he shook his head too, "how's a fourteen-year-old look like that?"

"Do you have any idea how much hormones n'shit're in foods these days? I'm surprised Frank's not just as big."

"Oh god, you're one of *them* too?" Harleson shook his head, "Y'know, I know a lot of Canadians and not a one of 'em talks like Mr. Tuath De."

"Ontario man, French accent... besides, he could be a transplant, maybe parents still have accents y'know? But yeah, as a person... he's definitely a little weird," Stern shook his head as Harleson put the car into reverse, "I want another look at that statement and the pic." Stern nodded then dialed from his own notebook, "Hiya Nick, this is Officer Stern, give me a call when you get this, I need to ask you a few more questions. Thanks."

He hung up as Harleson half frowned, "Five-ten, salt and pepper hair, soft but not fat, jeans and a dark jacket... sounds an awful lot like Mrs. Everett's missing pastor don't you think?"

Stern shrugged, "Sounds an awful lot like seventy five percent of white males in America."

"Austin PD said Mrs. Everett told them he was on a mission to bring the boys back..." Harleson pulled out of the drive and onto the main street, "yeah well Nick's home is here, so even if he ran away originally, he's back where he belongs now, and as for Mr. Brown, he's an emancipated teen, he doesn't have to go back if he doesn't want to."

"If you got something to say just spit it out."

"Any pastor, priest, rabbi, whatever's gonna know a 16-year-old with a background like Mr. Browns' is free to be on his own if his own parents won't have him, and runaways return home more often than not..." he shook his head frowning with his mouth, "something doesn't smell right and I'm not sure who broke wind."

—

"Do you know where you're gonna land?" Frank asked holding Nick's pack tight to his chest as they edged deeper into the woods. Nick searching for the place he'd passed out the night he got back.

"If I got the rotations and sizes right, this should put me right on the edge of the Bedowen closest to the Aine Haud."

"Are you gonna go to the tower?"

"Eventually, but I gotta..."

"Yeah, you gotta talk to Cathbad first, but I already told you, the other worlds are gone, dark killed 'em. I felt it from the others." Frank explained again.

"I know, but they were moving, their orbits were changing in the pendant, maybe they were wrong, maybe... it's gotta mean something."

"Nicky, I know what you want, but the pendant's just a watch," Frank argued softly, "everything's already set inside, so if our world moves then theirs will too, it doesn't mean those worlds or the people from them still exist."

"It's called hope, and I need it." He wasn't surprised at the depth of Frank's understanding, but something inside needed for them to somehow be wrong. Nick sighed, "I still gotta try, and if nothing else I'll get the pendant back."

Looking down, Frank built up a small pile of leaves with the toe of his shoe, "What if he tries to kill you Nicky?"

Unable or unwilling to meet his little brothers' eyes, he shook his head, "I don't know. If I can't talk him out of it, I might have to fight him."

Worry darkened the little one's voice, giving Nick an idea of what he'd sound like when he grew up, if he got the chance, "he's a wizard, one of the first ones..."

Shoving aside the idea of Frank dying as a child, Nick tried to lighten his own suddenly darker mood, "did you know even guys are really witches, 'wizard's a label the church gave 'em. They called boy witches wizards because they didn't want them to be confused with women."

"Really?"

"Mmm hmm,"

"Why?"

"Because in the mind of the church women are worth less than men, so calling a guy a witch was an insult."

Frank's expression twisted with a strange combination of confusion and a low level of exasperation, "Why?"

Turning in place, trying to get his position to match his memories Nick smirked, "Long and short of it... Because women don't have dicks."

"Well that's stupid, they make babies and make food for them... that's even more important than just... you know..."

"Takes both parts to make a baby, and I never said it made sense, but don't forget, dads take care of kids too," Nick's gaze scanning the tree line, confirming they were close to the right spot. From his reckoning, he should wind up within a few miles of the mound.

"'Less they get killed," Frank mused, "but moms," he felt the corners of his eyes start to sting, one of his last most comforting moments with his mother came after they'd gone to live with Nana, and he'd got sick from diving too deep into Ryan's pain.

He'd got sick and barfed, and mom held him and rocked him till his tummy settled down again. It was the last memory of the comfort of being in her arms. There was very little he wouldn't sacrifice to have just one more moment of it.

"Yeah, well, moms get killed too," Nick muttered, feeling the intensity of his little one's memory. He sniffed with a sudden deep longing to see their mother one more time too, he'd almost forgotten how much he missed her.

Knowing, more certainly than most there was no way to have another moment with her, he pushed out a sharp, deep breath and continued trying to distract them both, "...some guys are jealous they can't have babies, so they try to make themselves seem like they're more powerful, like they have the right to rule everything."

"But they don't," Frank shook his head. "Nobody should be able to rule over other people unless they want that person, then it supposed to be leading, not ruling."

Nick nodded, "well *we* know that, and when they're wanted, it's supposed to be a team effort."

"How come?" Frank asked as Nick finally found the spot Frank found him on the rainy night he broke free and came home.

"Because when there's two, they balance each other out, each one contributes something the other doesn't have."

"Whaddya mean?" Frank asked following.

"Look at you and me, you're the feeler, the thinker, I run interference, take the hits when I have to. Ry and Wee; Ry's the hitter, Wee's like you, he feels and uses it to think around violent situations," Nick smiled then added, "it's natural, besides, The History Channel did a couple documentaries on Ancient Egypt. 'The Golden Age of Humanity' they called it. There was peace, health, wealth, and nobody ever went hungry."

"Then what happened?"

"The priests started taking bribes to get people into 'heaven'," he made air quotes as he bent down to look at the remnants of his sooty handprint in the trunk, "finally."

He smiled and drew out a vial of his own blood from his jacket pocket.

"This is the one." Frank noted.

"Mm, hmm."

"Then what?"

"What, what?"

"The priests took bribes..."

"Yeah," Nick nodded as he started to draw into the air, the symbols and sigils to open the way between worlds, "well, they took bribes and started telling the kings they were supposed to rule everyone and women were only for giving them heirs, which for some reason, made them seem less important? Aaahhnnd it just kinda snowballed from there to where we are now."

Frank frowned, watching as the air held the sigils and gave a faint shimmer, "so they lied for power over other people?"

"Mm, hmm."

"That's stupid, no wonder Wee and Ry don't trust 'em."

"Yeah, that plus the tithing," Nick sighed then rose up and faced his little brother, who once again looked like an adolescent Sidhe, "alright."

"What's tithing?" Frank asked.

"It's a price churchgoers pay for their supposed 'salvation'."

"Whaddya mean? Like the bribe the priests did?"

"Yep, and then some, some even tithe their children."

"What?!" Frank asked feeling the same smokey dark, hot place inside his big brother he'd felt last night when he was talking about the guy he killed.

Nick shook his head, this wasn't the time or place for him to explain about the church and the travesty it'd perpetrated against children with the full consent of their parents, for the last several centuries. It was bad enough he knew there were guys out there like Pigg and Ezra. "When I come back kiddo," he smiled pointing to the opening in the curtain between worlds.

"'Kay," a tight frown twisted the younger Emerson's face while handing the pack over, feeling like doing so was somehow letting go of the older boy, "remember your power. Don't let him kill you."

Nick nodded, his hands on Frank's shoulders, "Harry, Mickey, and Jr., use them, let them protect you, and if the others start talking or trying to take you over, remember, YOU are the one who was born for this world, YOU are in control, it's YOUR power, YOUR life, YOUR TIME. It's going to take YOUR WILL to keep control."

Frank smiled, pulling his cell, and opening the walkie app Nick found.

"Okay," he nodded.

Nick did likewise noting he'd missed a call, but not caring since he didn't recognize the number.

With his pack over his shoulder he hugged his brother hard before stepping through to the first universe their soul called home.

There was a strange sense of relief when the 'curtain' between worlds closed behind him. As if by departing the world he'd been born into this time, somehow its problems were just a little less urgent. A faint smile crossed his lips, and a sigh swept the stresses off his shoulders. For all the problems facing them in this new world, they also somehow seemed more surmountable. There was no analyzing or acknowledgement of the sensation as Nick took a quick look around, saw he was alone and wiped the signs and sigils from the air, sealing the universes from one another.

"You there?" he asked.

"I'm here, you're coming through loud and clear. This is so cool!"

Frank's excitement was contagious as Nick grinned and started walking in the direction of the mound.

"Okay, I'm walking, you start heading home too."

"What about the car?" Frank asked, as he made his way back toward the sidewalk.

"Just tell junior where it is. I hope if those cops show up Vahl can handle them."

"He will, he's pretty smart. He kept his cover when we were with Sherry..."

The further they got from each other, the more their signals started to break up.

"Frank?" Nick asked.

"Yeah... I can barely hear you Nick, you're signal's dying."

Unbeknownst to one another, each boy stopped for just long enough to say what was most important to them.

"Yeah, no towers here. Be safe Frank, I love you little brother."

"You too Nicky, tell Wee and Ry I miss 'em and love 'em, but save some for you too."

And very like magic, with about a mile between them in each universe, the connection was lost. Still, knowing they could communicate if they were close enough gave them each a renewed sense of hope as they headed toward their respective destinies.

"...it's YOUR power, YOUR life, YOUR TIME. It's going to take YOUR WILL to keep control." Frank mocked through a hint of a sneer just before rounding the corner toward the house.

Catching sight of an unmarked police car, he ducked back behind a thick hedge watching the two detectives drive to the community exit. The fog of cynicism rolling over him with Nick's departure was swept away as an adrenaline surge made his corners tingle.

He wasn't ready to run into either of them yet and was going to play on his age as long as he could to avoid having to deal with them. After he and Nick ironed out the plan for the older boy to try and reach some of their other-worldly allies, whether they existed on Aderyn or not, Nick warned him to use his age to his advantage with the cops. *"You can't tell them what you don't know, and it's easier to convince them you don't know something if you really don't know it so..."*

"So..." he shrugged, *"you just asked Charles if he wanted to come with."*

"Right, nothing more, nothing less... I trust you shrimp, you'll know what's right to say and what's not."

"I won't let you down Nicky, never," he whispered wondering if it was all the things they'd been through making him so angry lately, or if maybe somehow Ne'Min left some of himself in his mind. Once the car was gone he moped his way home, feeling like he was walking inside a cloud even the sun couldn't burn away.

Nick sighed tucking the phone into his pack before breaking into an easy jog. The experiment was only a partial success. He and Frank could speak, but if they'd both been walking in opposite directions at the pace Nick directed, the range from one world to the next was about 2 miles total. Of course, being able to make contact at ANY distance, from an entirely different universe was huge and wonderful! He'd just hoped it could be more since Aderyn's energies were so pervasive. *Maybe Cathbad will know how to amplify them.*

Lost in his thoughts Nick stopped and stared, stunned to the point of disbelief. When he came up from having Cathbad remove the soul, the tree had been little more than a sapling, but now was fully grown.

It was nowhere near as majestic as it'd been before the darkness and the bolt from the light-spear destroyed it, but it looked as old as any of the trees considered ancient in Umatilla. "Wow," he smiled when a spark of hope flicked to life.

He cast a quick but intense look all around on the ground, then up into the skies before loping the last quarter mile to it, unaware of a set of golden eyes, not too different from Diagas' watching him, and wondering what these humans were going to do to their world this time. She wasn't ready to meet up with the others, she'd lived alone, fought in the first war alone, slept alone and awoken alone. She had no desire to interact with any of them, but still needed to know what they were up to.

Barely winded Nick drew to an easy halt in front of the great tree. He felt good, invigorated and light as he made his way around the trunk, until he found the entrance and watched the bark part in familiar woody curtains.

The stairwell was darker than even his vision could penetrate, and as he started his descent, he noticed a void of silence betraying a lack of activity in the druid's home.

"Cathbad!?" he called shining his phone's flashlight before him.

"Cathbad!" he shouted then whispered, "Where are you, you cranky old knothead?"

But there was nothing, no response as he reached the bottom and marveled.

There was no sign of the previous destruction, all the scrolls, books, beakers, test tubes, earthen jars, and everything were back in their rightful places on the shelves built into the walls.

Even the clockwork of the heavens was suspended, turning, and churning as if it'd never fallen, as if it'd never nearly crushed Wee and Ryan, as if it'd never nearly trapped Ilirya to her death. Not a crease or a crinkle existed in the metal ribbons representing the heavenly ellipses.

"Huh," he huffed watching the representation as its celestial bodies turned and moved however slowly, in their orbits, in the back of his subconscious something broke and sent a wave of chilling recognition over him, "No shit..." he mused noting how familiar it was, "how?" he wondered.

Was there a reason for the clockwork of the heavens to be represented both here and within the pages of the pendant, and if so, what was it? Had the old druid known the first war would come, and if so, when, and how?

"Really?" he sighed feeling at his neck for the heirloom. A couple weeks of its absence could do nothing to erase the years of its presence he'd grown so accustomed to. "I never should have taken it off, never should have left it," he shook his head and sidled off to the right, toward the depths of the druid's home. "Okay... where's my stuff," he hissed shaking his head, frustrated he'd missed something so obvious.

"...just 'cause it looks like a solar system doesn't mean shit... thirteen different worlds, multiple heroes from multiple universes, all dependent on each other. Did each world give thirteen heroes? Thirteen times thirteen...a hundred and sixty-nine... that's more like it, makes more sense... but Frank said they're gone now, us two are all that's left... how do we win this?" *CAN we win this?*

Lost in his thoughts while moving down the corridor, he didn't register the familiarity of the items displayed. There were rock hewn shelves lined with jars full of preserved things, animals, fleshy bits, vegetation, or any number of strange items he couldn't recognize, and a few he was pretty certain he didn't want to. "Sick," he sighed leaning toward an attention catching jar. It held a very large, silvery eye he was almost afraid would blink or look directly at him.

Thankfully, it didn't.

There were drawings, maps, portraits, most of which were of the world itself or many of its species; butterflies, dragonflies, that from the size of them seemed to have somewhere around a three or more-foot wing-span. There were hawks, pirini, dragons, and tons of other animals in their natural habitats, and still others more like the painting Frank and Vahl found depicting the leaders of the other races meeting, presumably as a united front.

There was one he found particularly beautiful. It was a rendering of a rose with petals of many colors all overlapping until they joined together into a rainbow-like stem. He smiled thinking it was oddly similar to so many of the early taxonomy drawings found in books and magazines of every pre-color photography era. There was even writing, though in Sidhe, he figured must describe the parts of the flower.

When he looked closer, he noticed the petals were all circular, and he recognized one of them, though quite how, he wasn't sure. The name of the bit he understood said "d'or o'edain". "Edain... edain...edain," he ran his hand through his hair as a chill ran through him, "Eden..." he breathed, "they called it Eden...that's where it came from...holy shit..." he huffed then counted the petals on the flower knowing before he was finished they'd number thirteen, and they did. "It's a triskadecagon, *the* triskadecagon," he whispered, looking back at the clockwork.

Stone on stone shuffled behind him, making him whirl, shining the light of his phone down the hall, but there was nothing.

He frowned noting the end of the corridor coming far too quickly with nothing telling in sight. He almost turned around but something told him to go directly to the far wall, to not stop till he touched it.

A sly smile slipped out as he looked to his left just before the corridor ended, revealing a slim dark opening, concealed until one was right in front of it. "Thank you 'Labyrinth'," a flash of a scene of the young girl in the beginning of the maze passing carefully camouflaged openings came to mind. He'd loved the movie when he was younger, but the goblins scared Frank who clung to him as if his life depended on it. Nick, however, had been mesmerized by how angles and perceptions had been used to create optical illusions, but aside from exhibits at museums or art shows, he never imagined any of it could come in handy in real life.

He stopped on the threshold peering into the citadel. It wasn't particularly large, but with the sudden shift in his awareness, he was able to see two other slim openings in either side of the back wall where both the casket and the sepulcher were inlaid.

A heavy puff of breath bounced against the walls just before he recognized the anomaly of the room. He rested his hand on the narrow divide separating the Druids hallway from the citadel and slid it around. Beneath his hand, fine grain, raw stone, not unlike limestone gave way to something colder and slick as a brand new white-board, even smoother than marble. The breath sounded again.

He held his, listening, wondering if he was alone or was there someone behind those darker than dark slits at the back?

'*s'just your…*' he whirled again, willing to swear he felt the wind of words tickle his ear.

"Imagination?" He barely breathed keeping one ear focused on his own sounds, the other on anything from any other angle as he stepped into the darkened room.

His head filled with blacks and reds, his nose filling quickly with the scent of smoke and old wood fires.

An image bubbled at the base of his gaze, revealing a tower surrounded by sand but bordered with a broad river no more than a couple hundred yards on its southern side. On its western, was the first strip of what would become a forest to rival anything earth had ever offered up, even during its most primeval days. The tower bore dozens of ornate arched balconies, most of them adorned with diaphanous silken draperies beckoning with seductive flutters in the breeze.

"My love..." a warm, honeyed voice sent delicious chills up his spine from the darkness behind one of the uppermost curtains, *"the people do not require your attention every moment of their lives..."* it was a good-natured chastisement, but it got the point across.

"They are different from their queen," his reply bore a knowing smirk, filled with the same good humor as her comment. Still, he turned behind the drapery, a tunic of forest green loosely draped over his shoulder to end halfway down his thighs.

"Only in their reception of your attention," she smiled, wrapping herself around him from the shadows of a corner, her hands sliding beneath the tunic, one gliding down his back to capture the firm curve of his buttocks while the other cupped his manhood bringing it to eager attention.

"Shit!" Nick panted, looking back and forth down the hall, certain he was alone, but almost driven to clutch his knees for the intensity of the vision, "Holy fuh huh hudge! Was that me? I should remember..." he wondered, trying to bring up the image of the woman. Had it been Ilirya? The voice hadn't felt or sounded like hers, it was thick, like honey but with the weight of molasses. He knew she was beautiful and somehow, he also knew she was a lover of consummate skill capable of making him quake on more levels than he could understand yet.

His hands shook and waves of sparkly sensation cascaded back and forth through him as he tried to focus on the task at hand. He reached for the sepulcher, nearly dropping it as it seemed to almost slide itself from its resting place into his arms.

Frowning with how light it was, he carried it into the hallway where the nearest two lightstones of those built into the walls instantly illuminated.

"They will have lives of joy and bliss." She sighed inside his head.

"And they will want for naught, the first ones are wise, and will educate their brothers and sisters in the ways of the worlds." He responded smiling. But somewhere, underlying these comments came the sound of metal on stone, and against metal.

In seconds those sounds transformed from healthy exercises to something far more earnest, and he knew they'd been wrong. Whoever these two were, there hadn't been the utopia they'd prophesied, something they hadn't been able to anticipate happened and Nick could only wonder if it'd been the product of the living dark's first forays into this realm.

"Wouldn't surprise me," he huffed startling when the lid seemed to spring open under his touch, "okay, that did…"

Looking from one of the lightstones to the other, then down into the chest Nick shook his head and began taking inventory.

It was as if whoever packed the chest knew what would be needed one day.

There was one more set of clothes, a light cloak he somehow knew would be as warm as he needed it to be, his bow and quiver had been returned, his long sword, another pair of boots, and a pack with all the accoutrements he and Frank found on the Fierowen soldiers he'd frozen when they first arrived. In the pack was their version of a first aid kit; parchments, what looked suspiciously like a modern pen but had no ink to it, "where IS it?" he growled then felt it. Even wrapped in leather the shape, weight, and energetic tone of it was unmistakable.

He unspooled the leather from around it, his eyes glistening at the first twinkle of light against the gold chain, then shedding several tears as the ancient bauble fell into his upturned palm.

"I'm sorry," he hiccoughed sweeping them from his cheeks, "I thought I was doing the right thing," he explained slipping the chain over his head and cradling the pendant in his hands. It warmed quickly with his touch, its front opening with the faintest brush of his finger against the latch, then behind the face, the first 'page', then another, and finally, with a feather light bend of the link through which the chain was run, the top knob popped open on a tiny hinge.

"I know, it's long past time," he nodded pulling his lock back and pricked the of one of his fingers. One at a time, three large droplets oozed up, running toward the open top, all he had to do was get it close enough.

Holding his finger and the pendant's reservoir together he squeezed until it was full then sat back amazed when the top snapped closed and the cut in his finger sealed.

"Wow…" he breathed flipping back to the previous page he'd not so long ago done a rubbing over. He'd believed the orbits and tiny spheres to be nothing more than planets, never even a suspicion that the planetary alignments could have had a matching alignment with adjacent universes. What he'd first thought were merely orbital paths for each of the planets to travel, he now realized, on tracing them back to their origins was far more intricate and infinitely more telling as he tilted the page in the light to draw a shadow along those trajectories.

With the interplay of light and shadow, his understanding of the consequences of this war became so much more complete than any of them could have anticipated.

If the dots he'd been calling planets, were actually universes, (as the book, the drawing and the clockwork seemed to indicate), then this page of the pendant was a cosmological model of thirteen actual universes that at one point in time seemed to have overlapped allowing for the original Heroes to interplay on a level no one could have imagined. It made so much sense he dropped back onto his butt and sat there, breathing hard, digesting, and assimilating the possibility. *This shit just keeps getting bigger and bigger every damned second!* Desperation cried deep inside. *Just like…*

"…the universes." Something started to click inside, some information whispering just beyond his hearing as he tried to draw it to the fore by going over what he knew while stuffing everything into the pack from home. "…they're expanding even faster now than it was back then, that's what the scientists say. If the others were alive, they'd probably be too. And we're sliding apart because of it. But we've all been expanding since the beginning… faster and faster, forever, if they're right. Eventually it'll all, THEY'll all be dark anyway." He frowned, "why doesn't it just wait? Eventually it'll win, won't it? What am I missing?"

He dropped the pendant into his shirt, feeling another shift when its warm metal touched his flesh, almost settling into the pit of the scar left by its removal. No matter where the soul was, or in which of them it was housed, the pendant at least, was home.

Bringing the chest back to the citadel, he noticed his hands having fallen into perfectly crafted grooves. He'd been so focused on retrieving his belongings he hadn't noticed the finer details now making themselves known.

"Huh," he pulled his phone again to access the flashlight but instead, all around the chest, in what he'd figured to be little more than swirls, and dots of decoration, lightstones started glowing in runes and writing he was able to identify as Sidhe in origin. He was surprised once more when some of the stones encircled what he'd noticed was a lock on the chest. Upon closer inspection he realized it was a lock, made especially for the pendant. And on the left and right end, where his hands fit to lift and grip the chest, were impressions that fit his perfectly. A shiver went up his spine as he set he box on the floor to get a better look, and dozens more stones burst to light all around him, illuminating the room till it was as bright as noon.

Tilting the chest up to take as many pictures of its designs as possible he began to turn it and felt an icy hot sweat break over him when he saw the molded circles for his hands, getting confirmation of the snub fingers. "What the fuuuck…" he whispered, wondering if Oemir'd had the same injury, or if it somehow changed to fit *him*, and if so, what could it mean? He suddenly had an excruciatingly clear understanding of Franks' fear.

Would it change anything? He shook his head, it wouldn't. They had to do what they had to do and if they got lost in the process, it was a small price to pay for the trillions of lives they could save.

"Alright, next things' next…" he pulled the pendant from his shirt and eased it into the impression on the sepulcher.

An audible click sounded, and the chest gave a wiggle as a drawer unlocked from the base.

Inside were three tightly folded parchments. He started with the smallest one, instantly recognizing it as a genealogy though he couldn't read the writing just yet. He could feel the information just on the edge of his consciousness. It was like trying to read a book in a language just different enough to make you grind your teeth. He couldn't do it, but knew he should be able to. He could, of course, recognize the family name on the second line from the top on the left, and he was fairly sure he recognized the names Lugh, Danu, Cathbad and Conchobar as well and did a double take.

"Well I'll be a monkey's... half-brother," he huffed then nodded, "Okay then," before folding it back up and sticking it inside the waterproof document pocket of his pack.

Next he opened one about the same size as the last one, but folded like a book.

It seemed it was a book, the writing was undoubtedly Sidhe and again, he found himself frustrated because he couldn't read it yet. *It'll come... it has to, there has to be a reason for this... Oemir wouldn't leave it to chance if he did all the rest of this on purpose.*

The third document brought with it a sense of relief, it was another map, also written in Sidhe but it was almost identical to the one Frank found in the fortress, though more detailed. This one was replete with illustrations of the different people who lived in the different areas, many of whom were part of Earth's own mythology. There were also strange markings easy enough to interpret as friend or foe. Friends were marked with a star formation and foes were struck through with a sword symbol, and there was a third mark, the tree of life turned upside down, which made him think the people of those areas might have either died off or been killed off.

His eyes fell to the Dragonbow mountains, and he smiled despite the heartbreaking losses he felt when the spine ridge fell, killing so many of their kindred in the cascade he'd wanted to follow them to the Summerland.

To his surprise, the symbol drawn there brought a faint smile, the tree of life, but it was neither upright, nor upside down, it lay on its side as if Oemir himself hadn't been certain if the people there were all dead or not. The people of the mountain were the dragons themselves, the offspring of the great mother who'd sacrificed herself to create their very world and bring life and light of all types to it.

Almost missing it in his whimsical reminiscence, his eyes fell to the area of the Nahroehn, it wasn't there. At least the fortress wasn't there, the earth was cracked in plates, those plates limned in red, so they resembled scales. The whole thing surrounded a thick river of magma with three small dragons emerging from it. One to the air, two to the ground, one of them with legs, the other without. Still there was more to it, but at the moment, the significance escaped him.

"Dragons… could there really still be…"

"Who's there!" barked Cathbad's crackling voice.

"Who do you think my old friend," he muttered hastily folding and hiding the map before snapping the drawer closed.

"What do you want!?" the druid demanded catching sight of Nick slipping the sepulcher into its resting place.

"I came for my belongings," he dropped a companionable hand onto the wizard's shoulder.

The ancient one leaned in sniffing hard at the boy, "You're different."

Nick nodded, "it's been a long few days,"

"Weeks down here!"

"How long have you been gone from here… up there?" he asked

suddenly understanding some of the differential between Cathbad's home, Aderyn's rotation, and Earth's.

His woody brow lifted, and a sneer pulled up a corner of his mouth before he shrugged, "a day… what do you think you're doing with this?" he asked palming the pendant.

"Taking it back, I didn't know any better."

"And you think you do now?"

Dropping it down his shirt, Nick cocked a half smile.

"I have to contact the other worlds, and I need your help to do it. It's good to see you old friend…"

"Only because you need something… always when *you* need something, what of others with needs? What of the sons who are HERE and need YOU or are you still such a selfish beast…"

Nick felt his lips turn down and his brow furrow, "The sons here? They're in trouble?"

That hard, wizened woody face leaned close to him, sniffing and scowling, eyes pinching tight as if to look right into the heart of him before answering with a nod, "from my understanding, the son of Conchobar, and several of his companions are taken by Leanna, who has thrown in her lot with…"

Waves of insight cascaded through Nick, whether it was the old being somehow sending him the information or whatever had come to him since his encounter with Leanna he couldn't say, but he turned his head to the side, "Tur…" he gasped frowning, "is there anything left of the Bedowen?" his hopes of grabbing a horse fading quickly.

"How do you know that?" Cathbad ground, "I only just sensed

the connection after leaving the navel."

Nick shook his head and shrugged, "it feels right... I mean it doesn't feel *right*, it just feels like I know it, like maybe I knew it when she was... I just..." then looking at Cathbad's face and reading the suspicion there, he shook his head and lied, "... magic's clinging to you maybe?"

The old wizard huffed, "Get out and do not come back unless you succeed."

"I need food and water," Nick cocked his head to the side before feeling the weight of his pack grow several pounds heavier. Looking at the carabiners on either side he saw two large skins hanging from them and smiled.

"Thank you."

"There's tonkfish in the pack. You will find the darkness in the eastern forest. Now get out, and don't get killed this time or there will be no time for you to find your way back."

Nick gave a quick nod heading toward the stairs then turned back, unable to stop his mouth, "You can be as angry with me as you want, but you cannot change the fact you are as much to blame for what went and what's coming as any of the rest of us. Your years and supposed 'wisdom' makes you even more culpable my old friend... you could have moved to prevent..."

The woody old wizard raced forward letting loose a shriek any respectable banshee would love to be able to wield as his fury took the form of a battering ram ready to crush Nick into the wall.

Inside, the teen was trembling with both anger and fear, but he did not move. He watched that smoky blunted end come racing at him, driven forward by the druid's charge across the floor, *so like the dark when it attacked us in the car…* he thought, wondering for a moment.

His left hand came up making a halt gesture to send the ancient creature catapulting over the suddenly stilled column of manifest rage, and into the wall.

"It was only a reminder of the truth of the past," Nick said softly, scooping his old ally up by his under arms and setting him on his feet. His hands lay gentle on the druid's shoulders, their eyes locked until those spindly arms came up, batting him away and his hands off him. "Get out," he hissed.

"Be ready my friend, try to contact the others if any are left. I think the time of our need is long since overdue." Nick turned his back on the old one and ascended the stairs knowing the first place he had to go was to the Bedowen. He had to assess the state of his homeland and see if he could find a horse willing to help him.

--

Despite seeing the sun come and go at least once while incapacitated by the dark, none of the heroes could say just how long they'd been captive of Leanna and her soldiers. Faces had come and gone, including hers, but it seemed within the dark there was no understanding of time's passage.

To Shep at least, it reminded him of the days on his voyage with Vahl to meet with Ula, *"I sure hope she's okay"*, while he'd been locked in the berth, drowning in grief over the loss of his nephew; but the others had no such frame of experience, and it showed on their faces.

So far as yet none of them had been tortured beyond their initial warning, and so far as yet, none of them was eager to chance what the next warning might bring.

They wondered what was happening on the battlefronts, who was winning, how many losses there'd been, and who they might be. Dylan was concerned about Howie and whether or not he was still alive, though in his darkest heart he knew the younger Emerson was. There was a terrible destiny awaiting him, and if Dylan couldn't get there in time to save him Wee would be better off if he at least got there in time to kill him.

Lou's gaze rode over each of his compatriots, his guts, for the moment hot and oddly light feeling. Today, whatever day it was, was NOT the day they were going to die.

He knew it as certainly as he knew he grew up in one of the most haunted towns in Illinois, beside Chicago itself. Something was coming, and in a flash he became aware of it.

It was the same ultra-low frequency he'd felt while on approach to the fortress with Dylan, the same kind of ultra-low frequency he associated with companies blasting in the quarry on the other side of town, giving him migraines as a kid.

With his eyes starting to feel the build of pressure, he shifted them to each of his comrades, catching theirs with his own, his excitement though was something they couldn't understand yet. Still, the son of Conchobar knew something very big was coming. The question now was whether or not it would get there before either the soldiers or living dark would do whatever they had planned.

The eternity it took for Lou to figure out what Leanna and the dark had planned passed relatively quickly. Through the trees, shafts of light and shadow from the setting sun were growing long. Soon those golden rays would turn orange, then pink.

Just before yellow turned to orange, each of the sons of heroes screamed as the dark squeezed them, raised them up into the air and slammed them down, spreading itself over each of them, stretching them out, pressing them flat like so much dough under a gigantic, spiked rolling pin. The tendrils of itself the dark used to keep them under control grew, with more spiny quills spreading and deepening their hold till each man was pinned, deep and, at various points, secured possibly into the very earth itself.

Their screams likewise pierced the oncoming dusk as writhing, smoky columns hovered over each of them. The first took Shep, flooding his screaming mouth, flowing up his nose and even pressing into his head through his ears. Beneath him blood flowed, darkening the ground as he bucked and thrashed against the invasion, fighting with muffled screams, as though through layers of void and time.

Dylan and Lou, each on either side of the older hunter, and helpless to give anything but prayers for a quick death if that's what it intended, were forced to watch as he stopped breathing for far too many agonizing seconds until Lou couldn't stand it anymore and screamed, "Leave 'im alone you motherfucking...fucker!" He braced for retaliatory pain, but nothing came.

"Motherfucking fucker," Dylan panted, gently flexing against the spines pinning him but finding no release. "That the best you got? Might as well call 'em 'assbutt'," he scoffed an instant before his own tendril pounced over and into his head the same way, cutting off his air and causing Lou to shout out again.

"So help me GOD I WILL KILL YOU!" he threatened as his too plunged, encasing him in the same oblivion as his companions.

Rage burned through each of the men, the best moments of their lives manipulated, warped, and mutated in memory with the worst. Hurts, grievances, perceived and received injustices were multiplied and amplified, wrapping those moments in a caustic veil of venomous fury, hate, and most importantly, fear so hot it could melt stone. Such a level of fury, over time, would burn out the soul of any living creature, leaving a deadscape of cold ash in its wake.

This is how it had succeeded in swallowing countless peoples, planets, and universes before, and how it would destroy this one as well.

In its last encounter with the beings of this universe, its center had been too far away; blown forward an eternity in time by the inopportune blast of a dying star, resulting in the creation of a nebula of epic energetic proportions, allowing even more light and creative energy in to delay its return.

In the immediate aftermath of the blast, it hadn't been strong enough to move backward through the current of time nor had it been pervasive enough. It had relied on those of its followers to soften the event horizon of light; to corrupt it from within so these worlds could be fractured with ease, a crown jewel of nothingness as it retook the universes, and brought existence to a halt; but they'd failed.

"Soon fledgling," Diagas whispered, raising a paw to block the young warrior as he tensed as if to slide down to the ground. Watching the sons of heroes being assaulted by the dark was a vile thing, their muted screams and howls were deafening to the old dragon, and made Torn's very skin want to crawl from his body.

To anyone on the outside it wasn't long before Leanna and her soldiers went from laughing and cackling at the expense of the men to cringing. Each of them privately grateful it was not his or herself in the clutches of the vestige. In the distance the dark slit of the dragon's pupil was fixed upon the Bedowen princess as she backed into the vestige's embrace. Within it, she became a pale silhouette moving sinuously and he realized the dark was playing her as it would an instrument.

A lustful moan rippled from its depths, catching the attention of the soldiers who turned from the humans to look and watch their mistress being mated by this fragment of living dark.

"Be ready to tend the men," Diagas instructed, his words whispers on the wind. Torn's quick nod was enough.

He set his paws firm to the ground, his claws, each of them the size of a Sidhe leg, sank into the woodland floor like hot blades through butter. His neck pulled back while he drew deep of the air around them then rippled forward with a hearty exhale, turning the night brilliant emerald.

The first target was the soldiers who, caught with the full force of the spire, turned to ash before they could draw breath to scream.

When he was certain he'd got them all, he turned his furnace toward the upper portion of vestige still trying to batter its way into the humans.

As the wall of intelligent void bucked and jerked in spasm to escape this killing surprise attack, and a torment it hadn't experienced in thousands of years, his lips pursed with pleasure. Attempting to save itself from agony, the firdur split across its girth, its upper portion turning back to Leanna, wrapping her deep in itself while whatever happened to the heroes was left to the abandoned lower section of itself.

Torn and Diagas watched as those columns of dark, each now more desperately than ever working to force their way into the humans, seemed to shrink, though whether because it managed to take refuge inside the intended hosts or because it had been burned away by the flame, they could not tell.

Eventually, the ancient dragon turned its flame to the last vestige of the vestige, still wrapped around, and now frenetically playing the princess of the Bedowen. Within it, she was oblivious to what had just happened, until the green flame burned through the outer layers of darkness, reaching the Sidhe woman whose scream nearly curdled Torn's blood.

"Tend the heroes... be cautious," the dragon ordered, as one more sound joined Leanna's screams.

This was the sound that wanted to splinter the night. A scorched metal on bone shriek capable of flaying the very air as the vestige, only partly done with its taking of the princess, caught fire. It left her a smoldering waste on the forest floor while thrashing and wilding its way deeper into the woods in a vain attempt to quell the dragon's flame.

The fiery smiting took only seconds.

Torn dashed to the men, each of whom lay still as death, their clothes smoldering, their flesh pierced hundreds if not thousands of times, but untouched by the killing flame, he wondered if perhaps they were too late, if they'd waited too long. Still, he trusted the dragon, its senses were far keener than those of most other beings, "cautious?" he breathed to himself.

"Whatever of the firdur managed to infiltrate is still within them, it will take you as well if it can."

The warning wasn't anything Torn was expecting, the idea of the dark consuming him as well, even after the rest of it had been exorcised set his bones to shaking.

"Bind them, one each to a tree then tend them," he ordered, a single claw scratching at the ground.

To the north and east an eerie, blood chilling green glow, reminding him of a book he'd once read called "The Tommyknockers", lit the night making Nick's blood run cold. "What the fuuuhh?" he whispered as Naiya, a kind and gentle chestnut mare he'd discovered patiently feeding just outside Tropus' rapidly decaying stable, veered toward the glow.

When he found the stable, his heart sank, it was so decayed he was certain no animals could have remained, until she turned the far corner, munching on whatever still living patches of grass dotted the area. She took her time, ambling toward a jumbled pile of equipment, while seeming to size him up. It was only a moment later when he realized it was her tack laying in a heap on the ground, her name emblazoned on the bridle and saddle.

She raised her head, cocked it to the side, still chewing the last mouthful and peered at him as if she'd been awaiting him.

Nick, for his own part bent down and picked up the bridle, "if you were waiting for me, thank you." He slid the soft leather piece over the mare's head, glad Wee and Ryan introduced them to a nearby stable owner a few years ago. Mr. and Mrs. Roberts taught them how to groom, saddle and ride as long as they mucked out the stalls before they left. Neither boy minded doing a little labor for the feeling of freedom riding brought.

When he finished saddling her he stroked her neck and met her eye, "The dark has come, the sons of heroes need us," he explained before swinging up onto her back.

The duo were on approach to the area Cathbad indicated when the glow burst to life. Naiya cast a glance at him and broke into a trot then, feeling his legs tighten around her barrel, into a fluid gallop he always figured must be similar to flying.

They came upon the scene sooner than expected, and while Naiya had long been accustomed to strange scenes, and was more apt to assess, she couldn't help noting her youth's legs clench and tremble. An involuntary shudder cascaded through her own skin when her eyes fell on a sight she'd never beheld in her life, a dragon, alive, enormous, vibrant and apparently, at least testy, had burnt a large part of this area of the forest with surgical precision.

Nick freed his sword from its sheath in the saddle and slid to the ground. His sword arm rose to mid-chest and a fearsome steel glinted in his eyes as he stalked toward the fledgling but balked within a few steps as though hitting a barrier.

Of its own accord, his body cringed and for a moment his mind retreated to blankness. Air stopped in his throat and his flesh twitched with the memory of thousands of needle sticks and razor-like slices firing through his nerves.

He forced himself to take a breath while his eyes scanned the darkness, looking for the vestige he could feel was still close.

Before him, the boy held his position in front of the bound heroes, his short sword out and, Nick noted, surprisingly steady for his age.

His tongue and throat were thick with nausea as he demanded, "What have you done!?" motioning toward his family. He forced his leaden feet to move toward them and saw, in the brackish exudate oozing from their wounds, the reason for his reaction.

"Th, th, they…" Torn stuttered, discomfited by his sudden inability to form a coherent sentence with the arrival of this newcomer.

Nothing he'd encountered in the last day and night had befuddled his mind, not the sneak attack on the tower, not coming face to face with one of the sons, not even meeting, befriending, or riding Diagas, or watching the coupling of the princess by the darkness; but this man, this *human* had him tongue tied. It was proof of the legends, the Oemir had been made mortal, and was standing here, now.

Deep in his soul, With Nick's arrival, Torn now knew the tales were true, and the end of all life was truly at hand.

Curious as to how the fledgling would react, Diagas simply watched, some part of him sensing something familiar in this newcomer, aside from the familial scent which also clung to the bound heroes.

Somehow certain the Sidhe youth was no threat, Nick's glance flicked back to the men; each of them peppered with dark bloody holes, their chests barely moving, their heads hanging forward. He knew all too well what each was going through.

Pursing his lips he swallowed hard remembering those holes being bored into his own body in his first line, and caressed the barely existent pock scars in the palms of his hands. "Until they either survive or succumb, they'll be very strong. Are they bound tight?"

Torn too swallowed hard giving a curt nod before choking out, "yes m'lord."

In the distance the scorched body of the princess inched itself into shadows, the Sidhe and the human unconcerned with her while

Diagas kept note.

The one closest was Dylan, but he was the one Nick was least interested in at the moment.

Instead, he moved to Shep, well aware the older man could be faking, if what he and Frank had seen the darkness do was real. Oily sweat covered him, drawing his clothes tight to his body at the same time nauseating chills made his belly quiver. A flurry of emotions rolled through his consciousness quickly morphing into a whirling dervish before trying to become a tornado of panic.

Closing his eyes and taking a deep breath he visualized it all stilling, folding upon itself, and growing until he could use it for his own purposes.

He crouched, sneering, "you call yourself a hunter..." his hand creeping toward Shep's neck.

"M'lord, they're possessed of firdur."

"I know..." Nick sighed, "and I'm not your lord."

"But you're Oemir," Torn half protested, "any of us would know you..."

"Hmm," Nick scoffed, interrupting the youth, and finally touching the man of the MacRoich line. His fingers settled in at the side of his larynx, pressing just enough to read the pulse thundering deep inside.

Splotches of dark wetness coming through Shep's shirt caught his eye again, as they flashed in time with the pulse. The situation was worse than he thought. "Fuck," he cursed, closing his eyes, and focusing on the timescape and his bound family. "Time to repay the favor."

He envisioned tendrils of will coming from himself, pushing against them, pushing them backward, but there was something wrong. None of them were budging. Where they should have been jostling like a movie played in reverse, there was nothing but the frustratingly familiar feeling of being blocked.

With a shake of his head he focused on Shep alone, trying to will him backward, to a point where he was uninjured.

He gritted his teeth and pushed a little harder. The agony he went through at Shep's sister's house was like none he'd experienced up to that point and he had no desire to feel it again. Sweat broke over him and his own heartbeat sped up as he tried just a little more, to no avail.

"When did this happen?" he demanded of the Sidhe who shook his head.

"They were already being possessed."

"And before that? How long did it have them?" he asked.

Torn shook his head, "we have no way of knowing."

"How long ago did you get here?" he asked wiping at streaks of blood. The ooze from the deeper wounds smeared, but many were only starting to grow tacky. "Mmm," he frowned.

"The sun had yet to touch the horizon, so…" Torn shook his head back and forth, "ten minutes ago?"

Nick was crestfallen, with the worst of everything obviously happening within those minutes, there was no way he could push the three of them as well as all the events back so far. At least not yet.

"Shhhit," he grasped Shep by the back of the head and the chin, putting his mouth perilously close to his ear, "Tommy would be ashamed of you!" and let the sentiment sink in, hoping the hunter would hear and be able to use it.

A dark frown twisted his mouth as he moved down the line to stand at Lou's feet. Once again he tried to single out the son of Conchobar and force his personal time backward, and again, he had the same result. Frustrated with his inability to do what it was in his nature to do, and angered by his supposedly strongest power's ineffectiveness, he swung a foot, kicking Lou firm in his booted ankle, wondering if pain could bring him around, it didn't. Gritting his teeth again, he moved further up his leg and, finding a place not currently bleeding, kicked him again, this time in the side of his thigh. Still nothing.

As he moved to the garage owner's side, the same pulsing dark splotches bubbling up through his clothes made Nick very nervous. *This is not good!*

He glanced over to his uncle whose shirt was fully glistening in the light of the rising moon and setting sun. *Can't free 'em till the firdur's out of 'em…sonofabitch!*

His eyes returned to the older man's lax face for just another moment before he leaned down and with a hammer fist punched him hard enough to make his neck pop. He put his hand over the garage owner's face, squeezing his nose and mouth shut, wondering if survival instinct could bring him back while he leaned close to his ear as well. His gaze now flicked between Shep and Dylan, hoping to see some sign of awareness of the outside world returning to them.

"You couldn't take me before and you can't do it now, you failed Rose, you let her die… your line is a failure and Lugh himself will spit on your ashes!"

169

"My lord…" Torn whispered aghast, inching closer to the dragon with whom he suddenly felt very safe. At the moment he was both awed and terrified by the brutality Oemir was showing. This person was nothing like the hero of lore, whose tales and songs of righteous battles and self-sacrifice he'd grown up listening to.

"You could NEVER best me!" Nick hissed as the face beneath his hand gave the faintest twitch. Letting go, he drew back his fist again and crashed it into the man's cheek, first on one side, then the other, "You never had the skill or the will! You're a failure! Worthless! You're not a hero, you're a waste of time and energy!" he finally cursed and let fly one last bone jarring blow as his gaze caught movement in both Shep and Dylan.

Shaking the numb and sting from his bruising knuckles he rose, "You think I didn't save something for you *uncle*?" He finally approached the man who'd abandoned them on the night his big brother was turned inside out, then left the man's wife and children to dangle in a world they couldn't have imagined, let alone been prepared for.

There was no reason to even try to move Dylan back through his experiences. If he couldn't budge Shep or Lou, there was no reason to think he'd have any more luck with his uncle. The only viable course of action was to piss him off enough to help him find his way out of whatever the firdur was using to keep him under control.

"Please m'lord…" Torn whispered taking an unconscious step toward Nick as he reached the long-haired man who seemed so much worse off than the other two. To his surprise, one of the dragon's claws curled around him and drew him back.

"Hatred must burn itself out," he tried to explain.

"They're helpless! Who could have so much hate in their heart?" the fledgling protested in a whisper.

"Only one who has felt it burn so hot in their own breast," Diagas whispered at the same time Nick also kicked his uncle's foot then approached his tied-up torso, grimacing at the blood-soaked rope.

Torn blinked hard, uncertain if his eyes were suffering the effects of the exposure to the dragon fire or if he was simply more disturbed by all he'd seen so far, than he'd originally thought.

The air surrounding Oemir had a shimmer to it, like the desert after sunrise. It seemed to be focused around his arms and hands as he leaned toward the last captive and punched him too, though with far less vigor and relish than he had the son of Conchobar.

"You abandoned your family, you abandoned your brothers!" he threw another punch leaving a thin splotch of blood at the corner of his mouth, again, far less than the trickle he'd left down Lou's face.

"You left your nephews prey for darkness and evils YOU could have prepared them for! You left your little brother to a task he was inadequate for! You left him alone, you broke his heart and if he dies it will be on YOUR SOUL!" He stormed into Dylan's ear, then watched as the eldest Emerson's chest hitched and bucked and his eyes moved beneath the lids. "Pathetic! Worthless! Useless!" Nick continued to berate the man, his fists now locked in his shirt, blood seeping up between his fisted fingers, their faces centimeters apart, "You're not capable of defying me or denying it! You turned your back on everything you could have been and because of that, they slaughtered your wife and child, and you DID NOTHING TO STOP IT!"

His breath caught in his throat and his eyes popped wide as Dylan's head moved forward, his lips coming to rest on Nick's forehead pulling a quick cascade of ferocious, fiery red images from the boy before he backed away with a cockeyed smile on his mouth. Molten red and black emotions were dragged through his head and chest, taking him by surprise. He'd never experienced Dylan's power before, and hadn't expected him to be strong enough to use it.

Containing his relief, Nick clasped his hands to the sides of his uncle's head and slowly released the heat of his rage and fear into the older man. *Please let this work.*

"Merciful Danu!" Torn gasped watching the captive's flesh redden almost to the point of glowing.

"Interesting," the dragon mused.

Heat shimmer pulsed and grew around the two until the elders head flew back, his mouth open in a silent scream, this time accompanied by a stream of darkness on fire. A scant second later the holes in his flesh erupted in burning darkness as well. He was a living torch for what seemed a killing length of time as the darkness, working to keep its foothold in him, was driven out.

When it was exorcised Nick sat back on his heels watching his uncle as he gasped and panted, slowly working his way back to consciousness.

Once the elder man's breathing leveled out Nick moved behind the tree and cut him free. D listed to the side against the ropes even as Nick clawed at them, tearing them away before grasping at the hem of his shirt and pulling it up to his armpits.

"Goddamn hairy mother…" he muttered pulling off his flannel and using it to wipe his uncle's chest and belly clean. He had to see.

A moment later, and weak with relief he sat back on his heels, his fingertips moving from indentation to indentation where the holes the vestige had obviously kept control of them with, had been burned closed. "Thank god," he breathed, unaware of the water moistening his eyes.

In just another moment Dylan's eyes came open landing on Nick, his face twisted in curiosity.

"C'mon, you can rest later, Lou and Shep need you," he urged, helping D to his feet.

He couldn't focus and couldn't think straight, he was smoldering inside with rage and the last bits of the vestige; and this man before him was impossible. His big brother was dead six long years ago, it had to be a trick.

Still though, he was free, and his hands grasped the visage of his big brother, working hard to pull himself up.

"I tried Nick… you never shoulda… you never shoulda tempted 'em, they wouldn'ta killed you."

"Fledgling! Bring my water!" the over-grown teen ordered before meeting Dylan's eyes, having a hard time keeping him on his feet, "Wrong Nick."

When Torn dashed to him with the canteen in hand, his young face was bright with wonder,

Nick couldn't help but want to smile at it as he let Dylan take a few sips.

Naiya watched the youth take her rider's pack then turned toward one of the few patches of grass left even this far from the stable. She meandered as she munched toward the distant woods while keeping a sly eye on the gathering. Bipeds were easily

173

distracted.

"More!" Dylan gasped even as his nephew took the canteen away.

"No, you've been on fire," he dismissed then frowned as his elder whined but nodded, he was obviously much worse off than Nick first thought. "I take it you have the flame?" he asked, motioning to the few trees still burning green, and finally turning his eyes to Diagas, who gave a faint nod.

"You've already done so much, I have more to ask."

"I remember you son of Danu, we were allies long ago," he smiled.

"I pray still are," Nick smiled and was almost pulled off his feet as Dylan slumped, losing his footing until his nephew righted him and moved him to Shep.

"D, you're going to have to pull it from him."

Dylan's face crumpled in horror as he looked back and forth between the two remaining captives, "both of them?"

"'Fraid so."

"I can't," he shook his head, his breath trembling and hitching, "don't ask me to Nick, I never wanted this, I can't live that again, not two more times…"

"I can't do what you can! If I could I'd do it myself," Nick ground.

"They're not blood, and I still gotta save Wee! You don't know what's gonna happen, but I saw it! I saw it do him like it tried to do us, then it made him… it made him…" he hiccoughed then fell into the overgrown teen's arms, "it made him…*un*make him…" he shook his head, rubbing his face against Nick's chest, "and he's all that's left!"

"Jesus fucking Christ," Nick sighed holding the man back so he could see clearly, "Dylan, without these men… everything is dead! Not just Wee, not just Nick and Frank, entire worlds! UNIVERSES!" he snarled, trying to play on D's delusion that he was Nick Sr. He grasped Dylan's hands, thrusting them over Shep's face, in spite of his uncle's resistance.

"Please don't make me Nick, please…" he sniffed.

"We're out of options and maybe out of time! Now PULL IT OUT!"

"I CAN'T!" he screamed back, but the reflex was too powerful for him to control in his current state. His body trembled as the first tendrils of living dark started to move from the hunter into the reluctant psychic and trickle out into the night.

"You let his mother, your SISTER die! You let HIM DIE! And then you gave in! You gave UP! Tommy's gonna hate you, you pathetic sad sack of shit!" Nick ground into Shep's ear, heartened when the first twitches began, and the trickle became a raging set of rivers exploding from the eldest Emerson and were almost instantly incinerated by yet another surgical blast from their ancient ally.

When Shep was as cleared as he could get, and his breathing was once more back to normal, and his eyes were wobbling through the night but reacting to the reality around him, Nick motioned to Torn.

"Get your resin and get him out of his clothes, you're gonna hafta patch up the biggest bleeds." Nick ordered.

"Resin m'lord?"

"The orange powder in your kit!"

175

"Ahh her blood, aye," the fledgling nodded, hastening to do as asked.

Inside Nick another thing clicked into place, "Her blood, powdered, that's why it burns so much. And gimme mine!" he added, ushering Dylan to Lou's side where the splotches of blood had grown to nearly saturate the front of his shirt.

"Nick? S'at you?" the older hunter mumbled.

"M'lord," the boy nodded tossing Nick's pack to him while grabbing his own then moving behind the tree so he could undo the knots binding the hunter.

"Be CAREFUL!" Nick snapped, "and I told you…"

"Right, of course," the young fledgling dismissed, making Nick smile and shake his head in a spate of sudden good humor. The kid had spunk they were going to need before they got these men back to the tower of the sun or to the Dragonbow mountains.

He smiled at Ryan's old friend, "Yeah Shep, it's me. You gotta help the kid, he's gonna heal you up but you gotta get outta your clothes. It's gonna hurt."

Nick turned on his cell's flashlight, "fledgling!" He barked then tossed it to the youth who grinned.

"It has its own light!" He wondered setting it face down on the ground to keep their position hid while he got everything ready.

The hunter's face twisted in confusion as he struggled his way out of his soaked shirt while trying to return order to his internal world, "yer dead…"

"Yeah," the elder boy nodded helping Dylan sit for a moment, "wrong Nick, maybe." He shrugged succeeding only in further confusing the exhausted man, "nevermind. Jeans too Shep, you got some heavy bleeding on the right."

Grumbling, Shep did as he was told with Torn's help then asked, "how come he doesn't have to strip?" Pointing to Dylan.

"I cauterized him from the inside out…"

"Like you blew up the tree?"

"Bush, but yeah," Nick nodded, "you're not directly related, I don't know if you could've handled it."

He frowned looking at his uncle. A twinge dared to make itself known in the pit of his stomach, "Just one more time D, this one's gonna be the hardest, but then it'll be done," he encouraged softly as the older man shook his head palming away a slip of blood from his nose, his face twisted in fear and hurt.

"Don't make me Nick… please," he whispered.

"We don't have a choice," he returned wincing with the words before frowning in wonder, "Dylan, look at me," he grasped his uncle's face turning it toward him, but his eyes wouldn't meet the boy he thought was his big brother.

"Look at me! Could you do it by using me?"

The new twist morphing through the eldest Emerson's face was almost comical in its intensity, "crazy?"

"I can handle it."

Dylan shook his head as Shep's head rolled toward him, his eyes squinting in disbelief, "no Nick, no you can't," just before he sucked wind and gave a mighty growl as Torn sealed the first pulsing wound and the first molecules of the scent of scorched flesh hit the air. "Whathefuck'eryoudoin'!?" he howled.

"Sealing your wounds, it will hurt less if you lay back and breathe," Torn admonished.

Something inside Nick seemed to snap as he grasped his weary uncle by the chin and leaned in, his teeth clenched, and jaw muscle jumping, "you know NOTHING about me! NOW can you DO IT?"

Dylan's glance flicked to Lou then back to the young man he suddenly realized was his nephew. Nick Sr. didn't have an angry bone in his body, unless of course something hurt someone he loved, but mostly he was made of good humor and kindness with a hint of mischief thrown in. As far as Dylan could see, his son had become the exact opposite. "Nicky?"

"Lou is too strong for you, you can't handle him, I can."

"Use me kid," Shep muttered trying to sit up even though Torn pushed him back down, "he's been through hell."

"So have you," Nick shook his head.

"You can't know what it's like," Shep protested.

Nick huffed, "You're not in any condition Shep, so, no."

Dylan slumped against the tree, his head wagging back and forth, "Okay."

"Good," Nick nodded, "tell me what to do."

"Don't let 'im kill Wee," he muttered.

Taken aback, Nick frowned feeling his tummy twist again, "What? Don't let *who* kill Wee?"

"Don't know yet," D shook his head.

"Okay." Nick nodded. "We'll protect him, all of us. Now tell me how to drive this shit out of Lou."

Dylan rose to his knees and shoved him aside, "get out of the way," then closed his hands over the garage owner's face.

Nick scrambled to Lou's other side leaning toward his ear. "Rose is dead because of you! Because YOU FAILED HER, you LET her die! It tore her apart because YOU weren't GOOD ENOUGH," he sneered, the cruelty of his words making both Dylan and Shep cringe, though they understood what he was doing.

Neither of them had any idea how he knew so well to counter the dark inside them; it created an amorphous, constantly shape shifting, writhing fury subverting and perverting life's joys by splicing them with tragedies, hates and enmities. It warped its victims' experiences so intellectual and emotional footing couldn't be achieved let alone maintained. It was like being caught and rolled by a crushing tidal wave of every bit of hell a person carried inside and never getting a chance to take a breath.

Nick's accusations provided a coherent stream of thought a victim could grasp like a lifeline and use to channel their guilt, anger, and rage to fight against the tides trying to suffocate the soul inside the meat-suit. Didn't mean the words didn't hurt though.

They thought they wanted to know how this overgrown kid knew how to fight this thing. Nick knew they really didn't.

Even with his hands over Lou's face Dylan seemed to be struggling. Exhausted, in more pain than anyone but Nick might know, and more importantly, terrified of being forced to feel the hates and failures of someone else's life when his own were almost more than he could bear, Dylan on his own was going to fail.

Nick shook his head, *One last trick…* he thought. Biting his lips and taking a deep breath he moved behind his uncle, placed his outspread fingers at his temples and focused his energy on letting them sink in.

Inside his mind Dylan felt a brief crowding, as if someone had shoved into him, but in a breath, it became more like someone was standing with him, supporting him, holding him up even, *"breathe D,"* he heard and felt his body do it.

In another moment warmth moved through him, turning to a comfortable heat before slowly becoming uncomfortable heat that exploded into blistering, stinging agony.

"You FAILED LOU! YOU LET HER DIE!" he heard then felt the rumble rolling toward his hands, propelled by a rage so deep it almost made him pee himself, at least he thought it was, 'almost'.

"I will KILL you!" the rage snarled just before the living dark bypassed Dylan.

It erupted from Nick instead, sharing every detail about Lou's life, ravaged from his soul, everything no one would ever want another person to know.

The rupture from Nick took everyone by surprise. Diagas was quick though and just as accurate as he'd been before. His green flame burned the streams as if it were fuel erupting from the son of Oemir. The flow and burn lasted longer than it had for either of the other men, leaving them to wonder if there'd be anything left of Conchobar's kin when all was said and done.

As the darkness and the fire petered out Nick lowered himself to his knees behind his uncle, slumping on his shoulder while D slumped into Lou's chest, gasping and heaving. He thought Nick was crazy when he offered to use himself, couldn't see how it could be done, but there were many things about his eldest nephew Dylan didn't know. "Nick?" he grunted.

"Gonna barf," the teen breathed into the tattered ruins of Dylan's shirt then pushed himself away, his corners tingling as fear sparked through him, awaiting the agony of springing back to his natural age and size, awaiting the burning through his veins as the dark they'd put into him tried to exert its control over him. He panted hard, wincing while his heart skipped in his chest.

"Not on me," Dylan warned with a weak shrug.

A violent shiver cascaded through Nick, his entire body remembering the horrible, nauseating feeling of every bit of him stretching back, almost curling in on itself in an effort to put him back to right. Panting through his mouth he waited, trembling with sweat covering him from head to toe.

"Where is he!" Lou barked coming back more quickly than even Shep had.

Pale and startled, Nick peered around his uncle putting on what he hoped was a brave face, "save it for later, we gotta fix you up," then nodded to Torn who set to work untying the knots in his bindings too.

"Get me outta this!" he demanded wrenching and straining against the straps holding his hands behind the tree, causing the pulsing in the holes of his chest to gush even more.

"Hero! Behave like one!" Torn admonished, "the more you struggle the tighter they become, you want your freedom, you must be still."

"Kid's got gumption," Nick muttered pushing off Dylan before helping him to sit down once more.

"Takes one to know one," Shep added.

"When I get loose so help me…"

"Enough!" Dylan barked, patted Lou's shoulder, then groaned, "save your energy man."

Despite his feet still being bound, Lou found himself free enough to push up to his knees until he was within centimeters of Nick's exhausted countenance.

"You gotta let me help you," Nick admonished holding up the crystal resin container.

"Help me!? HELP ME!? What like you helped..." he stopped, his eyes falling on Shep, "what the hell're you doing to him and why the hell are you down to your skivvies? What the fuck's going on here!?" he demanded.

Anger once again rising to a head, Nick grabbed Lou's shirtfront in his fists, "You need to get out of your clothes so we can get you fixed up so we can get the hell out of here."

"Bullshit!" Lou argued, trying to jerk out of Nick's grip as the others looked on, unsure what to do about the pea-soup thick hostility between the two.

"GET THE FUCK OUT OF YOUR GODDAMNED..." Nick yelled before his clenching jaw stopped him. None of the others even had time to think let alone react when he stood up, and with a growl from somewhere deep, yanked the older and much heavier man onto his feet.

At almost the same instant he had him up, he pulled Lou close then virtually threw him backward.

There was only one person aside from Nick who showed no reaction at all when the garage owner stopped, suspended in midfall while everyone else watched, incredulous.

Nick kept his eyes on Lou letting the fall progress in small increments until the older man was horizontal, his feet on the ground, but from his thighs up, looking very much like he was laying on an invisible plank.

"That's more like it," Nick sighed, stilling him again.

He pulled the garage owner's shirts up and over his head, then set about dabbing bits of the caustic agent on his deepest and bloodiest holes. The closer he came to being done with Lou's chest, belly, and arms, the shakier his hands and breathing became.

His eyes flicked to the older man's jeans which were practically soaked in the thighs. Nick was going to have to, in effect, pants him. The worst of it was Nick wasn't even giving him a chance to consent to being helped. He'd used his most effective power on an ally if not friend, and now he was going to strip him down to his shorts in front of everyone.

Just because he'd learned a level of indifference to his own nudity didn't mean others felt the same way. He knew he was different, he knew if it were him he probably wouldn't give a damn, but it wasn't, it was an ally, and even worse he was going to have to touch him, again, without his consent.

The more he thought about it, the more nauseous he became, and the more he knew he just had to do it and get it done. Keeping Lou alive was more important than any possible embarrassment or vulnerability he might suffer.

"M'lord… the light…" Torn offered.

"I can see fine," Nick's voice was soft as he double checked all the holes in his upper body, ensuring they were sealed, the scent of burning flesh thick and acrid in the air.

At Lou's side, his hands over his waist and almost quaking now, he whispered, "I'm sorry man, we just don't have time for your bullshit."

As quick as he could, through his fumbling and shaking fingers, Nick undid his jeans pushing them down with one hand while the other held the waistband of his shorts up.

Having forgotten his feet were still tied, Nick took a moment to free them and noticed several of the holes in his legs must go all the way through the meat, and the streams of blood still connected to his body were frozen in mid flow.

"That's not good," he muttered looking over to Lou's locked in surprise, expression.

"When I let you go, this is gonna hurt like a motherfucker," he warned.

"M'lord you're not…" Torn looked horrified.

"Yeah," Nick nodded rolling his finger in the resin until it was well coated, "I am."

"Danu be merciful!" The fledgling shook his head.

"Oh kid that's just wrong…" Shep winced.

Dylan and Diagas just watched.

He glared at Shep and Torn, his face pale and twisted in obvious uncertainty, his voice grew tighter as he barked the facts of the situation, "Both femorals have been nicked in at least a couple places and I don't have any silk, and even if I did, I'm not a surgeon! I don't know how to save him any other way!" he yelled, his voice cracking several times as he did, reminding at least Shep of his true age.

Turning his focus back to the injuries he muttered, "I won't let him bleed to death just because I was afraid to do *something*."

No one noticed as he set the case of dried dragon blood onto Lou's thigh, made sure his index fingers were in the proper places, then rammed them into the first wound from top and bottom, the dragon was smiling with approval.

When he was sure Lou wasn't going to bleed to death, and all the worst wounds were sealed, Nick shimmied his pants back up, secured them, and righted his shirts as well, while streams shimmered down his cheeks to drop off his chin. "I'm sorry man," he whispered around a tiny catch in his throat.

He strode several yards away, his back to the group, his breath and shoulders quivering while he collected himself. For a few moments, all eyes watched, curious, not understanding why he wasn't celebrating having healed one of the heroes until finally Dylan's voice croaked through the night air.

"How long can you keep him like that?"

"Long as I want, long as I'm conscious…he's just one person." Nick muttered. He took a deep breath shoving his despair deep inside. He never imagined there'd be a time when he'd use his power to make an ally so powerless. Even though it was for a good reason, and even though it was done he was still sick to his stomach.

He huffed out a great rush of air and returned to the group, moving behind the son of Conchobar and joined by Torn who was happy to help catch the hero.

"Ready?" Nick asked.

Torn nodded.

"It's gonna get loud for a bit," He warned the others just before all of Lou's two hundred-plus pounds of solid muscle came crashing into them.

They eased him down as the fires from the dragon blood hit.

Torn returned to Shep when the screams came.

Dylan eased himself back against a tree and gazed at the moon when the groans began.

While gasps and pants peppered the night air, Diagas kept a look out for enemies.

When he curled in on himself, trying to squeeze away the agony Naiya stood watching from within shadows.

And when he finally fell somewhere between wakefulness and unconsciousness, Nick sat beside him, silently wiping sweat, and blood streaks clean until he returned to them.

"What the hell did you do to me?" Lou pant-grunted a few minutes later, when the worst effects had subsided, and he could sit up on his own.

"He saved your life," Shep answered.

Wincing and cradling his jaw, he asked, "Why does my face hurt?"

"It was killin' me," Nick shrugged with a weak smile, "so I beat it up, it's better now."

"You saved my life?" he asked, puzzled.

"Mmm," Nick nodded, rising to his feet, putting some distance between them.

"Huh, what the fuck wasssss…" he started, following Nick's movement until a very large, very green figure caught his attention, "wha…" he choked on his own air and swallowed hard, "wha," he coughed then tried again, "wha…"

Nick leaned down, his lips close to the garage owner's ear, "he's a dragon. You know… breathes fire now and then…" and in that quiet declaration, Dylan, Lou and Shep all fixed eyes on the giant emerald colored reptile whose head, even though resting on the ground between his paws, was still taller than any of them.

To their credit and in spite of their physical and mental conditions, no one fainted.

"Fledgling," Nick called, "what's your name?"

"Torn m'lord,"

"Thanks for your help," he shambled to the kid, his hand extended, "I'm…"

"Oemir m'lord, I know."

"We call him Nick," Shep smiled offering his hand to the youth, who helped him to his feet, "thanks boy."

"He's a MacRoich," Nick winked then faced the dragon, "and you are?"

"Green Flame Clutch, Diagas," he tilted his head. If not for the leathery opalescent green plates and feathery looking frills, his countenance would have been knee shakingly fearsome, the slight bend of his lips and upturned corners of his golden eyes indicating good humor helped too.

"The fledgling will stay with you and yours firstborn, we have much to do." He met eyes with each of those present before seeming to disappear into the background, the only evidence of his passing faint disturbances in the dirt.

As he continued his previous mission he paused, leaving one cryptic whisper behind, "have great care sons of heroes, the spawning has come.”

“Spawning?” Shep shook his head, “You know what he’s talking about? He talks… that’s weird.”

“He speaks English,” D noted, “that’s weirder.”

“Naiya?” Nick called shaking his head, bewildered because he wasn’t as agog as Lou over the meeting of a dragon.

“That was a dragon!” Lou pointed in the direction of the departed being with Dylan nodding his weary head, he simply lacked the energy to be impressed just yet.

“Shep… a *dra…gon!*”

“Yeah,” he breathed, “they got leviathans launching the ships out of the harbor Vahl took me to, they’re about as big, but far as I know they don’t talk, just work with the Sidhe captains. Maybe that’s what he’s talking about? Oh god! Ula? Any word on Ula?” He turned desperate eyes to Nick who shook his head, shrugging, while edging toward where he’d last seen the mare.

“Dylan? Draaaagon?” Lou persisted while Torn cocked his head in curiosity at Shep.

“Watch them,” Nick instructed, levering up the grip of the sword with his shoe. He’d been so preoccupied with the others he hadn’t seen Torn move it far away from where any of them could get it if they couldn’t be saved.

“MacRoich,” the Sidhe youth nodded then caught Shep’s eyes.

“Shep,”

“The queen of the Akirowen was last safe at the tower of the sun in her grotto, she and her people fought nobly be assured.” He was pleased by the visible relief in the hunter’s face as he scrubbed it with filthy hands, succeeding only in making himself dirtier.

Still far too slow to recover, Dylan reached over to the side and slugged hard from the canteen before passing it to Shep first, since he was the older of them and Lou seemed more energetic.

"Motherfucking fucker," he mumbled.

Lou's head snapped around and met his eyes, a grin burst forth, then a chuckle. Dylan too chuckled hitting the canteen again before passing it to the garage owner.

"It's dead," Lou shrugged swigging a mouthful before getting a good look at Dylan. They looked at Shep, then back at each other, chuckles bubbling out into full blown laughter making both Torn and Shep look at them as if they'd lost their minds.

"Yeah," Dylan breathed, "wasn't you who killed it though," he teased.

Lou shrugged, "next time."

Long moments later, Nick returned with Naiya and the three other Bedowen mounts, two of which Julius bade his comrades leave behind, and one more who'd stayed with its stablemates when the princess returned with the vestige in tow.

"M'lord, the tower of the sun must certainly be under siege again and your kin are in no condition for battle. None will come back to the wood while Diagas' fire still smolders, they should rest. The Oemirkin sent me to learn what I could last daybreak... he's holding the tower against forces he cannot anticipate..."

"And the return of at least one ancient ally... are there other dragons returned?" Nick asked.

Torn gave a quick nod, "He spoke of 'we, and us' so I do

believe."

"Khazeer, Wellyn, and if he's still alive, Wee, need to know they're back…" Nick nodded.

"The Heru and Master Wellyn are felled, the Elder healer will certainly not let them return to battle so soon."

Nick sighed, his chin fell to his chest as he remembered his and Frank's shared vision. "They need the light of Aenor, it's gonna be a massacre unless they got the light spear fixed or re-mounted…"

Torn frowned, "m'lord how could you know that?"

"I don't like repeating myself." Nick scowled.

"Aye," the youth nodded with a dismissive wave, "Oemir, how could you know of the status of the light spear?"

"We saw the aftermath," he muttered then turned to the wracked men, "camp or ride?"

But it was the horses who made the decisions, each of the three moved before a rescued hero while Naiya nudged Torn in the back.

"We ride then," Nick nodded.

Dylan looked between Shep and Lou and sighed, "the heroes ride; take two," then let Nick help him into the saddle.

"Take two what?" Torn asked gravitating to Shep.

"Second attempt to ride the fuck outta here," Lou smiled needing no help.

"Leanna's men and the firdur took them just before they could flee," Nick explained.

Dylan's head swung loosely toward his nephew, "just how the

fuc'could you know that? S'just like a motorcycle," the eldest Emerson gave a loose smile and waggle of his head, "except there's no engine, brakes… well, kinda…"

"He got it from us dumbass…" Lou explained, "and the breaks are called reins."

"Motherfucking fucker," Dylan sighed barely above a whisper.

Nick cast a curious glance at him but for the moment said nothing. Instead, he mounted Naiya then helped the fledgling swing up behind him. If the horses wanted to move, it made sense to listen.

--

"Hold tight my king!" Julius shouted; his fingertips hooked tight over the time-eroded wood of the bridge. Up on the ruined platform Errmot and Boaz, lay flat spreading their weight out as they moved toward their Captain. Errmot's vice-like grip clamped around Julius' wrist, keeping him suspended in the space between realms with the Bedowen Heru dangling from his own grip when the wood finally crumbled.

Tropus knew he should've been paying more attention to this borrowed mount who'd initially balked at the passing of something none of them could see, but the animal most certainly sensed. His war stallion, Majek, was recovering from pirini poison back at the tower of the sun, and for his lack of attention he'd been thrown.

The bridge, a perpetually suspended fistula between realms was shrouded in mist meant to fog the mind, shearing it away from its true purpose, exposing travelers to their demons and devilments, making them face their follies before allowing passage. The structure itself appeared as whatever those approaching thought it should be, but the act of crossing through the mist must come from a place of truth in purpose.

191

Without such strength, the bridge could choose to thwart any attempts at crossing.

Usually each rider faced their shortcomings, fears, and failures, but in this case the bridge seemed to have reacted barely an instant after Tropus' mount set hoof on it, meaning, the king of the Bedowen bore enough guilt and failings to have nearly cost all their lives.

"Be still!" Boaz ordered reaching toward his own mount, Aaroch, who approached and knelt beside him, giving him access to his saddlebag where a fine coil of Sidhe rope hung. He slipped a knot around Errmot's ankle then tied a section off onto the saddle horn before cutting the rest away.

The group moved with a precarious jerk as Aaroch rose to his feet and pulled backward, away from the rapidly encroaching mist. Boaz, however, ran forward, already creating a slipknot with which he hoped to secure their king.

"Whatever you have in mind Boaz, now would be a good time!" Julius' voice strained over his shoulder before he turned back to look at their king who now had his wrist in both hands, "Heru! Can you…" he started then lost the words he wanted. It was as if his mind went blank. He knew Tropus was exceptionally powerful, knowing some of the oldest magiks and taught by Cathbad himself when he'd been no more than a fledgling, but he couldn't remember what he wanted the king to do.

The giant king shook his head and felt an old sensation some would have called fear when he rose several inches as Aaroch strained to back up. In front of them, and coming from the depths of the crevasse below, more mist sped forward, unfurling, racing to surround them.

"For Danu! Pull Aaroch!" Errmot encouraged though the horse threw its head side to side and reared up in confusion.

Boaz lurched to the edge of the cliff, one end of the remainder of the rope tied tight around his wrist while he undid the slipknot. Instead, he retied a traditional one to the far end and swung it to their king. The extra bulk wrapped around his forearm, giving him a chance to loop it under until it was snug, and he was more secure.

Through the unfurling fog, each member of the quartet felt their mind lose their sense of purpose. Several times one or another panicked demanding to know who the others were. Aaroch barely kept his own senses, in some moments he went from rearing against the rope binding him, and at others, pulling enough to raise both the king and Julius almost back over the edge of the precipice.

They'd been moving at a steady pace when the soldier's mounts all stopped and refused to continue. Nick, Naiya and Torn all turned at the same time, frowns on their respective faces as Dylan fell unconscious from his saddle, a single foot stuck in the stirrup even after he hit the ground.

Nick leaped down, arriving at his uncle's side at the same time as Lou whose mouth turned down in a severe scowl.

"They fucked him up bad," he muttered easing the eldest Emerson's foot free.

"I know," Nick nodded, "I didn't help."

"Did you have a choice?" Lou whispered.

Nick twitched his head to the side and cast a quick glance at the others, "Torn, build a fire, we rest here for a bit," a shiver ran through him as Naiya's ears perked forward and she nickered then stomped her fore hoof. "What is it?" he asked pulling Oemir's cloak from his pack and rolling it under Dylan's head, but Naiya simply stomped again and motioned with her head. "Alright," he nodded and met eyes with the fledgling, "keep watch, I'll be back."

"M'lord, but Diagas said…"

"Yes, and as you ride with me, you'll do as I ask. Care for them!" he ordered swinging himself up into the saddle only to feel Lou's heavy grip hard on his forearm.

"You're not goin' alone."

Nick reached into the back of his pants and handed over his .45, "I need you to protect them. In spite of everything, you're still the strongest here."

"Where are you going?"

"I don't know," Nick shook his head, "but she does."

Dumbfounded, "she knows… what if you get into trouble?" he whispered.

Nick's hand dropped to the pommel of the sword, "I'm covered," he motioned to Shep and Dylan, "they're of the line too, and they need someone to watch over them."

"He can do it, he's steady as a rock," he urged motioning to Torn.

"He's a fledgling, he can't do it alone."

Lou grunted and shook his head, his bright green eyes driving hard into Nick's sky blues, "who's gonna protect YOU?" he hissed through clenched teeth. He was mortified knowing this kid knew all the wretched details of his life, but something about this reckless, headstrong, duty-bound, and inspiring young man drove him to act with the same determination, even though part of him hoped somehow none of this was real.

He'd give anything to be back at home with Rose watching reruns of one or another of those ghost hunting shows, picking out facts from fallacy while cruising his way through a six pack and half a fifth while they argued over who got the last piece of pizza. God how he wanted that.

In answer to his question Nick's hand stroked and patted Naiya's neck, "stay with them… please," he whispered an instant before a gentle clamp of his knees signaled her into the forest ahead.

"Son of a bitch," Lou spat combing his hands through his hair.

At his side Torn, eyes on Nick and Naiya, handed over a skin of water then clapped him on the back before helping Shep unload what they'd need from the other horses. Lou, shaking his head, began to collect kindling for a fire.

--

Ilirya jumped, nearly tripping over the heavy skull deep in the overgrown grasses. There was no body nearby, the gnaw tracks in the bone were grown deep green with moss while a cluster of prickleberries sprouted from its single empty eye socket.

"Nuh," she breathed crouching down, her imagination filled in the flesh over the skull and though the face she saw was not one of her personal friends, it was familiar.

Her heart skipped a beat when the air pressure around her changed though not so much as a blade of grass rustled.

With one hand on her short sword, she rose up.

"Show yourselves," she ordered and froze, the color bleeding from her as no fewer than a dozen feral faces poked up from the grasses, the triangular heads and glistening razor-sharp incisors a dead giveaway.

They'd once been allies though not truly friends, they were a semi-civilized race who understood most of the languages of the world but didn't have the least bit of caring for diplomacy, or interactions with most others. They clustered in small family groups or prides and were not only territorial and aggressive, but they were also prideful to the extent an insult could result in one becoming a feast for the family. The Felesians were not who Ilirya was hoping to meet first.

"What has come of the Cyclopes, Gregaria? Steropes? I've come to speak with the matrons, firdur has returned and another war is upon us," she proclaimed as they closed on her, their voices whispers of sandpaper on stone.

She shook her head, their words making almost no sense, leaving her wondering whether a language could change so much in only a few thousand years, or was this one she'd never known. As a group they stepped forward, spears or swords stopping within millimeters of her cloak and revealing another layer of Felesians behind them. Even if she wanted to flee, she may not make it out of their territory alive if they chose to pursue her.

With her only option being to continue the path, she handed over her short sword and went where they poked and prodded her to go.

--

"Hey, wait…" Charles called to the driver and leaped up from his seat, "Sir, can you let me off?"

"What're you doing?" Mickey whispered fiercely.

"Help wanted sign," he pointed back toward a small t.v. repair shop they'd just passed.

"A job?" she scowled.

"No can-do kiddo," the driver called, "we're almost at the station anyway."

Charles returned his attention to Mickey, "you got endless bank?" he asked cocking his eyebrow, "my roll's almost gone," he explained referring to the money he'd stolen from Ezra, money they didn't need to know anything about.

"We'll come with," she nodded, rising to stand at the back door as the bus pulled into its "station", which was a small, covered bench right in front of the post office.

"No man," Charles shook his head, "you guys go home, I'll catch a ride to the house later, or I'll call if I'm too beat, maybe I can make some scratch y'know?"

"Dude, the town's about 3 miles long, no public transpo here," Harry scowled.

"Truckstop might be hiring," Mickey offered pointing in the direction of home, "it's right behind the woods."

"Who needs a bus for 3 miles?" Charles gave a small smile then nodded at Mickey, "I'll check it out, thanks."

Harry frowned, "you sure you don't want company?"

"Look, I just gotta do something, and maybe there's more than one place hiring y'know? And it's not like this place is downtown Dallas 'er something... can you say, 'Po Dunk'?"

Mickey and Harry looked at each other, then at Charles, "Fine, but you call if you need a ride, remember you haven't had sleep in almost 48 hours man," Harry piped up, "and you're not from here."

The young man huffed and flung his hand north to south, "lettered streets," then east to west, "numbered streets... names just on the edge of town... grid system, not that hard."

Harry shook his head, "just be careful man."

Suddenly more tired than he realized, he nodded with a grateful smile, "I will. See ya' in a bit."

Heading toward the small subdivision they called home Harry and Mickey walked companionably, wondering if they were doing the right thing letting their newcomer meander around all on his own.

"You think he's gonna bounce?" Harry asked.

Mickey shrugged, "he's probably thinking about it."

"Probably won't make Nick too happy if he does."

"Mmm,"

"Would you be?" he asked.

She shrugged, "he's a good kid, he could be a solid asset."

"You know what I'm talkin' about."

She sighed, "it doesn't matter, I've always been for Nick, every line I've ever seen or remembered."

Harry stopped and looked at her, "he ever been gay in any of the lines?"

She smiled a gentle satisfied twist of the lips, "he tends to be... flexible, I just didn't even think about it for some reason."

"So... bi?"

She shook her head, "natural, we call it natural," shrugged again, "it's you guys that have to put a label on everything so you can stigmatize it and use it to make other people seem inferior."

Harry's curious expression turned deeper, "Hey, hey, whoa there!" he pre-empted the head of steam she was obviously building up, "I ain't labeling anything or anyone, and neither do any of the brothers… I don't care, I'm just curious."

"I mean *humans*, that 'you'," she smiled with a nod.

"right… like you're not?"

She shook her head, "not entirely… neither is Nick, or Frank for that matter."

He stopped, eyes wide and expression open, "wait a minute…you weren't shittin' when you told that guy you were…"

"Part Sidhe? No. I thought you… nevermind." She nodded more to herself than to him, "we're all part Sidhe. How much do you know about the history of the worlds?" she asked.

"Same shit they teach everyone in school."

"So, nothing," she nodded and sighed.

"Exactly."

--

"I need to get back there! You don't understand!" Ryan ground out as he pushed himself up using the wall beside him.

Since regaining consciousness, every moment he'd been awake was filled with attempting to regain control of his body and move his way through the agonies of healing. Areen checked on him when she could, but she was busy ensuring the safety of the refugees, arming them, and preparing them for the eventuality of an onslaught even here. He wasn't sure, but he thought he also heard something about dragons, which spurred him to continued action, he always wondered if they'd ever been real or if they were just mis-named dinosaurs.

Dunkun spent as much time as he could with Ryan but as the First Acolyte to the Elder Healer, he was often needed by other patients. It was one of those other patients who'd actually brought news of Wee, ensuring Ry the love of his life was still alive and commanding the defense of the Fierowen tower, even though the news was two days and more importantly, a whole night ago.

No one could tell him about Nick or Frank, and there'd been no new news of any kind since the previous evening, which left the mountain cave practically singing with tension.

"You are long away from ready Ry," Dunkun called from across the common room.

"Doesn't matter," he grunted, "my boys need me."

"They need you well and whole, you must trust in the will of the bloodline,"

"FUCK THE GODDAMN BLOODLINE! THEY'RE KIDS, MY kids!" he bellowed falling to his knees, sweeping a faint line of blood running from his mouth and nose away like a petulant child, "They're just kids," he slumped as another acolyte made her way to him.

"Until you are healed you are more likely to get them killed, is that what you want?" she asked, her voice soft but her words cruel.

"Don't even know if they're still alive," he shook his head.

"You are still damaged inside, if they are dead you cannot help

200

them, if they are alive, you are not well enough to help them," she reminded him, "for the sake of those you love, you must tend yourself first!"

To his surprise, and not for the first time since his return to the world, great bulbs of tears waddled down his cheeks, "you don't understand, you can't understand..." he choked. The despair filling him was worse than the injuries he'd suffered. Being kept from Wee, and unable to see their boys, touch them, hold them, and know for himself they were all alive and well enough was a torture he couldn't wish on his worst enemy.

Images kept flashing through his mind; Wee beaten, bruised, and bloody, and cradling his broken arm after they'd been attacked on their way back to the house the night Nick returned. Nick scrambling in the shower, then quivering in his arms, naked more than just physically, so terribly vulnerable while locked in the torment inside his own mind in the tiny hours of the night, trying to cleanse himself of whatever had been visited on him during his captivity.

"They *need* me," he pleaded clawing at the wall again, trying to pull himself up.

She stood beside him levering him up, "yes they do, but they need you whole, give yourself the time to serve them properly," she urged, this time her voice gentle and understanding.

He'd learned over the last few days many of the Sidhe were at least empathic like Wee if not having some level of actual psychic skills. He'd also seen evidence of what many would call magic, and he was deeply intrigued by it, wondering if what he'd always supposed about "magic" was true, that it was just a different level of energetic frequencies the learned were able to access and manipulate, "mages?" he asked panting over his knees.

"Most of them are certainly at the tower helping fortify it and protect those within."

"None here?" he asked, spocking an eyebrow at her.

"Possibly, but most magiks for healing have already been used on you, and your… guest will only allow us to use so much… I think it fears you will…" but he shook his head, so she stopped.

"A deal's a deal…" he lurched toward the stone bench, his daily goal to get to and from as many times as he could, "if there's a mage here… can you bring them to talk to me?" he asked, easing himself down.

"You wish to talk with one? You will go to them," Dunkun nodded from beside his next patient.

"Fine," Ryan nodded pushing himself back up to his feet, "which way?"

--

Movement from the bathroom caught his attention as he wiped the steak knife with his napkin and slipped it beneath the sheet and under his thigh. He couldn't say how long the damned thing had been in his room, if it'd been there when the boys came in the morning or not, but he'd rarely been happier for their creativity. Keeping an eye on the thing lurking in the shadow as it watched him, waiting for the room to go dark so it could do whatever it was planning, he reached to the night table with his other hand, slipping the black light along his other thigh. When it moved, he'd be ready.

--

Charles straddled the stool at the counter, gracing the waitress with a shy smile.

She gave a nod, holding up a finger as he nodded in return, an image of a large satellite view of a bit of ocean off the southeast of the U.S. came up on the t.v. He watched a line drawn from Miami to Puerto Rico, then up and East to Bermuda and wondered what got lost in the triangle this time. To his surprise, another boundary was dawn over that bit, this one coming in from much further east, it's south western end dipping into the triangle as the chyron below the graphic came up, "Mystery Dark Patch Growing in Sargasso Sea".

"How can I help ya hon?" she smiled.

He shifted his focus, "You know anything about that?" he nodded toward the set.

"Sorry, I don't get much time to watch the old boob tube, too busy puttin' m'dogs up between rushes."

Charles nodded looking around at the three other people in the restaurant, two of them obviously truckers, and the last one probably a Lakeview resident, he pulled out his last two dollars and laid it on the counter, "will that cover a cup of coffee and an application?"

Her weathered smile seemed to glow at him as she pushed the cash back, "You wanna work here? You're gonna need this."

She sort of twirled on the spot and strode away then returned just as the news story switched to one about a small town in Kansas experiencing a full technological black out.

She poured him a steaming cup, sliding over a handful of creamers then fished a pen out of her apron, setting it across the application.

Wordless she patted the back of his hand, dashing to one of the tuckers who's elevated hand held his own coffee cup.

--

Camouflaged by soot and shielded by the dark, Leanna rested in the depths of the forest, tormented by the visions brought on with her seduction by firdur. The world she'd always known to be lush and green, vibrant with color lay before her, a scaled, scorched plain limned by red molten rock where the only thing still standing was a flat plain. Tur's stronghold, in the distance was ablaze and the corrupted Sidhe within were naught but ash. She tossed and whimpered, surprised she hadn't been destroyed, and suspicious about what could've caused such a precise and devastating fire. There hadn't been a dragon on Aderyn in just over three millennia. At least, not a free one. Her fevered mind even wondered if any of it had really happened at all.

--

"Errmot?" Nick slipped from the saddle dashing to the body closest to him. It was one of the faithful Bedowen soldiers who helped him, and Harry escape the palace.

Relief filled his face as the Royal Guard pushed himself up on his elbows and nodded, reaching forward to untie a length of rope from his ankle, "aid the Heru my king."

Nick lurched to his feet, his gaze on the comparatively gigantic ruler of the Bedowen who was struggling to push himself up and pointed behind himself to his men.

"Tropus…" he confirmed the ruler's status, helping maneuver him into a seated position, then checking his pulse and moving on.

Rolling the next closest soldier over he gasped, "Julius," then pressed his trembling fingers to the Captain's throat, his own snapping closed so hard he almost couldn't breathe.

"Please…" he whispered, something hot and hard in his chest. It took far too long but he finally found the pulse and leaning close felt breath against his cheek. A grateful gust rushed out of him as he pressed his forehead to that of the unconscious soldier then pointed to Tropus, "watch over him!" and moved on.

"Hey," he rolled the next one over, "Boaz." He tapped the soldier's cheek, grateful when his eyelids fluttered, and his breathing came deeper. Nick unwound another length of rope from his wrist, wincing when it came away bloody and layered with meat.

"Shit," he leaped up pulling the dragon blood from his pocket and handing it over, "you'll be alright," he assured.

"Heru?" Boaz mumbled squinting at Nick then smiling and taking the resin, "Tropus?" He looked around grinning large and bright when he spied the Bedowen king with his fingertips pressed to Julius' brow. "Tend the Captain my king," he admonished sweeping a dusting of the orange powder over his wrist, the smell of searing flesh becoming something he was reluctantly getting used to.

Nick reached over, cradling the soldier's cheek with a grateful smile, and returned to Julius directing over his shoulder, "Errmot, Boaz, when you're able, gather your mounts and make sure you have your needs, you'll camp with us tonight."

He shook his head, his fingers lightly stroking the Captain of the Guard's cheek.

"…thought you could clear the bridge with things as they've been." He muttered toward Tropus before his eyes turned to the king, Nick trying to soften the glare eager to burn the Heru to the spot. "You should have left them to go alone, did you really think *they* wouldn't have known what's been going on for so long?"

Shamed even for a moment by this human, Tropus gave a single somber nod, "I could not ask them to risk what I was not willing to myself…"

Nick sighed his understanding, "yeah, never was your style." As much as he wanted to chide the ruler for his pride, almost getting his personal guard killed by going with instead of sending them alone, the eldest Emerson held his tongue, there was no reason to antagonize the giant other than spite at this point. "It's good to have you back," he breathed instead.

Beneath his fingertips, as Julius took a deeper breath, he grinned while his eyes welled with gratitude. "Are you ready to ride?" he asked the Heru.

"We need to make contact…"

"We will, tomorrow, in the light."

"For millennia I hungered to wash in your blood," Tropus pushed himself to his feet, not knowing quite how to read this young man before him.

"Business before pleasure," Nick quipped tapping Julius' cheeks. When his eyes began to flutter Nick could've sworn his heart sprouted wings. "Thank Danu!" he sighed, "put him on Naiya's saddle," he commanded climbing up and situating himself behind so he could hold the wounded soldier in place while they rode.

Tropus did as directed then mounted up, "Where are your people?"

"Errmot, Boaz, take the rear, we don't know what's in this part of the forest," he directed, securing his arms around Julius. The Captain of the Guard's head lolling back on his shoulder, his warm green scent stirring an ache deep in Nick's chest. He nodded at Tropus, "Heru, stay in the middle. It's not far."

Naiya set a firm pace bringing them back to the campsite only moments after Julius regained full consciousness. Three sets of eyes bulged on their arrival.

"What the hell?" Lou muttered.

"Looks like he made some friends. They were supposed to have joined the battle…" Shep breathed.

"Heru Tropus!" Torn gasped then whispered to Lou and Shep, "The king of the Bedowen," he leaped to his feet, "m'lo… Oemir… where… how?" he asked reaching up to help Julius down.

"The guy who had the death warrant out on the kid?" Shep asked.

"Mmm hmm," Lou growled, meeting eyes with the king before taking measure of the eight and a half foot tall Sidhe ruler.

"Naiya must've sensed them," Nick shrugged casting his eyes on Dylan who was still unconscious. He looked at Lou, "did he wake at all?"

Silent, the garage owner gave a nearly imperceptible shake of the head, he was worried about the eldest Emerson, the things he'd suffered while captive and the lasting effects of those things he could barely contemplate.

Turning once his feet were planted on the ground, Julius waited for Nick to dismount before wrapping him in a quick embrace, "My king," he grunted trying to hide a grimace of pain with a smile.

No matter whether initially forced or not, his smile turned radiant as Nick's soft gaze caressed his face and one hand came to rest on his flank while the other dragged a gentle sweep down his chest.

Blushing, Nick dug into his pack and grabbed the walnut shell by feel, then stuffed it into his pocket next to the resin. He knew there was some kind of salve in there, having smelled it when he and Frank first arrived here and took a pouch from one of the Fierowen soldiers.

From the corner of his eye, he noticed the son of Conchobar's jumping jaw muscle and the narrowing of his eyes at Tropus. He turned, dropping a hand onto Lou's shoulder and gave him a companionable squeeze coupled with a slight smile and a tiny shake of the head. *"It's alright,"* he thought to the older man and began helping them get their gear down.

In what seemed no time at all, the new additions made places for themselves around the fire, portioning out rations for everyone. From water to dried meat, vegetables and fruit, all was shared over news of happenings over the last few days. In time, even Dylan finally woke and took in what he could.

Sitting next to Nick, Julius pulled a flask from inside his cloak, took a swig then handed it to the young hero.

After a sniff Nick smiled and took a hearty gulp, "Oh, I needed that," he said softly, visibly relaxing.

"Don't hog it kid," Lou smiled reaching over then looked at the Captain of the Guard questioningly.

"Of course, son of Conchobar," Julius nodded, "you of all appreciated a fine distillate more than most," he joked.

"Often enough to find himself on his face in a mud puddle the next morning," Nick added softly while receiving a gentle nudge at the shoulder.

"The last feast..." Boaz drawled with a sly smirk from his

position on Tropus' side, his reminding making even the king chuckle.

"Ahhh the feast," Errmot, Julius and Nick grinned together.

Taking on a drunken affect Nick turned to Julius, "My lady… would'st thou care to share me'…"

"Meal," Errmot suggested with a smile.

"Drink," Boaz tempted.

"Me' big baldie!" Nick finished, motioning suggestively with his hand and hips before mocking falling onto his face, to the delight of the Sidhe present and the humor of the humans.

Despite the giggles even Lou felt, being very well able to imagine his ancestor behaving in just such a way, there came a strange little twitch to his stomach. Every interaction with the eldest of the junior Emersons' told him the kid had a stick up his ass a mile wide and two long. The only kind of humor he could imagine the teen having was intellectual and dry, if indeed he had any sense of humor at all, and about a million miles away from ribald.

Catching a curious scowl on Dylan's face, he shrugged miming tipping the flask up and chalked it up to the teen riding the effects of the Sidhe liquor. Even with his own tolerance his first slug of the sweet-hot apricot nectar lifted some of the weight from his shoulders for a very comfortable long moment.

Bouncing to his feet with an easy smile only familiar to the Sidhe present, Nick took another swig before passing it around once more.

"Be right back," he spun round, heading for a secluded spot just a couple dozen yards away, his fingers fumbling at his zipper.

"Pairs my king!" Julius urged, barely a hint of a wince on his features as he rose up, meeting eyes with his men, all of whom nodded.

"Aye Captain, pairs," they agreed.

"Have any of the others given you proper thanks for your aid?" Julius asked while they attended business.

Nick shrugged, "Tropus didn't wash in my blood so that's a plus," he zipped up and leaned against the tree, his gaze roving over the captain of the guard.

With the danger currently passed, he let himself think about the feel of Julius' body leaning against him, the rhythm of Naiya's gait building a comfortable friction he hadn't had time to consider at the moment. His nose filled with the scent of wood, and earth, and spring green while he noted the Sidhe's planes, the way his breeches stretched so perfectly around his hips to the curve of his buttocks. He delighted in the sweet torture of warmth filling him from his belly to his root as the Sidhe took his time.

Julius sighed, "I have missed you my king," he righted himself and faced the human man, "my brother," he smiled, his expression turning soft, "neen eri meleth," his hand shook as he raised a finger to caress Nick's cheek.

His eyes glassy, Nick reached out and touched the soldier's chest, "take off your shirts," he whispered the command. Only the most extreme age, or injury could make a Sidhe soldier's hand tremble.

Without hesitation, but with obvious discomfort Julius did as he was told and stood before his eventual king, the garments draped over his forearms.

Nick winced and gasped. Julius' shoulders were both bruised, almost black with deep purple climbing up his neck as well as down his upper arms. "Lemme see the rest," he commanded taking the garments and noting the same depth of color through Julius' wrists and forearms. "What the fuck happened?!" he demanded, throwing the shirts over his shoulder, and pulling the walnut from his pocket.

"The bridge… I could not let him fall," he explained.

"He's at least five or six times your weight, if not more! What were the others doing?"

Julius smiled, his hand cupping Nick's cheek while his thumb stroked the frown on his face, "saving us."

At the gentle touch, his anger softened, Julius was, after all, the Captain of Tropus' personal guard, he was doing his duty and couldn't be faulted for it.

He took both of Julius' hands in his and examined his palms. One of them was torn in several places with deep needles of ancient wood buried in the tissues.

He cupped the Sidhe's face, their eyes locked as he huffed and scowled, commanding, "on your knees."

As if someone had struck him from behind, Julius complied, a soft smile on his lips even as he ducked his head.

Something sparked inside Nick as he turned the soldier's head till they were eye to eye again, "never turn your gaze from me," he whispered, his voice too thick to make tone as he opened the shell, scooped out a finger full of the jelly-like liniment and warmed it between his palms.

"Left arm," he said assisting the soldier in raising it up till his hand gripped Nick's shoulder.

Once the ointment was hot enough to bring immediate relief he started at Julius' wrist and worked his way up to the elbow, squeezing and draining the bruising up toward his shoulder. Then with another finger full doing the same with his upper arm, deep into and over the shoulder and along the outer chest and upper back.

Nick repeated the process with Julius' right arm, then took a good long look at his hand.

"Meleth," Julius breathed, rising to his feet so they were on the same level while Nick started pulling the needles from his flesh. The fingers of his other hand stroked Nick's cheek, his heart beating so hard and fast they could both see it in his chest.

Another wave of warmth blossomed through Nick as a shimmer followed the trail of those fingers before weaving through the stubble covering his jaw. It was more than just the memory of Julius striding to his bedside, his face contorted in an expression Nick hadn't been able to understand.

At the time, he'd been paralyzed by some concoction Leanna's handmaid poured down his throat, his muscles were just starting to burn again as the Captain of the Guard whipped the sheet Harry had just draped over him, off him. The Sidhe's face had twisted, and grimaced at the sight of Nick's clawed raw, bruised, and bloodied body, but there'd been more. Something in his expression baffled Nick until he'd seen Julius unconscious. It was then he felt the same expression twist his own features. If he could have the moment in Leanna's suite back he'd invite the soldier to join him and see if he could make the expression go away.

His heartbeat matching the Sidhe's, he reciprocated the gesture, "neen eri meleth," he nodded drawing a shaky breath and pressing his cheek to the Sidhe's leathery calloused palm.

A still-frame came to mind, a half-dozen Sidhe fledglings capering at the beach on the banks of the Winding River where it caressed the elbow of the Bedowen. Most of them were naked, splashing in the cool playful waters, some of them sunning, others making love. He and Julius were sunning, drinking in the sights and sensations of one another in an afternoon of perfection shared with the brothers and sisters of their homelands, "if you'd been further harmed by his foolish, vain, arrogant…" he ground but found himself silenced with tender, relieved and needy pressure from Julius' lips.

"Many things are uncertain," he smiled taking Nick's hand with its snub fingers and pressing it to his chest, "save this. Say it again," he pleaded against Nick's mouth.

Nick's thumb stroked over his nipple as it hardened while his other hand stole into his hair. The thumb of this one giving a gentle rub along the steep angular crest of the captain's ear before sliding down the back of it to end by supporting him at the nape of the neck, "neen eri meleth," his smile sighed before pressing their foreheads together, "my first love."

"I felt you in the woods," he traced a finger over some of the angry bruises still on Nick's face. "We arrived as soon as we could," he breathed.

Nick's cheek still in his hand, nodded, "I knew someone would come… but Fetik's nature had to be…"

"Revealed, yes," Julius whispered taking Nick's hand from his chest, bringing it to his lips.

"Yes," Nick drew a tremulous gasp. His mind clouded, and hot pressure forced the breath out of him. He could feel himself dodging Fetik's blows, letting some of them fall while nailing the cruel soldier

213

with some of his own. He knew someone would come, he knew he had to stay on his feet as long as possible, but though he'd felt those certainties, he had no knowledge of Julius at the time, or Errmot, Boaz, Xian, or anyone. He found now, having not known of them then, hurt worse than any beating he'd experienced this far.

"I thought you to be safe in the infirmary, but Leanna," Julius continued his own catharsis, his eyes glazing before the rims shone with moisture. "Then from her suite I heard your torments," he choked, "and when I saw the aftermath, I had to see what she'd done," he hung his head, so their foreheads were resting together.

"Blank...the way you looked at me...I feared you'd never know me again," he gasped before returning Nick's hand to his chest and stroking it down his quivering stomach and around to his low back while touching his lips to Nick's then under his jaw and down the front of his neck.

His own hands eased their way down the young man's wiry muscled chest to the hem of his shirt where they lingered on his hips. He shook his head, his heart breaking with the memory of the sounds of Leanna's sinister deed, "what she did to you... the *PIRINI!*" he spat daring to slip his finger into the waistband of Nick's jeans, making his low belly quiver as the digit moved from one side to the other and back again.

Nick shook his head, "S'not important," he panted running his hands over the Sidhe's torso having released his injured hand to trace his lines and drink him in. For the second time this evening he shuddered at the feel of the Sidhe's rose petal smooth skin, his own aching to feel it against every part of him even as Julius popped the button on his jeans, pushing his hand further along the dark line of hair.

"I have so missed the feel of you," he sighed, his fingers

214

sweeping to the side then angling down along Nick's jutting hip bone.

Between the Sidhe's silken skin warming the palms of his hands and luxuriating in the captain's every texture, Nick found himself bobbing on a sea of sensation, accentuated by the warrior's light caresses. He was so full he ached for release even as he reveled in his lover's tenderness.

Breathing hard, barely able to think, he simply nodded, his lips pulling gently on Julius' jaw and neck while his fingertips reveled in the warrior's naked skin exploring the places he hoped would bring his love the most joy.

"Meleth… I must…" Julius muttered, his eyes closed, his own breath short through his bliss-filled smile. He slipped his hand further down, riding the crease between Nick's body and leg. He grinned as the young man's muscles jumped, his over full member spilling lubricating fluid even as he avoided touching him there just yet. He wanted to see ecstasy instead of emptiness in the young man's face. He wanted to heal the hurts that kept them apart through the ages.

He smiled when Nick leaned back, his hips shifting forward, and his legs spread open. He lowered the zipper coaxing the garments down, giving himself unfettered access.

"God yes…" Nick gasped slipping out of his boots, "I have so missed you," he dared to whisper, stepping out of his jeans. "Your smell, your taste," he kissed the Sidhe, drawing him in and wishing, "to forget where I end and you begin…" when Julius' warm, calloused hand found its way under him to the little platform just behind his scrotum his knees nearly buckled, and he gasped.

His overfull manhood twitched with his stomach muscles, and

his whole body seemed to seize when the captain began to stroke the almost unbearably delicious spot, his pressure alternating between firm and feather light, keeping him wholly distracted from anything but the explosive sensations within.

"Too long," Julius sighed, absorbing every smile on his lover's lips, every vibration through his body. He reveled in every squeeze and possessive caress from the young human's hands. Every touch, every breath brought his own erection closer to bursting, he looked down to find Nick's fingers already beat him to the buttons and ties of his breeches.

A heartbeat later, he too was free, and Nick's palms were taking him in, gliding over his thighs and hips, then under his buttocks to wrap himself in one or the other of Julius' legs, almost desperate to try and hold him up against the tree, to feel himself become one with the love of his first life.

Finally, skin to skin, Nick's heavy pants grew more urgent with every caress. He pulled the warrior tight against him, wrapping him in one of his legs, his hardness pressed next to Julius', unable to control his trembling while fulfilling his need to feel their bodies together, and wishing for a night that could last forever.

Holding Nick securely, Julius sighed and shook his head. "You said you would... and you did... you came back," and braced him there, keeping him captive by mouth and hands as his caresses sped up and deepened, his other hand finally alternately going from the base of his scrotum to encircling his silken shaft. At the base he gave it a squeeze then spread his fluid over the head.

Nick gasped. Nothing had ever felt so perfect. Even when he and Charles made love, as incredible and satisfying as it had been, nothing had ever made him feel this whole.

"Julius… please," he panted, stroking his face as his plea filled the Sidhe's heart.

"Soon meleth," he grinned against Nick's mouth, reveling in the warm hands voraciously exploring him.

"I need…" he whimpered against the almost fearful desperation in his heart.

"I know," he swept Nick's lips with his own as his finger moved back under him.

"You," Nick confessed then grimaced, his jaw clenching with self-recriminations even as his traitorous hips arched forward while Julius continued to bring him joy. "I need you…" he bit his lips shut, fighting back a sense of desperate wanting, having nothing to do with the simple act of sexual release. It came instead from something so deep his trembling grew to shivers and quakes clinging to the crest of a fear holding him captive.

Sensation burst through the fear, electricity running along every nerve in his body, bringing a primal growl of delight rolling up his throat as his teeth nibbled the soldier's shoulder. His arms wrapped around the long, sleek torso, the leg curled around him pulled him even tighter, so tight he could feel the Sidhe's heartbeat against his own breastbone. Soft billows of warmth swaddled them together as Nick gasped.

His breath held again, his eyes on the moon, one hand gliding up into Julius' hair before angling his head to press their lips together, while the other slipped down his back, fingers stroking feather light, the separation of his buttocks before perching on that same spot beneath him, drawing pants and gasps into the early evening.

Overwhelmed, Nick's heart raced, a pounding so fierce he didn't know if he'd survive it. He was ravenous, desperate, and dizzy while something gargantuan burst open inside and began to fill him, suffocating him, though he had no desire to stop it. His lips moved over Julius' jaw to his neck where he buried his face, and clung to the soldier, a continuous flow from his eyes he couldn't stop.

He couldn't breathe, he could only vibrate as everything he was, was possessed by this terrifying thing.

"…my heart," Julius whispered, fighting his own shivers brought about by Nick's gentle starving caresses over every part of him.

He ducked his mouth to blaze a path down his chest and belly, lingering for a delicious moment over Nick's belly button before grasping him once again, his own steely hardness quivering as he pressed his lips to his love.

"Julius…" Nick pleaded in a whisper, clutching a handful of the captain's hair as vacuum threatened to send him over a now familiar precipice again, "please…" he whimpered, "I can't…" he grasped the soldier by the chin, bringing him up, "wait…" he asked.

His smile was tight, and his eyes closed as he leaned forward drying the last remnants of the rivers on the Sidhe's chest as he pressed his lips to his silken flesh again, and again.

Wet tremulous gasps gave Julius pause as he tenderly stroked the human from neck to waist, then held him close breathing him in and giving him room to recover.

"Have I hurt you meleth?" he finally whispered.

Nick finally leaned back against the tree shaking his head. His eyes still closed; his lips stretched into a soft smile while his breathing evened out. Julius' fingers slid down the glistening whiskers of his cheek then into the soft fine coating of darkness on his chest and belly.

"Your hair is thicker," he sighed with a smile rubbing his cheek along the softness. "But still soft as down."

"S'the human in me," Nick whispered, bringing Julius back up to hold close again while absently stroking the lines of every muscle he could reach.

Julius sighed, his gaze gentle on Nick's as his back arched before his hips thrust forward, eager for loving touch.

"I wish to wake with my cheek against it," Julius smiled, his eyes falling to half as Nick's tender touches and strokes lit searing fires deep inside him.

They took a moment to breathe, peering so deep it seemed they each sought their history in the other's eyes, Nick smiled, "ever the romantic," he whispered before kissing his way down the warrior's chest. His hands wrapped around his hips, cupping the hard muscles of his buttocks before his lips landed at the base of his erection.

Julius gasped, his hips thrusting forward "And you'd not have me any other way," his breath held as Nick dropped his lips over the slick dome and drew sharply while his fingers kneaded those perfectly formed muscles then moved back under him.

"Ahh, Oemir…" he panted, his fingers running through Nick's hair, his hips bucking in time with the pace and rhythm he set.

When he was almost certain Julius was ready to climax, he rose up and grasped the soldier at the hips, finally turning them so it was Julius against the tree.

"I'll have you any way you'll allow me," He swept one of the soldier's legs back up and around him, devouring the long-muscled limb with one hand while the other tormented and teased his aching erection, drawing gasps and mewls from his Sidhe love.

They chuckled, explored, and sated one another, jockeying for dominance with caresses and kisses their weapons of choice.

"They should've been back already."

Lou pushed himself to his feet and helped Dylan to his, "I know, but you're not…"

"He's my blood, Wee'd never forgive me if…"

"Alright, just shut up, don't even put it in the air in a place like this," Lou admonished.

"Julius will die before he would allow harm to come to Oemir again. They are quite likely reacquainting themselves," Boaz smiled with Errmot nodding at his side, and offering, "It has been many an age."

"He's a kid, no matter what you all think, he's a *human* kid, he's NOT your Oemir!" Lou shook his head.

Tropus looked to his guards, an eyebrow arched and a strange twist at the corner of his mouth as he shook his head with a sad sigh, "mortals."

Shep rose to his feet grasping Dylan's upper arm, "You stay! If something's up you'll get everyone killed kid…" he angled the eldest Emerson back down and pointed at Boaz, "keep him here," who nodded.

"Let's go," he slapped Lou on the chest.

The garage owner shrugged, "Why me? Kid fuckin' hates me…"

Shep gave a mighty and highly parental frown making something inside Lou wither, "You a descendant or not?"

"Throw the goddamed line at me… I never asked for any of this…" he groused while they headed off in the same direction Nick and Julius went.

"Kids that age hate everybody, you get used to it…" Shep comforted. They moved as quietly as possible, eyes peeled for any signs of firdur or other enemy incursion. On high alert, they stopped just a few yards into the tree line.

In the deep grasses, a long line of black stitching down the side of a naked back told them they were looking at Nick. The supposition was confirmed a second later when Lou noticed another cluster of black stitches, just above his hip where the arrow had gone through. Almost at the same time they saw the stitching, Julius sat up, clasping his hands to Nick's head, and running his lips from the young man's mouth down his neck. Realization crashed into them, and they turned away, meeting eyes.

"I thought he was with the girl?!"

Lou shrugged, "Double your pleasure?"

Shep's eyes snapped wide, "he's fourteen."

"He can change his age."

"Physically. Inside he's still just a kid, isn't he?"

"After everything you've seen you really believe that?" Lou asked, "that's gotta fuck with the hormones."

"Hmm…" Shep grunted again.

Lou gave a quiet groan, "Man, I hope they're not barebackin'."

"Oh man…" Shep grunted, his eyes grown wide as he made to lurch toward the lovers but found himself captured by Lou's elbow with the garage owner's hand over his mouth.

"If he is, harms already done. Leave 'em be Shep, the kid needs to burn off some steam anyway, get his head together…" he stopped and shook his head releasing the older hunter, "you know what I mean."

Shep nodded, "yeah," then his gaze went back to Nick and Julius, and he shook his head, "I really didn't see that coming," he whispered taking just another second to re-analyze the situation and assure himself it was loving going on instead of anything unwanted.

"Dude… really?"

"Shit," Shep whispered, shaking his head, realizing what he'd just said.

"Yeah, well, me either," Lou whispered also having turned back and watching the two together with open curiosity.

Shep shrugged, "guess everybody's experimenting these days."

After another moment Lou chuckled, "got news for ya man, that ain't experimenting, that's *experience*."

Shaking his head Shep sighed, "never thought I'd have to give 'the talk' again…"

"Ships sunk. Besides," Lou sighed, "I'll do it."

With a spocked eyebrow Shep couldn't help but smirk, "you'll do it?"

"You're old enough to be his grandpa, you think he's gonna wanna hear anything from an old man? Besides, he hates me. It'll be easier for him to act like he doesn't care what I say, y'know?"

In the distance Nick whispered into Julius' ear, causing the warrior to beam an unexpected smile before their eyes met and they disappeared into the tall grasses.

Shaking his head Shep huffed, turning the younger man away as the lovers disappeared from view, "Boy you're not just a perv, you must be 'bout as dumb as a box 'o rocks too…" he motioned back toward the campsite, both of them relieved there'd been no trouble.

"Did you find them?" Dylan asked, struggling to push himself up until Lou's hand fell light on his shoulder.

"Like he said, they're okay," then reached over and sipped from the flask again meeting eyes with Boaz who raised a curious eyebrow at him. He gave a faint nod, passed the flask to Shep and smiled back at the Bedowen soldiers knowing grin.

--

"Did Oemir get off well?" Vahl asked once Frank shuffled from the kitchen to the patio where the Sidhe was watching a large bonfire burn.

Frank nodded, his hand on Vahl's shoulder, the barest tips of his fingers dipping into the flesh, "Yeah, there's a range on the cells which is cool, but that's not important, I need to know everything that went down with the cops."

"Of course," Vahl nodded before Frank's fingers slipped into his head.

"Sorry Vahl, I need to see it all," he apologized softly.

The Nahroehn Sidhe hadn't given much thought to the idea Frank could, let alone might invade his mind.

When he'd done it to the young Emerson at Sherry's apartment

223

it was to wake him from a possibly murderous night terror. It had been very much self-defense; use of a tool he was so uncomfortable with he couldn't help but believe everyone who could do it felt the same way. It wasn't the first time he'd had someone invade his mind and it probably wasn't going to be the last, but as much as he didn't care for using his own gift, having someone else do it to him was a sensation he'd never wish on anyone. The easiest way through it was not to fight it, until he felt the boy turn.

It wasn't what Frank intended when he sought the memory of Vahl's interaction with the detectives, but once he'd watched it all, from greeting them at the door, to listening to their banter before they pulled away from the house, something else happened.

He felt it deep in the pit of him, a hot tingling at his armpits and groin with a memory, blades shimmering and swirling in the air, dark forest surrounding him as blood spilled from precise and tiny cuts meant to torment and torture. *"What's this?"* he thought before catching a glimpse of the victims.

A slice into Wee's cheek and another down the length of Tommy's forearm. The heat and tingling were a blast of joy to Semet's soldier. A blade sliced through the muzzle of what looked to be a .45 as if it were cake, and someone inside the youngest Emerson seethed.

"Track them, watch Kieren… if HE is with them, bring him, if he is not… then strike at the foundation before it takes root," Semet had whispered into his mind.

"You meant to kill them, and you toyed with them like a rabid wyvern!" Frank heard himself accuse, and wondered what a wyvern was.

"I did," Vahl acknowledged, *"every drop of blood a prize I'd not claimed in a thousand generations, so many millennia without a kill… I was invigorated!*

224

I even entertained using the old tools... but Kieren... then Owain and Petrouk..."

Frank watched the scene unfold as the other two riders came upon the spot where Kieren was holding Wee and Tommy down amid gigantic foliage.

But Frank already knew what happened, Mickey arrived with Lou and moments later so did Ilirya, instead, a prickle of curiosity poked him, *"old tools? You mean magiks don't you?"*

A sinister smile turned up the corner of Vahl's mouth, *"you once knew them as well..."* a deep, dark chuckle sent a shiver through the body of the youngest hero, *"I knew you were in there, using the child... always simply taking whatever you desired without a thought for the needs of any other!"* Vahl charged.

"Teach me?"

"Teach me?" Frank asked both inside and outside.

Even as he felt the Sidhe begin to nod, Frank heard a dark and sinister chuckle again just before his fingers slammed deep into the warrior's mind and he heard a thought, *"no need..."* hiss through both of their heads.

In his grip, Vahl bolted upright and back, leaning hard on Frank, and choking as information flowed from him into the boy's mind. Formulae, plants, recipes, spells, incantations, blood, and sex magiks, sacrificial rites, as well as those less destructive, less poisonous to the soul.

There was no telling how long they stood like that, information pouring into Frank while it was copied from Vahl. When Frank came back to himself dusk had arrived and no matter what he tried he could not rouse the Nahroehn warrior. Vahl lay still, barely breathing, his eyes open and an unvoiced scream lodged in his throat.

Struggling with the height and weight of the Sidhe, Frank somehow managed get him up to his room. He stacked pillows beneath his head so he wouldn't drown on his own saliva if his swallow reflex failed and stood staring into empty eyes.

As if in a dream Frank closed Vahl's eyes with trembling fingers and blood running from his nose. He had to go to the bathroom but couldn't move, his bowels were roiling. His stomach was sick, and he wasn't sure if he was going to throw up or if he was going to explode from the other end. He wasn't sure, but it felt like there was an axe planted squarely through the center of his skull.

Reflex is what sent him careening into the bathroom to empty his body while his mind made room for everything he'd stolen from the Sidhe he considered, kind of a friend.

"I killed him; what did you do!?" he demanded of the other voice inside him. Aside from the sinister chuckle he swore he could still hear, he wasn't really sure was the voice there at all. It wouldn't respond.

"shit… I gotta do something… I can't call the cops… 911? Stroke? I don't know… what if he remembers? What if he tells? Shitshitshit, god Nicky what do I do? What did I do?"

Back at the bedside he paced up and down, his teeth gnashing on his bent forefinger. He opened Vahl's eye and waved his hand in front of the Sidhe. He pressed his ear to his chest and listened to the slushy lub dubbing of his heart along with the almost imperceptible rise and fall of his chest confirming his breathing.

"Damn you! WAKE UP!" he shouted, shaking the warrior by the shirtfront.

"VAHL!" he barked then pleaded, "please wake up Vahl! I'm sorry, I didn't mean it, it wasn't me I promise!" he whimpered with tears running down his cheeks and blending with the red snot still running from his nose.

His fingers stole into his hair, squeezing and pulling by the handfuls while tight mewling sounds came from the back of his throat. The room was a cage, and he couldn't leave it. Every circuit around caught him glancing at the unmoving Sidhe on the bed, hoping for a sign of wakening as dusk fell to evening.

Finally, he sat, his back against the desk, his eyes fixed open and watchful. His heart considered the warrior a friend even though he'd started off as an enemy. He'd looked after Frank, he'd allowed himself to be led by a child for whatever his motivation had been, he'd helped them and now a deep and sinister part of the littlest Emerson had stolen him.

He heard the front door open and saw the refraction of light slither into the upstairs hallway, and he couldn't move. He heard Mickey and Harry Jr chatting as they arrived and called out to see who might be there, and oddly enough, he felt a wave of trepidation roll out from Mickey.

"Stay here," he heard her order even though she spoke in nothing more than a whisper.

He heard her flip open a butterfly knife she'd decided to keep, as she crept up the outer edge of the stairs.

"Frank?" she whispered, her own very sensitive eyes making out his shape against the desk just before she flipped the light switch and blinded them both.

"Frank?" she asked again noting the crust of blood down his face, "what happened? What's wrong?"

A split second later she noted the fallen Sidhe and pressed her finger to his throat, ensuring he was alive before kneeling at Frank's side, stroking his hair, trying to capture his distant gaze.

"Frank, talk t'me buddy, what happened?" she asked turning his face till his eyes moved and fixed on hers. "Harry get me a couple paper towels," she called then refocused her attention on Nick's brother.

"Talk t'me Frank."

"Stol'im" he whispered, unable or unwilling to meet her gaze.

"Stolen? Like 'stole' or like the pastry?" she asked unable to feel much but muffled numbness, like his psyche was wrapped in dust bunnies and cobwebs.

His head cocked to the side and his eyebrows pitched inward in curiosity, "Stole… I stole him," he clarified before his voice dropped to a haunted whisper, "but it wasn't me."

"Stole him? What do you…" she caught him by the wrist as his hand came toward her forehead seemingly of its own volition, "hold on…" she held him tight but finally got him to look into her eyes, "you read him?"

The boy shook his head as another flow of tears started down his face, "I don't think he's in there anymore," he choked.

She held out her hand behind her when Harry emerged in the doorway with one damp and one dry paper towel.

"Is he inside you?" she asked, starting at his cheeks, wiping away the tears and working her way down, cleaning him as best as she could while he nodded, his chin in her hand, his eyes flicking from Vahl to Harry.

"I didn't… it wasn't me… is he gonna die?"

Mickey glanced back at the warrior, then to Harry, and finally back to the boy.

"Tell me what happened," she insisted and once again had to hold his hand away from her head, "use words Frank."

He shook his head, his eyes saucer wide, "I only needed to see. The cops left so they talked to him. He did what I told him, then I saw what he did… and *he* got mad, and we knew it but seeing it was different and he didn't care, and he was mad at us, then we remembered magiks…"

Desperation clung to him like skunk stink, his words came faster and faster with his heart hammering in time. "And we remembered, and I asked him, but he wouldn't wait, he wanted it *now!*" he gasped before continuing. "And it was just like it used to be and we took it, and we stripped it out of him, and I think we broke him too…"

He gasped and panted, his hands swiping at himself, at his face and his chest, his fingers pulling at his hair. "And we stole him and now he's gone and in me with the others and they hate him, and they want to kill him, but *he* wants to kill him too…"

All the while Mickey was trying to grab his hands and hold him still, to keep him from hurting himself. "And it's mean and evil, so much of it, using pain, killing for nothing, killing for power, and sacrifice of innocents and innocence…" and as it dawned on her, what he was talking about. He screamed a guttural, feral, wounded animal sound, batting and clawing at himself and at her even as she tried to restrain him.

"Harry, help me," she strained against the 9-year-old boy who, thanks to some of those ancient magiks was just a little stronger and just about the same size as her.

Harry moved into the room, trying to grab at the boy too until Mickey looked at him, "get cuffs or something."

The harder she tried to restrain him, the harder he fought, pulling, and pushing and jerking even as she sought to hold him close, to trap him in her embrace, to soothe him and ease the pain in his battered psyche.

Harry returned just a moment later with a pair of handcuffs and a length of rope.

By the time they had him bound securely enough so he wouldn't hurt himself, both Mickey and Harry were panting hard and sweating like they'd run miles.

He shook his head as she retrieved her butterfly knife and drew it down the length of her finger, scrawling the triquetra she'd used on those two hunters to freeze them, on the top of the desk while incanting once again, "*I'essa 'en Danu amin naia lle a'putta!*"

"Spell comes in handy," Harry smirked as Frank froze.

"We need something to keep him out, if what I think happened happened it may not be long before he breaks it."

"There's scotch in the cabinet," Harry offered.

"Save that for us," she muttered, "hit the master bathroom, see if there's some antihistamines in there, or some pm pills or something," she instructed, "I'll take the hall and the downstairs one."

"What exactly do you think happened?" Harry asked as he headed across and down the hall.

"I think one of the Oemir's stripped out Vahl's knowledge and infused it into Frank."

Harry's eyes went wide, "for real?"

"Yeah,"

"They can do that?"

She shrugged and shook her head.

"That *cannot* be good."

"No," she agreed.

6

Standing on the balcony watching the mages below continue to work one of the more powerful protection spells he knew, Wee drew a shaky breath. His knees were trembling and from the inside out, there wasn't a part of him not vibrating. They'd survived the night and another assault from vestiges, schades, an assortment of flying, creeping and slithering allies of the enemy as well as Sidhe from the Nahroehn. The same place Frank and his team went to rescue Lou and Dylan. The same place none of them returned from.

He occupied his mind with being amazed by all the efforts the Fierowen, Bedowen and Akirowen people and soldiers put forth to get the light spear mounted on a mobile platform in defense of the tower the previous day.

To Ula's surprise Khazeer gave his blessing to Wee's strategy. He understood they lacked the resources to organize an offense, so protecting the tower, city, and its inhabitants was the only alternative.

Taking a moment alone, exhausted, and nauseous, his fingers curled around the sandstone banister as water ran from his eyes. *I can't do that again, and they can't keep it up forever, we need to evacuate, and we need to know their plans, where they're hiding, we know nothing… we need intel, or we won't survive. Where are my boys, please give me a sign they're okay.*

A light hand fell to his shoulder, "you did well Wee, not a single soul was lost this night."

He nodded but couldn't turn to face her, he didn't care so much about being seen crying, hell, Nick, and Dylan broke him of any embarrassment about that well before he hit puberty; it was the fear of what two little boys might be facing all on their own in the night, and what might happen to everyone and everything when night returned. Far as he was concerned, it was all coming way too soon. It wasn't the possibilities that had him terrified, but the probabilities.

"The king and his master of arms will be allowed to see you once you've rested."

Again, he nodded wiping his face dry on his sleeve and steeled himself before turning to face the Elder Healer and the acolyte beside her.

"There isn't time to rest, dusk will come fast, could the firdur be doing something? Can they make night come faster?" he asked.

She took his hands into hers, a soft and kind expression on her face as she nodded behind him, then blew a deep breath into his face, giving him the rest she knew he needed but would otherwise not be able to obtain.

The acolyte lowered him onto a cart and accompanied her to a darkened set of rooms not far from the convalescing suite. Here they tucked the young man onto a bed and left him to dreamless sleep.

"Where did you put him?" Khazeer asked when the Elder Healer returned.

"The family suite m'lord, he'll sleep soundly for a while."

The Fierowen Heru nodded, allowing himself to be helped to his feet, then to a table where another acolyte was escorting Wellyn.

"Bring us a map," he then commanded.

"M'lord," she nodded taking over care of Wellyn and waving the acolyte toward the hall, "get it from the war room."

"Aye elder," came the fading response.

"And find Tierus!" she ordered.

"Aye." Echoed back.

She shook her head, "that fledgling is going to be more useful than he knows. You're to use him to liaise with the Oemirkin," she ordered then wagged her finger, "and if I learn of either of you so much as…"

"Healer," Khazeer addressed softly, "certainly you haven't finished your rounds with all the stations so soon…" it was his way of reminding her of her duties to the rest of their charges, not just him. He knew she could become so preoccupied with a single patient her acolytes may become overburdened trying to cover for her singular vision.

She gave the expected 'harumph' but left him and Wellyn to their planning.

"Heru!" came a rough bark from down the hall as the ruddy faced Janell ran into the room. "Heru! Master Wellyn!" she gave a quick nod to them both while skidding to a halt beside the table, "Glad you are well… where is the Oemirkin? There's a happening… in the distance… East of the navel… a burst of what can only be…" she shrugged, "well it *must* be, it could be nothing else," she seemed to assure herself.

"What must be what my lady?" Khazeer asked.

"Fire! Of *color*!" she burst as if she'd already told him, "m'lord I cannot say... nor those of others... but the legends!" she gasped.

Khazeer and Wellyn each cocked an eyebrow at one another and faced the woman.

"Well?" she asked, "have you seen him?"

Wellyn frowned, "The Oemirkin Wee?" while her head bobbed up and down with frightening speed.

"He is... otherwise occupied... fire of color you say my lady?" Khazeer asked.

"Sire..." she curtseyed showing only the faintest hint of fluster, "Yes! Green! Spring green, bright as first buds! It was beautiful yet made my bones to shudder!"

"Near the navel you said?"

"East of it, near the... near the... it. Near *it*, near the way to... you know...*them*," she nearly whispered.

"The bridge?" Wellyn asked with half an eye on his king and the other on the woman.

"Tropus and his guard left for it this morning... my lord what if they did something? Fire and destruction, this was..." she shuddered, "terrifying... what if he destroyed the way? What if it destroyed them? I must tell someone!" she urged looking around and hoping to see the human she'd come to equate with protecting the palace.

"My lady, you *are* telling someone," Wellyn gently reminded ushering her to join them.

"If Tropus and his guard have gone to the bridge it is possible the light you saw was them traversing the way, those who are destroyed by the bridge have always disappeared without an inkling. More likely they were able to cross," Khazeer tried to soothe.

"It has been long since any of us have seen a crossing, from either direction my lady, disturbance of atmospheric nature is sure to be expected after so long…"

"Lightning?" She grasped at the idea, visibly relieved by it.

"Very possible," Wellyn nodded, "we will send a rider to assess the situation."

She nodded but kept looking around, almost oblivious to the presence of the King of All Sidhe, it was obvious Wee had become a touchstone among the citizenry.

"What are you called my lady?" Khazeer asked softly.

"Janell Heru."

"Janell," he nodded with a light smile gracing his countenance, "when did you last rest?"

His question took her by surprise, her head snapping back to center and her eyes piercing into his. She thought for a moment then shook her head, "after the first siege ended," she shrugged.

"Perhaps then it is time for you to do so again, we will have the light investigated, and it is certain once the Oemirkin and we are through, he will require those who have come to know him best, at his side," Khazeer instructed as Wellyn motioned an acolyte to the table.

Janell nodded and stood, her eyes already falling to half-mast with the relaying of her news and of the certainty she'd be needed again soon.

"Lights! Several Heru!" she turned, "two for certain, then two again…"

Khazeer and Wellyn nodded, "we are grateful for you Janell."

"You will tell me what you discover?" she asked, still unnerved by not knowing what it could have been.

"I will," Khazeer promised as she finally left with the acolyte.

"Think you they made the crossing?" Wellyn asked when they were alone once more.

"It is difficult to know, it would make sense if they had, though why *they* would allow Tropus himself to cross…"

"Maybe the fourth was one of the mounts?" Wellyn offered.

The King of All Sidhe nodded but his slightly pursed lips gave away the depth of his uncertainty, "send Tierus and his friend to investigate."

Wellyn's eyebrow seemed to disappear into his hairline, "two fledglings rather than seasoned soldiers?"

"Tierus kept watch on Wee through the night, he's an impressive fledgling," Khazeer smiled.

"Beezle will most certainly benefit from his influence," Wellyn agreed, "what troubles you?" he asked, quite able to read the darkness of his king's expression.

With a sigh, Khazeer admitted, "the Oemir, I fear, is not fit for battle command, it will take a desperate toll on him."

Wellyn, not certain he shared Khazeer's assessment cocked his head to the side, "he will meet whatever demands are made of him my king, carbon must endure crushing pressure to become diamond."

"Pressure that comes too quickly will shatter the carbon rather than bind it. He's in despair for his love and for the sons. He's been distracting himself since the children disappeared, no one has heard word from his brother or the other hero sons and now he feels the welfare of all those in the Fierowen are upon his shoulders alone."

Wellyn nodded, "he seems not to know we all must act as one to survive and win this war, rather than one bearing all the burden…" he gave a sly smirk to his life-long friend, "very like a Heru I know."

Khazeer chuckled as the original acolyte came jogging back with a stack of maps and chest of inks.

"Always mincing your words Wellyn… truly one of these days you must learn to speak your mind." He grinned while thanking the youth. "Now, let's prepare to help this human bit of carbon become a diamond."

"Aye my king."

--

They knew in their hearts what they'd find when they crested the rise which lent shelter to the town, and saw no signs of smoke, animals, or habitation. The grass was overgrown, the grains also, and there was a silence whispering of things unnatural.

This was not how Gargol lived. They were embodiments of life-light, some of the earliest children of the great dragon, hewn from the very stone of the world itself.

They were incandescent with all things joyous, and bountiful.

Though their visages were often terrifying to the softer, rounder, younger species, their hearts shone with generosity, mirth, and celebration. And from what he and Arabelle could feel in their very bones, he knew with certainty, this most ancient of species, at least in this town, had been extinguished.

Crouching at a roadside hillock Minya muttered, "This is recent." He motioned to a severed stone head. Her eyes were open, her fangs extended with a droplet of venom frozen forever in stone at its tip, but the horror of her expression was what struck him. Whatever had severed her head, she'd seen it coming and she'd been terrified.

"There is nothing over here, emptiness appears to span the entire town," Arabelle called from a nearby house where she knelt to inspect a deep impression with a fine dusting of sand at its bottom.

"I'm not even sure firdur could do this… were you there Minya? Did you see it?" she asked, her voice almost accusing as he rose to his full height and made his way to her.

"Did you?" he returned.

She gave a quick shake of her head. She'd been a child during the war, too young to take up arms to defend her world and its people, but she'd never forgotten the loss of the brothers and sisters, both literal and figurative, who'd been the asking price for those who continued to live. She'd almost had an extended family with the Gargol, like most others she'd been drawn to their light, a moth to the proverbial flame.

"This was strategic," Minya sighed, "it's been moving in secret… I fear the attack on the tower may have been a finale rather than an opening salvo…"

"When two parties are at war, but only one knows about it, the others have already lost," she nodded wiping away the droplets from her eyes.

"We are not lost yet!" the strange Sidhe ground through his teeth.

The memory of Ilirya using the tip of her dagger to free one of the eggs from the dragon's wall popped into the maiden's head. "No. No we are not lost yet."

He glanced to the lengthening shadows and rapidly encroaching darkness, "we'll scout the town, gather whatever lightstones we can find and in the morning head to Fauxston, I feel time suddenly moving a lot faster than we thought."

She gave a curt nod, no longer caring what his game was, no longer caring what secrets he was harboring, he was just as repulsed by the carnage as she was and right now, they were at least allies.

A short time later, Arabelle emptied a pouch of powder into a bowl, "This was all I was able to find."

Minya nodded, "Other than the head, there's wasn't so much as a single intact stone in any place I looked."

She shook her head and met his strange bright eyes.

"Have you energy…" he began only to find her nodding and slinging her bag back over her shoulder.

"I do."

With the disturbing sense of time having slipped so far away as to leave them in a void of stagnation, the pair left the once beautiful lands of Gargoloth for Fauxston and the hope of finding living allies.

--

Officer Stern sat back, satisfied with his now tidy piles of files. The desk had been a mess for a couple days, and he'd finally got it under control. He was equally glad Harleson had gone for the day. The detective was a good enough guy, a little crass, a little gruff, but most cops from larger cities took a while to decompress.

He took a sip of long cooled ginger tea and reached for an interdepartmental transfer envelope dumped into his inbox while they'd been talking with "Mr. Tuath De" as Harleson called him.

He told himself he didn't need assurance, and he'd never admit it to Harleson, but knowing the detective had a funny feeling about their case validated some of his own misgivings.

He liked the kids, talking with both Nick and Frank hadn't rung any of his alarm bells. Same with Charles, and Harry Sr. Sure there was the incongruous story they got from the orderly who helped bring Harry in, but the fact was, it wasn't uncommon for Emergency Department intake stories to be muddled in the beginning, family members were like sea gulls, they each had their own story, and they all loved to squawk.

Very like Harleson, he wasn't sure where his wiggly gut was coming from, but wiggly turned squirmy when he focused his attention on Mrs. Everett and thought about the pastor chasing the kids all the way up the country to bring them back.

Mrs. Everett's assertion their concern was based on having sheltered Mr. Brown for the last three years and hoping he was going to take a more prominent role in the church, just didn't have enough legs to keep the story from shaking. There was also the story about the murdered 'alleged' child trafficker (who was frequently associated with the Everett's church), and the finding of his stolen car on the Texas-New Mexico border. The story had come his way via a conversation with one of Austin's finest.

And last but not least, there was an ancillary report, including cell phone vid, from the very same officer, showing a blurry image of a young guy who just seemed to 'appear' in the middle of 6th Street wielding a medieval looking dagger, against himself. The vid, as bad as it was even after cleaning it up, showed a guy who looked an awful lot one Nick Emerson Junior.

He opened the folder and slid out a pair of traffic reports about a couple of accidents on 183, about a day apart. One was a blue Prius that got rolled several times off the side of the road, and the other a green and brown station wagon, also rolled, though this one didn't look like a ball of tin foil. The registration of the vehicles was what got the reports sent to him. He'd flagged the names sure, but this not only grabbed his attention, it set something dancing a mad kind of jig in his belly.

The Prius was registered to Howard "Wee" Emerson, and the Brady-like station wagon belonged to Harry J. Armstrong. Both went off the road in virtually the same place, and both had been respectively 'squashed', though, as yet there was no indication of how.

"Son of a bitch," he sighed swigging hard on his tea before reaching into his drawer and dropping a dollop of Jack Daniels Green label into it. "I'm not gonna like this," he shook his head and started organizing his notes so he could whip through the computer searches quickly and still get a good night's sleep.

Something inside laughed at the idea of a good night's sleep, and whatever it was, made him very uncomfortable.

--

Sheltered by gigantic leaves, in the depths of the forest Leanna rolled onto her back and breathed deep. She wasn't in much pain,

242

the vestige had seen to her protection, but she was drained, both by its coupling with her as well as the trauma of finally realizing a dragon had somehow survived all these millennia and it hated both her and the firdur.

It wouldn't be long before her mount returned with Fetik. He would see to her needs until she was ready to return to Tur and give him the gift likely to secure their victory.

She'd been part of the crusade from the beginning and now, with their plans about to come to fruition she couldn't help but breathe a sigh of relief.

Everything from the taking of Conchobar and using him to lure Oemir to his doom; to her recent victory had been millennia in the making. No one could have known how long it would take until she could defeat Oemir for his betrayal, but she knew it would happen and now she could claim her victory over Tur and his doubts as well. Firdur would finally finish its consumption of him, and she would rule the few survivors who would swear fealty to the dark while they worked to ensure the onset of multiversal oblivion.

--

Drawing to a halt as the tail of the great mother came into view, a single teardrop gathered in the corner of each of Diagas' eyes. He hadn't seen her in millennia, but finally returning to her after so long moved his heart like never before. The drops fell to the ground, flaring to quick lightning like brightness before hardening to become two more of the first newly formed light stones since the last war.

In the height of moonlight, Zu stood out, prominent with his ruby red scales and fiery golden crest which now stood tall and proud, truly the visage of a leader of the ancient kind.

The other eight they'd freed, lounged, or stood sentinel, possibly waiting for Diagas' return. His suspicion was confirmed when several snouts turned in his direction, and all of them rose to their feet.

Such a formal acknowledgment of his arrival could mean one of two things, either they were likely to drive him away, or they would accept him and his role in their survival. He could not say which it would be, but given what he'd seen while with the fledgling, whatever option they chose made no real difference. They must work together, or everything was doomed.

With a deep breath he strode forward, after all, there was more at stake than his feelings, and the others had to be told there was a spawning in the offing.

--

"You sure you don't want a lift?" the smoke stained, but kind gap-toothed smile asked as he washed his hands and turned away from his reflection in the truck stop mirror.

"No, thank you sir, just feel free to give me a call next time you roll through," Charles nodded with a smile unable to touch his eyes.

"You bet," the trucker grinned, unfurling two twenties and a ten and handing them over, "remember, I got a king cab son, we can get comfortable."

"Yes sir, I look forward to it."

He turned and headed out the door knowing the lonely long-haul trucker would wait a couple more minutes before emerging too.

He felt surreal, a different kind of 'not there' than he'd always felt after shambling back to the pastor after Ezra.

When it was Ezra he'd felt somehow stronger inside for having endured his torments, he'd also felt betrayed. A deep, heavy loathing came alongside thoughts of the pastor and how he could subject his 'best boy' to such heinous acts. He'd always lied to himself though, believing, or at least wanting to believe the pastor didn't know what Ezra did, even though he frequently told Charles Ezra was one of 'The Lord's agents'. Often saying he was sent to test the faithful, and reform the wayward of the flock, turning them back to God and the righteous path.

I'm a fucking idiot. He thought wondering how Nick let himself be saddled with such a blind, *loser*, was the only word he could think of.

But leaving the truck stop, waving at Fran who'd taken his application and promised to forward it to the boss, he felt a strange combination of things.

Sure, he felt dirty, but he also felt what it was like to have power, even if it was just a little and only over himself. It was new, exciting, and scary, and a twenty minute back and forth got him fifty bucks, all his own. Not a "gift", not an "allowance". It was money he earned with nothing more than himself, and for the moment, he was okay with it.

Why then, he wondered as he headed down the darkened street, back to the little subdivision Nick and Frank lived in, did he feel like he wanted to cry?

--

Thankfully the schade was just as reluctant to call attention to itself as Harry was to draw someone into the room.

When it came from the shadow of the bathroom, he was ready. He'd been resting with half an eye on the door, the tip of the steak knife between his fingers, and wondering if he was up to the challenge.

There was no way to know what to expect, but it came at him with a short sword, taking him by surprise. The weapon was immune to the effects of the calcite ring, turning what the boys hoped would be protection into a possible cage if he let himself be trapped.

Instead he rolled off the far side of the bed, glad the night nurse shut the door on his way out so he could lower the rails; and flicked his little knife at the schade. It hit the being's shoulder, flinging off bits of dust into the air before clattering to the floor.

The ghoulish creature smiled, its gum rubbery lips stretching over splintering teeth and tried to stab across the bed only to burn its face and hand against the power of the red light.

Grabbing one of the pillows, Harry slipped it out of the case, wound the case tight into his fists, and with his non-slip hospital socks giving the traction he needed, dashed toward the oncoming creature.

It'd been a long time since he'd gone toe to toe with a schade but with his heart hammering hard in his chest, and adrenaline pumping, he couldn't really remember the last time he had so much fun.

He feinted to the right, forcing the schade to swing its blade closer to him, it was close enough for him to swing the pillowcase up under its sword hand then twist the fabric hard and fast, gaining control of it. Moving the weapon aside he stepped in close to the being, slammed its sword arm into his knee, barking in pain even as the blade rang out against the tile flooring.

The schade was fast though and palmed him in the nose, knocking him back a step. As it ducked to retrieve its weapon his knee came up once again, this time hitting the creature in the face.

A stab of pain shot through his leg, one of his hands reflexively rubbing the spot though the other held tight to the schade as he hopped and hissed through his teeth, "ow, damnit damnit! Son of a bitch!"

With a snarl he returned his other hand to its other ear, keeping its bald head in his control as he ran its face again and again into the same throbbing joint before it swept his leg out from under him. They landed in a heap on the floor, the other worldly creature atop him, its forearm across his throat even as it tried to reach for its sword one more time.

Harry's left arm came up, boxing its ear, but it stayed lodged atop him, its elbow colliding with his jaw, making him see stars and spit blood.

He grasped the loose end of the pillowcase and wrapped it around the schade's neck, wringing the ends together as its eyes bulged and its fingers clawed at his face, scratching, and tearing his skin, one finger perilously close to his eye while he pushed the creature further away, still trying to strangle it.

It took quite a bit of time, several minutes in fact before the schade stopped struggling and its weight went limp against his outstretched arms, held aloft by the same bit of fabric that squeezed the life out of it.

Harry lay panting as dusty flaky bits began to fall from the creature.

Why they disintegrated he'd never known, but he was always glad for it. After all, explaining this kind of a body to anyone in authority would be hard enough, but knowing they'd just take it to some top-secret government place without knowing much of anything about it at all was untenable. After all, everything the government got its hands on never failed to go sideways, and they were trying to save two universes, not destroy one for the sake of the other.

When the schade finished flaking away, and the flakes themselves became no more, Harry grabbed the short sword, rolled himself to his feet and looked down. There was a quarter-sized splotch of blood on his jonnie and a burning sensation in his side.

Sweat broke over him as he pulled the gown up and bent back the soaked dressing covering his surgical site, sour breath full of the smell of fear gushed out of him. Several stitches had pulled, and the wound had a pencil sized opening, but it wasn't as bad as it could have been.

He sat heavy on the side of the bed wiping sweat and blood off his face then took inventory of the room. There were speckles of blood in several different places he could deal with easily enough. The hard part was going to be explaining the cuts, scratches, and bruises on his face.

After cleaning up he sat back on the bed, black light sweeping the ring around him to illuminate the calcite. The overhead light gave him an extra measure of comfort and protection, allowing him to finally drift off to sleep where memories of past lines mingled with instances from this one, and ambiguous fears from all they'd faced so far.

In those visions where dark was a living thing trying to kill his two best friends and all the world around them, there was no rest.

7

With the moon angling toward its descent Nick's gaze was drawn up. There was no pain like when the sun hit his eyes. He knew he was supposed to be more than cautious in the dark, maybe even afraid of what it harbored, but over the years he'd come to find a sense of peace in the nighttime.

For Nick, he couldn't say he'd ever really been afraid of what schades would do to *him*, but considering what they'd done most recently, his fears were for the people around him. His main concern, of course, was always Frank and his well-being, but oddly enough, it wasn't the schades and Frank either. He knew his little brother could kill them when pressed, but the fear that sometimes ambushed him in the quiet times, was the memory of those often-nightly visitations from Pigg. The threats he made to start with Frank. The memory Nick had of the first line, and a used up little brother who'd been raped and abused till he became little more than a wraith, never left him. He doubted it ever would.

Still, their years with Wee and Ryan, coupled with whatever the cranky old knothead of a druid had done, had worked several kinds of magic on him.

Without a soul he was free to do what was necessary to save the universes, a fact which brought him great comfort. Without a soul, he had clarity, and clarity brought a particular concern he just couldn't get out of his head. His concern, especially after what he'd done to Lou earlier, was what Tur, Ne'Min, and the others in the fortress had turned him into, and what it might mean for the few heroes left.

He glanced at each of the companions as they slept during his watch. He could feel the sons of heroes restless inside themselves. The torture they'd endured at the princess' order having caused deep wounds in their minds which couldn't be healed as easily as their bodies. During this time which should've been restful, each of them was once more at the mercy of every horror of their lives.

He looked deep upon Torn's sleeping face, the fledgling was strong, brave, and true, earning Nick's trust right away, thankfully the others were following his lead.

Warmth moved through him with the thought of Errmot, Boaz, and Julius willing to be at his side once again, and though he was still disturbed by Tropus' actions at the bridge, he couldn't find it within himself to be angry with the King of the Bedowen. He'd been trounced by the bridge itself and would not dare risk his personal guard again, at least not with Nick around.

A gasping sniff and a quick bony 'thump' snapped his eyes to Lou who bolted upright trying to quiet his heaving breath while his frantic gaze took in everything around them, making sure they were all safe.

"Psst," Nick caught his attention and tossed Julius' flask to the terrorized hunter.

It seemed to fly right into his hand just as he cursed, "shit," in the faintest whisper and pushed himself fast to his feet. He stumbled behind the nearest tree just before a rasping cough presaged a belly full of vomit splattering the ground.

Naiya's head came up for a brief moment before settling back down to rest. The human would have to tend himself, there was little she could do for him, or any of them.

It wasn't long before Lou shambled back, his hand wiping his mouth before he dumped the remaining contents of the flask down his throat.

How hard the last days had been on him was obvious in the slow stiffness of his movements and the weight with which he just sort of 'plopped' down beside Nick.

"You'll be alright," he assured even as Lou gave a doubtful twitch of the head.

"I dunno," he muttered.

"I do."

But the garage owner dropped his head to his chest, still shaking it side to side, "you don't know shit kid."

Expecting a flare of temper similar to the one he'd been unable to control earlier, when Shep and Dylan said the same thing, Nick was grateful when it didn't come. Instead, a smile tilted the corner of his mouth.

"I knew before you, or either of them did…"

Lou tilted his head, his bright green eyes frowning along with his mouth, "yeah you said they had you, was them scarred you up?"

"Some," he whispered reaching toward Tropus' pack and digging quietly until he found the king's flask, which was just a little smaller than his head.

"Holy shit that's huge," Lou sighed.

Nick couldn't help but smile and think of a running gag from some of his favorite movies before he took a swig and handed it over, "…'it's good to be the king'."

Taking a solid gulp Lou nodded, "no shit." He hit the flask again then handed it back, "God that's good… how'd they get you? And when?"

Nick inclined his head, his finger running over the first spiral of the triskele engraved on the polished metal, *life,* then onto the second one, *death,* and finally over the third, *rebirth. Past, present and future; can there be a future, do we have a future, or is this the future?*

"'bout a month before we met, Terra-time, one of Ne'Min's flunkies tried to grab Frank… almost got him too, but I got lucky."

"They got you instead," Lou realized, "Jesus kid…"

"Better me than Frank. I'd just got back the night before Wee and Ry got rolled, that's the day we met," Nick shrugged, "important thing is I got away."

"You used blood magic to open the veil."

Nick nodded.

"How long you been practicing?"

"The spell? Just since they took me… I dreamed of it from the book, then just kept trying to work it till it worked."

"Fuck," the garage owner sighed, "and they did…" he motioned up and down his forearms, "to you…?"

Nick gave a soft knowing smile and nodded.

"So, you really *do* know…"

"Yeah."

"And that's how you knew how to throw us a lifeline?"

"Sometimes it pays to be a rage filled teenager." Nick nodded.

"Lemme ask you something else," in fact there were at least a dozen questions he wanted to ask the teen-in-a-man's-body, but he went with what popped out of his mouth first. "What did you do to me?"

Nick bit his lips, his gaze holding fast to the moon.

He leaned in close, anxious whispers between them. "One second I'm comin' around after feelin' you inside my head sniffin' around my life's dirty clothes hamper, the next I see Shep in his skivvies with that kid screwin' around with him…"

"Healing what the vestige did to him," Nick corrected keeping his eyes on the orb in the sky.

"Whatever. And I can still hear you in my head blaming me for Rose, rubbing salt in what I already know's my fault!"

Nick shook his head, "S'not your fault."

"Shut up and let me finish!" he demanded then rose up onto his knees, "look at me! At least have the decency to look me in the fuckin' eyes!"

Nick did, his gaze steady.

"So, I get why you said what you did while I was in there, I get why you took advantage of the situation to pop me in the face a few times… I do." He swilled from the flask again then handed it to Nick, who took a hearty gulp as well.

"Then you're screamin' in my face, and the next thing I'm on the ground on fire from the inside! What the fuck did you do to me!?" he demanded though he kept his voice low, wanting to keep this between the two of them.

With the moonlight shining full on Nick, Lou watched his chest quiver while he took a deep breath, and felt his own insides start to get hot and gurgly when the young man's eyes misted over.

No matter what he said to Shep earlier, the teens reaction was proof, deep inside, he was still way too young for the burden fate dropped onto his shoulders, or at least part of him was.

Nick shook his head, "I said I was sorry… you were being a dick, and waiting wasn't an option."

Lou took another deep breath and leaned in, their eyes uncomfortably close, "one more time kid. What. Did. You. Do. To. Me?"

"You didn't give me a choice…" he whispered handing Lou the case of dragon blood from his shirt pocket. The confused hero examined it then put it back.

"What is it?"

"It seals wounds. It's the blood of the great mother," Nick's breath trembled again, "take a look." He motioned with his head to Lou's chest.

Leaning back to see where the holes were in his shirt, he pulled it up, almost reluctantly looking at his chest and belly, where in those same places, fingertip sized scars had formed. "You treated me?" he asked dumbfounded.

Nick nodded as another layer of mist congealed under his eyes.

Easing a suspicious eye to the overgrown teen he growled, "what else did you do?"

Nick closed his eyes, took a deep breath, and bit his lips before finally letting it out, "I stopped you. Then I stripped you down to your shorts and sealed the rest of your wounds, you were losing too much blood, I had to do something!" he insisted, needing to make Lou understand why he did what he did.

"I was scared you'd bleed to death, the way you were fighting everything. It was pulsing out the holes." He shook his head, this time the mist became drops, and he gasped, "I'm sorry." He apologized again.

Lou sat back, his brows bent, and his mouth pursed in confusion, "that's it?"

Nick nodded.

"No, really... that's it?" he insisted, "you stopped me...what is that part of what you can do?"

"Uh huh," Nick nodded again.

"Okay so you can freeze people... then used that shit to heal me even after I was being..."

"A dick," Nick nodded.

"Combative," Lou corrected, feeling his guts start to unwind as the kid huffed a half smile.

"I used what I can do and made you..." he shook his head, "I did something you didn't consent to," Nick mumbled, his arms crossed on his knees, and his chin on his arms.

"Is that what *this* is about?" Lou asked thumbing dry one of the tracks under Nick's eye.

"Mm hmm."

Now it was Lou's turn to bite his lips. He shook his head and rolled his eyes toward the sky as if asking for help, then looked into the young man's eyes once more.

"You ever woke up in a hospital?" he asked.

Nick gave a curt nod. "When I was a kid… a schade stuck his fingers in my head and they couldn't wake me up," he explained.

"Like you did to the one you two captured?"

Nick nodded.

"Jesus," Lou hissed horrified at the thought, "one of the first things they do in the ER is strip you naked so they can find any external injuries you might have… you know that right?"

Nick nodded, "when I woke up, I was in my underwear and a jonnie."

"Did you consent to it?"

"I was just a kid; it wouldn't have mattered anyway."

"Irrelevant, did you consent to it?"

Nick shook his head.

"Exactly. They did what they had to do even though you were unconscious, right?"

Nick nodded.

"Well, if you froze me, I wasn't exactly able to consent, was I?"

"Mm mm."

"But you still fixed me up anyway, right?"

Nick nodded, "that's what Torn was helping Shep with too."

Lou changed his position, so he was sitting next to Nick, "Well, thank you for helping me. Even if I was being…"

"A dick?"

"Hmm." Lou grunted.

They sat in awkward silence for a few minutes, sipping on liquor before Lou motioned to Tropus.

"So that's the guy had the death warrant on you yeah?"

"Mm hmm."

"And you're gonna trust him? And his personal guard?"

Nick grinned, his eyes on Julius, "mm hmm."

"What makes you think they won't throw you to the wolves, or those pirini things at the first chance?" he asked, taking another long draught from the flask.

When Julius and his men had come with Frank and Shep to rescue him and Dylan from the stronghold, he'd been more than willing to trust them, and honestly, he still was, at least with his own life, but Nick had a destiny and because of it, Lou wasn't sure he was willing to trust them with the kid.

"They're only on loan to Tropus."

"Whaddya mean?" Lou asked, a slight slur to his speech as the liquor and all the events of the last few days hit him hard.

"They've sworn their fealty to the King of All Sidhe, when he's ready for them, they'll be *his* guard," Nick explained then added, "besides, they want to live."

257

With another slug on the flask Lou leaned back, his eyes drooping closer to closed, "how d'you know that Julius guy?"

Nick nodded, and sighed, "most recently he, Errmot, Xian, and Boaz helped Harry and me escape the palace after we... absolved the warrant."

Lou's brows furrowed, "if it was absolved why'd you have to escape?"

"Leanna," Nick began, gently removing the flask from Lou's grip, taking another sip, then putting it back in Tropus' bag.

A different voice from deep inside continued to explain, "the princess who had her men and the vestige take you all... her emotions are a contagion that have turned my homelands to decay, you experienced it yourselves as you were marched through them. Best to escape rather than risk Tropus still under her influence after so long."

But Lou's eyes had closed, and his breathing turned smooth and deep. Nick didn't know how much he'd heard or digested, but had a feeling his curiosity was satisfied, at least for the time being.

"We have a hard day in front of us brother, sleep well," he admonished, easing back, and staring at the moon to get his thoughts organized for the coming day.

"I will not fail this time," he sighed letting both memories, and visions of things to come commingle until it was time for his relief.

He would wake Errmot. Lou, Shep and Dylan would be angry one of them hadn't been awakened but they were all in compromised condition, and needed to recover.

"How are *you* feeling?" Lou groaned when he hefted his mount's saddle settling it onto his withers.

Nick shrugged, "Fine. You?"

"Mmm" Lou grunted.

Nick couldn't help but smile. He'd slept a few hours and awoke oddly refreshed and with the beginnings of a decent plan.

They were to split into four groups with himself, Julius and Lou going to appeal to the ancient ones.

Errmot and Torn were to capture one of Semet or Tur's people and bring them back to the Tower of the Sun. There, whatever they knew could be extracted and relayed to the refugees in the mountain, where Tropus and Shep would go to fill in the queen. In the meantime, Boaz would get Dylan to the Tower of the Sun as quickly as possible in order to get him to the Elder Healer. In the night he'd developed a worrying fever and from the smell of him, something was festering.

Torn was only to relay the news of Diagas' existence to the king and Wellyn, in otherwise complete privacy, all others were sworn to secrecy. The more who knew of this fortuitous circumstance, the less potent the element of surprise became. After advising Khazeer and Wellyn, Torn was to take the fastest mount he could and get to the tail of the mountain where the dragons were sure to have congregated, and meet with them, hopefully his affiliation with Diagas would serve him well.

Once we learn where Semet and Tur are hiding their forces we can beat them, splinter their ranks, attack where they have no expectation… we must make them think we are trapped and weak. Khazeer and Wellyn will understand.

"No hangover? You were kinda hitting that juice pretty heavy."

"Nah," he shook his head, "if it was Ry's scotch I'd probably be puking my guts out."

"So you're an experienced drinker already huh?"

Nick cocked his head to the side, his eyebrows furrowed, "you think it really matters? Long as I'm not driving."

A chill ripped through the garage owner at the sound of finality in the kid's voice, but he really had nothing to counter his assertion.

"I dunno, but I bet Uncle Wee's not gonna be so happy with you getting all alcoholic on him… probably take it out on me."

"I'd worry more about Ry…" he said and stopped, a tight and unusual look on his face Lou didn't know for certain how to read.

"You think he's still holding on?"

Nick's mouth turned up at the corner, and his brows down, each by a hairs' width, "yeah, I do."

"My king… a word?" Julius motioned Nick off to the side.

"Y'know," Lou groused at the Sidhe guard, "you keep calling him 'my king', but just a couple days ago you were making pretty big business about Frank being the 'house' of the Oemir… what's your game dude?"

Julius shook his head getting the gist of Lou's question but not understanding what had him confused, "there is no game son of Conchobar, your brothers are my king, are *all* our kings," he motioned to himself, and where the others had been, even Tropus.

"Huh?"

A confused smile twisted the Captain of the Guard's mouth, "the soul has found its home in the youngest, in Frank, but him, who you call Nick, IS Oemir himself."

"The soul is the soul, you can't separate the man from the soul, and for the record we're not brothers."

Julius cocked his head to the side, "but you are, all of you are of the line of Lugh, know you not your own parentage?"

Nick grimaced, he hadn't wanted to let that particular cat out of the bag just yet, but here it was, and catching Lou's dumbfounded look, he nodded, "yeah. Our mother... Danu...your mother, Nessa. She later married Fergus MacRoich, but both born of Lugh."

"Wait, what?" Lou shook his head, his brows furrowed, "you called me the son of Conchobar, everyone has always called me son of Conchobar, everyone KNOWS Conchobar was Cathbad's son... all the LORE says Conchobar was Cathbad's...now you're telling me it's all wrong? That I'm the same line as him?" he demanded of Julius, while jacking his thumb at Nick, "Make up your mind man."

Confused and uncertain how long the charade was going to endure, Julius looked at Nick, "...does he truly not know my king?"

Nick pinched the bridge of his nose.

"Kid?" Lou asked.

The overgrown teen nodded at the garage owner, "yep, we're family. Nessa and Lugh... but she and Fergus were set to marry..." Nick shrugged with a sad smile, "So she set the wedding for the spring, and once you'd arrived, she left you,"

"Conchobar," Julius corrected.

"Conchobar, with Cathbad to be raised, everyone thought you were his from one of his dryad lovers. Given his love for Danu he did raise you as his own."

"What's Danu got to do with it?"

"Nessa was one of her favored devotees, she appealed to Cathbad to raise you to be the next king." Nick shook his head, a frown unsmiling his lips, "you said you read your book… didn't it tell you all that?"

"You do realize it's Conchobar you're talking about, not me right?" Lou shook his head mystified and more than a little concerned about the teen's apparent inability to keep the times and people separated, "and the book didn't go into the begating shit, just the history of our worlds, I gotta admit though, I'm not sure I ever believed any of it," he sighed, "what'd yours say?"

"Bits and pieces, none of us can read it," Nick shrugged as if it didn't make any difference and smiled as Julius confirmed what he said.

"Wait a sec," Lou frowned, "I thought 'cause Frank's a little young, you were just keeping it from him."

"Why would you think that?" Nick breathed, "We had some pages translated, but when pigg… when the house blew up we lost a lot of it. After that, Nana never managed to get more than a few more pages translated…" a glaze covered his eyes and was blinked away, "she was killed before she could get much more done."

Who's pigg? He wanted to ask but wouldn't. When a person changed tack that fast, there was nothing good attached to the thoughts.

"Blew up?" He asked instead.

Nick's eyes dropped down as his lips twisted in a wince, clearly pained by the memory, pained by his part in the explosion that cost their mother her life.

No matter what anyone else said, or how many times Harry told him it wasn't, he knew it was his fault. *If I'd just done what he said, just let him take me, she wouldn't be dead.* He once more berated himself as this time a pair of unstoppable tears dropped over the rims of his eyes. "Yeah," he managed to grunt then fingered the wetness away.

Watching and listening, Julius felt the cascades of guilt slamming through the human his love had become. He once again caught glimpses of a slovenly, depraved man, and felt a barrage of the agonies this youth had endured. He had to still every urge to grab him into his arms to soothe away the pains of his human upbringing. With luck he'd have a chance to remind this Oemir, offspring were not meant to bear the wrongs of the adults around them.

A slow crush pushed hard on Lou's chest, the look on the young man's face spoke volumes. Not wanting to pry, he shook his head, his face twisted in a wince, "okay so… I still don't get how him and Frank can both be king, no man, no *being*, can serve two masters."

Julius nodded, "this is why we serve Tropus until the king takes the throne."

"Yeah? And which one of 'em's gonna do that?" he half demanded. The only answer forthcoming was a glance between Julius and Nick. It was both too much and not enough of an answer.

"Shit," Lou's hand swiped down his faintly green-tinged face, "So if you can't read your book, then how do you know all this shit? I mean I've read plenty of the lore about Conchobar, Cathbad and Lugh and even Nessa but nothing, nothing says anything about Conchobar being Lugh's…"

Looking to Julius, uncertainty written on his face even as the Captain of the Guard nodded.

Nick gave a sheepish shrug, "well… Lugh… let's just say

discretion was NOT one of The Shining One's finest attributes… Nessa though…a lady of honor. She would never have openly betrayed her oath to Fergus… but our senses are more keen than those of men."

"It was an open secret among our kind," Julius smiled, "after all, we champion love wherever it can be found."

"And…" Nick's head bobbed in a nod, "we were there when you were born."

"When Conchobar was born," Julius corrected.

"When Conchobar was born." Nick amended.

"Excuse me?" Lou wobbled himself down to sit on a stone.

Nick nodded, "Julius and I were with Nessa when she went into labor with you… your father… ancestor. We weren't the only ones, most of our kin were there, waiting to meet our new half-human brother."

Lou's jaw dropped and a layer of greasy sweat shone on his face, "who the fuck are you? Are you Nick or are you Oemir?" he whispered then shook his head, "I don't feel so good."

With an indulgent but sympathetic smile Nick patted him on the shoulder, "it's alright, if we win, it'll be fine."

"And if we lose?" Lou grumbled.

"There'll be nothing left to know we ever existed," he admitted, "excuse us."

Lou gave a nod even as the two stepped just a few feet away.

"I would rather we bring Errmot and Boaz as well, three of us alone are no match for the ancient ones."

"We don't need to be, the bridge will know. It's bad enough we have to divide again so soon but Dylan needs the Elder, and we need information on Tur and his forces. Khazeer and Wellyn must be told what we know, so must the refugees in the mountains. And, if I know Liri she will have gone or sent others to try and re-establish contact with our old allies so then Areen must be told, there is too much to do and too little time."

"We could send word with ravens or nightbirds…" Julius started then stopped at a skeptical eyebrow from Nick.

"And leave none sure of where or from whom word actually came?"

"Aye," the captain nodded, "I no sooner said it… we could look for a crystal? Or maybe the first ones have one?"

"It'll be worth asking, but barring that, we have little other means than face to face to brief the others. I feel it slipping away Julius… everything, it's happened too fast," he stopped, wondering somehow if his childhood friend knew of his powers, and exactly to what extent of them, he was aware.

Then he began to earnestly wonder what he might be able to do, if anything, on such a grand scale.

"Of that I too feel certain… something feels… wrong meleth. You *are* my king, but as the son of Conchobar has also said, you are of a human youth. How then are you knowing the things you know?" he whispered, his brow furrowed in confusion.

Nick gave a half-hearted shrug, "Cathbad woke me."

He breathed deep and swallowed hard, having to force himself to keep his hand at his side instead of letting it stroke the cares from the Captain of the Guard's face, "As for the feeling of something 'off', yeah, I feel it too. We didn't know we were at war and because of that we were caught off guard, we may lose but not because we won't have given everything we can!"

Julius' eyes popped wide, "Heru we cannot lose! We MUST win this war and fight back the firdur!"

"What if that's not the right way to go?" he mused more to himself than to the Sidhe. "Isn't that what we did last time?"

"Aye."

"And all it did, was get us here."

Julius frowned, "What would you have us do?"

"Whatever we need to," Nick shrugged. "I just wish I knew more. Why is it so hell bent on destroying all life in both universes? What did we do to deserve it?"

Frustrated he turned, his fist at his mouth, forefinger flicking at his lips while he paced, thinking aloud, "It's immortal, it's eternal, it's half of the daily celestial cycle. I mean what the hell have we got that's got its proverbial panties in such a bunch!? Unless it's just plain evil, like the FIRST evil…"

A scant second later he stopped and wheeled, a faint glimmer of the beginnings of an idea came to a simmer while a dark smile crossed the teen's adult face. He squeezed the Sidhe's shoulder then returned to Naiya whom Lou just finished outfitting.

"You're fourteen," he said with a shake of his head.

"Not anymore," Nick shrugged while checking the saddle and his pack.

"Bullshit," Lou hissed, shaking his head, "Jesus fucking Christ."

266

"What?"

"Fuckin' fourteen," he sighed, still shaking his head, "it's not my business…"

"Nope," Nick shrugged double checking his sleeping area for forgotten bits.

"Jesus… I'm an idiot," Lou muttered wondering why he'd told Shep he'd talk to the kid.

"Not gonna get an argument from me," Nick teased under his breath but still smiled at the older man, wondering if he'd heard him.

"Little shit…" he grunted then finally took a deep breath, "c'mere."

"You really wanna start the day this way? You're not up to par yet," Nick reminded him, just in case he was feeling feisty.

"You know you got a real shitass attitude kid."

"Maybe it's just personal," the overgrown teen admitted.

"Why? What the fuck did I ever do to you?"

Nick shrugged, "tried to get in my way on a bad day, then tried to get between me and my brother. Got yourself captured, and tortured, just like them," he motioned to the campsite and the others who'd left earlier, before continuing. "Almost cost two universes not just one, but two more of the descendants who're supposed to help save everything against the dark. And now I gotta babysit your reckless ass till we can get you back to the tower and I can get on with business…" Nick squinted his eyes at the man, "you want me to keep going?"

Lou's blonde eyebrows shot so high in surprise they were hidden under his hair, "You babysitting me? That's rich!" he barked.

"If the shoe fits…"

"Wow… you got some fuckin' ego on you…better be careful 'er one day the universe is gonna show you who's really in charge."

Something dark passed over the youth's expression, the same as had set Lou's teeth on edge from their first meeting. He knew magiks were done to the kid but other than the lines of his history being awakened, what else might've been done, he wasn't privy to, and he didn't like not knowing.

Reminding himself he was supposed to be the adult here, he let the boy's assessment roll off his back, and held out his closed fist to the young Emerson.

"Listen, it's none of my business who you wanna screw," he grasped Nick's hand, placing something into his palm, "but never bareback!"

He hadn't missed the subtle cue when he grabbed Nick, he felt the muscles twitch and knew the youth was ready to fight if necessary.

To his chagrin he felt a perverse pleasure when instead, the boy's face showed surprise at the sight of caring in the form of a condom.

Slipping it into his wallet Nick nodded, "We didn't, and I still have one left, but thanks. So is that your 'talk'?" he asked smiling at Lou's upraised eyebrow, "you don't whisper as quietly as you think."

Lou smirked, "sorry."

"S'okay… we just needed to get our heads' together," Nick said.

A moment of companionable silence passed while Nick checked his pack, taking inventory as the older man did the same.

"Lou?"

"Mm?"

"Potassium nitrate…"

"Yeah?"

"We use it in a lot of spells,"

The son of Conchobar nodded, "wards, summonings, bindings, expulsions… what about it?"

"Ry and Wee call it saltpeter."

A grin broadened the older man's face, "Mm hmm?"

"Sometimes they kinda giggle about it… they always said we'd understand when we got older…"

Red crept up Lou's neck to tinge his grin just a little pink, "ahhhh, I gotcha," he nodded, "there's an old wives tale that if a woman didn't want her husband to screw around on her, she'd put saltpeter into his food or drink, and he wouldn't be able to… you know."

"Get it up?" Nick asked.

"Yeah," the older man chuckled, "what made you think of that?"

"Harry… when I told him Ch… when I told him I have a…partner, he said if he ever caught us not using rubbers he'd dose us with so much we wouldn't be able to for a decade," he explained, blushing quite bright as he did so, "then he gave me Wee and Ry's box of Trojans."

Lou gave a good-natured chuff, "I think he was just trying to get a point across that with any sex, you and your partner need to be using them. There's diseases that'll kill you, or whoever you're messing around with."

Nick nodded. Just before Wee and Ry pulled him and Frank out of public school, they'd gone over most of the STI's including HIV, AIDS and the Hep's, and how important protection was. Thinking about the sex he and Charles had on the way home, and how they hadn't bothered to use protection, his eyes turned down just enough make Lou frown, "what?" he asked.

Nick shook his head, wrestling with another idea rolling through his head between waking and this very moment.

After last night with Julius, and the things he'd felt; the breathtaking, enormous, and overwhelming sense of suffocation by need, he felt like it could have killed him. The several mind-blowing orgasms were something he'd never known could happen to a guy, and it was spectacular, but it was the crushing need while in the arms of the Sidhe that felt like some kind of sinister monster lurking inside.

He wasn't sure it was safe to ever feel it again and if salt peter could make sure he never got hard again, then maybe he'd never have to face the searing intensity again either. Thing was, the last person on any planet he'd want to ask about getting turned on, or being able to come whether there was an erection or not, was Lou.

"What?" He asked again.

Nick shook his head and shrugged, "I don't know... do you think he was... I don't know if... maybe," he latched onto the conversation he and Frank had with Harry the other day when he told Frank about Nick's "sex cooties" in the first line.

"Who he, your partner?" Lou pressed.

"No," Nick shook his head, "Harry."

"Harry?"

"Yeah. What if he uh… what if he stops being… you know…"

"What? Stops giving a shit just because you're gay?" Lou asked.

"Bi, but yeah, what if it matters to him?" he mused aloud knowing Harry would forgive him for even pretending to think he'd give a shit if he was gay, bi, pan or whatever.

He didn't care if Lou thought he'd think something so stupid, but he just couldn't bring himself to allow the man to know what happened to him last night. It was way too intimate. Still, he was glad the older man wasn't holding any grudges. Apparently, their talk had done enough to cool the garage owner's dislike of him, and maybe the revelation of their three-thousand-year removed kinship hadn't hurt either.

"Bi," Lou nodded. *'That's not experimenting that's experience,'* he told Shep just yesterday. He shook his head, still smiling as he brought a friendly hand up to the boy's shoulder and met his bright blue eyes, "You think he's gonna stop being your friend because of who you're attracted to?"

Nick shrugged, "people are effed up, they'll kill a person just cause they're gay. I mean Wee's been challenged just 'cause. And a few times there's been bullies even went after Frank thinking he's queer, just cause he's small and kind. But he's not… like me."

Lou turned to face the young man fully, "Look, whatever you're thinking kid, there's nothing wrong with you. And there's always gonna be judgmental scumfuckers who think they have a right to tell you who it's okay to love or even just to fff… have sex with. If Frank's got half the skill I've seen from you, he's gonna be able to take care of himself just fine no matter which way he is. As for Harry, he's your best friend right?"

"Yeah, mine and Frank's… he's been with us through

everything, and in the first line… well… shit I guess he knew everything about us…"

"And as far as I gathered, almost a lifetime trying to rewrite your history yeah?"

Nick gave a curt nod.

"And you really think it's gonna matter to him when he's stuck with you all through so much?"

A weak smile tilted the corner of Nick's mouth, "probably not," he nodded. "You said it's an old wives tale, so saltpeter doesn't really do that?"

The son of Conchobar, overtaken by a sense of camaraderie, and perhaps a longing for a family long lost to exile, found himself warmed by a sudden flush of affection for this teen who'd been so hard and cynical and confrontational since the moment they met.

But, now the kid seemed to have let him in a little bit, he couldn't help himself and gave the young man a good-natured shoulder shove.

"Nah, just gives your heart palpitations and your ass the shits."

"Speaking from experience?" Nick asked.

"Something like that," He chuckled.

Easing himself away from the older man his twenty something expression oddly enigmatic, he gave a nod, "good to know. Thanks."

"Y'know," Lou shook his head, "I never woulda figured you for the promiscuous type, I mean, sheesh," he ran his hand through his hair and tried again, "listen, we're all gonna be in for some weirdness if this really is the start of the war. So, whatever happens, you can talk t'me about anything okay?"

Nick nodded, "Thanks."

After another slightly awkward moment Lou shook his head, "I can't believe you're the kid I met just a couple weeks ago, I mean, you are, but you're *not*." he muttered sweeping his hand down his face.

"I'll tell you a little secret…" Nick offered.

"Mmm?"

"Time… It's relative. About three days here, is about two at home."

Lou cricked his neck, "You got it down that good?"

"S'what I do." Nick shrugged.

He peered deep into the young man's eyes, looking for something; some tell-tale sign everything was alright, or everything was all wrong, "everything you've done, yesterday, today… not a hint of you going back to your real age… you stay this way I think you're gonna get stuck."

Nick nodded and sighed, "Harry's worried the same thing. I think you're right. But I'm different now, there's a thousand lines inside me, awake, waiting to tell me what I need to know, when I might need it."

He swallowed, "but it's not like it is with Frank," he shook his head, sadness in his voice, "I don't know if he'll survive them, but I have to believe in *his* strength to do *my* part in all this. The part of me? The angry part, I'm still here, still angry, at least a bit, but mostly I'm just done with giving a shit about it, none of it matters," he hissed then took a breath. "Trying to save whole universes kinda puts things in a different perspective y'know?"

Lou nodded, he got what the boy was saying, but as someone who didn't trust or take kindly to magic or magical beings, he just couldn't bring himself to trust the process Cathbad unleashed. But Nick, or Oemir, or whoever he was, was right, if they survived and saved the universes they could set things right and if they couldn't, there'd be nothing left to know or care.

He blew a hot frustrated breath out but nodded, "alright, I'm gonna ask you to be careful, and I don't just mean with your dick, we don't know these people or what they want, I mean what they *really* want y'know?"

"…and you don't want to see me get hurt?"

"I don't wanna see ANY of us get hurt… at least not any more than we've already been."

It was on his lips to tell Lou not to worry, he'd been broken before and managed to get put back together but given what he learned while clearing Conchobar's descendant of his firdur possession yesterday, he didn't see any need in adding to his burden. He already blamed himself for Rose's death, which turned out to be just the latest in a string of losses stretching back to his very birth, and Nick having had to play on his hurt was bad enough. Lou was just as scarred as any of them, and it wouldn't be fair to lay anything else on him.

"Thanks," he nodded, also knowing this wasn't the time to explain the history he and Julius shared. How, as children they'd been inseparable, then as fledglings they'd fallen in love and remained so for centuries. No matter whoever else either of them came to love, their feelings for each other never changed, and they seemed to always find their way to one another again. It was the way of many of the children of Danu.

"So… the bridge?" Lou started.

"Yeah?"

"What do we do when we get there?" he asked.

Nick cocked his head to the side while a beaming smile lit his face, "we cross it."

Lou rolled his eyes and chuckled but shook his head, "aww c'mon."

"You stepped in it."

"Shaddaap," he drawled with a smile.

Nick shrugged trying to hide his own as they mounted up and headed out. Whatever would come next would depend on the forces they and the others could muster.

--

"There is no time for dawdling! The firdur has returned, it and its allies have attacked the Tower of the Sun! Heru Khazeer and his forces have sent us to warn our old allies!" Ilirya explained through the small mesh window in the door of the otherwise pitch-black room they'd ushered her into.

"…and where was Khazeeeeeeer when we needed *our* allies?" the Felesian guard mewled without even giving her time to answer before striding away toward the center of the village.

"Licking our own wounds." She sighed, raising her gauntlet of lightstones to start searching the room into which she'd been locked.

The need for diplomacy and patience was intense, and without it she would be tempted to either try to pick the lock of this makeshift cell and find her way to the Queen's den, bruised feelings

275

be damned, or find some other way out.

But this was not the time to think about crossing the Felesians, they were ferocious, superb hunters and skilled at many different modes of combat as well as stealthy operations, in short, they were necessary. She just wished she'd been able to reach the Cyclopes first, as neighbors to the Felesians they were likely to have had a better relationship with the royalty here.

Frustrated by the need to wait, she took a deep breath and sat on a bale of straw, braiding several small groupings together while taking in the details of the structure and deciding where the best place for her makeshift wick would be, if indeed she needed to burn a wall down to get to the Queen.

--

In a place to the North-west, where the green of the Bedowen gave way to a spindle of Fierowen desert betrothed to a delta at the mouth of the Akirowen, what started out as a thread of black, had days ago, become a river.

It turned toward the lands of the Nahroehn, carving a bed that grew broader and deeper as more and more of it moved into this world.

This time, there was nothing to stop it, no light from the sun could turn it from its path, no heat could turn it away or dissolve it, or burn it away.

Over the millennia since its last attempt to infiltrate this universe, it had learned; some would even say evolved. And as it devoured the other universes, making them devoid of life, it grew even more powerful.

As it flowed toward the tower of rock slowly crushing its way into the Bedowen, it enveloped every living thing in its way, for its own needs.

When it was stable enough, it would spread itself over the land, seep into the ground, stealing and usurping every life-giving element and nutrient and when it was done, the ground would crack and the fires in the center of the world would bubble to the surface. Waters would boil away, trees would turn to ash, the world once called Aderyn would be consumed until it was no more than a faint memory of a lifeless grain in a universe of blissful void.

And when there was nothing left here, it would pierce the veil between worlds, finally able to turn the life energy of the last of the triskadecagon of universes against itself, setting off a chain reaction of eradication of all things life and light. The destroyer of life in this universe was the world ancient living things called Terra, and younger living things called Earth.

--

"Yes, we have some wards similar to these," Rae and her fellow mage Alain nodded.

"These are…" Alain nodded looking between Ryan and Rae.

"Blood magic," she finished "…like the ones the Oemirkin had the others using on the tower to help it resist the onslaught," she finished.

"Oemirkin," Ryan cocked his head, his heart leaping into a painful gallop making him wince, "Wee… Howie Emerson?" he asked, but they only shrugged.

"We know only he was the one left to defend the tower when Khazeer and Wellyn fell. We did not learn his name," she smiled softly at the burly man's let down.

"Short human, about yay high?" He held his hand up to just under his chin, "dark curly hair just below his shoulders?"

But they shook their heads, "we received our pleas from the other mages, we did not meet him."

Ryan shook his head, "my kingdom for a horse… or better yet, a transporter," he sighed.

"These spells, they work on your side?" Alain asked.

Ryan nodded, "yeah, they're pretty powerful over there, so I'm guessing they're gonna be a whole lot more so here."

"Of a certainty." Rae nodded, her respect for the work obvious, as well as her trepidation.

"Say, you guys got any way to help me finish up healing here?" he asked, "I gotta get to the tower, find out what's up with Wee and the boys…" his hopeful expression was easily read between the two, as were their own looks of uncertainty.

"Heru," Rae started but he interrupted her with a shake of the head.

"I'm not one of them, I'm just a guy in love with one of 'em," he explained.

"You are the other father to the Oemir himself?" Alain asked.

"Yeah me 'n Wee are their, well… they're our kids."

Rae dropped her head, "then you have our sorrow, word came that the elder succumbed to a death warrant on him."

Ryan gasped, literally backing up, folding over the emotional gut punch, "what?" then shook his head. His blood turned to ice and tears covered his eyes. His arms folded around himself, remembering the feel of Nick clinging to him, the emotions of his experience at the hands of the schades a tangible field that had hurt Ryan's heart, "no… not my boy…"

"We are truly sorry Heru," Alain offered with a hand on the man's shoulder.

"Nicky," he sniffed, burying his face in his hands, something inside screaming while the Aeshema drank it all in, "What about Frank? Any word on Frank?"

"Other than he is now become the Oemir and gone to rescue sons of heroes from the Nahroehn, no other word."

His face crinkled, "…gone to rescue? He's a kid for god's sake…" he wavered on his feet, his injuries and grief a weight he could barely sustain.

The two mages sat him on a bench, Rae offering water from the skin dangling from her hip.

"Where… where's his body?" he asked, bloodshot eyes begging between the two.

"We do not know, though Tropus may have kept it," Alain offered.

Rae leaned toward him, "he came to the summit with his guard, none sensed pretense, he would be bound to return it to the birthplace of his bride."

"Think you after all this time he would readily part with such power? Or such a powerful talisman?" Alain hissed.

A grotesque vision of Nick's body, shredded and crucified, being carried like a war banner through towns came to mind, making his throat close in reflex.

"He's not a *talisman*, he's a…" his voice broke, "kid," his face stained in shimmering ribbons and his hand over his mouth, "he's *my* kid… *our* kid, whoever this Tropus guy is, he doesn't get to keep Nicky!"

Rae put a hand on his shoulder, "he is the king of the Bedowen lands, the birthplace of Oemir," she explained nodding, "if his motives are true, he will return the body, it is a matter of honor."

Alain scoffed but held his tongue.

"I need to be healed, to be able to get to the tower and help Wee, can you help me?" he whispered, wiping his running nose like a kid with a cold, "please?"

"All that can be done to help you heal, has been done, time is the only magic left to you now," Rae assured him.

"There has to be something," he choked feeling as if he were being crushed all over again, all he wanted was his family back, "please."

Rae shook her head, "I am sorry hero, we do not have the means, time is the only thing that can make you whole."

"No," he sniffed, "my *family* is the only thing that can make me whole… what's the fastest way to get to the tower?"

Alain shrugged, "you have magic like this but cannot make a portal?"

"Portal?" he asked, remembering Mickey casting her spell on the patio, opening the way for them to all come through after the boys and Harry.

"Only the most powerful among us could do it," Rae explained holding up the paper with the warding spells on it, "even these will exhaust our resources for a time, let alone collapsing distance."

Ryan's head was spinning, *collapsing distance? What? Like 'folding space?' Is it their way of saying 'wormhole'? What else do they know? How much technology do they have here?* He wondered feeling his stomach roil and clench. *Nicky I'm so sorry kiddo, I shoulda been there for you, I shoulda protected you... God... Wee, he's gonna be a wreck, and my little guy... he's nine for fucks' sake! Rescuing? Who?*

It was all too much, the information overload, the grief, the agony of his half-healed body. Shutting down for a time, he slid from the bench to a heap on the ground where Alain and the accompanying acolyte hefted him onto a cart to bring him back up to the makeshift infirmary.

"Dunkun warned you it was too soon," he sighed shaking his head.

Alain and Rae watched the two visitors disappear into the mountain then turned to collect the other mages.

"These will be most beneficial, though I do wonder how a human came to have such powerful spell work, perhaps when the veil grew, not so much as we thought, was truly lost." He mused.

"Apparently." Rae smiled turning in a flash, her short sword slicing through his throat down to the vertebrae, arterial spray passing her head by mere inches as she slipped behind the body, catching it as it started to fall.

Noting a small outcropping of petrified dragon scale, she'd seen on their way to speak with Ryan, she dragged Alain's body behind it before sweeping dirt and debris over the huge blood stain.

None were likely to come this way any time soon since the others were marching and chanting their spells, circling the nearest entries into the caves. Her lips pulled tight over her teeth as she slid a small metallic looking rod out of a pocket, flicked her thumb nail across it and held up the resultant flame to the paper, watching it burn while a satisfied smile grew over her face and a flash of darkness coursed along the veins of her neck.

--

"Wow, that doesn't sound good at all," Charles shook his head and sipped from his soda, "any ideas what to do? I mean, should we call an ambulance for him?"

Mickey peered at him through an amber inch of scotch in the glass her lips had yet to touch, "to be honest I'm more worried about Frank."

"Yeah, freaky as shit, poor kid was just," Harry shook his head, "it was like he snapped or something."

"Well, I imagine having a whole 'nother person inside your head can't be good for anyone, even someone who's got a gift." Charles surmised.

"Yeah," Mickey nodded, "well, you've got a gift too, if I remember right, you're pretty observant, do you know anything that could help keep Vahl, or the other Oemirs quiet in his head?"

Charles shook his head, "shit… anti-psychotics?"

"Wait a minute, you're part one of them," Harry jacked his thumb toward Mickey, "you know spells, you bound that thing in the hunter, can't you bind the other minds inside the kid?"

She shook her head, "I don't know. I don't know that many spells, just the couple I've managed to grab from the other lines I've seen."

"So? Stitch something together," Charles suggested.

"What about contacting Jack?" she asked.

Harry shook his head, "oh heeeeeelllll no! I ain't gettin' anywhere near that crazy sack o' bastard, especially not after how he got his head effed with."

Mickey nodded, "yeah, and he did shoot Nick."

"I told you we shoulda taken those books."

Mickey nodded, her hand out to Harry as he pulled his phone, "Dial 'em up, see what they can scan to us."

"Don't enjoy it too much," Harry smirked.

No clue what they were talking about Charles corrected them, "By the way, Nick was grazed. Shot's when the bullet stays in," He shrugged when the others cast their curious eyes at him, "what? I'm from Texas."

"Y'know you don't have much of an accent," Harry offered.

"I'm from Austin, we only got the tiniest bit o'drawl," he demonstrated.

"Left in or grazed, it's all the same to me," Mickey hissed, clearly not a fan of Jack Masters.

"Not to the person who gets hit it's not," Charles smirked gently, though he understood exactly how she felt. After all, he was in love with Nick too.

"This is Mickey Farrell, in Lakeview Oregon, we met a few days ago when your brother was dealing with a… hitchhiker. I need some information that might be in some of those books. It's an emergency," she breathed then added, "don't make me have to find

283

you."

"Voicemail?" Harry asked.

She nodded.

"Damn," Charles nodded, impressed, "pretty tough."

She cocked her head to the side, her smile slightly predatory, "it's not good to fuck with the witches, especially when one's part Sidhe."

Swallowing hard Charles nodded again, "good to know."

"Okay, so Mick, till they get back to us you need to find a binding spell to help Frank stay Frank…. Or be Frank again. Maybe even find one to put Vahl back in his own head. Charles, you're gonna need to…"

"Get some damned sleep," he groaned before adding, "and run interference with those cops remember?"

"Shit!" Harry cursed even as Mickey dropped her head into her hands, shaking it side to side.

"So, it's gonna be on you to find out what you need to take care of a comatose…"

"Sidhe," she sighed, "where the hell am I gonna find that level of spell work?"

Sliding one of the laptops over to her Charles gave a tight smile, "it's called the internet. Nick was talking about putting word out on different sites about schades and vestiges and shit while we were coming here, I bet you can find some of the more hardcore ones in the history."

The young woman nodded and smiled, "yeah, alright."

"And you gotta have some of your own resources, right? Maybe someone from your hometown?" Harry frowned, "which is where, by the way?"

"I can't go back there," she mumbled.

"Did I say you should?" Harry sniped.

"They got phones there?" Charles asked softly, fully aware of how it felt to be unable to go home again.

As much as he wanted to undo so much of what happened, from the pastor getting killed, to Harry Sr. getting stabbed; now having to face the cops and try to lie to them, AND make them believe him, he knew it was impossible. *'Let's not forget all this stuff having to do with demons and other universes, and spells and magic... and even whoring myself out for fifty bucks,'* Even if he could, he wasn't sure he'd want to. He just had to find a way to live with it all.

Charles pushed himself away from the table, "I'm going to bed, I'll be in Nick's room."

The other two nodded, Mickey opening one laptop and Harry the other, each focused on their tasks.

At the top of the stairs Charles peered into Frank's room, his glance moving from Vahl to the magically immobilized youngest Emerson, he sighed and once inside Nick's room, locked the door, just in case Frank broke free.

"Oh gross…" he groaned at the sight of the blood-stained sheet on the bed.

Pinching the sheets at the corners, he rolled them off the far side, grabbed a pillow that smelled like Nick and collapsed onto the bare mattress, barely able to draw the comforter over himself before he was out cold.

--

At the head of the path leading from Gargoloth to Fauxston, the very air began to shimmer, tiny tightly packed concentric circles growing before their waves overlapped in a moving collage of universal energy.

Molecules moved with increasing speed sending the circles cascading into each other until the molecules themselves seemed to separate and a tall, statuesque warrior woman with a burgundy storm of waves and curls stepped onto the path with a familiar raven on her shoulder. Behind her lay a panorama of black with fracture lines of hot orange stringing the plain. The sky was suffocated with tumultuous, sinister grays, and a baleful wind chased fine grains of ash into the nothing. With nothing but virtual oblivion behind her, her gaze locked onto the backs of the two travelers while her finger stroked the breast of the bird,

"Watch them, tell Oemir what they have thus far encountered. Lend help wherever you are able." her dulcet voice left no room for disagreement though the creature did chirp a melodic string in retort.

She shook her head, "They are mortal. I, like the She, cannot see what they will do." She reminded her companion, only to receive another reply from the avian.

Glancing behind them she let out a heavy breath. "Far too many possibilities, as you well know," she shook her head. "No, I fear the future of all life is in the hands of children."

Poe chirped again and she nodded, "…as it should be in any universe. When you have told Oemir, you will bring the news to Areen, to the refuge in the dragon, and then you may go to the soul, give what aid you can, but be swift, the first ones will not wait to pass their judgment."

Poe cocked his head to the side, his clear coffee colored eye with its gray ring gazed deep into her emerald eyes before unleashing what sounded like a tirade of squawks, and chirps, making her smile and shake her head.

"I miss it too, but such is the nature of universes born together. Like children growing to adulthood, they go their own ways. It is truly a most grand example of life itself."

He squawked again, scoffing at her assessment.

"We have no choice, what the firdur wants flies not just in the face of the *cycle* of life, it seeks to end it all. The suffering has already been immeasurable. Every life is a building block upon which new and often profound forms come to exist. It must be allowed to flourish while it can!"

Seemingly satisfied, Poe rubbed his beak against her cheek before launching from her shoulder and climbing into the sky. He banked to the southwest, heading toward the Oemir and at least one of his kinsmen.

--

"What happened?" Dunkun frowned as his apprentice maneuvered Ryan to his pallet, the large human grunted and twitched, his eyes fluttering open, his gaze darting around the area.

"Wee? I gotta talk t'Wee... Nick..." he sniffed, "they said he's gone, they killed him," he pushed himself upright, his elbows on his knees.

Frowning Dunkun glanced to his apprentice, "contact the tower, and if you can... Wee."

The apprentice dashed across the infirmary to a trunk where something seemed to glow beneath a skylight.

Ryan's brows furrowed and his mouth pinched first, then pursed in a small 'o' as the apprentice made some motions then brought the plate of crystal to them.

"He is meeting with the Heru and Wellyn, but this fledgling is awaiting instruction," he handed the device to Dunkun.

"Phones? You've got PHONES and you DIDN'T TELL ANYONE!" Ryan roared, "WHAT THE FUCK IS WRONG WITH YOU PEOPLE!?" he demanded, lurching to his feet, and gazing into the crystal with the First Acolyte. "WHERE THE HELL ARE MY KIDS?" he bellowed doubling over with pain.

He didn't see the young soldier's face crinkle with suspicion at him, but Dunkun did, "he is Ry, a father of the Oemir, he has been told the elder boy is fallen. I am Dunkun."

"First Acolyte," Tierus nodded, "I have heard of you. I am Tierus," the fledgling gave a curt nod, "I've not heard of either of them falling, though the younger is now the Oemir. He and others left to mount a rescue at the Nahroehn fortress, though that was two days ago, and I have not heard any other news."

"Would they have phones too?"

Tierus' brow furrowed, "I know not what a…"

"THIS!" Ryan stormed thumping the crystal, "this thing! The thing we're talking on, we call it a phone for fucks' sake!"

"They *may* have a crystal with them, but…the ravens, crows and nightbirds are far better suited…"

"You can carry these! Jesus fucking Christ!"

"They are delicate," Dunkun explained, a firmness to his tone Ryan hadn't heard thus far, "and thumping them may damage the lattice within, which would then change the resonance frequency and make them less effective if not useless, do you understand?"

A frustrated roar ground out of Ry's throat, his hands grasping tight on Dunkun's robes while his face pressed to the Acolyte's shoulder but nodded, he did indeed understand.

"When the meeting is done, have Wee make contact..." Dunkun started but Ryan lifted his head up with a bark.

"NO! Don't you tell him anything! Don't you tell him I'm awake! If he's running the show over there, he can't afford to get distracted, it'll get him killed and I didn't come back just to lose him, do you understand me?" he demanded.

"Aye. I will learn what I can of the elder son and advise you..." Tierus' mouth turned down and he pointed to his nose, "uhm... you may want to rest father of Oemir,"

"Ry's fine," he grumbled allowing himself to be led back to the pallet where he fell to his side, his knees in his chest, squeezing his bleeding nose shut while his breathing settled down. Whatever else they might be saying beyond his caring.

--

"It's beautiful," Lou mused, taking in the sight of the bridge. To him it appeared as a small town covered type that usually crossed a tiny river. "It's like that one in Beetlejuice, you ever seen it?"

Nick nodded, "yeah, it's one of Ry's faves."

"S'it look like that to you?" he asked.

Nick shook his head and swallowed hard, "no."

"My king?" Julius asked, but Nick just shook his head again, his eyes locked onto whatever it was he was seeing.

289

The color had drained from his face and sweat was running over him.

"It's okay."

"Whaddaya see kid?" Lou asked.

"Just, a bridge," he answered, hoping by not acknowledging the details of it, he could somehow change its appearance.

While Lou's appeared stable, short, and obviously wholesome, what Nick was seeing would give even Indiana Jones pause.

It was a mist enshrouded rope and plank bridge, with open spaces of about 3 feet between each plank. It was bowed down deep at its middle with long runnels of moss and vines. There were areas where it was obvious some of the boards had been broken, and what made matters even more unnerving was his inability to see the other side.

"Our cause is true," he muttered swallowing hard again and looking to each of his companions, "if I'm not back in an hour..."

"What if time runs different on that thing, or the other side?" Lou asked.

Nick raised his eyebrows, "pretty sure I got that covered."

The garage owner frowned, "Maybe, but how do we know if it rejects the one who goes over?"

Julius shook his head, "those who are rejected are never heard from or seen again."

"So, if I'm not back in an hour..." Nick shrugged into his backpack, then slid from Naiya's back and stroked her neck, "thank you Naiya," his breath hitched but he shook his head and looked from Lou to Julius, both of whom stood before him.

"My king, let me go, you are the one who will carry us through this war if indeed we are even capable of winning."

"I can't ask someone else to do what's my duty," his voice was soft as he took the Captain of the Guard's hand.

"Tropus too felt that way," Julius half warned.

Nick's lips twisted in a small smile, "He was my king before I was his. If I fail, you must follow Lou and Frank."

Julius tilted his head, "we will."

Next, he took Lou's hand in his, "if I fail, you two get to the tower, tell them we need to work without the first ones..."

Lou shook his head drawing a deep and tremulous breath. "Kid..." keeping hold of Nick's hand, he swung the young man around, pressing his arm to his back before shifting his grip to a sleeper hold. Nick was unconscious before Julius' sword was fully drawn.

With the headstrong teen out cold, a look of hardness settled onto Lou's features when he met the Captain of the Guard's eyes, "No matter what or who you think he is, or how old he looks, he's a fourteen-year-old kid man, a HUMAN TEENAGER! Not even what you'd call a fledgling! You should have known better!"

Without missing a beat, or so much as batting an eye Julius smiled softly, glad of the older man's caring, "he is the first love my heart has ever known, and likely the last it will ever cherish so wholly."

Lou gave a hard swallow even as his expression softened, "Look after him," he ordered lowering the hero into Julius' arms before slinging his own pack and taking off at a steady jog across the bridge. "...there when I was born...shit."

Once under its canopy the bridge stretched forward like something from a dream, "ahhh fuck, 'cause why wouldn't it?" He grunted but kept a steady pace, dozens of yards stretching out both behind and before him. "I got this…" he nodded to himself.

"Yeah right, the only thing you got is a way of gettin' people dead! It shoulda been you, then she coulda had another that wasn't a curse…" a long gone gravelly gruff voice called from behind, the sound of it causing a falter in his step while chilling him to the bone, although he'd actually expected it.

No matter how prettily they were dressed, places like this never brought out the happies.

"There's no time for you old man," he breathed and kept on jogging, "there's more important things at stake here."

The next one stopped him in his tracks and birthed gooseflesh all over his body. It was soft, warm, and cool all at once and reminded him, for some reason, of pink tiger lilies, "what about me? Aren't I important to you?" she asked, a slight pain in her voice bringing tears to his eyes.

"I only knew you from pictures and stories," he gasped turning to see if she was really there.

She was, and she was wearing a bright pink sundress with red flowers. Her hair was the same free-flowing strawberry blonde he had, and her eyes as green as his. She had a smile that rarely crept out onto his face, coming only in those few, unguarded moments when he was alone or with Rose, but he recognized it, nonetheless. Looking at her, standing in front of him, his heart reminded him of what was lost with her. It was worse than what the firdur had done, there was no hate to provide a barrier between his love and his loss, but at least those were still pure.

She died not long after his birth, a cruel crime committed by the universe, for which his father, and the rest of his family blamed him. His father married again, and had more kids with his second wife, but none of it mattered. He'd lost the only person he ever loved without hesitation, the only one who never betrayed him. His second marriage had been one of convenience borne of loneliness.

"Do I matter?" she asked.

"Always," he nodded, a slip of wetness skating down his haggard face even as he forced his mind clear, "but you're gone, a long time now, and you can't help here."

"Your father blamed you, so did the family."

He shrugged, "Their baggage. I'm not any more responsible than you are…were. Sometimes shit just happens, sometimes good people die, and right now I'm trying to keep two kids from getting themselves killed in order to save two universes, so," he shook his head, choking on the next words, "I gotta run."

She strode toward him, her hand reaching for him, "can't you stay? Just a minute?"

He shook his head, "I can't, maybe I'll find you when my time's up," he chuckled skirting her image. He knew enough to avoid being touched, to avoid being dragged into her death. Instead, he turned away from the infinite promises of her open hand to continue down the darkening pathway, heading for the light at the end of the tunnel.

He couldn't have said how long he jogged, he'd got a good stride going and was fully into the sensation, just like when he was a teenager, running the fields for fun, wondering if flying could even feel so good! In time he noticed he was finally making headway against the lengthening platform, the brightness growing to the point he couldn't look at it any longer and had to keep his eyes averted.

He wondered if it was going to be hot, but the only heat he felt was coming from within.

Finally, he was coming to the horizon of the light field when a shadow cast itself forward.

"So, you're gonna try and save them, like you couldn't save me?" she asked.

The son of Conchobar skidded to a halt, "I thought you might show up. I would've died to save you Rose. I never should've brought you with, shouldn't have taught you anything, shouldn't have got you involved in any of this," he sighed as another duo of tears slid down his face mixing with his sweat, "I'm sorry."

She nodded, her elfin face still rounded with her now eternal youth, a dusting of light freckles forever over her nose and cheeks, "I know."

"Why haven't any of the others shown up? I expected a gauntlet of hate, curses, and torment... Aunt Joan, Jericho, Elias, Rebecca... I mean I'm a fucking ghost hunting atheist from the edge of the bible belt, it doesn't get much more black sheep than that..." he wiped his face dry-ish.

"No Lou, you're the descendant of one of humanity's earliest heroes," she smiled and shrugged, "besides...they might be waiting for you out there..." she pointed into the light, "or maybe Toto... it's that you're not in Kansas anymore... or maybe..." she paused, a mischievous smile curling her pert pink lips, "there's no time for that anymore."

"That's what the kid said," he muttered.

"Told you you're a good guy," she stepped back to let him pass, "go save the universes Lou, maybe when your time's up, I'll come find you."

"That's a lot of maybes,"

She shrugged and blew him a kiss, "that's universes for you."

And then she was gone, and he was once again, broken out in gooseflesh, "shit."

He shook himself free of the heebie-jeebies, re-settled his pack, and with a deep breath, walked into the light.

--

"Ungh, son of a bitch!" Nick cursed holding his head in his hands, "how long have I been out?"

Julius shook his head, "only moments."

Nick looked from the bridge to the timescape, trying to superimpose them both, only to find he couldn't see the entrance to the other realm, at least not from this one.

"I can't believe I fell for a sleeper hold..." he grumbled then choked, "I can't see him," his heart thundering toward panic.

"None, not even my king can see another's path across the way," Julius explained.

Nick swallowed hard with a nod, "any sign he made it?"

"No."

"Any sign he didn't?"

"No."

Nick glanced at his watch, "maybe I could pull him back, it's not up to him to do this!"

"Heru, each of the heroes has their path, did you not help cleanse him yesterday?"

"Cleanse?" Nick questioned then nodded, "I guess."

"And are you rid of your own... scars?"

"I don't know... probably not. But I don't have a soul to worry about."

Julius frowned, his expression questioning even as he remarked, "My king how could such a thing be true?"

Nick shook his head, "You weren't there."

Still frowning, his mind full of the ecstasies and intimacies they'd shared the previous night, Julius shook his head, feeling it best to leave the discussion to another time. Instead, he simply took Nick's word for it, at least for the time being, "If you are correct, then perhaps the son of Conchobar IS best suited to this task."

"Maybe I should speed things up?" he muttered seeming not to have heard Julius, "get him back faster?"

The Captain of the Guard smiled shaking his head, "As well skilled and empowered as you are, you are not now, and never have been, blessed with the virtue of patience."

"So, you're saying sit down and wait."

The chocolate haired Sidhe pursed his lips, trying not to smile.

He couldn't fault Julius's point of view, or logic. Instead, he checked his watch again, sat up straight, crossed his legs, turned his palms up on his knees, closed his eyes, and sighed, "shit."

--

Deep reds, browns, blacks, and highlights of gold set off a

barrage of memories as Mickey scrolled down the homepage of the Pacific Northwest Wiccan, or PaNWic Society, to the "Share a Spell" thread.

She could smell patchouli and incense and feel the fake bear skin rug under her. The last time she was there she'd been wearing jean shorts, a cut off shirt and her favorite rope-strap sandals. The rug was off white and so full of various fragrances that Mistress Morningstar and her consort Wolfbane, (Beth and Dave Turner to the public), didn't even have to burn incense anymore.

Nubs of flames danced on their wicks scattered all over the otherwise dimly lit apartment. The altar was draped with a midnight blue cloth embroidered at each corner with protective sigils and seals of Solomon. In the center was the traditional pentagram within a circle of silver.

Upon that, sat a brass chalice, a gleaming athame, and a Tibetan singing bowl used to harmonize the surrounding energies.

This was the day Mickey was moving up the ladder from novice to maiden. Of the others in their 'coven', she was also expected to be the first to make high priestess.

The others, even the Mistress and her consort couldn't work the magiks she could. Not a single one of them had the will to do what needed to be done sometimes, none of them had the talent, the connection to the harmonics necessary, the knowledge she had garnered from her memories of multiple timelines, and most importantly, none of them was of a bloodline born to utilize such powers.

Mickey knew the ceremonies they'd orchestrated so far were pale and impotent, relying on little to nothing more than whispering a wish to the universe and hoping it would be heard and granted from 14 billion years away. She also knew in order to cultivate the relationships she would need as she grew older and more powerful she would have to go through motions, many of which had all but lost their meaning and potency to humanity.

She jumped onto the thread with a new identity and a simple introduction, "MissSidhe100: Need a spell to separate or isolate multiple entities in a single host."

Leaning back, she watched the greetings and questions roll in, answering them as best as possible while remaining as vague as possible.

--

Wee sat back hard in the chair, his glance flicking from Khazeer to Wellyn and back again. The scouts he'd sent out had returned with information, all but Torn, of whom no one had seen hide or hair since his departure.

Wee couldn't help feeling responsible for anything bad happening to the fledgling. After all, it was his fault.

As if reading his mind, which may well have been the case as far as he knew, Wellyn nodded, "he is a promising fledgling, clever and resolute, he may well still be alive."

"Let's hope." He took a deep breath, his heart aching for Ryan, or whatever comfort he might glean from Nick or Frank. What wouldn't he give for one of Nick's icy stares, or his pursed frowns, or the hum of general intensity constantly rolling off the boy, he couldn't think of anything.

His mind turned again to Ry, the nights they cuddled on the couch watching "cuckoo for coco puffs" conspiracy shows and laughing. The times they watched the show about alien astronauts and wondered if any of it could be true, how he longed for those easy years. He felt a deep cut of guilt for wanting to return to those days, before the boys came to them, when the idea of the family destiny was nothing but folk tales and "bullshit".

God I want him back, his spirit seemed to cry as he choked, "it's never easy losing someone," then returned his attention to the map that now showed the locations of several camps for both schade and firdur. There were also camps and beings headed this way from the western pole, though what exactly their destination might be, couldn't be said just yet.

"We know they're traveling light; horses, camels, a few wagons, a few battering rams for when they break through the mage's shields." He looked between the king and Wellyn, "they're not going to last much longer, and the wards they've put up are going to need to be reinforced, and I don't..." he stopped and shook his head.

"You don't what?" Wellyn asked.

"I don't know your kind so, it's probably just nerves."

"Kin of Oemir..." Khazeer started to urge.

"Of course... everything could be important... We have to think about infiltration. We've seen the dark infiltrate the dead or dying, usurping them, but what about sympathizers? I feel... well, I feel... betrayal..." he shook his head, "duplicity? I don't know... darkness."

"In what *way* do you feel darkness?" Wellyn asked.

Wee shook his head, "it's like nothing I've felt... kind of a darkness of spirit, malaise, more than ennui, but less than depression. When I was a kid, we went after a colony of thoughtforms on the brink of becoming wraiths, a friend of a friend got… I don't wanna say possessed, but more like usurped by it so we had to…" he shook his head again, remembering the trail of destruction the thing used the hunter to cause. The kills it reveled in.

It didn't matter the hunter was used to kill evil doers, a rapist, a wife beater, a bigot who road hauled and hanged a black kid for walking through the wrong neighborhood on the wrong night. It'd used the hunter, and what it had done to its victims was mortifying.

"Wee?" Wellyn asked, snapping him out of his reverie.

"Mist, amorphous, everywhere and nowhere," he snapped back to the moment. "'Course, it's darkness, pervasive by nature," his brows furrowed, and he swallowed hard, trying to refocus.

"What supplies will they either need, have, or be waiting for?" He asked. "If we can cut off their supply lines that'll be a start. After that we're going to need to make sure our forces are ready to move in once we distract them. And we're gonna need a loooooohhhhht of those lightstones. In our universe, fire works against vestiges, does it hurt them here?" he asked.

"Indeed, as does light itself," Wellyn answered.

"Has anyone taken stock of the armory?" Khazeer asked.

Wee nodded, "Yeah, I had a few of the young ones clean it out and distribute the weapons among our people and the troops Ula brought in to help defend the city and tower."

"And why have we not brought out the stones? Tell me they were not damaged?" the king asked, obviously dreading the idea.

Wee shook his head and explained, "Folks just used what they had, but when the seedlings enveloped them they turned out to be fairly useless. If there were more, they were probably already distributed too."

"Seedlings?" Khazeer asked.

"That's what we call baby vestiges… a swarm of them attacked us in the forest…"

"Firdureen," Wellyn sighed hanging his head, "TIERUS!" he shouted with a wince, gladdened by the sight of the fledgling dashing into the room.

"Yes, they stripped Raziel of his skin while he protected the Oemirs." Khazeer nodded.

"Yeah."

"Master," the youth nodded greeting each of them in turn.

"These, however, are no ordinary stones," Khazeer frowned, "Tierus, have you ever been to the armory?"

The lad shook his head, "No, though I do know where it is."

Khazeer nodded, a prior nagging hunch from when the fledgling managed him so deftly into the tower, was back. "What, with your sight, do you recall of the last war?"

The question caught both Wellyn and Wee off guard, but sent the boy's blood plummeting to his feet, the first sign of any real emotion anyone had seen.

He swallowed hard but otherwise remained stoic, "Far too much to account, what are you asking of me Heru?"

Wellyn, taken aback by both Khazeer's question as well as Tierus' answer, nodded in sudden understanding.

He now knew why the fledgling had a reputation as a half-mad unclaimed bastard. If he had memories from the previous war, there were really only two ways he could know the things and people many said he did. He was either such a strong psychic he could read the information from those who'd been there, and had acquired the knowledge while in the womb, or he'd been born of a soul who'd been lost during one of the battles, but most likely had no knowledge of who he'd been before.

Either option was rare, to be sure, but was known to happen once in a while.

"Behind the wall of shields…" Khazeer said, his gaze curious and gentle on the youth's expression as it appeared he was almost watching something in his own mind, then brightened with understanding.

"There are tunnels! Heru Ula's entrance is one of the nine to end at the outer wall. The other twenty-seven somewhere within the tower, but all, at ten-degree intervals…" his voice trailed off for a second before he seemed to choke on his own air and stumbled backward a few steps. "Oh my king!!" he gasped, coming fully back to the moment, "Could they still be there? Did anyone else know of them? Did Semet? Tur?"

His fingers steepled at his chin, his head nodding, Khazeer felt a strange and almost guilty twinge in his chest, "You must find out, and while you are down there, there is something else you must do."

"You have only to speak it my king," Tierus assured, something inside him clicking into place, as though he'd been waiting his whole life for this moment.

"Bring a large scoop, and in the hub of the axis you will begin to dig. YOU and you alone! No one else must know what you are doing or looking for."

"Aside from her tears what will I be looking for?" Tierus asked.

A strange expression twisted the king's entire face and for a moment Wee thought he was having a stroke.

Khazeer ducked his head and looked to his best friend who eyed him with keen curiosity. "You *will* know it when you find it."

"Who will we send to the bridge?" Wellyn asked.

"Janell and Fern should go," Wee offered, anxious to contribute now that the King and his Master at Arms were on the mend, "they're both smart and tough and really hard workers. They'll do us proud."

With a look to each other, Khazeer and Wellyn nodded.

"Is there anything else my king?" Tierus asked.

"After you've either found or not, what you're looking for, you're to speak with only the three of us. No one else, not Beezle, not the Elder Healer, not Ula, no one but any of the three of us is that clear?"

No one made mention of the obvious relief flooding Wee as he leaned back, feeling more secure in his place. He couldn't imagine trying to cope with everything without some kind of distraction.

"Understood m'lord," his stoic expression not lost on any of them. One day, if any of them survived this war, he'd come to make a superior soldier if he chose such a path this time around.

With a nod of the head to each of them, Tierus strode with purpose out of the chamber.

"What's he gonna be looking for?" Wee asked once the door closed.

Khazeer took a deep breath, "It came into being before Aderyn, and was here long before the birthing of our own kind. Legend says the tower itself was hewn from it."

"My king…" Wellyn drawled, his brows furrowing together in curiosity, wondering if the king could be saying what simply couldn't be possible.

"What is it?" Wee asked, enthralled and noting the same expression on Wellyn's face as he could feel on his own, a look of curious consternation and possible implausibility.

Khazeer leaned in, drawing them both closer even as he looked around, assuring himself there was no one, and nothing to overhear.

"Oemirkin!" a voice none of them knew slipped through the door just before it was flung open, a junior acolyte running into the room, an easy dozen or so yards in front of a shambling, obviously exhausted shape.

"Shep!" He leaped to his feet, casting an apologetic look back at the king and his master at arms then ran toward his old friend, only to be intercepted by the acolyte.

"Oemirkin… the senior son has been taken to the elder, she needs you."

"Nicky?!" he gasped.

Shep shook his head, "Dylan… go!" he directed, waving the young man away with the junior healer while he continued shuffling toward the table where Khazeer and Wellyn stood to see if they'd be needed. He plopped unceremoniously into the chair Wee just left, and just as quickly nearly fell from it.

"We got 'em." He panted, "Lou's with Nick and Julius, they're goin' t'the bridge. Tropus and Boaz went to fill in the queen. Errmot and Torn're gonna capture a schade, bring 'em here for questionin'." He leaned into his hands, breath wheezing hard, fever heat pouring out of him as he wondered how Lou was holding up or if he was suffering too. "Was s'posed t'go with Tropus," he muttered shaking his head, "Boaz wouldn't hear it…" he grunted before sliding out of the chair in an unconscious heap.

"Sit!" Khazeer barked pointing to Wellyn as he made to move. The king bent beside the fallen son of MacRoich. He found the humans pulse and felt his flushed cheeks.

"He needs healing as well," he muttered retrieving a pillow from Wellyn's cot and slipping it under Shep's head before covering him with a blanket.

It took more time than he would've liked before he could push himself all the way back up and head to the window where a small communication crystal was charging in the sunlight.

"He spoke of Nick, but where is the youngest Vanwah feya? Where is Frank?" Wellyn asked.

--

"Our patrols smelled your approach and sent word for the others to come," Jinx, the smoky blue furred leader of the Felesians leaned forward, her forepaws crossed on the tabletop in front of her, her sleek, angular chin resting on them while her one blue eye, and one green eye held their gaze on Ilirya's.

"We were caught unawares, have you seen evidence of firdur moving through your territories?" she asked.

"The scent is half a world away, but it *is* on Aderyn. Once again, firdur has penetrated our world." Her paw slapped out to the side pressing down on a small insect unfortunate enough to have made itself known to her, "and it is growing."

She let the bug go, watching it before slapping it down again, this time taking it between her jaws, holding it firmly before crunching through its carapace even as its spindly legs flailed.

"Yes," Ilirya nodded, her face expressionless as her hostess ate its prey, "we encountered firdureen at the western edge of the Bedowen where it meets the Nahroehn. We must all come together again. Life itself is in danger."

Snapping her jaws in rapid succession to draw the rest of the insect in, Jinx chewed while nodding, then took a moment to lick her paws and clean her face before responding, "the old allies... many of them are no more. Not so much as a Cyclops has been whiffed in centuries... though they did migrate toward the lands of the Gargol as we grew our borders. The dwarves were beset with a plague that slashed their numbers only a handful of decades ago."

She licked her whiskers and winked at one of the guards before purring, "As a whole, we hoped your kind had suffered a similar fate... after all... what else could keep our deeeeeeaaar allies from us for sooooo long?" she mocked.

Ilirya, keenly attuned to the mercurial moods of this branch of the feline genus nodded, "we fell into ourselves after the war. Our leader was..."

"Butchered by Tur," Jinx fairly slavered over the idea, "we continue to tell the stories, split in two, its soul made mortal and eaten by the schades under Tur's command..."

"No!" Ilirya breathed as the matriarch arched an eyebrow at her, "made mortal... made human, yes. But humans are different, it was newly born, rescued by Conchobar, raised by him. It knew nothing of its heritage, what it lost...what we all lost," she explained, "we despaired, and with the great sacrifice the Gargol made, the loss of the dragons, and the last push with the light spear and her tears...

the dark retreated, Tur and his schades fell back to their fortress."

"And you failed to pursue them, to eradicate them, or even bother to seal the way!" she accused.

"Yes," Ilirya sighed softly.

"In fact, you allowed them to propagate. You allowed them, as a matter of fact... to use Tur's fortress to rupture doorways into the universes of humans AND heroes. So long as they moved through our world you were willing to allow them to continue to the world of men, willing to sacrifice your brothers and sisters so long as your own world was left out of it."

Ilirya sat still, the only movement, the red of shame climbing to her cheeks, "Our numbers were depleted beyond understanding as were those of many of our allies. We went from a population of millions to less than a tenth..."

"As did many others," Jinx hissed, "our world has been dying for millennia, since your kin made way for the dark, even the sea cow's realm has grown thin of life, why should we sacrifice our own when you and yours have done nothing but sit on your paws and wait for rescue from one who could never be reborn?"

The woman often called, the She of the All, swallowed hard as her heart thudded heavily in her chest. Everything the leader of the Felesians was saying was true and not only did her words cut as deep as their claws or spears could, but as intended, they left her feeling very small as well. "He has been reborn, the line has returned."

Jinx licked her teeth, "in a human child... yet another sacrifice you are willing to make to save your own skins."

"No!" the Fierowen Princess protested, "He knows who he is, that he is destined to lead whatever are left of the heroes..."

"The other universes are dead! You are as aware of this as we are!"

"We could not help them, our ranks are too few, and now the war has come back to us, if our universe falls then the human universe will as well, they have billions of souls at stake!"

The smokey blue shoulder shrugged and was treated with a cursory lick to straighten the fur, "they are self-destructive, even if we were able to turn back firdur, they would not last another century."

"You do NOT KNOW THAT!" Ilirya admonished sternly, her patience wearing thin.

"Of course we do, it would not be the first time they attempted to eradicate themselves, the last time, they nearly succeeded," she smiled, "there were only a few thousand... yet... they reproduced like rats... mmmm bountiful times..." she purred.

"Bountiful times when they worshipped your kind! The mother of your kind, Bast herself."

Jinx smiled, "the point Ilirya, is that your kind did nothing, in fact you sat by and allowed firdur to infiltrate universe, after universe while you waited, inactive, and through that inaction... complicit in whatever fate will befall the human universe, just like the fate that befell the others. So tell me... why should we risk our numbers when you chose not to lead?"

The eventual Sidhe queen maintained her eye contact with the leader of the Felesians but did nod, "I can give you no good reason other than the saving of the universe we share."

Jinx's lip curled up, "we do not require this universe, my kind can live quite comfortable in the lap of luxury in the world of man, fed, coddled, asked only to do that which we normally would to keep our homes clean of vermin, so again, why should we risk our numbers?"

"Because without you, we will almost certainly lose, and then, so too shall Earth." Ilirya admitted as the leader of the Felesians broke into a very satisfied grin.

--

The road from Gargoloth to Fauxston wasn't a long one, or particularly treacherous but, as they'd both admitted, they no longer knew what lived in the woods. Knowing it would be best to reach their destination as close to sunrise as possible, they stepped up their pace, jogging in companionable silence the last few kilometers unaware of the right hand of the Emissary watching and pacing them as he'd been instructed.

Just as Lou was passing through the far end of the bridge and into the light of the first ones, Minya and Arabelle arrived on the edge of Fauxston. To their heart-pounding relief many of the farmers were already out tending their flocks or fields.

"Thank Danu!" Minya breathed.

"Indeed," Arabelle nodded, grasping his sleeve, pulling him faster toward the town while they waved at those who noticed them and waved their own greeting.

So long had it been since the town had such enthusiastic visitors, many of those in the fields started to make their way toward the town proper, wondering what was coming and whether it would be for good or ill. They'd spent millennia living in peace, practicing their therianthropy and building a strong community alongside those who sought to join them. Whether they could shape shift or not made no difference, only whether they sought to be part of a caring

309

community.

Even as they neared the town square, gathering residents as they continued inward, they were greeted with skins of water and warm, fresh baked bread.

"Welcome to Fauxston brother and sister," an elder woman ushered them toward a courtyard table near a hand pumped well, "I am Wereiwyn, my husband has gone to bring the Keeper, they'll be here soon."

"Thank you," Minya nodded gladly taking the bread, and water skin.

"Many thanks... this is Minya, I am Arabelle of the Northern Horn of the Fierowen," Ilirya's chosen introduced them.

A whispered muttering went around the circle of now gathered residents, many of them wanting to know what someone of the Fierowen was doing in their lands.

"Quiet please..." Wereiwyn urged, "we've not seen a Sidhe in millennia, we were under the impression they'd been all but lost in the great war."

Arabelle shook her head, "We thought the same of you."

"Well then... perhaps our seers are not so," the aged female's mouth gave a wry twist, "...mistaken as we had thought."

"Pardon?" Minya asked after taking a gargantuan swig on the skin to wash down the last of the bread. He wiped his hand on his breeches and offered it to the woman. "Pray lady, tell us what they have seen?"

Two men, one large though light on his feet, and the other smaller but also outwardly energetic wove their way through the throng surrounding them.

"I am Talmai, the town Keeper," the larger one introduced himself then motioned to his escort, "this is Wyle, husband of Wereiwyn, and the seer with whom you'll be wanting to meet. Minya, Arabelle," he nodded a greeting to them then motioned them toward his Inn. "Come, Wyle tells us you've been traveling without rest for days, let us have you fed and rested."

The quintet moved through the crowds, "As soon as we know something, you too shall know it," Talmai's voice boomed through the street, effectively dismissing the townsfolk back to their daily work while information was exchanged.

"I told you!" Wyle whispered; his lips turned down in a troubled frown as did his wife's. "It's back!"

"He is correct," Arabelle acknowledged in the quietest voice, "firdur, schades… once again they are in league and have infiltrated Aderyn. The Gargol have been slaughtered, naught but dust remains of them, nary a tear or so much as a shard of crystal to be found in their village."

Ushering them into the earthen and woody smelling structure Talmai locked the door behind them all as Poe perched on a ceiling lamp to listen.

--

For the first time since his return from schade captivity, Nick paid attention to his breathing, allowing his thoughts to move through his mind without judgment.

The Aderyn timescape folded, and furled, dancing, turning, and twisting through its place in the universe. There were large fields of life energy, small packets of it, and tiny dots moving on the landscape. From his vantage he tried to find the bridge but even though it was easy enough to locate himself and Julius, there was still no indication the passage between worlds existed.

He thought about Dylan and found himself peering into the Tower of the Sun where a handful of outlines moved among the floors, fulfilling duties, preparing for another onslaught. He was able to discern two carrying another, and yet another falling in a room not too far away. There were few details available to him, and no real images, just feelings accompanying the outlines. There were differences though between Sidhe and human and for that he was grateful. He also now knew Shep had been sent with Dylan.

"Boaz must've insisted," he muttered while Julius watched over him, wondering what the young man might be seeing. It was obvious he had many of the same talents Oemir had, as well as many of the same personality traits. Such was a greater reason for Julius to love him, and fear for him.

The scape moved this way or that, depending on what he wanted to see or who he thought of, especially if there was some kind of underlying relationship. When he thought of Ilirya, he found her, a larger outline surrounded by several smaller ones, appearing to be meeting. "Gathering the allies," he sighed and wondered about Frank.

In an unexpected move, the Aderyn scape was joined by an overlay of the Earth scape, an outline that could only be Frank for its prominence, laying on its side with a shape, most likely Vahl close by.

"Stay safe shrimp."

Movement caught the corner of his inner sight. His eyes popped open, and he leaped to his feet, turning toward the bridge as he did so, his right hand outstretched, his expression fearsome and familiar as he met eyes with Julius, who stood with his sword drawn.

"Firdur!" the captain of the guard whispered, motioning to a darker than normal shadow at the far side of the entrance.

"Waiting for Lou," he breathed.

"Almost certainly."

"How could it know?"

But Julius just shook his head, unable to fathom how it could know anything other than by spying on them.

"Leanna I'll bet, she may well have gone to join Tur," Nick wondered aloud while chewing his lip. "I should have killed her."

"Heru!" Julius gave a harsh whisper, "to have done so would have undoubtedly meant you own death, Tropus would not have stopped until your skin was a banner shredded by the desert winds on its way to the Fierowen!"

Nick nodded, "I know, but this is the mistake in movies that drives the plot to where it never would have had to go if the hero would've just done the right thing in the beginning, consequences be damned."

Julius' brows furrowed, "I do not..."

"S'alright," Nick shook his head, "point is, if it comes down to it, at least I know the soul is safe."

The dark smile he gave was exactly the same as it'd always been. It quickened his love's blood, encouraging him to face whatever may be in the offing. "Julius should a time come when she forces the situation, it should be me. No one else can be allowed to pay for my mistake."

The Sidhe Captain frowned but nodded, understanding all too well the events between Leanna and Oemir responsible for bringing them to this place at all. Her bitterness had all but destroyed their lands.

Peering deep into the woods from even this far out on their edge he could see the decay liquefying the trees of their homelands, earthbound beings that were ancient when even the Gargol were new.

From what he could tell, if Leanna had indeed gone to join Tur, the Bedowen was dying, the magic of whatever her driving force was, had likely gone with her.

In a flash within his minds' eye Julius saw the dragons being herded toward the canyons and ravines of the Bedowen's southern border, and turned his gaze to Nick.

"You told Torn to bring news of the dragon you met, and others he mentioned?"

"Hush!" Nick scowled, "there's no telling what else may be listening!" his outer gaze stayed fixed on the vestige wondering if it understood speech, while his inner gaze sought evidence of any other of the firdur's servants nearby.

"Did he say from where it came?" Julius whispered.

"No. We shouldn't speak of it again in the open."

Julius nodded, "Aye Heru."

--

"Get the healer!" Tur bellowed, his blade soon to be white hot in the fire as Leanna walked circles around the tent, the singed tatters of her gown fluttering around her. One hand cradled her growing belly helping to support the excess weight pulling on her back, the other reaching for pillars of support within her lovers' refuge.

"On his way Heru!" One of the Nahroehn soldiers replied, barely turning his head to try and peer into the tent.

"This was NOT an auspicious time for you to carry an offspring! You of all Sidhe know the time frame within which we are working!" the king of the schades growled, "I've no time to tend a newborn!"

"Then you will simply have to assure my survival!" she spat, "and this is no ordinary offspring. Born of firdur there will be none who can stand in its way! Your war that could go on for years will end in mere weeks if not days!" she explained, panting, and reaching for her next handhold.

His crooked and stern, ghoulishly pale face twisted into a scowl capable of cowing any of his soldiers, though it had little to no effect on the Princess of the Bedowen. "And how have you managed to keep this… offspring… a secret for so long? Or need I…*speak*… to Fetik?" he bit.

He had no concern for who she chose to bed, but if his own Bedowen informant had withheld such news of her pregnancy for so long then he certainly deserved whatever Tur decided to mete out.

Her sharp gasp snapped his mind out of the list of punishments he might prescribe and deepened his already mighty frown.

"Leanna?" he asked, looking up long enough to finally see her, to see the contortions of pain on her face. Never in the thousands of years they'd been consorting had he ever seen her thrown off by physical discomfort, and there had been more than enough instances where they'd sought to test one another's limits. Even from his vantage he could see something different about her offspring filled belly, it looked as if it'd grown considerably in just the few hours since she'd been brought to him.

Tur was no stranger to the measures females used to determine when to let their eggs be fertilized, but Leanna was no common female. Their ambitions were equally matched. They both wanted an end to the travesty called life, or at least whatever life they themselves did not allow to survive. The firdur was well aware of their desire too and was content to devour the dragons' other creations first, allowing Semet and his most loyal Nahroehn soldiers, Tur and his schades and the firdureen to feast on and eradicate the majority of the Sidhe, and anything else left.

Their plans were already ahead of the game, the birth rate since the last great war had stagnated where the population should have climbed. Tur and his schades were to thank for that. The corrosive effect the existence of the cursed had on those who'd not been compromised was a side effect Oemir could never have anticipated when he unleashed his caustic spell on Tur and his people. Those affected found themselves compelled to retreat to the fortress where atmospheric conditions couldn't do away with them so easily.

Their attempts to evacuate to the world of man had proved even more detrimental. Whether it was due to the wider spectrum of electromagnetic energies the human world was subject to, or some other factor like it's gravity, or even the pull of the other planets still in the system, to the composition of their sun, his schades couldn't survive long enough to determine. So far, their attempts at using the human bodies for protection had resulted in temporary but short-lived success.

The humans also had an array of people they called 'hunters' who were the knights of the realm, defending the world and its people from other worldly invaders, many of whom were also a concern to the schades trying to gain a foothold in Terra's universe.

He sighed, even the experiments to grow firdureen within a newborn human host, in the hopes it could overtake the creature inside and evolve within it, had proved fruitless, resulting in the death of the hosts. Ne'Min's most recent attempts to infuse a hero with the firdureen had almost reached success.

The son of Oemir had been the first to survive, in spite of how they'd weakened him.

He'd been starved for longer and longer periods of time, and deprived of water nearly to the point of death, and still he'd survived, remaining strong enough for his system to reject the majority of the firdureen. But some of the firdureen were able to resist expulsion, a fact which sowed hope.

Leanna told him of having watched the Oemir clear the other heroes before making her own escape. Once he was recaptured, the boy's strength may help him survive when the infiltration was attempted again, perhaps at a slower pace this time. If they succeeded, this war would be won before the final battle even arrived. The heroes and herus would be destroyed from within.

"Tur," Leanna breathed, reaching down to catch the new arrival, "be ready."

The schade Heru nodded, standing near his almost white glowing blade as she breathed deep and pushed; a few tight grunts and the occasional sound of strain the only evidence she may be enduring any discomfort.

The birth, like the gestation, was fast as the offspring slid out of her body, landing soft into her hands. She laid the comparatively tiny being onto the cushions below and knelt closer.

317

"Blade," she panted, her hand out for the hilt as she inspected the infant. It was male with almost black hair. It had the proper number of fingers and toes and was perfect in shape even if it was small.

A dark, smugness twisted the corner of her mouth as she motioned to the new arrival, "fertilized by firdur," its veins black beneath its pale flesh.

"Summon Ne'Min, tell him to bring the traitor's bits," she ordered leaning back as he motioned a guard to do as she instructed.

"What are you planning?" he asked.

Sitting on her heels, she grasped the cord, the hot knife cutting through it with no effort, the heat cauterizing it instantly. Even so, as she tied it in a knot, a few drops of black squirmed into the fabric of the cushion before she handed the blade back to her lover and began to clean the offspring.

Most Sidhe births were relatively smooth even when the gestation was the standard nine to twelve months, the newborns rarely cried, but unless they were in distress, all of them came out awake, Leanna's did not.

"What's wrong with it?" Tur asked frowning at the mostly rounded ears.

"Nothing," her mouth twisted as she continued cleaning him. When she was finished, she swaddled the infant and held him to her breast, angling her nipple into his mouth as his eyes finally opened and took a long look at her, then his surroundings.

Peering into the newborn's gaze Tur gasped.

"Yes," she smiled, "for now, it has its father's eyes."

8

"It is you who should lead us; Zu is an ancient," whispered a younger of the dragons whom Diagas learned was called M'pet.

"His eons are the greatest treasure we dare hope to have. You will become a far greater dragon at his frills than you would at mine." The last of the green flame clutch explained, far too aware the youth would be far safer here, than with Diagas on his quest to counsel with the Sidhe king and queen.

Congress with humans could be dangerous enough, but as the last war made plain, some of their Sidhe brethren had proven themselves unworthy of trust as well.

Of those they'd rescued from the bowels of the Bedowen, all were angry and spoiling for revenge against Tur and his schades; against the darkness, and most importantly, against Leanna herself for her part in luring, trapping, and murdering so many of them for use as feed for her forest.

Diagas even heard whispers considering the "accidental" slaughter of all Bedowen Sidhe as penalty for their part in the near genocide of the dragon race. Zu, however, with some effort, managed to refocus their attention on the situation at hand, reminding them if the dark won this time, there would be no chance for justice, or revenge.

As he made his way into the three-thousand-mile-long mountain range the body of the great mother had become, Diagas wondered just how much influence Zu would have to keep those youths from taking revenge on those who were innocent. Then he wondered if anyone who'd been there could be considered innocent at all.

The nearer he drew to where he knew Areen and the infirm of the Fierowen to be sheltering, his scales began to rise or ripple, fluffing themselves in response to the scent of so many sheltering in such a comparatively tight space.

As he ventured further into her remains, two of the scents he moved through, both warmed his heart and gave him another set of shivers. In seconds, an underlying scent caught his attention, creating a honeycombed image deep in his mind.

His lips curled up and his frills stood on end as he backed up and took in the sight of the walls of the chamber into which he'd arrived. His heart galloped in excitement as his snout followed the scent of the She of the All to a single, newly vacated space. He drew a long deep breath then let it out in a sigh, his eyes half closed as he drew yet another breath, and angling with great care, set fire to the interior of the alcove, his electric green flames clinging to every surface until the walls themselves began to glow.

--

Chewing his lips Nick glanced at Julius, "I have to try and reach him, if it moves…"

"I'll be ready," the Captain of the Guard nodded. If the vestige moved from its place, he'd nudge Nick and grab Lou the instant he began to emerge from the bridge IF he began to emerge.

Closing his eyes Nick saw himself, Julius, and the vestige on the timescape. He was still unable to see Lou so he reached out with his consciousness in the direction of the pathway between worlds, hoping the half bloodline they shared would make it easier for him to connect.

"If you're there, if you can hear me Lou, there's a vestige waiting for you, you have to be slow, stealthy... can you hear me? Please be there, tell me you can hear me... if you think it, I should be able to hear you..." he tried to instruct. He was fairly sure there was little if any inherent psychic ability in the garage owner, but given he'd been hunting paranormal things most of his life, it was possible he could have acquired some latent abilities.

Hmm, maybe... he wondered.

If Lou survived his passage, but couldn't hear Nick from this side, maybe, just maybe...he opened his eyes, looking at his version of the bridge, his heart pounding in his chest, his breath coming short as Julius looked at him and shook his head. He had no idea what his Oemir was seeing, only that he did NOT want to share or face it, and yet he was willing.

His was the same recklessness and unyielding need to do the right thing that inspired so many Sidhe so long ago, and made Julius love him so much his heart wanted to break... again.

Nick gave a weak smile, as if he could read the captain's expression, and maybe, after all their centuries together, he could, a little.

"I have to." Didn't mean he wanted to.

The ancient and treacherous causeway scared him almost beyond reason. He thought of the darkness flowing through his veins, thought about Frank's assertion of the soul not going back to him because there wasn't room for it. He took a shaky breath.

It wasn't going to let him cross, and he knew it, but to be what he needed to be, he had to face the fate he'd created for himself. Whatever may happen, he had to try, after all, the only certain way to fail was to assume he already knew Lou was lost and continue on without him.

"My king…" Julius warned in spite of his understanding. Once again, they were in perilous times and all existence may be on the line.

He couldn't think of anything he wouldn't sacrifice for them to have just one more lifetime together without the universes trying to tear them apart.

Nick dropped a hand onto his love's shoulder then pushed the fabric aside to see how he was healing. Overnight, the bruising had turned light green thanks to the salve. Smiling he cupped Julius' cheek as their foreheads came together, "I'll be right back," he assured with an easy and rakish smile leaving the Sidhe to do little more than nod.

As he approached the first plank, the vestige seemed to shudder and almost dance, as if it wanted to reach out and grab him but for some reason, couldn't.

"Huh," he wondered, then swallowed and laid his hands on the ropes before disappearing into mist.

"Lou! Hey asshole!" he called in a pre-teen voice he barely recognized as his own. Thankful for it or not, the sound didn't seem to go any further than his own ears, *"Lou!? Can you hear me?"* still no… *okay,* clenching the ropes so hard they burned his hands, he took another tentative step forward, feeling for the next board with his toes. He knew it should be about three feet in front of him and angled sharply downward, but when his foot landed, it landed flat, jarring his knee as his weight came down hard.

"Wha..." he asked the air as the mist began to roll away, revealing a strong, sturdy, and very tight wooden crossing, no steep slopes, no broken boards he'd have to navigate over, no slippery moss or mist slick spots to drop him into the abyss, "cool," he sighed.

"Lou!" he shouted, taking off at a steady jog toward the far end. "C'mon man, hear me," he pleaded reaching out with his mind again, hoping as he drew closer to the far side, to make contact.

"He's coming for you," the warmth of the representatives of the Heliosons smiled at the left side of Lou's head.

"Told you he would." *Wish to hell he hadn't.*

What if he didn't make it? Of course he made it. He's strong and good... he's not like me... the word *"broken,"* whispered in the depths of his mind, *No... he's just a little chipped here and there,* Nick thought, unaware those who awaited his arrival could see everything he could, and hear everything said or even thought.

"You're okay kid, you're gonna be okay," Lou dared to breathe, as on his right, a beautiful woman with tumultuous thick black hair, sky-blue skin, and lightning streaked storm cloud eyes grinned, a forked tongue flicking out to wet the daggers that were her teeth.

"Hope is like a hint of sweet in the salt of mortal existence, and this one is a feast!" she murmured.

"You don't get him," Lou warned through a sudden inexplicable wave of ferocious protectiveness.

"That will be up to the soul," an undeniable, authoritative voice of the elder of the Gloamare warned from behind him.

"Yeah well, what if he doesn't have one?" Lou whispered recalling Julius' assertion the 'soul' was within Frank, which left him to wonder how Nick could be Oemir without having his. *Maybe Sidhe don't have souls, but when Tur killed Oemir he had to... what, manifest one? Make one from scratch so he could make it mortal? Nah...what the hell kind of fucked up shit would that be...?* He wondered as the representatives of the three ancient races chuckled amongst themselves.

"...I'll start with him if you don't do what I say..."

Lou felt something in his stomach flip as he suddenly understood everything he needed to about Nick. One look at the puffy slavering face with the tiny porcine eyes, and a little boy in his underwear on a cot in the background and he felt like he wanted to throw up. "Uh nuh," he breathed as the others fell silent while the first of the deep scars within the boy came to life on the bridge.

"Fuck you," Nick spat, *"you're dead, dead and gone you filthy sick prick... it was better than you deserved!"* just before another came into being.

"I knew Dex sent'cha... couldn'ta been the pastors' new boy, too bad cause you... you got the devil in ya'boy... cuttin' up a man after slittin' his throat, s'what those serial killers do..."

"You stole and sold kids to rich sicko's... if killing you means I'm evil then what the fuck does that make YOU?" Nick challenged.

Lou grinned, happy the kid was holding his own, glad he wasn't falling to the guilt the ghosts of the past were trying to dig up before thinking, *Jesus Christ what the hell has this kid been through?* Even though he knew he was about to find out.

"I touched him..." the first accuser was back, *"I touched him, and you didn't do a thing to stop me! I made him dirty, just like you... I made him MINE! Just. Like. You."*

324

"Shut up, you're worm food," Nick's voice trembled.

"You made it soooo easy," the piece of filth's slimy voice grinned, *"sure 'they' told me what to do, but you just stood there and let it happen, everything they said you'd do, you did. You ran away, if you hadn't done that, I never could've got that whiney little bitch of your mother out of the way!"*

"Not my fault! YOU killed her, NOT me!"

"You made it possible. You made it possible for me to mark him, you made it possible for your grandmother's murder, just like you made it possible for your fathers.' If it wasn't for you, every single one of them would be clean, whole...alive," he chuckled as a crack of belief marred the teen's expression. *"And happy."*

Glancing over the poker faces of the ancients, finding himself horrified by everything he was seeing and hearing, and even more so by their refusal to intervene on the teen's behalf, Lou couldn't help himself and yelled out, "Don't you listen to 'em kid! Not a word of it!" He wondered if the teen could hear him but was somehow certain the ancients wouldn't allow it. This was Nick's darkness; these were his own perceived failings he had to face and overcome or fall to.

"What would you give to undo it all?"

It was a different voice speaking this time; one Lou had never heard before though it somehow sounded familiar deep in his genes. He threw another glance at the ancients and his heart fluttered in his chest. They recognized the voice, and it was obvious in their expressions they hadn't expected it.

"Not possible," Nick whispered, *"I've already tried."*

"Many times we tried to give you the power child, to give you the ability but you refused, you struggled and fought," They were suddenly surrounded by

images of Nick's recent captivity, chained to the slab, Ne'Min or any of his assistants tormenting him. Slicing his veins open in small increments, layering his naked arms and chest in firdureen as they ate at his flesh and others tried to find refuge within him. All the while Ne'Min kept him immobile and distracted by feeding cruelties and their visions of the future into his mind.

"Each time you refused to embrace the chance to choose your own destiny. Instead choosing to follow what others have dictated for you."

"No," Nick panted and shook his head, *"you tried to kill me and use me to grow your firdur, like you did with D's wife and baby…"*

"You could re-set everything. That is the potential greatness of the gift you possess."

"Everything?" Nick's heart skipped as he gulped, his fingers absently caressing the scars along the undersides of his arms.

"No kid, c'mon, don't you buy that snake oil!"

"EVERYTHING!" Ne'Min's voice insisted.

"You're a liar," he shook his head, but the protest was weak.

"How far?" he asked.

"All of it, to the eternity before the beginning." Ne'Min's ghoulish smile, full of cracked and splintered teeth beneath his stretched balloon flesh, leered close.

"Bullshit! Time would resume and it would all happen all over again; you know it as well as I do, probably even better!" he argued.

He could almost hear the flesh around Ne'Min's mouth stretching before the ghoulish creature spoke again, *"And if another path were carved?"*

'Wee and Tommy' he thought, literally halted by the possibilities being dangled in front of him.

He'd created new branches before, but only by mere seconds. What Ne'Min was suggesting was impossible. It was a grandfather paradox time wouldn't allow, similar to what happened when he tried to push things off the line at the Daykin house.

Still, he couldn't help but wonder. All around him, the history he knew, of both worlds spooled backwards; it ran like a movie in reverse, words, sounds, screams warping in nightmare audio accompaniment that made his spine quiver. In seconds it was too much to take in.

He tried to slow it, to watch as things went back, to watch Nana return to life, to watch Frank become un-touched, to watch his mother come back.

Nausea twisted his bowels as he turned in circles, watching line after line after line reverse itself, all the times he'd died, been killed, or killed himself. The times Frank suffered the same abuses he had at Pigg's hands. The times he'd been too much of a coward to stop the bastard from fouling the boy, not just dirtying him but using, abusing, and in a way, erasing him. The threats he'd whispered in their ears were somehow louder than the screams playing from other areas around him, those were the histories that hurt the worst.

Then there was Harry, he once told them no matter what he did, no matter what he changed when the boys first came into their powers, someone always had to die, and someone always did, but he'd never told them the horrors of how.

In a matter of minutes, the eldest of the junior Emersons watched 18 years of failure, slaughter, and a fascinatingly sinister array of cruelties perpetrated against anyone who got close to him.

Schades tortured and tormented his friends and their families, hunting them down, tearing them apart in every way possible, not just literally.

They destroyed relationships, trusts, reputations and sowed misery and strife in whomever they touched, in whoever's life Nick touched. They turned it all inside out so even the smallest of achievements or victories wound up polluted to the point of meaninglessness.

Aside from the whispers, the accusations, the doubts, the screaming and fighting and fury; it was the quick dawning realization slithering up from his low guts, clawing its way into his brain that was most sickening. Ne'Min was right.

For the entirety of his existence as Nick Emerson, in all its iterations, he was to blame for every lost or ruined life touched by his, whether directly or indirectly.

"...shall we take a look at some of your other incarnations cousin?" His personal boogeyman grinned at his ear as the scenes in the mist rolled even further back.

He'd been an only child, never aware of the reason for his existence, or the origin of his line.

He'd been unwanted, unloved by either of his parents, both of whom thought him a pariah; his father, abusing him and his mother, beating them both for the slightest misstep. At various ages he'd been jailed for battery, theft, breaking and entering, grand theft auto, armed robbery, and time after time, incident after incident, upon release to his parents, he was beaten near to death, until the last one, coming moments before he finally ate a bullet.

While the scenes played out for all, including Nick, to see, Lou watched as the boy stumbled backward as if struck. His head snapped to the side in some sort of grotesque "play along" as the boy in the bloodline image was beaten again and again.

"Stop it…" he hissed watching the teen cringe and crouch just as the one in the vision was doing, his hands and arms over his head, cowering before a tormentor who no longer existed.

He looked again to each of the ancients, "Stop this!"

But they wouldn't.

Stings set up shop in the corners of the son of Conchobar's eyes as he watched Nick take another invisible beating that would've left anyone face down, only this boy crawled, clawing his way toward something Lou couldn't see yet.

His lips disappeared and his face contorted in horror when he saw a .45 in the hand of the incarnation and watched Nick move as if putting the muzzle into his own mouth.

When the boys' skull splattered in the image, he barked in surprise and gulped his relief when he turned his eyes to the teen whose head was still, gratefully intact though he lay on his back, gasping as the next lifetime of despair began to show.

This time, he'd been a girl, a latch-key stoner whose little brother got hit by a van racing down the street and got blamed for it. She hadn't been able to bear the guilt and loss, so ran away from home learning to kill the pain with harder and harder drugs, until one night she died bad in a sleazy motel room, murdered by a trick with a fascination for asphyxiation.

Once again, they all watched the darkest moments of this incarnations' life roll forward while the boy on the bridge suffered the last indignity, clutching and grasping at his neck, on his back, kicking and trying to hit at the invisible presence pinning him down while he gasped her last breaths.

As more and more of the incarnations and their tribulations unfurled, Nick recognized the common thread, the common darkness knitting them all together.

Lifetime after lifetime, incarnation after incarnation, despair formed the core of his being. It stole any hope of joy from him, stealing light from his life. Chances for love or camaraderie were torn asunder, and behind every incident, he now knew; he'd seen over and over again, the eyes of his tormentors flicking white, their faces going lax for just a split second before their torments bore down on him, usually due to the influence of one particular schade.

He shook his head, *"all the lifetimes…"* he gasped through a throat so tight every breath was little more than a wheeze.

"ALL of them," Ne'Min grinned, *"from the moment of your curse to this very instant… all of it done just for you cousin…"*

"Sick fuckin' bastard…" Lou croaked, his heart burning with hurt and hate even as he wondered if it could all be true.

"So much… so much for so long, why didn't any of you…" he thought, but knew the answer. The information was there, it'd been there since Cathbad woke the lines.

"And you can undo it aaaaalllllll," Ne'Min hissed rewinding his own memories even further with a wave and a smile of cruel delight, until the very beginning held still on display in every direction he could look.

Oemir captured, bound to a sacred oak, stripped bare before silent cackling hordes of schades as Tur stepped forward, his Sidhe blade gleaming against the moonlight as it swung up in an arc, splitting him wide open, straight up the center. The only sound, the slick, globulous slurping gurgle of intestine sliding from its security out into the open, then followed by the sound and rending pressure of Tur's hands plunging into him. He screamed, panting against the grotesque agony and pull of his sinister cousin's calling forth, capture, and rending of his very soul.

A shiver ran up his spine and gooseflesh broke over him as Nick seemed to be jerked up to his feet, his arms forced open and bent backwards, held as if he were bound as his progenitor had been.

Lou watched him stare stoically ahead, presumably into the very eyes of whoever was tormenting the origin of the boys' soul. "No... don't... don't..." he shook his head as the schade's sword came up to split the Sidhe open. In the same instant the teen jerked and cried out, writhing as if the schade hands were once again, inside his body. "For gods' sake STOP THIS!" he demanded in a growl an instant before the boy slumped forward and fell to his knees, his arms wrapped around his torso.

"STOP!" Nick cried, his arms clutched around his body, trying to hold himself together, trying to keep himself whole as he fell to his knees and beneath him the bridge gave a mammoth shudder followed by a ripple to quake the universes it still touched.

Lou felt the shudder through his feet, he heard the sound of thick wood cracking, his heart lurched into a gallop. After everything he just witnessed, it'd be a miracle if the kid could continue to hold his own, no matter who he was descended from.

"Nick, don't!" Lou pleaded, "hang on kid... don't give up..." his gaze moving from ancient to ancient, none of whom seemed to know, remember, or care that he was there as they watched history begin to repeat itself.

"It never had to be this way cousin… you could put an end to all of it, none would ever suffer. Your gift of time and its ages could quell the grief of every living thing…" Ne'Min whispered, its arm around his shoulders as the teen, though physically undamaged, tried to keep his insides from spilling outside. *"How many times have you sought release?"*

"So many," He gasped, his eyes on one of those examples, one of the most recent ones. The Sedona Vortex, the first line of this incarnation. Losing Frank broke him, seeing Ne'Min turn him inside out in slow motion, somehow able to move in spite of Nick's will, extending the torture and torment of his twenty-four-year-old baby brother being ripped apart by the schade's bare hands.

The horror caught him by surprise and by the time he realized he couldn't stop it, but should accelerate it, Frank's last scream was the only sound in his memory. Not even Harry could keep him alive after that.

"How many times have you sought to save those you loved but failed?"

Nick shook his head, sweat running over him in streams despite the chill coming on the heels of the sensation of Tur's sword slicing him open, *"too many…"*

Another shudder rippled out from the teen; wood splintered beneath his knees. Mist and the stink of something festering wafted through the plank boards while leaves above curled and fell, freed by the quaking radiating from him as its epicenter.

"You must choose Vanwah feya… a destiny of YOUR choosing or the failed plans of those who came before?" the schade's urgent whisper tickled his ear.

Around him the torrent of images swirled, loosened from their ethereal moorings to encircle him. They squeezed toward him until they flowed into him, becoming one with him, making him a man with an ages long history of misery and failure to call upon, to be tormented by for all eternity, or perhaps finally find a way to obtain the release he'd longed for since the beginning?... choices...

Splintering made its way along the bridge, now accompanying the thunderous quakes shaking it apart.

In a breath, his inner world went dark. There was no more bridge, he was floating, relief permeating every atom of his existence. He felt himself smile. *"Peace..."* he sighed.

There was nothing left, no pain, no sorrow, no grief, it was a state of being in its purest form. No love, no light, no hope, or joy.

"Empty." The word came unbidden, and with the thought, the memory of the feel of Tur's hands ripping the soul out of him. A hollow, cold, memory bigger than all of space and time followed by another word filled with despair, *"Alone."*

An explosive burst of images papered his interior landscape until he was tightly surrounded by as much of the visible universe as he'd ever seen. Bright wonderful hues of planets and nebulae, whose colors and potential stirred his soul filling him with wonder. With the next breath they floated nearer, closing in on him. Everywhere he looked there was some celestial thing, moving closer, squeezing until he could barely breathe, pressing against him, keeping him prisoner.

A memory of Pigg, holding his arms above his head, his knee on his lower legs to keep him still, his body weight pressing him so hard he almost blacked out, flashed in his mind. His heart raced again, his lungs wheezed trying to take a breath, his nerves fired while he tried to break free but couldn't. He screamed without a sound for someone to help him, to save him, but no one came.

"You MUST CHOOSE cousin!" Ne'Min ground between

splintering teeth, *"NOW!"* he demanded.

"God…" Lou gasped, then bellowed, "No you don't! You don't have to do a goddamned thing he says!"

On either side of him the others glanced from him back to the tortured child slumped on his knees, his long, sweat soaked hair hiding his face, hiding his despair from the view of those watching. Beneath him, the bridge between worlds, crumbling.

"LEAVE ME ALONE!" He cried out.

When he opened his eyes again, the objects were racing away into eternity, until not even one was visible within his line of sight. He gasped relief.

There was an itch in the back of his brain, like a memory long forgotten trying to come to the fore. There was nothing but him. Ne'Min's voice was gone. The cacophony of existence was gone, but no matter how great his relief was, there was something missing. Beneath him, another board cracked.

Lou twitched as several of the wood planks beneath the teen snapped under his scant weight and started to separate. He could see Nick on his knees, still hunched over, oblivious to the danger he was in.

"Come on kid! Come on…" he urged then railed at the ancients framing him, "For fucks' sake do something! He's just a kid!" But they stood transfixed, all three of them with expectant expressions.

Another image came to mind, blossoming in the void, a strange, bulbous flower, its thirteen petals joined together by a woven stem. *"I've seen this."*

One by one the petals became stained with darkness, falling away until only two remained.

It clicked after the first couple petals fell away, *Yeah, we're the last two, bound together, even with the others gone, it's failed against us, why?*

On an endless loop he watched over and over again, his heart breaking a little more each time. Despair, futility, and desperation filled him. Seeing so many universes being extinguished he thought about the cruel ends each of his soul's incarnations experienced and couldn't help wondering why. But he knew, somehow, this time could be different, it had to be. Never before had they come this far or been this capable in the face of the destiny awaiting them.

Finally, he looked down, gazing into the gaping maw of oblivion below and felt his fingers relax.

He knew what Ne'Min wanted him to do, but none of them knew what epiphany was about to explode with the power of a nova within his mind.

"MAKE YOUR CHOICE!" Ne'Min ordered though he was nowhere to be seen, still, Nick could feel him.

He thought of all those who'd been ruined, devastated, and destroyed by Tur and his right hand, because of him; and as the last plank beneath him gave way, Nick finally understood.

--

"Mmmm?"

"C'mon, go get some coffee, I'll watch these two," Harry Jr. offered, shaking Mickey awake.

She'd crashed in Frank's room. By the look of the mess, she'd been busy through the night.

"Did it work?" he asked as she unkinked herself from a tiny alcove at the far side of Frank's desk, where she'd wound up.

"I don't know… what time is it?" she asked glancing at the clock.

"7:30. I got no clue when those cops are gonna show… I'm thinkin' to take Charles to them, see if we can avoid them coming here."

Something in his expression brought her full awake, "what happened?" she asked lurching first to Frank and checking for a pulse. It'd been touch and go through some of the bloodier aspects of the spell, but when she finally sat back to wait, she was pretty sure he'd be okay. So far as she could tell, he was, at least physically, fine.

Next, she checked Vahl, who also had a pulse and was still breathing.

"The blood's back."

"Huh?"

"The glamour, it's gone, I cleaned up what I could on the walls and stuff, but the carpet, shit, it's fuckin' brown man."

"Shit," she shook her head, "alright, first things' first…" she grabbed a sticky note and pen from the desk and jotted down a quick couple things. "This is the best I can do on short notice; we can't rely on glamours forever so make sure we've got these, then get to work marking the spots we need to clean." She shook her head, her crystal blue eyes meeting Harry's gentle and frightened browns, "We're gonna be okay, but we need to be fast, I just gotta check out Frank first… then pee. I'll be right down."

"If the glamour's gone that means he's gone too, doesn't it? I mean that's how magic works right?" he asked.

"Depends on the spell, whether it's sigil or other graphic based, spoken, potion, a contract… but a glamour… yeah that's gonna mean he's not on it anymore," she nodded taking a closer look at

Vahl after confirming Frank was still asleep.

"I'ma call pops," Junior frowned wishing he could be anywhere else as he dialed Harry Sr. on his way downstairs.

--

The armory was dark and almost completely empty, the remnants of a few shattered lightstones lay here or there, the odd broken bit of spear, or leather or shield strap as well.

This was one of the few times in his life Tierus could say he felt cool and true purpose, he smiled closing the door behind him and raising his light gauntlet overhead, comforted by the weight of the scoop over his other shoulder. He made his way through rows and rows of empty shelves and stands upon which armor usually rested. In the farthest depth of the armory stood a small door anyone could easily overlook, unless they were on a mission from the king.

--

"I don't know for sure," he shook his head, "I been gettin' night terrors on and off since I got stabbed as a kid… last night was one nasty motherfucker…I mean sum bitch," he blushed.

The kindhearted, slightly younger woman across from him nodded, "I can see that," she waved her hand over her face in the same areas his had bloody scratches. "The stitches that ripped were external and the doctor assured me your internal stitches were just fine," she sighed watching him nod, something almost desperate in his expression.

"What I'm most concerned about Mr. Armstrong, believe it or not isn't your stitches, I'm worried about how this episode will affect you in the long run."

Harry couldn't help it, his chuckle was accidental but genuine,

"You're worried about PTSD or some of that?"

"Yes, I am."

He shook his head, a grin on his face she'd seen far too often in her twenty plus years as a trauma counselor, "Miss, Ma'am... back in my day, what you call PTSD... we used to call the School of Hard Knocks. When you survived, it meant you beat it, and if you didn't... it didn't matter."

"Things don't have to be that way Mr. Armstrong, please don't take this the wrong way but back in our day, things were different, they didn't know the things we do now."

He nodded, "Oh I know, sometimes though this younger generation, and ma'am that includes you, you all gotta learn something... sometimes too much information ain't a good thing. Sometimes in fact, being able to fool yourself is the only reason we survive... call it a kind of a psychological 'placebo effect', you dig?"

She smiled, it was bright, warm, and humble, all the qualities he'd ever found wonderful in a woman, she tilted her head down at an angle while nodding, "I do," she scratched a note on her clip board then finalized everything with a surprisingly confident signature ending in an unexpected flourish. "My contact information is in your discharge paperwork, please, even if you just need to vent or... anything... please don't hesitate to call me Mr. Armstrong." She rose, turning the clipboard toward him and handing over the pen.

"It's Harry miss, my daddy was the only 'Mr.' I never knew, and you can bet your bottom dollar, I'll be more than happy to have a cup of coffee and to bring you up to speed... my dreams are..." he sighed, "sometimes nightmares... maybe it's about time I got some insight from someone else." He pushed himself to his feet after signing off on his release and stuck his hand out, smiling when she clasped it with a firm, warm grip.

"It'll be a pleasure… Harry," she nodded, clutching the clipboard to her bosom as she smiled her way out the door and left him to get dressed.

"Sweet kid," he muttered looking at her business card, "Joanna Robinson," he huffed a little chuckle, "coo coo kachoo."

Outside, she was only a few years younger than him, but inside, he was darn near ancient and felt every moment of it. Glad to be leaving, he slipped from the johnnie into the jeans and a sweatshirt Harry Jr. brought before taking Charles to talk with the cops. His smile tightened as he shook his head, hoping the kid could play it cool and not bring trouble to their door, at least no more than they already had on the way.

--

Officer Stern set the cup of water next to Charles' elbow. The kid looked like a deflated balloon, very like he hadn't recuperated much from his ordeal.

"Thanks for saving us the trip out," he offered.

Charles' smile was weak as he winced then sipped the water, "light still kinda bugs my eyes," he muttered. "Harry made me. He said it wasn't good to mope around all day, not when we got stuff to do. And he wanted to see pops."

"Jumping right back on the horse huh?" Stern asked, just a little glad Harleson wasn't in yet.

"Yes sir."

"So, what kind of stuff you got going on?"

Charles shrugged wondering how much it'd take to get him on

339

a bus back to Austin, or if he could just work himself a long-haul ride with his gap-toothed friend, then there was the question of whether or not going home would get rid of the gnawing rats in his belly.

"Collections I guess, he says it's kind of a never-ending cycle, was for us at the church too."

"Church?"

"Yes sir, New Day Ministry."

"How long were you there?"

"Three and a half years, does it matter?" he asked.

"I'm just trying to get a little background, see what makes a young man tick these days, see I'm a little curious about the work all you kids do."

Charles nodded but shrugged, "to me it's just what I been doing with the ministry, just a different bunch of people."

"Okay, so I get Mr. Armstrong coordinates everything," Stern began.

"Armstrong?" Charles asked before his expression lit up, "Harry Sr. got it, yeah, from what Nick told me it's Harry's contacts keep the donations flowing."

"But you're the newest member of the team, right?"

Charles nodded.

"Where are you from?"

"Austin sir."

Stern nodded scribbled a note on pad at his left hand then asked,

"One of the others said you've only been with 'em a few weeks... s'at right?"

Charles nodded again, "About a week sir."

"You're a long way from Austin, what brought you here?"

At that, Charles looked down and shook his head, a soft and somehow insecure smile stretching his lips, "I just ran."

"Away from the church?"

"Mmm hmm."

"Can we talk about that?" Stern asked.

"I s'pose," Charles nodded and glanced at the entryway where Harry Jr. sat reading an honest to goodness newspaper. "What do you want to know?"

"Well, I guess the first question's the most obvious," Detective Harleson asked emerging from the side door into the bullpen, "why'd you run?" he nodded to his partner, "Stern."

"Harleson."

"Coffee?" the new arrival asked looking toward the back of the room and grinning, "Thank God!" then glanced at Charles, "You up for a cup kiddo? I mean it's got water in it and no offense you look like you could use something with a little kick to it."

"Sir, y'know on second thought a cup of coffee would be nice."

"Cream and sugar?"

"Just cream please... about two shades lighter than me," he smiled.

"You got it," he moved to the machine and glanced at his

341

partner, "Stern?"

"You know how I take it, thanks," the older officer smiled. This was definitely going to be interesting.

Harleson brought over three cups and set them all up while pulling his chair right over, just close enough to Charles to tell the boy he had the detective's undivided attention.

"So… why'd you run?"

Charles' smile was tight as he took two deep swallows of the brew, "thank you sir," he nodded.

"It's crap but it gets you through the day," Harleson smiled.

Charles nodded again, "yes sir, s'pretty much what I'm used to."

"You could always pitch in and buy us some of that big city stuff that peels the enamel off your teeth," Stern admonished.

"You guys wouldn't know good coffee if it bit you in the… butt," Harleson bantered before casting his most charming "city" smile at Charles.

The young man took a deep breath then looked from one officer to the other knowing all too well they were trying to show him they were just 'regular guys'. "Why I left, well then, there's a lot to it, and some of it's not at all savory if you get my meaning."

Both officers sat back, each with his own cup, literally giving the boy room to speak whatever he would.

"Most important reason's simple enough. I fell in love."

--

Frank's eyes fluttered open and flicked around the room. Vahl's body lay on the bed, exactly where he left the Sidhe, but there was a stinging all over his chest and belly. He craned his head to look down at the blanket covering him and tried to pull it off only to find his hands cuffed behind himself, and to the leg of the desk.

"Smarter than they seem," he breathed wondering where everyone else was. He took a moment to close his eyes and reach out with his senses, feeling for other life energies in the house but it seemed there was only one, and she was in the backyard.

The corner of his mouth tilted up as he gazed deeply at the body on the bed reaching into its otherwise empty mind.

"Get me out of these," he ordered.

Vahl's eyes opened, the body rolled to its side and got up. It immediately lifted the corner of the desk so whoever was using Frank could slip free.

Once he was loose, he rolled the blanket off and looked down at the myriad of foreign symbols carved into his flesh, some of which he recognized, others were so foreign and from so long ago, he wasn't sure he could read them.

He chuckled softly and nodded, "she may pose a problem," he hissed rolling onto his back so he could get his hands in front of himself. The Sidhe warrior's empty shell simply watched him.

"Back to bed till I say otherwise," he ordered noting the cuff keys on the desk and setting himself free while the body did as instructed.

He took a moment to pile some pillows under the blanket then glanced once again at the handiwork and frowned. Whatever she'd done, it was certain she complicated matters to a dangerous point with her spell-work, and he was miles away from happy about it. Shaking his head he donned a sweatshirt and kept his mind on her presence while he crept down the stairs.

--

"My lady! Heru Areen!" one of the villagers nearly ran face first into her while running down the corridor as she was running in his direction. She'd been briefing the mages on pertinent information brought from Tropus and Boaz's arrival earlier this morning when a vibration through the ground coursed its way up through her. It was a sensation she hadn't felt in far too long, and it lit the fire of hope in her breast. *Ilirya was right!*

"Green fire!" he urged, changing course, to run with her.

"Green?" she breathed.

"Aye."

"Is it spreading?"

"No," he shook his head, "can it be?"

"Pray it is! And bring only those you can trust! We may need stewards," she nodded pouring on another bit of speed, leaving him behind, panting and nodding as he clutched his knees.

"Green flame!" she called, pulling out another bit of speed from her depths.

Still at least a hundred meters away from the womb she could feel the change in temperature, and grinned when the air around her began to shimmer with a faintly emerald hue.

"In the name of Danu, please…" she breathed.

"Please what?" came a voice that set her hairs straight up and brought gooseflesh over the whole of her.

She wheeled, ecstasy on her face as she leaped at the giant head, one arm wrapping up the side of the snout and the other grasping at the raised corner of his lip, "Diagas! How large you have grown!" she cried, tears of joy streaming from her eyes, "I thought you gone with the others! So many of us searched after we finally turned back firdur…"

"Too few of us survived my dear friend," he sighed, tilting his head to rub his cheek to the top of her head, "but the time has come at last… Ilirya has an egg?"

"We too suffered greatly, though not so in numbers as others. And yes," Areen nodded, "she sensed life and at the touch of her blade to its follicle, it nearly leaped into her hands." She looked back down the hall, "others are coming, we will guard them with our lives!" she promised.

"I know you will, but be certain your kind remain wary, those few of us left have little care for much but revenge, All Sidhe are vulnerable should Zu lose his hold on the others." He held a claw to her, allowing her to climb to his shoulder. "We have much to discuss, and much to relay to your husband." He paused to cast a mischievous glance at her, "Did Wellyn survive?"

"He did," she grinned, "and I am certain he'll be joyful as a fledgling to see you again! First however, I must advise the Elder's first Acolyte lest he think I ran afoul of something."

"Her wing?" he asked camouflaging them both as he made his way through the great mother.

"Yes… and if I may ask a favor… one of the humans has been quite… distraught…"

Diagas nodded, "One of Oemir's sires, he is concerned for them."

345

"You spoke with him?"

"I will tell you all I have seen when there are fewer to hear… until the time is right, the fewer to know of recent actions, the better, many among you are not what they seem."

She gave a shallow nod with a tight expression, having sensed, and feared their infiltration by the dead or dying who'd been possessed by firdur. She was glad to have confirmation. "How I have missed you my old friend," she sighed as joyful tears sailed out behind them, such was the speed at which he moved through the miles toward the shoulders of the great dragon from whom their world was birthed.

--

"Aww fuck you guys! Nick!" Lou yelled breaking toward the bridge, just knowing one of the ancients was going to somehow interfere or stop him. For every step he took he was sure he'd be held back. And then he was diving toward the entrance, reaching over the precipice where Nick's hands disappeared almost half a heartbeat ago, with the last board breaking.

"NIIIIIICK!" he called looking down, his heart hammering, sweat breaking out all over him, "god no… no please…" those stings at the corners of his eyes started up again as he pulled himself further forward, hoping the kid was hanging on just below his line of sight.

"Hey," a soft voice accompanied a hand dropping down in front of him, "s'okay."

"Son of a bitch…" a grin broke over his face as the mist cleared and he saw the bridge returned to its solid state, as it had been for him, and at the beginning of Nick's journey. "Son of a *bitch*…" he grasped the teens hand pulling himself to his feet, "god*damn* son of a bitch!" he hooted grasping the young man tight and swinging him around.

"I thought you were gone, I saw you fall! I thought they'd stop me, how are you here? Was it real?" He pulled the boy to him, then off the bridge, and back onto what he hoped was solid ground.

Once safe, he stepped back, seeing the young man as if for the first time as Nick smiled, bright and full, his eyes alight almost to the point of glowing. Till this moment the only hint he'd got the boy knew how to smile was last night when he'd been joking with Julius and the other Bedowen Sidhe, but even then, it'd been nothing so warming as this.

Nick nodded, "Yeah, it was real." He looked at the three ancients watching them with curious expressions on what he could see of their faces.

He knew their species each by sight though he'd never seen them with his human eyes, and standing before them he inclined his head.

"Helioson, Gloamare," he greeted them each then turned his gaze to the human form female, "and the eater of darkness, Vetala, thank you for meeting us."

The three beings exchanged glances, one of them asking the others, "could he be?" before whatever their conclusions were, were couched in some language he couldn't understand.

"I am." Nick nodded. "And I have a few questions."

--

"He's not up here!" Harry called, pulling the blanket off the pile of pillows before turning to Vahl's inert form on the bed, "What the hell did he do?" he whispered but knew he wouldn't get an answer.

347

Mickey raced up the stairs, "His jacket's gone. How the hell…" she shook her head, "he was cuffed to the desk Harry!"

The boys' oldest friend shook his head, "yeah well he's not now," he gazed deep into her eyes, so very like Nick's it was spooky, "you didn't hear anything?"

She gave a quick shake of the head, "I was in the back pulling bones out of the fire from the spell. Can't really do to have even possum bones in a family bonfire y'know."

"Mmm," Harry nodded checking Vahl's pulse and pupillary reaction to light. "He said he stole him?"

She nodded, "Yeah, from what I got, one of the Oemirs apparently pulled at least Vahl's knowledge out of him and into the kid, maybe even his whole psyche 'cause right now he's about as responsive as a frozen turkey."

"And you couldn't get anything else from Frank?" he asked.

"Mm, mm," she shook her head, "he was so freaked out Harry, he was on the verge of hysterical, and he was starting to fight… and he was strong, I mean *really* strong… *scary* strong. Like more than a kid his age should be. I could barely hold him down, we had to do something." She explained.

"You did the right thing Mick… what do you really know about Oemir? I mean *his* life? Who *he* really was?"

"I've been trying to figure out if I was there since I was a kid, s'why I crossed even knowing they'd capture me, I thought, maybe I could…" She shook her head and chewed her upper lip.

"Did you know, you know… back then?" he asked.

She sniffed, wiping her eyes. "I'm not sure but a lot made a lot more sense when you told us it took you 18 years trying to save them. It explains all the dreams."

"Whaddya mean?" Far as he knew, this was the first time he really got to ask her any of the questions he'd had for so long.

A small huff came with her tight smile, "I see the lines. For every time you reset things, you created another line, you all just didn't live it, but with each one, who you each were at the moment you created it, continued in that line, creating just as many different possibilities."

Harry's expression popped with a new depth of understanding. "You mean, like literally the whole, 'every choice creates a new universe' idea of the multiverse?"

"I'm pretty sure." She nodded.

"And we only stayed in this one because...?"

She shrugged. "The most powerful aspect of magic besides focus, is intent, maybe the pendant kept you tethered? I don't know."

They took a moment to contemplate the implications.

"Anyway, what do I know about Oemir, they referred to him as the first-born son of Danu. He was a lover, but he was a fighter too, he brought the others together, saved Conchobar, trading his own life for his..." she stopped and hung her head then looked up into his expectant face, "but when he fought, he could be savage, merciless, just like any of the kings of old. I know more about Nick than him, at least, I think I do. The first dream I ever remembered was of Nick."

She shook her head, "You can't know what it's like..."

Harry pursed his lips, his hand squeezing her shoulder, "eighteen years of do-overs and just about four more wondering if there was some way to try again if I had to… been plenty of times I wasn't sure what was real or a nightmare, or even knew which try I was in. I get 'cha."

As if they were of the same mind they nodded, "…and there's nothing in this world for him," Harry mused.

"Yeah," she nodded.

"Shit."

"Yeah," she nodded again.

--

Tierus stared all around the hub in wonder before closing the access door and sliding down to the floor against it. Khazeer told him he'd know it if he found it, and he was right.

He looked all around the enormous room where under normal circumstances, enough armor, and weapons of varying types, for no fewer than a full brigade of warriors, were stored, and effectively hid the entrance to the tunnels. Each held one of the great dragon's tears.

Nine of them extended out from the hub for no fewer than ten kilometers. Each tear large enough to fit securely into its notch at the outer wall, in effect, surrounding the city in its entirety. Only Ula's grotto entrance had been left open, though that tear was used to illuminate her comings and goings. The other twenty-seven fit into ventilation notches in the base of the tower.

"My goddess," he gushed, his heart hammering in his chest, pounding so hard his whole body trembled with each beat. All their lives, all their history, every Sidhe knew the origin of their world, they all knew the three-thousand-kilometer length of the Dragonbow mountain range was said to be comprised of the mothers' body, but to find this, here… put an entirely different scale on the greatness of she who writhed and smote in the chaos of creation. The truth of it was dumbfounding.

--

"Oh god, pull over!" Charles muttered, the blood dropping from his face, leaving his skin lax and ashen as the car skidded to a stop on the gravel shoulder.

There was just enough time for the boy to throw the door open and scramble on his hands and knees down onto the grassy roadside where he could heave in relative privacy.

Sitting in the drivers' seat Harry grimaced at each retch, watching his back arch until he was empty. If it was him puking like that, he'd want to handle it alone, so gave Charles the same respect. While waiting he pulled his cell, sending a group text they were on their way home.

"How'd it go?" Mickey responded.

"dk yet."

"?" she replied.

"L8r."

"k."

Charles slinked into the seat as Harry slipped his phone into his pocket, "sorry," he clicked the seatbelt on.

"Should I ask?"

"I didn't give him up," he shook his head back and forth against the seat back.

"Not used to cops then?" Harry threw the car into gear, easing back onto the blacktop.

"Not like this, not for a long time." Charles pushed himself further upright, trying to focus on anything but the slimy feeling in his bowels.

He shook his head, "I know how to lie man, I'm goddamn good at it, but shit..." he shook his head again, "it coulda been so easy to slip, I'm not sure I didn't, but I don't think I did, it was like there was something inside me screaming to tell 'em it was all in self-defense..."

"So what *did* you tell 'em?"

"It was so close to the truth... see there was this guy who used to give money to the church, he was a sadistic fuck... used to hurt people like me... least I figure there had to be more than just me..."

"Like you? Black or queer?"

"Queer for sure, loooooooved Leviticus, didn't give a shit about Jesus' teachings though... maybe black too, who the fuck knows? But Nick... it was like he knew something was off with the guy and the night before, he asked if I wanted to come home with him... he was beat to shit, like it was all fresh, said he got jumped, but didn't seem to care. He... it was like he *knew* me, knew the pastor was in cahoots with this fucker, so when he sent me to "pick up some funds" ..."

"Short-hand for pimpin' you out?" Harry asked.

Charles gulped and nodded, it was close enough, "well Nick said I didn't have to, he said there was nothing wrong with me... I fell for him like a ton of bricks... only other person made me feel I was okay as just me was Emilio...my first boyfriend," he explained at Harry's questioning eyebrow. "So we ran."

"And that's what you told 'em?"

Charles chewed his lower lip and nodded in a yes/no fashion, "Just told 'em Nick caught up t'me b'fore I even got to the top of the hill and asked if I wanted to come with him... he made me feel okay to be me. I think the pastor almost tried to but never could. I admitted we boosted cars along the way, only ones that were already from out of whatever state we were in y'know...they didn't seem to care about that."

Harry nodded, a slick smile turning up half his mouth as he chuckled with appreciation, "they'd already crossed state lines... that's fuckin' genius man."

"Nick's idea," Charles sighed.

"So why the puking?" Harry asked, almost amused at how wide Charles' eyes popped and how far his jaw dropped down.

"The guy Mr. Armstrong stabbed... the guy Nick... the guy he..."

Harry nodded, "yeah, was that the guy?"

Charles shook his head, "No, the pastor."

Harry sucked wind, wondering how he'd missed the connection even as everything clicked into place. He didn't understand how Nick could do some of the things he could. He hadn't been really sure he'd seen what passed between Nick and the man who stabbed his senior self; but it was as if everything swirling around him from the moment, he met the eldest of the junior Emersons suddenly became real and sent a massive shiver up his spine.

353

"Fuck."

"That's why the puking," Charles sighed a relieved sound as a small smile crawled out onto his lips, glad he was no longer alone in his new understanding of the little part of this world so recently revealed to them both.

"It was so hard to act like we never even made it to the fuckers' house first."

Harry's heart gave a couple quick, body quaking thumps as the implication sank in, "Say again?"

9

"What have you done!?" Tur demanded, wanting to both storm and be amazed.

"I have brought to bear the weapon to win this war." Leanna smirked swiping the blade's keen edge down her hand, filling her palm with a pool of blood.

"It is of the Oemir?"

Stripping the swaddling from the infant, leaving him naked to the world, she looked at her lover, incredulous. Even seeing it with his own eyes he still questioned its origin. She found it unbelievable. "It is, and I have done what your people have failed to do for centuries!" she sneered pointing to some flecks moving on the pillow where the infant lain when she cut the cord.

As Tur leaned over, his milky eyes popping wide at the sight, she painted the infant with symbols drawn in her own blood and afterbirth, he gasped, "no!"

"Yes," she growled, finishing the spell to camouflage the child and protect it from being revealed prematurely, "the epitome of what you have coveted since the night you stripped him of his soul. An offspring of the Oemir's soul fertilized by firdur itself."

"But will it have his gifts to wield?" the king of the schades asked, his eyes pinching tight toward her. It was indeed everything he'd been trying to achieve, but Leanna accomplishing what he or Ne'Min hadn't been able to, stuck like a bone in his throat.

Ne'Min slinked into the tent, passing a satchel directly to the princess. "The genetic material we collected.

"From his recent captivity?" She asked.

Ne'Min nodded.

"This incarnation, not any of the others?"

Again, he nodded. "Yes."

"He is a child," she hedged, uncertain how effective her spells could be to grow the child's power within the newborn.

"He has no knowledge of the full potential of his power," Tur, understanding exactly what his lover was about to do, cautioned, then asked while motioning to the infant, "do you really think this one will come to them any sooner?"

She set the infant into Ne'Min's arms turning her attention to the blood, skin, and muscle samples and began the process to allow the infant access to everything descended from Oemir, to this current incarnation of him, exactly as it existed in Nick.

In response to her lovers' question, the corner of her mouth angled up, "only time will tell."

--

"In spite of all they have done, his nature has not been changed." The Gloamare noted, watching the two descendants disappear into the mist of the bridge.

"More than you think," the Vetala shook her head, "the firdur within him will make quite a meal when he can no longer control it," she grinned.

"Perhaps. Perhaps he will decline to use it." Gloamare mused.

The two ancients cast their gazes on Helioson who watched the mortals leave and said nothing. Enigmatic as always, it kept its thoughts to itself knowing both of its junior siblings were incapable of seeing all the first son of the great mother's fire could.

Enveloped in the mist keeping the dimensions apart, Nick frowned and stopped, a strange series of burning and stabbing sensations racing over his chest and belly.

"Jesus… what the fuck?" he snarled lifting his shirt and looking down.

"That happen when you fell?" Lou asked peering close at the scratches growing more vivid under the fine layer of dark hair.

"What do you mean fell?" Nick asked, his finger gingerly rubbing at one of the spots then finding its way to his mouth.

"Definitely blood," he met the son of Conchobar's eyes, "is it just me or does that look like symbols?"

"It does," Lou nodded, then frowned, "what do you mean fell? When did you fall?"

"You're the one who said it," Nick shrugged.

"Did not."

"Did too," Nick pulled the shirt back down nodding toward the far end of the bridge.

"No, I didn't." Lou insisted.

"Did so," Nick grimaced, his hand rubbing his chest and belly, "stings though," he frowned as they started walking once again.

Another couple steps forward and Nick doubled over, arms wrapping around himself, "Fuck!" he cursed, Lou crouched at his side.

"What the hell's goin' on with you?"

The eldest of the junior Emerson's shook his head, "I don't…" he stopped abruptly, the color draining from his face as he met and held Lou's eyes, "firdur!" he grunted forcing himself to his feet and racing for the end of the bridge, "Julius!" The fear in his voice unmistakable.

"Kid wait!" Lou caught up and kept stride with him, "If it's a vestige you can't just go racing…"

"It's got Julius!" he argued while pouring on even more speed, leaving the older man behind, panting.

"You can't know that…" he shook his head, straightened up and raced to follow.

He skidded into Nick's back, grasping him by the shoulders to keep from bumping him out into the open.

The young man's hands were in front of him, a look of hate darkening his face as he brought his hands together then pulled them slowly apart.

Lou couldn't help gaping in amazement as the cloud of darkness holding Julius in its clutches was first compressed with Nick's squeeze, then in spite of the fight it was putting up, pried apart, screaming like hot twisted metal, as he drew his hands apart.

Lou shoved the teen to the side, poising himself to dash into daylight to save the soldier.

"Don't you move!" Nick ordered as another tendril of his will spooled out on the timescape binding Lou to the spot.

"What the fuck!" he grumbled, pushing against an invisible force he hadn't yet experienced. It took a moment before he realized what happened, "Lemme go Nick! You can't do this alone!"

"Wrong," he muttered. There was a feeling, like the springtime airing of a winter stale house, inside him. He wasn't sure what it meant other than the feeling of possibilities somehow awakening within, even as a new layer of sweat dripped down his face and he met eyes with the love of all his lives in the distance.

"Apologies meleth…" Julius' blood-filled whisper might as well have been a stab into his heart.

"Oh no you don't…" he shook his head, the now familiar sensation of heat growing as it moved through him toward his hands. As it did, he envisioned yet a third tendril of will, this one wrapping around his love, using time itself to slice through the tentacles of firdur working to destroy something, anything of the world of light.

The pike sized holes that marred the captain were left full of darkness as Nick's will encompassed him from head to toe, holding him still in time while he tended to the vestige.

The focus of his will, mirrored in the movements of his hands, flowed outward in two rivers of shimmering rage. Lou's eyes popped wide, he thought about the night Nick returned from their home world, after they'd lost so grievously to the vestige at the Aine Haud.

That same night, Nick went after Ne'Min, who'd taken Frank to try and learn what they had planned, or turn him to their will. Nick had been so furious and probably so afraid, he'd manifested a literal ball of heat, leaving a nearby bush in smoldering embers in seconds. Lou could almost still feel the heat on his upper arms from when Nick grabbed him.

The manifesting rage in the young man was beyond anything Lou could have imagined. He was watching as something like bands of pressure wound around the vestige, squeezing, and lighting it on fire everywhere it touched.

It writhed and bucked, its movements spasmodic and frantic as it fought Nick for control of its own time and fate. Slowly its entirety was engulfed in flame. As it succumbed, Nick cracked a sinister smile giving Lou a squirrelly feeling in his guts as the kid froze the vestige's existence, keeping it burning, unable to fight, or to flee.

"Get Julius," he ordered setting Lou free while he relished the living dark's protracted destruction.

"Shit." Lou lurched, his heart pounding war drums in his head as he grasped the Captain of the Guard under the arms and returned to Nick's side.

With the wounded soldier on the ground he nodded, "h'okay," then knelt, checking for a pulse while watching, transfixed as Nick let the thing's time progress again.

Little by little, flames ate away the darkness he held captive, unable to do anything but suffer the light burning its existence away.

"I will set the universe ablaze to destroy you if I have to." The teen-in-a-man's-body promised.

Lou couldn't tell how long they both remained still, watching Nick torture and torment the entity. They watched it burn away in slowed time, Nick savoring every second of its incineration. When it seemed most of the vestige was gone, he glanced at Nick, his eyes falling to the boy's arms, lined with bulging black veins, the same as those climbing up his neck and wrapping beneath his jaw, and he gasped.

Leaping to his feet, he grasped the teen's forearms, "Jesus Christ Nick, fuckin' kill it man, just be done with it."

"Suffer..." he hissed as it writhed yet again, though miserably weak now.

Frightened by the darkness running through the kid's veins and what it could mean, what he suddenly found himself praying it couldn't mean, he grabbed Nick's chin, turning him so they were face to face, "we need to help Julius."

With a wringing, twisting motion of his hands the vestige disappeared in a final, thin rail of flame, dead and gone.

"Shit kid... what the hell?" Lou whispered, a mighty scowl on his face as he held the forearm, inspecting the blackened veins. "They did it didn't they?" he asked rhetorically.

Nick's other hand squeezed his shoulder before he moved to Julius, took a deep breath, and focused on his frozen frame as it was on the timescape. Gathering and redirecting his will, he began to nudge Julius' time backward.

The first few times he'd brought himself or others out of time were clumsy in comparison to what he now understood. He was so much closer to his origin, his desired effect was far more precise. He only had to separate the strands between the firdur and Julius while he and Lou existed on a metaphorical sideline. It was no more difficult than unbraiding a lock of hair.

He willed Julius back along the strand of his experience and watched as the points of darkness withdrew from his body. As they did, they dissipated into nothingness leaving him curious as the stab holes became whole, healthy flesh again.

When he was sure all the captain's wounds were un-done he drew a harsh, shaky breath before slumping back hard on his heels and letting out a deep, tremulous sigh. There was a faint, somewhat pained smile on his lips even as his heart felt like an elephant was stepping on it. Reluctant to show this sudden discomfort he perceived as weakness, he looked at Lou and gave a curt nod, his gratitude unmistakable.

"Now why the hell didn't you just do that for us yesterday instead of setting us on fire with that dragon blood?" Lou asked even as he realized something was wrong with Nick. It was obvious he'd overtaxed himself.

Nick shook his head, "I tried, it had you all too long," he said softly, trying not to show his fatigue.

A surprised grunt burst from him, his head turning down, eyes squeezing shut, breath stuck in his throat as what felt like a rapid-fire cascade of fireworks went off in his mind, in a way blinding him from the inside. When the after-images turned to darkness again, another cascade, this one of pressure waves of emotion seeming to radiate from deep in his core, similar to the way it did on the bridge, but instead of continuing outward, it hit the barrier of his flesh, then rebounded back inside. It was a nauseating, erratic feeling making him want to cry and scream, kill, and heal all at once. Then it was gone, leaving him gasping exhaustion.

All of a sudden more attuned to the overgrown teenager than he reason to be, Lou crouched at his side, "What is it?" he asked, a nagging certainty in the back of his brain he knew more about

Oemir's descendant than either of them realized.

But Nick only had the strength to shake his head and release Julius, who cast his gaze around frantically, his brows furrowed as he patted himself down, feeling for wounds.

"I'll give you a thorough checking out later," Nick's softly panted promise making the soldier blush.

"My king," he half stammered, "the firdur!" he leaped to his feet.

"It's dead," Lou assured rising to his feet and frowning as Nick stayed where he was, giving a faint shake of the head.

"How?" Julius asked dumbfounded then frowned as well, his expression grew severe even as Nick tried to break out his most charming smile.

He crouched behind the teen all too familiar with the laxity after over-exertion. "Meleth…" he barely breathed lifting him to his feet, "are you able to stand?" he asked turning Nick's limp-noodle body around. His frown deepened when he noticed a strong line of darkness slow to fade within the veins of the boy's neck.

He held Nick up, so they were eye to eye, "what have you done Oemir…why?" he choked.

"It's not his fault," Lou shook his head, "the schades…when they had him…" he explained, quick to defend this new half-brother even as Julius drew a deep, angry breath and let it out slowly.

Taking his weight onto his own legs little by little, Nick changed the subject, "why did it go after you?"

"I fear I may have got too close to the bridge, it moved like never before, not even during the war could darkness move with such speed."

"Hmm," Nick grunted.

"And what of the bridge? What happened, you'd barely been gone but a handful of moments."

"It was a bust," Lou shook his head, "I went in and a few minutes later ran into Nick, and here we are."

Nick huffed, curious if Lou really didn't remember. "It's possible the separation of universes may have severed the link between our worlds," Nick covered.

Aghast at the thought, Julius looked between the two men, "What you say cannot be."

Nick nodded, "I went in to tell him about the firdur, it was foggy."

"Thick like pea soup," Lou added, "it did seem to go on for a while but, there's really only two directions to walk, in or out y'know?"

The soldier's brows furrowed deep, "How then was it we were almost cast into the abyss?"

Nick shrugged hoping a half-truth might be enough, "the bridge chooses who it allows to cross… maybe it's like we said last night, it judged all of you because of Tropus… maybe it just didn't want to deal with us."

"If that is so, then we no longer have even the hope of the ancients at our sides. I pray your father-in-law has something greater than the light spear… though you must tell me later how it was you killed the firdur."

In spite of the resurgence of the suffocating feeling creeping up on him, and the fear he felt about letting it in again, he couldn't help himself. He was drawn to the soldier like a moth to a flame and he could feel the desire to hold him returning. He wondered if he could control the terrifying need or fight it off to save the relationship they might be able to build.

"It angered me," the young leader smiled with a gentle squeeze to the back of Julius' neck, "it had my Captain captive... an untenable situation," he half whispered, his lips millimeters from Julius', both of their hearts pounding the scant air between them, the scent of desire thickening as well.

"Hey," Lou smiled and shook his head, "I hate to break up a party, but don't 'cha think we oughtta get back and tell Khazeer the mission was a bust?"

"He has a point," Julius smiled, barely able to stop his lips from reaching toward Nicks.

"Ass hole," Nick smirked at Lou even as he rested his forehead against Julius', "just gotta make the right argument don't cha?"

"Comes with age kid. C'mon," he grinned, glad when the horses joined them, returning now with the danger in abeyance, if not gone.

--

It didn't take long for Frank to get his bearings. It didn't matter if he didn't know the rotations or timing of either of the planets, where the universes still overlapped, he didn't need to. He knew what landmarks to pay attention to and adjusted his course accordingly. It was time to pay Vahl's homeland a visit, something no one would ever expect.

--

With the sun leaning toward its resting place, dark eyes stayed glued to the door to the armory wondering what the half-mad bastard might have been doing in there. She was well aware he was suddenly in company with Khazeer and Wellyn, several of the villagers had been whispering about it for days, so much so she was determined to learn why. Night would be soon upon them, and someone needed to know how they were planning to thwart the firdur for another night. But first, she patted the large satchel over her shoulder, the hard lumps of several dozen schade created "light-stones" needed distribution.

Noting a gathering area where many groups of Khazeer's people mingled with those of the Akirowen and Bedowen she moved among them, smiling, singling out either mages or others with various useful powers, who would take one.

Once they were activated, Tur and Semet's forces would experience another population burst, with none but them any the wiser. If the warriors of the light were taking too long to succumb from without, then the schade life-forces would do so from within.

Tierus took one last deep breath then eased it out before leaving the armory in its emptiness and darkness.

"There's no time yet," he sighed to himself.

"There you are! Time for what?" Beezle came jogging up to him from an arched passage encircling the tower where, under normal circumstances, artisans presented their wares to their fellow Sidhe.

Steeling his features so as not to betray his surprise Tierus shook his head, "to set more wards. They held last night but the mages are exhausted…" his voice trailed off, "what have you been busying yourself with?"

The fledgling smiled and shrugged, "whatever has been needed, running, gathering, peeling…" he frowned with his mouth and thrust his thumbs toward Tierus to display numerous cuts and nics in the flesh, "indeed I enjoy a meal as well as the next though if I should never be required to peel again, I could be quite happy."

Grasping one of the youth's hands and smirking at the cross hatched digit, Tierus shook his head, "did no one tell you when peeling you must cut away from yourself... not toward?"

This time the youth blushed and shrugged.

"Come, perhaps the Elder Healer can use you, I must report to Master Wellyn," the half-mad son of none wrapped his arm around Beezle's shoulders maneuvering him back into the palace.

"Report what?"

"That the armory is, indeed, empty... come."

--

"I've no intent to mislead you, but there will be many who refuse to march under Khazeer's banner again, especially after the king's abandonment of us after the war," Talmai apologized.

Minya's head tilted in a slow nod, "Then they should march under the banner of whomever they feel most comfortable. A banner is merely identification of friends from enemies, if life is to continue, all, will have to make a choice."

"It's a shame there wasn't more of that sentiment a thousand years ago when the allies of the dark began their campaigns against those of us who remained." There was bite in Talmai's tone.

"We fought alongside the Gargol," Wereiwyn's voice was soft with sorrow and the horrors they'd seen, "it wasn't just schades, it was the Foenwyn, pirini, all of the day-walking darkness lovers, they massacred the Gargol, smashing them up into dust..." words caught in her throat even as Wyle took her hand in his, kissing the back of it.

"What they did… it was… grotesque." He offered, choking back tears of his own, "it was savage. A barbaric genocide against such an ancient, peaceful race," he pulled himself together, a steely glint reforming his countenance for not just those at the table to see, "we annihilated as many of them as we could!"

"We decimated their numbers, by the body count," Wereiwyn's whisper was full of still, unfulfilled malice.

"None have returned since that last… battle,"

"You said it was about a thousand years ago?" Minya asked, nodding as they did before explaining, "that would be about mid seventeenth century Earth time, huh." His lips pursed as he mused for a long moment, the possible implications of his thoughts lost on them.

"And you are being true when you say only ours and the world of man remain?" Wyle redirected the conversation.

"The lines of heroes are gone with but a handful remaining, led by descendants of Oemir himself but still, so few," the mysterious Sidhe added with what seemed a depth of remorse in his voice.

Even so, those at the table didn't fail to notice a wave of surprise cascade through Arabelle's face, as if his news was new to even her.

"Wyle," Minya asked, "as if crushing them up wasn't bad enough… what else did they do to the bodies?"

Wereiwyn's head drooped, chin down, "whatever magic they cast, many of us saw… explosions of life-light, until there was nothing."

"Explosions?"

She nodded, "as if it was exorcised from the… pieces they took, then snuffed out… as if killing them weren't enough they had to eradicate their light as well…. It was sickening!" She dabbed at tears with the edge of her sleeve.

"I'm sorry to bring up the memories."

"What are you thinking?" Arabelle asked, her expression as pointed as her tone.

He looked between them for a moment, "they wouldn't get that close to any level of lightstone unless it served some purpose to them or their masters… I'm not sure I can imagine what purpose could be served by taking their pieces and driving the life-light from them, other than pure sadism."

"Unless their sole purpose was to ensure no one could use the light against them… it would be in firdur's interest."

"Very true." He nodded, feeling they were missing something.

Conversation continued for a time before Minya and Arabelle were given rooms in which to rest while Wyle, Wereiwyn and Talmai brought the villagers together for consultation.

Once their plans were outlined Poe took wing, drawn toward the West, but not to the elder brother. He sensed the soul of Oemir heading into the Nahroehn, but also something wrong about it, and determined to investigate. The emissary had charged him with many things, but this particular avian sometimes knew more than even the gods did, and its instincts were rarely wrong.

--

'Night… again? Already?' his heart thumped hard, his throat ran dry and metallic. The creatures called pirini were throwing themselves against the energy field the mages had raised around the tower. The scouts he'd sent out hadn't

returned yet and he could see, in the distance, a wall of undulating darkness behind every schade and predator in the land, waiting for them to break through the barrier so the firdur could consume every living thing in the Fierowen.

For a desert, the night air had a surprising amount of moisture. He'd marveled at it, if only peripherally on his first night there. It was nothing compared to the pervasive humidity of Oregon, but as someone who was highly attuned to the presence of water, he reveled in it.

"Hey, I heard Nick's coming," Ryan smiled, dropping a hand on his shoulder.

He turned to face the man he'd chosen as his mate so many years ago, and smiled, so grateful he was alive, "it's been so long, I can't imagine…"

"Just keep your head to yourself, he'll tell us what he needs us to know," Ry suggested.

He was just about to agree when a stabbing pain shot through his head, right though his eye in fact. It was followed by a grotesque sensation of vacuum within his head as something was drawn out of him through the socket. In the periphery of his vision he realized what was being pulled through his eye, was… his eye, and it was being drawn out by some invisible force. There was a sickening feeling somewhere between delirium, vertigo, and a concurrent nausea. He watched, with his remaining good eye, as his skull, the surrounding flesh, and everything else he could see was pulled apart by that unseen force. Tissues, organs, and cells were reduced to their essential elements and finally into atoms. There was pain. It grew like a spark into an ember and finally into a flame… he knew there'd be an inferno soon and it would devour him from his socket out. He had to stop it and reached for Ry, but the older man just stood there, his body ruptured down the middle, his flesh the color of someone weeks dead, mottled gray, black and rotting purple, his eyes clouded so neither the irises nor pupils were visible.

He reached for Ryan as he fell away, hitting the floor like a felled tree, but behind where he'd just stood… "no," he gasped, finally recognizing this horror.

370

He hadn't wanted to see it, not when they first arrived in this world, and not now.

"Nick…no!" he shook his head but couldn't take his eyes off his eldest nephew who stood like a statue, his hand outstretched with a pillar of living dark having traversed the distance between them, the seedlings the Sidhe called 'firdureen' devouring his very atoms as they were drawn from his body. The only problem was that it wasn't HIS body. This was Wee's body, and he was trapped in it. Stuck inside the experience of his little brother being un-made by one of the boys he'd spent the last four years raising.

"NICK! STOP IT!" he demanded while the firdureen continued their feast toward him.

In another breath, he wasn't inside Wee's future anymore, he was watching it from outside, and as it usually happened, he knew it would come to pass, and he knew there was nothing he could do to stop it.

Frozen, unable to wake, unable to shake himself from this abominable sight, he watched his eldest nephew, his dead big brother's first son feed Wee to the living dark. And when it was done devouring him, it grew; the tiny, insect like specks of it grew together, joining into one monstrous, collective whole they'd all come to know as a vestige.

When Wee was gone, Nick motioned to the darkness. It approached him, wrapped him into itself until he wasn't visible at all, and retreated into the distance, taking the teen with it, or maybe the boy was taking it with him, Dylan couldn't tell.

"You better run you fucker! When I find you I am going to KILL YOU!" he screamed after the enemy his own blood had become, then for a time, the world inside him was quiet, and he was, once again, alone.

"How's he doin'?" Shep grumbled from across the room, his eyes at half-mast and trying hard to focus on Wee who sat at his brother's bedside.

371

"He's furious, beyond furious," he shook his head, "enraged," he hissed then whispered, "and in despair. I've never felt anything like this from him before," he scrubbed his hands with his face, "not even when they killed Nick, or took Maggie. It feels like... drowning in hate," he muttered more to himself than to the hunter who'd been a family friend for ages, "I almost saw something," he shook his head rubbing his temples with his knuckles, "but it was too deep."

"Young'n, y'can't trust anything y'get from him. He was already in shitass shape when we pulled them out of the fortress..." he rolled his head back and forth in the depths of the feather pillow, "then what it did... what *she* did..." he rubbed the string of tears flowing down the side of his head, "she fucked it all up. Everything," he choked, "it's all rot now... corrupted... can't even remember what's truth..." his voice fell to a whisper.

"You will Shep," Wee comforted, "you all will."

"You don't know..." he shook his head back and forth again.

"I know YOU." The youngest of the senior Emersons moved his chair to the hunter's side, "why'd they cut him up?"

He'd watched the Elder Healer tending his brother while another acolyte brought Shep up to what he figured was a triage infirmary. The acolyte tended Shep while the Healer tended D.

When she unwound what was left of the singed and burned-into-his-skin bandage from his forearm and Wee saw the seared flesh with those fine shards of obsidian, looking like they were woven into the skin he'd almost tossed his cookies. When she wrenched them out with tweezers, pulling bits and strings of meat and skin with them, he felt the bile rise, burning in his throat. Then, when she sliced the dead flesh away leaving the meat and tendons exposed to clean everything and cover it with some kind of milky gel before rewrapping it, he swallowed it down.

"That's how we found him, I don't know."

"Did any of the others say anything?"

Again, Shep shook his head, "we were… I heard the kid talking last night,"

"Kid? One of my boys?"

Shep nodded, "Nick."

A gust of relief burst forth, to have an indication at least one of them was okay, "what about Frank? Was he there?"

Shep shook his head, "he never joined back up with us. I don't know…"

Wee shook his head, a tight smile pulling at his mouth, "S'okay, he's okay, if he wasn't I'd know it. I'd feel it. I don't have that with Nicky. So… you heard him talking…" he prompted.

Shep nodded trying to push himself up, but dizziness almost overtook him and forced him back down. "He said he cauterized him from the inside, that's why he didn't have to use the dragon blood on him. At least that's what he told Lou."

"What?" Wee asked then cautioned, "You've got a fever, not as bad as D but it could get there if you don't rest."

"The dragon blood, that's what Torn used to patch me up, I'm not hurt," the hunter protested.

"That where the pocks came from?" he asked, "like the ones on Nicky's hands?"

Shep nodded then told him the story of how they'd been captured and tortured by the princess and her troops and the vestige, then how Nick and Dylan rescued them from the torment.

"Jesus Shep," Wee sighed wincing for what he could feel the experience had done to the older man. "You may be patched up, but you're exhausted, and that leads to sickness, we need all the lines we can get, as healthy as possible."

With a reluctant nod, Shep hitched a sticky, raspy breath, "Anyway, what they said, I didn't make it all out… I was kinda… dozing… him and those Bedowen guys, and Lou…" his breath shuddered, "I mighta been dreamin'."

"Shep, please."

"I'm not sure…"

Wee took a breath, thinking back to the night Dylan returned to them. The night after Nick fought his way free from this world back to their home. What Dylan confided to him and Ryan, what Frankie saw in his dreams and what Nick later demanded Dylan tell him.

"Dark," Wee whispered, "they tried to grow it in him didn't they? That's why they cut him up."

Shep's eyes squinched shut and he bit his lips closed even as he nodded his head, "I think so," he gasped turning his fierce but fevered gaze to the young man before him, "what kind of shit is this? What kind of things wanna grow dark in us? It's not like we don't have enough of our own t'deal with! What's the fuckin' endgame?!"

"Annihilation Shep. They want it gone…they don't want to take it over, they don't want to rule it, they want life itself stamped out." Wee hung his head, scrubbing his face with his hands, "At least that's what I gathered from the mages and villagers, some of them were here before, during the first war, others no…but that seems to be the general consensus."

The older hunter's face creased into a bunch, "for the love of God why? Don't they get that if all life gets snuffed that means them too?"

"Far as I can tell… it's almost like a cult. The schades… some say they think the dark will spare them… others think they're just tired of being immortal, done with it all…"

"So they're gonna kamikaze themselves and take everything else with 'em? Fuck that! Fuck THEM!" he snarled pushing himself up till he was sitting, "I didn't lose my best friend, my goddamned NEPHEW to those fucks so they could wipe out entire universes…"

"Lay back down. It'll be night soon. The defense of the tower is all we can do till daylight."

In short order his old family friend's eyes fell closed, and his breath wheezed and rasped evenly, giving Wee time to return to Khazeer and Wellyn to learn what Tierus discovered and what the next step in their plan would be.

--

Spreading his psyche out as he approached the Nahroehn fortress, Frank paused as a dark smile twisted one side of his mouth. There was much more in front of him than he could have dared to dream. His powers combined with Vahl's knowledge of Semet, and his movements could afford him a crucial edge in the upcoming battles. He could feel Vahl's psyche squirming in his mind, pinned deep within like a bug on a board.

He was furious though, oddly enough, his anger was neither directed at the boy, nor at the Sidhe who'd lived his life in service to Semet. His only fault was having been betrayed by his Heru, his redemption came in his oath of fealty to the She of the All, the very

Sidhe those of the Nahroehn had been ordered to thwart at all costs. Vahl wanted vengeance, and if *he* wasn't careful, the angry soldier might break free to usurp control over the child, destroying all of them to get it.

But it didn't matter, the body he was using had gifts more powerful than the Nahroehn soldier's had ever been, but if he lost control, giving the soldier any kind of opening, the boy would not be the only one to lose.

He snapped out of his reverie, the child's belly twisting as he sensed something on their approach to the fortress. There was pressure, as of something closing in on the decaying structure, and if he was lucky, he wouldn't have to work too hard to make it do his bidding. So with the fortress before him, he veered to the left, to the area where the Nahroehn and the Bedowen overlapped, not too far from the navel of the kingdoms where he'd be able to confirm his suspicions, and from there, set his plan in motion.

--

A grimace crossed Nick's face just after his chest and belly started to sting again. He'd forgotten about the pain while dealing with the vestige and saving Julius, but now it was back, and those stings grew into slashes and stabs. Whatever carved itself into him wasn't his own doing. He was pretty sure it might be Mickey. Part of him knew it was a spell, but the work and carving of it was so crude not even Oemir could quite make it out just yet.

To take his mind off it as they rode toward the Fierowen, he studied the timescape, searching for and marking in his memory places of congregation where he could see vestiges, schades, pirini, and frightening quantities of the 'consumed' awaiting the nightfall flying toward them. He even found Tropus and Boaz making their way toward the Fierowen with a prisoner, as well as Errmot and

Torn several kilometers away and seemingly lying in wait near a small cluster of minions of the dark.

His vision flew out, taking in a more panoramic view of the world's largest continent with all of their positions in relation to the encroaching natural evening.

"We're not gonna make it," he breathed, noting the guards stationed around the campsites, keeping alert for the approach of any who'd dare oppose Semet, Tur, and their allies.

"Huh?" Lou asked having been lost in his own thoughts when the overgrown teen mumbled.

"Dark will come with the night…we won't make it to the tower before it arrives," he clarified as something on the 'scape caught his attention. His mind's eye riveted to something hidden just beyond his sight, in a place where 3 beings were meeting. Two of them were schades, he could tell by the strangeness of their essences. The third, however, was a Sidhe, her presence unmistakable and impossible to misidentify so haughty was her demeanor, and unnaturally large the stature she inherited from her father.

"So, she did go to him…"

"Who went to who?" Lou asked.

"The princess?" Julius asked.

"She's left the Bedowen and joined Tur…"

"Our homelands are turning to decay, her spells have been left to deteriorate," Julius explained, his words covering a faint grunt and moan from Nick as he tried to ignore yet another electrical volley of needle like pain, this one shooting from his belly, across his ribs, and up to his shoulder where it caused a cramp in his neck.

Nick was just about to tell them about the state of the stables when he'd met Naiya, when a wrenching sensation cruised through his intestines, up to his stomach and down through his bowels.

"Naiya stop!" something barked deep inside him.

"Mmm shit… be right back…" he grunted slipping from the saddle and, with his arm across his stomach made his way behind a thick stand of shrubbery.

"Y'alright kid?" Lou called, his face turned in a deep frown as he met eyes with Julius, who shrugged but also seemed disturbed. "He alright?"

"Let us hope." Julius nodded though his expression remained tight and visibly concerned.

Once behind the shrub Nick kicked off his boots, scrambled out of his jeans and shorts, falling to his knees with his stomach and bowels clenching. There was no way to tell what would explode first. Breath hitched in his throat, which seemed to stop working just when he needed it most, and cold greasy sweat appeared out of nowhere, sealing over his skin in what felt like a plastic vacuum pack.

"Fuck…" he managed to get out before his stomach clenched again, right in time with another series of stabbing scratches, these more like slices, not unlike the cuts the schades made in him while he was captive.

There wasn't much in his stomach; food and the act of eating didn't seem to hold much allure or importance for him, and so he wasn't completely surprised when whatever might have been inside him, felt like it should have jetted out, but was in reality little more than a mouthful of spit. The other was much more what he expected.

378

"Y'alright kid?" Lou shouted.

"M'okay," he felt like he shouted in return, though to his own ears it sounded more like a whisper.

"Nick?" Lou shouted again, then after several long seconds slid from the saddle as did Julius.

"M'okay!" Nick grunted though there was deep pain in his voice.

"My king?" Julius headed around the bush while pointing to Naiya, "get his pack."

"NO!" Nick shouted, hoping he was sufficiently empty as he pulled off a sock to clean himself up before righting his clothes. He swept his forearm across his mouth and nose then wiped his face with his increasingly bloody shirt before he forced himself to his knees. "I'm alright, gimme a minute…" the last was weak but enough for his companions.

"You get sixty seconds kid! No fuckin' around with it either!" Lou warned, his arm across Julius' chest, holding him back. "Give him the minute."

Breathing through his mouth Nick pushed himself to his feet, his hands on his knees, "just need about ten…" he grunted, stumbling out with his boots tied together in hand. "Sorry," he whispered, heading toward Naiya.

Lou stilled his urge to help and kept his distance. Julius, however had to be held back as the young man reached up, draping his hikers over the grip of his sword.

"Release me human! Hero or not I will not…"

"Julius!" Nick barked, his back still to the men, his forehead resting for a scant moment on the soft sweaty neck of the mare.

"My king," the Captain of the Guard instantly stood at attention.

"Leave him be." He panted, turning toward them, "we need to find a place…" he choked then, holding his head in his hand breathed, "till morning…"

Overtaken yet again, Nick gasped, thumped his chest, and fell to his knees a haggard rasp ripping out of his throat, his fingers clasping at the ground as he tried to breathe but failed.

Frightened by whatever was going on, Lou let go of Julius and nodded, "Okay," as Nick went down. "Shit," he crouched on one side with Julius on the other. "What's wrong kid? What's goin' on?" he placed a hand on the teen's back, and another on his chest, helping to hold him up. "Jesus Christ you're soaking wet…" he looked at the Sidhe, "anything like this happen to Oemir?"

"Never like this," then helped sit Nick back on his heels, "breathe my king…" he urged through the gasping, choking, barks making both men more nervous by the second.

Unable to look at either of them, and unwilling to let them see his growing desperation and fear, he gulped hard and squeaked, "Try…ing…" while his heart thundered far too fast and hard for any of their liking.

Pushing aside Nick's dripping hair, Lou turned the boy's face to his, "Jesus Christ…" he sucked wind at the sight. The bruises he'd stopped noticing were deep green and yellow, but there was virtually no other color to his skin. His face was so pale it looked like it belonged on an exsanguinated corpse, but Nick's eyes made his stomach flip. Usually bright, ice blue, the irises almost looked white with just a hint of blue inside the black ring.

His own heart tripped in his chest, "fuck me… hold on kid, hold on," Lou urged shifting position while Nick nodded. "I got an idea," he slipped behind Nick and once again put him into a sleeper hold, lowering him to his back once he lost consciousness. Much to Lou's relief, it only took a couple more gasps before his breathing returned to normal.

Both Lou and Julius sat back on their heels, relief evident in their faces.

"Had to be killing the vestige," Lou muttered.

"Or saving me,"

"Or both..." Lou nodded, "and what about yesterday? I mean I've seen him do things... but that and this morning was 'orders of magnitude' next level... this shit's gonna kill him Julius."

"Then we must ensure he has no need to use his gifts again, at least not to any such extent."

"Agreed," Lou nodded, noting color returning to Nick's skin, and more oozing up through his shirt, "what now?" he asked pulling the shirt up, "holy shit, what the fuck?" he breathed at the sight of what had initially looked like scratches on Nick's chest and belly, but now had become more obviously carvings.

Julius shook his head, his hand stroking down the side of Nick's face, "my king..." he frowned, "get this off him," he ordered, flicking the shirt before returning to his mount for his first aid kit.

"This is definitely spell work," Lou noted, doing as instructed even as Nick started to come around.

"What're you doing?!" he demanded, trying to back away from the garage owner's red streaked hands, "what'd you do to me!?"

Lou tossed the blood-soaked shirt aside, "Easy kid you're all cut up."

"Stay still my king," Julius urged, kneeling beside Nick, trying to ease him down onto his back.

"No!" Nick barked, scrambling backward, away from the men, "get the fuck off me! Don't touch me!" he ordered, and when he was far enough away, flipped over. Leaping to his feet and with a hand in front of him warding them off, he started backing away. His chest and belly dripping blood as a glop fell from his nose.

"Easy kid, we're just tryin' t'figure out what's goin' on..."

"Don't!" he barked again, "don't you fuckin' touch me!" his voice cracked while his outstretched hand shook violently.

A dirty and slick sensation crawled into the back of Lou's mind, greasy, slimy puzzle pieces spinning around, trying to come to some kind of order he suddenly didn't want to contemplate but couldn't help. *He's been abused, 'I did it without your consent...'* he recalled Nick saying. *Without consent. He's been fuckin' molested...a lot! Howie or Ryan?... or was it that mind raping motherfucker? 'I touched him, I made him mine...'* he almost remembered hearing somewhere.

Though the voice didn't sound like Dylans, he couldn't help wondering at the depth and thickness of the animosity between Nick and him.

"S'okay kid, s'okay..." Lou urged, reaching forward, "I'm not gonna hurt'cha... just take it easy."

"Fuck easy!" he spat, "back the..." he started just before his voice broke and it seemed as if a switch had been thrown inside. He looked from one companion to the other, a deep frown on his face, as if for a moment he wasn't sure he knew either of them.

Julius' brows furrowed deep on his face, "Oemir?" he whispered looking to Lou for answers neither of them had.

"Alright, alright… here…" Lou set the kit on the ground before stepping back toward the horses with Julius in tow, "clean yourself up, we'll wait."

But Julius shrugged off Lou's hand and took a hesitant step toward Nick, "My king we want only to help…We need to see the spell to know how to do so."

Grabbing a water skin and his shirt, he doused himself and started dabbing at the blood, "just startled me is all…" he muttered, "I think this is Mickeys' work, something must've happened to make her cast it, but did she cast it on me, or did she cast it on Frank?"

Frowning but glad to have something else to focus on for the moment Lou swallowed and shifted mental gears, "Frank? What makes you think…" he started to ask.

"We're entangled. He looked like a fledgling Sidhe last time I saw him…" Nick flipped his shirt around, looking for a clean spot on it but there weren't any left, "fuck…" he sighed.

Striding to Naiya, the marks of his tortures were plainly visible for the others to see, and though Julius knew them; both from having seen them in Leanna's suite, as well as their lovemaking last night, the true quantity and viciousness of them was new to Lou.

Seeing the crucible of his young life etched into what should've been pristine skin in the waning daylight sent a pain through the son of Conchobar, but helped him understand where the boy's steely inner strength came from.

Rifling around in his pack, Nick pulled another t-shirt and returned to his companions, "s'as clean as I'm gonna get without a swim or a shower… either of you recognize any of it?"

10

"How far has he progressed?" Areen asked, glancing around them, making sure there were none close enough to spy on them.

Dunkun pursed his lips and gave a 'neither here nor there' nod, "he is in no way ready to fight, if you bring him to the tower, he will die."

"That is not what I asked." The Fierowen queen clarified.

Frowning fearsomely the First Acolyte's lip curled, "he can urinate without assistance."

"Good," the queen gave a nod, "make him ready."

The look flying across the First Acolyte's face would have set any other Sidhe's heart pounding and forced them to rethink their plans, but the queen had never been easily quailed, and though Dunkun had no knowledge of her plans, he didn't care to either. She was about to take one of the fathers of the Oemir's incarnation and put him in a place where he most likely would not survive.

He inclined his head, "the lamb will be ready for the slaughter shortly my queen."

Areen's skin prickled and her hackles rose along with her

temper.

If this had been any other time, any other series of events, she would have been more inclined to explain her rationale, but given what those defending the tower were about to face she had no patience nor desire to share what was moving along the threads of energy she could feel weaving within her soul.

Still another part of her wanted to thrust her fingers into his throat and pull it free for his sinister inference, and it took far more will than she cared to admit, to force the desire down, to force it away until she was certain she wouldn't give in to it.

The last time she'd felt so much desire to kill was the last time living dark had come so close to infiltrating their world, and she hadn't liked it then either.

Dunkun gave a quick shake of his head, his brows furrowed, as if he had no idea from where his words had come, "My queen... I apologize... I know not..."

She reached for his shoulder but stayed her hand only inches from his flesh as she forced her expression to soften back to her natural stoicism. "'Tis the dark Dunkun, and its servants... there must be troops nearby. Be wary of it and spread the word, do not give in to it."

Sweat beads emerged over his upper lip, "aye my queen..." he bowed, "my apologies."

The vision of his larynx clenched in her blood covered fist aside, she swallowed hard and gave a curt nod, "none needed my friend. None needed."

With her own light pack secured to one of Diagas' thornier frills, Areen breathed deep, the weight of her rage held at bay by the living energy of the great dragon's own kin, and her love for the last of the Green Flame Clutch, the last of the dragon family with whom she'd grown up so long ago.

"I am afraid my friend," she whispered listening and watching for Ryan and Dunkun.

"You have always been wise," he praised, though she found no consolation in his words.

"Children," she shook her head, "between them a mere twenty-three human years when we have over two hundred-fold the time in their own years, and are virtually helpless… our allies are gone, the other heroes are gone… Ilirya, for thousands of years has tried to guide the soul, to return him to us, but even she has…" her breath caught as her throat crimped closed. She shook her head and covered her mouth, hoping to stop the words of doubt from coming out and tainting the very air around them.

Diagas nudged her gently with his cheek, "Have you forgotten the ways of the universe?" he asked.

"In what respect?" she returned, not quite giving him her full attention.

"That in every world containing life, there is a perception of time moving in its own way, all determined by everything beyond our scope to manage. Each system's central star, its composition, its size, its age, the distance of the world from it. The composition of the world itself, each of these drive the life spans of the beings inhabiting those worlds…time moves in its own way, but it is the perceptions of those bound to each world that defines the meaning of the measurements."

She nodded, remembering her earliest lessons, "of course, objectively a second may be a second based on picos and nanos, but once the connection between worlds was lost the comparative macro measurements changed, an Aderyn day became only hours for Terrans."

"How do they know that? Does everyone?" Ryan's voice asked, echoing from several yards down the corridor, his feet shuffling between the stuttering clacks of a poorly managed walking stick.

"Of course everyone understands the basics…" Dunkun responded, "is it no longer so on your world?"

Ryan shook his head, paused, and panted, "no, sadly most folks don't even know how electricity works, let alone time. There are specialists though."

"How do you know what you know?" the First Acolyte asked.

"Nicky," Ryan panted, "his power is tied to time… we had to learn a lot real quick when the boys came to us, even if most of what we think we know is only theoretical… his daddy never told any of us much… makes me kinda wonder why? Maybe he didn't wanna know? Maybe he never thought there was too much to it… or maybe he knew too much and didn't wanna know he knew y'know?" Ry mused.

"What are you saying?"

"Maybe he knew what was comin'… knew it was headed for his son… maybe he couldn't face it… or worse, maybe he thought by acknowledging the possibility he'd make it happen… humans are kinda stupid that way. We like to think if we pretend something ain't happenin' it ain't happenin'… sucks, stupid, but it's kinda one of the things that make us, us."

Dunkun shook his head and sighed, helping to support his human charge, "how horrible! How has your kind survived?"

"Sheer will, secret societies, the illuminati…reptilians for all I…" He stopped, his breath caught in his throat as his eyes took in the sight of the 'hall' as his healer had called it.

The majority of the room literally filled with the prone form of a dragon whose head lay on the floor directly behind the queen, who stood with an arm embracing around its temple.

"Wha'the…fudgebar…" he breathed as he felt himself get dizzy and lean hard between the stick and the Acolyte.

"You've impressed many of us father of Oemir," Areen smiled, moving forward to take charge of him. She turned and motioned to her old friend. "This is Diagas, of the Green Flame Clutch," she introduced them, "Diagas, Ryan, Son of Steven."

Ry's head swung loose toward her, his brows furrowed, "how'd you know my last name?"

She smiled and motioned him toward Diagas, "I know many things… come, we must move quickly, night and darkness will come far too soon. You must promise to stay far from the fray else I will be forced to leave you here."

"Ma'am I can hardly handle this cane…" he panted, "I'm not good for anything right now. 'Cept maybe a dirty joke or two."

With his oblique promise, Diagas lifted his snout and swung his head till his right nostril was directly in front of the human, and almost the same size. He sniffed hard enough to make Ry wobble, then blew back and sniffed again before he smiled.

"Didn't know dragons could smile…" Ryan muttered, his heart beating hard, giving him a whole body tingle before breaking out in a light sweat.

"You are… interesting… for a son of man," the dragon mused.

"Didn't know dragons could talk…" He muttered again, leaning just a little harder on the queen.

"Come, time is…" he chuckled looking Ryan up and down once again, "… short."

Diagas held out a paw, straightening his jointed claws while Areen wrapped her arm around the human and largely lifted him onto the dragons' digit, navigating its hand, arm, and shoulder until the human was nestled between its shoulder blades. Once he was safe, she leaped down, retrieving the small satchel Dunkun prepared for him. Some herbals for infection and inflammation, some bandages, and plenty of pain relief.

She returned in two fleet bounds, mounting behind Ry, holding tight to some of the softer, downy frills between the hardened, more sword-like ones.

"Lean onto your elbows," she directed, laying herself over his back to keep him as safe as possible. "We're ready."

"Hold him tight," Diagas directed.

She nodded assurance just as Ryan turned his head to ask a question and Diagas took off, his body low to the ground while he squeezed through the tunnels. Stony walls raced by at rollercoaster speeds, with him taking turns unerringly and without pause.

The movement, the speed, the turns shifted Ryan's entrails back and forth, leaving him queasy and not sure he wouldn't throw up. He opened his mouth, breathing steadily through it, and let himself relax into the body of Areen's companion. He took comfort in her weight pressing down into his back, stabilizing him as much as possible.

Keeping his eyes closed, the only reason he knew they'd emerged from the mountain to the outside was the darkness behind his eyelids was no longer so dark.

He groaned with every turn, pitch and yaw indicating the dragon's progress over the terrain. He bit his tongue with every leap or landing, and tried to make note of the differences he could sense in the air.

Moisture, dryness, heat, anything to keep his mind off the movement, and off the very real possibility he could be making a killing mistake by going to the tower. Wee was there, running the show almost certainly believing him dead or on the road to dead.

Knowing his sudden arrival and presence could kill the young man he loved, he returned his mind to focusing on the atmosphere and its changes. After all, what was done was done, for better or for worse, he was on his way to be with his husband.

--

Frank's body stopped, Oemir's eyes looked down to where his feet met the ground then peered out toward the horizon. There were fingers of rivers of black where firdur had clawed the land, and it seemed those scratches were either filled with or had dark boiling up from beneath the ground. Streaks of orange rimmed the slashes while the earth itself had begun to crack at its edges.

"I've lived for ages, there is no other to stand against you…" Frank's mouth whispered as the voice of the boy whispered deep inside *"what do you want?"* "what do you want?" the mouth asked, crouching down, the right hand of the body moving toward the river of darkness, *"how do we win?"* "How do we win?" he asked reaching forward, submerging his hand and allowing himself to roll forward until he somersaulted in and found himself sinking without a means of orientation. In his ears, his heartbeat slowed, beat by beat until it stayed still.

"How do we win?" he asked again before the darkness wrapped itself around him, pressing the air out of his lungs until sparklers went off in his eyes and he was sure death itself was calling his name.

--

"What's it say?" Nick asked, his brows furrowing, his stomach clenching while he forced himself not to back away from the hands on him trying to trace the cuts through the hair.

"I can't tell... it's... weird..." Lou shook his head.

Julius too shook his head, "I'll get my shaving blade..." he looked into Nick's eyes, "apologies meleth... though I enjoy your softness, we have needs must see the carvings..." then rose to retrieve his razor.

"Hold on Julius," Lou pre-empted then looked at Nick, "how old are you kid?"

Nick cocked his head to the side and nodded, understanding why Lou was reminding him.

It was the same thing he'd done to hide himself from the police in Austin, he just needed to remember himself as he was supposed to be, "fourteen," he answered and felt his skin start to pucker as it drew in on itself, "five six, and about a hundred and ten pounds." He finished.

His skin itched and in spite of the sting along his chest and belly, he scratched with the nubs of his fingers as the adult hair thinned away leaving him with a small patch over his breastbone. In proper time, it would become the fine, light coating over the majority of his front side Julius found so enticing.

"Weird…" Nick breathed looking from Lou to Julius.

The Captain of the Guard, having forgotten the form of the boy, looked fast between Nick and Lou, his eyes misting over for a moment before he took control of himself. What Lou said was true, he was in love with a human youth, he had bedded a human youth, no older than a fledgling, and now he could only wonder what harm he might have done, all in the name of loving him.

He met Nick's eyes and then Lou's before turning away, his expression enigmatic and curious with the faintest hint of uncertainty while Lou nodded and leaned in, pulling his phone, and taking a couple high resolution pictures of the carvings.

"Julius…" Lou said meeting the captain's eyes, "apparently nothing is what it seems," he turned his eyes to Nick's, "the girl… Mickey you said? You think she did this?" Lou asked.

Nick shrugged, "Yeah, maybe," pulling the fresh t-shirt over his head.

Arching an eyebrow Lou scowled, "You know anyone else who could?"

Nick spread his arms wide and huffed, "here? Name someone."

"Shit," Lou's scowl deepened, "alright… let's do this…" he shook his head, sending the images to Mickey, for a translation and practical application of the spell work, hoping once they returned home, they'd automatically send.

"How do you… I mean… you HATE this shit…" Nick hissed.

Lou shrugged, "doesn't mean I don't get it… or appreciate what we can learn from it."

"Why do you hate it so much? You're descended from a god…"

Lou shrugged, "anything been easier on *you* because of it?"

Nick shook his head, "not in any life I've ever had."

"Exactly… it's just jizz kid, people think cause it's from a god it's something great? What the fuck do they know? It's a fucking curse! You know that even better than me!"

"Yeah," Nick agreed, "I thought I was normal once. It was kinda nice."

Lou pocketed his phone setting his hands on Nick's teenage shoulders. He'd forgotten the boy was a handful of inches shorter than him until he returned to his true age. As an adult, he might be almost as tall, but if he stuck with his Sidhe heritage, he'd wind up taller than Lou by a couple inches.

"Kid… Nick…" he started, turning him away from Julius, walking him a little way to the side "you gotta be careful, you know that right? What you did earlier… I know you did it to save Julius but… whatever this thing is you can do, it's not good for you, I'm pretty sure you know that right?"

Nick gave a quick nod, "yeah." He swallowed hard, "it needed to be done though."

"Yeah," Lou nodded, "but it didn't have to be done the *way* you did it."

A wave of darkness crossed the boy's features as he motioned to the Captain of the Guard, "You see him?"

"Mmhm," Lou nodded.

"He's mine. It tried to kill him! Nothing fucks with what's mine!" he bit.

Lou shook his head, his voice vehement but quiet, "…and if he dies in battle? Or Frank does? Or your uncles? Harry? … what're you gonna do when you lose someone during a fight? You can't let your temper get the best of you! We're going to war Nick! And from what all the signs are pointing to… YOU are the one who's gonna be a major part of our success or failure, whether you like it or not!"

"I AM aware of that," he acknowledged, his voice also soft, "but if there's something I can do and I choose not to, I may as well be killing any of them myself, and YOU know that. You know the responsibility better than you let on. So you don't get to tell me not to do what I know's the right thing to do."

"I know," the garage owner shook his head, wrapping the youth into a one-armed embrace, "god help me I know but you can't throw yourself away."

"He wasn't just supposed to be my Captain of the guard, before Tur killed me, he was supposed to be my husband! Ilirya my queen, my wife…"

"You didn't even *know* him, OR her, before these past couple weeks!" Lou hissed.

"Someone in me did," Nick argued, "I felt him in the forest while fighting Fetik, he saved Harry and me, got us out of the palace in case Tropus's fury hadn't cooled, swore his fealty to me yet again…"

"Do you love him, or do you think you owe him?" Lou asked.

Nick shook his head, "Frank has the soul, I'm not capable of love anymore, not for anyone… but if I was…" he cast a wistful glance at the soldier, "I would."

Warmth spread through the son of Conchobar as he shook his head, "you're wrong kid." He turned him so they were eye to eye,

"Frank may have the soul, but if you think you can't love... whatever was done to you before, whoever hurt you... you're wrong and the sooner you know it, the sooner you can protect yourself against maybe losing it."

Nick shook his head, his brows furrowed as he raised up a companionable hand to Lou's shoulder, "do you think I don't know? You think I don't know what's going to happen? Do you even have an idea what the firdur wants, or why?" he asked feeling a dam inside about to break, about to let something horrid loose through his whole being.

Lou gave kind of a half twitch, half nod, "yeah it want's the destruction of the universes, of everything."

Nick nodded, "yeah... one life for hundreds of trillions in both of our universes combined, that we can imagine... maybe hundreds of trillions times more, I don't know, but I don't have any delusions about how this is gonna end, I just have to figure out how to make sure none of this ever happens again. My death in the first line only postponed it and brought us to the situation we're in now... that can't happen again," he took a shaky breath, his gaze falling to Julius's horrified expression a dozen yards away.

He knew the Sidhe heard everything, with their exceptional hearing they could've been twice as far away and whispering and he would've heard them, "only this time, it's for universes instead of for a brother, or a lover."

Julius wiped his face with a faint nod only Nick saw. At the same time a drizzle of hot lead seemed to hit Lou's bowels as a series of events scrolled through his mind.

In his minds' eye he saw Conchobar, bound by his hands to an ox's plow yoke across his shoulders, prodded forward to a hilltop by a group of pale, wasting Sidhe soon to become schades. They neared an all too familiar looking tree and positioned the famed Celtic King to be bound to it. His back to the trunk, the yoke still over his shoulders, his arms strained back, the bones threatening to come free of their joints.

A faint fluttering sound drew nearer and louder before a rage filled cry tore the air and ropes fell away, freeing the half human as though he'd never been bound.

The yoke listed to the side enabling Conchobar to throw it off before using it to make short work of the closest schades and capturing their swords to join his brother.

With teeth clenched and ferocious grins decorating their faces, he and Oemir fought back-to-back, slaying any of the enemy who came within a hairs breadth of their sword points. Then something neither of them could have anticipated happened.

Darkness itself fell like a curtain between the warriors, separating them, wrapping Oemir against the same tree, pinning him with thousands of spikes of itself to give Ne'Min the chance to bind him as they'd done the half human king.

Lou couldn't see what else happened, everything was blocked out for a time as the world around him changed and he found himself alone, far away from any other warriors, away from schades or Sidhe.

And when a handful of his own troops finally arrived, the veil of dark undulated away leaving them staring in horror at the sight; Oemir, stripped naked, bound with his arms straining behind him, his torso cleaved open, his innards pulled out to the ground draped over what appeared to be a newborn boy child. Their horror was compounded when they realized the Sidhe was still alive.

"Gods get him down!" Conchobar ordered, pushing Oemir's head up till their eyes met, ice blue to emerald green, "eyes to mine brother," he turned his head, "get Cathbad NOW!" he bellowed.

Oemir's head swung down, his gaze falling to the infant, "bring it..." before he lost consciousness, upon his release from the bindings.

Lou gasped horrified, "they captured you because you came after me..."

"No," Nick shook his head, his body once more changing to accommodate the weight of his ages and responsibilities. They were so accustomed to his adult visage, they didn't even notice it happening as he explained, "they used you as a lure, it was the only way they could stop me from stopping them... and it worked for a time."

"It gave the firdur enough time to destroy the other eleven universes, gaining in strength before returning its attention to both of ours," Julius offered, joining them.

"But I'm back now, and no matter who they try to use, I cannot, I *will* not make the same mistake not with war upon us once more."

"And this time," Julius interjected, "the firdur is stronger, faster, and it has without a doubt, evolved."

Clasping a hand on each of his companions' shoulders, Nick cracked a little sneer, "So have I."

--

Racing to beat the setting sun, Diagas and his passengers took in as much information as possible, noting gatherings of enemy troops, and walls of deeper than natural shadow, from which foreboding was stoked within the dragon and the queen.

"Schades, and firdur…" Areen whispered.

"and pirini," Diagas murmured.

"Oh my," Ry breathed, knowing he was the only one to get the reference.

The last time Diagas had been so grateful for his camouflage was when the dragons were rounded up and fed to the Bedowen forest.

It wasn't long before the spire of the tower of the sun came into view, though it seemed they would not beat the arrival of night.

From the corner of his eye Diagas caught a swiftly rolling darkness moving toward the tower, headed directly for the path they were on.

"Hold tight," he urged leaping into the air before angling his body down and into the desert sand where he swerved in the direction the wall of dark had come from, emerging into the open, now behind it.

Flipping sand off the hood of her cloak Areen frowned, "You'll have to use Ula's grotto entrance and emerge from beneath, perhaps some of the fortification spells will not reach too far down."

She felt a ripple of acknowledgement move through the dragon's scales and frills as he swerved once more, tight to the left, pouring on another burst of speed as another phalanx of enemy troops was carried by firdur, toward the palace.

"My goddess," she gasped catching a glimpse of several faces borne within the darkness, faces she recognized as having been people of the Fierowen.

--

Poe turned, curving his wings, calling out for every other avian within hearing distance, to join him. He could not believe his eyes, though he'd seen it for himself when the house of the soul cast itself into the flowing river of darkness. Even as he called out, the human child still had not emerged leaving fear pounding within his breast.

In moments, he was joined by ravens, night birds, crows, owls, a pair of hawks and a pair of falcons. Together they followed his lead to where the boy went under and searched for some sign of him.

With the keen sight of the hawks and falcons on their side, they identified their quarry in spite of its submersion in the ichorous looking substance. The nearly twenty other avians dove and darted, keeping their eyes on the raven's charge as Poe tucked his wings close to his body and angled downward, diving head first into the darkness. He was taken aback when the splash he expected did not happen.

He jerked his head up, bowing his back, angling sharply toward the sky, his wings flapped through what amounted to brackish air while his talons grasped the back of the Oemir's covering. The instant his head emerged into the clean air, the other avians descended, each grasping and clutching at the human child, pulling it out of the dark and onto the ground.

He gave a call of thanks as most of the others left, though a few of the cleverest of the corvid family raced to a nearby water stream, filling their bellies to regurgitate on the human, providing it wasn't dead. Poe himself wasn't sure.

High above the plain they took the time to note the earth cracking and blackening toward the Nahroehn tower where veins of the same darkness seemed to create a corrosive web of itself spreading toward the west and south, eating away at any living thing in its path.

They called out to Poe, telling him what they saw then darted in, landing on or near the human, his heartbeat almost inaudible even to their keen hearing.

Were it not for the visible pulse in its throat they most certainly would have given it up for dead, maybe even made a feast of it. But, one by one, and for several trips to the stream and back, they dumped their bellies full of water until finally, just before sunset the human sputtered and coughed, his dark blue doveish eyes rolling around, noting his location, and his numerous companions.

Its soft flat beak turned down before it squawked, "Poe?"

The companion of the goddess hopped to his shoulder and nipped his side 'head flap'.

"It is you!" The human smiled and caressed the raven's breast, making the other family members chatter with surprise and maybe even a hint of envy. "Thank you!" it chirped looking from the lead raven to the other assembled corvids, "thank you all!"

The one it called Poe chirped at the others, thanking them for their service, and letting them return to their nests for safety in the night. He then grasped the human by its head flap, drawing it to its feet, and toward the shelter of whatever was left of the nearby slip of Bedowen forest. After all, he had news to relate.

--

"The bulk of our fighters will be ready in the morning my friends, till then please take rest and comfort among us," Talmai invited.

Arabelle looked to Minya with a pinched expression, "we should head out before darkness falls... there may be others..."

"My lady," Minya smiled faintly, "there will be safety with the new day."

Wereiwyn nodded with enthusiasm, "and in all fairness, our people do know who's closest and who's most likely willing to join in the fight once more."

"And," Talmai added, "those who may not welcome such long-lost kin."

A quick and silent flick of the gaze between Arabelle and Minya forced a deep sigh from the lady of the Northern Horn before she flopped into a chair, "of course you are right. Thank you."

And for as grateful to be welcomed in such a fine town as they were, both Minya and Arabelle could only wish for night to already have passed. With another look between them, there was no doubt they both felt time slipping away.

"Oh to be able to 'alter time, speed up the harvest or teleport me off this rock'." He sighed.

"Teleport?" Arabelle asked.

The corner of the strange Sidhe's mouth turned up even as he shook his head, "just some dialogue from an old bit of theater from my youth."

"Theater?" she asked perking up, it'd been a long time since she'd seen any kind of theater.

"Yes, a story from a long time ago in a galaxy far far away."

She nodded, "Ahh from the time of the first heroes… you never did answer my question… were you there during the war?"

His lip crimped again though he answered carefully, "I was very different then…as were most of us in those days."

11

Julius looked at Lou, his mouth pursed tight as their eyes met, the son of Conchobar chewing viciously on a hangnail.

"You were right."

"Yeah well, sometimes being right isn't what's important," Lou muttered around the digit, his gaze flicking to Nick who lay still as a stone, in a sleep so deep it had both men troubled.

"I've seen guys with his mindset."

"It never ends well."

"It never ends well." They chimed together.

"I heard what you were talking about," Julius admitted, "we have exceptional hearing, particularly when compared to humans."

Lou nodded, "You and Oemir…"

The captain of the guard cocked his head to the side, listening.

"Did he ever say anything? Give you any ideas about what he might be considering to hold back the dark or stop it?"

At the mention of the dark, the Sidhe couldn't stop his gaze from hitting all the points of the wards surrounding them, keeping them safe from any prying eyes or overly sensitive ears. It was old magic, but the oldest spells were the most powerful, and very few could penetrate an inter-world pocket they did not create themselves.

Julius shook his head, "he spoke of so many possible ways, so many choices, so many… things, impossible things, probable things, *improbable* things… worlds of things beyond the understanding of almost all Sidhe." Julius hung his head blushing, "especially someone as uncomplicated as myself."

Lou's eyebrows jumped up nearly into his hairline, "uncomplicated? Yeah right."

"No matter how it may seem son of Conchobar, my needs and desires are very simple. To be able to live my days with the love of my life, to protect my king, my queen, and the peoples of our world, little more or less."

Lou shook his head with a smile, "Oh yeah, easy as pie. So, those things he talked about…do you remember any of them?"

Again, the Sidhe shook his head, "it was so long ago Heru."

"His life could depend on it."

"I shall try."

He stood in the moonlight, surrounded by desert. The tower of the sun before him, surrounded by impenetrable darkness blocking his view of all but the uppermost levels and the freshly remounted light spear. His sight, so keen in the dark began to penetrate the firdur, drawn by flecks of brightness he realized were those who'd been usurped through the last few assaults. Both allies and un-dead enemies of the dark moved within it.

From behind, a wind of incredible power slashed the night air, knocking him to the balls of his feet as it seemed to move over and around him passing him by as if he was in a tunnel of it. Then his face was burning, scrubbed by a blast

403

of sand before all went still for a moment, the world holding its breath.

He gasped, his lungs filling with scents old and familiar, until under his bare feet, he felt the sand tremble while beyond the shroud of darkness, energy pulsed over and around the tower.

'Even he cannot penetrate the wards, they go through time and space… beyond the bedrock….the impact will kill them all…'

Nick sat up, his eyes wide, a ragged breath heaved in his chest, "they won't make it." As quick as he'd awakened, he was back down, eyes closed as if it hadn't happened.

"The fuck was that?" Lou frowned.

Julius shook his head, "He said something similar earlier."

"Yeah, but earlier he said, 'we'…this time he said 'they'."

"Perhaps a vision. They came often enough in his sleep during the war," the Sidhe nodded, "I will watch over him son of Conchobar, you also need your rest."

Lou nodded, "wake me in two hours or if anything changes with him." He scooted down, arms behind his head certain he wouldn't get a moment's sleep before soft snores brought a comforted smile to Julius' face.

There was nothing Lou or Julius could do, they knew nothing of the dragon's passage after all, or its charges. Purpose filled him as he turned, the backside of the great being nearing the outer edge of the Fierowen's perimeter wall, heading straight for Ula's grotto with darkness closing on his tail.

"That makes sense, though it won't help," he said to himself knowing the queen most likely thought there should be a weak spot where water entered the tower. He felt his brows furrow, "how does she not know?" But this was not the moment to wonder what the queen might have forgotten about elemental magics.

He focused his mind's eye on the grotto entrance, the words flowing from his lips very like water themselves, "Tempero a celesta, chilith anandemo obieri nin connuluga na nee nana. Tempero a celesta, chilith anandemo obieri nin connuluga na nee nana." Again and again until the focus of his will reached through time and space, as he bade them make way. Bending to his desire, a ripple, as of a stone into a pond pushed out from the center of the grotto entrance. An opening at its center whose radius cascaded in waves of energy, keeping all darkness at bay as the light from the great dragon's tear, lit the way, filling the void. It stabbed at the darkness even as it strove to embrace the dragon and his passengers.

"Tempero a celesta…Dive Diagas! Now! Chilith anandemo obieri nin connuluga na nee nana." He shot the thought at the dragon and heard the great creature speak.

"Hold him tight Areen!" before he leaped once more into the air, his tail flicking away out of reach of the vestige as he again soared into the sky then angled downward, aiming himself like an arrow into the center of the light.

The iris of the event snapped closed as he filled the void, sealing the ward once more with their passage as the vestige flattened against the energy barrier, the allies and enemies shielded within its darkness crushed by the force of its collision.

"My king? You must awaken Oemir…" it was a gentle but insistent voice he knew well, but the speaker was not here, not on this plane, and he sounded afraid.

Lou shook his head listening to the strange Sidhe language slipping from Nick's mouth, "what the fuck's he saying? What is that? Some kind of spell? What the fuck's he doing?" he demanded, looking around them, through the wall of their protected pocket, watching the world and skies literally changing. The clouds were on fast forward as night sped through its course to become pre-dawn, then the lavender of dawn's arrival came and what it showed made his stomach roil.

"WHAT THE FUCK IS THIS JULIUS?!" he demanded, his eyes wide with panic as the copse of trees within which they'd established their pocket no longer surrounded them. In fact it was retreating behind them at a speed he was at a loss to understand.

The Sidhe guard swiped away a layer of dripping sweat making him look like melting wax, the sight of which sent Lou's heart crashing into his bowels, he didn't like the idea of the Sidhe being unnerved.

"Oemir! You MUST AWAKEN!" the soldier demanded, holding Nick's head in his lap, watching with horror as his already sunken cheeks drew even closer to his skull, wrinkles and lines appearing where there'd been none, where there SHOULD be none. "Please my king!" he begged listening to the words pouring from Nick's lips over and over again.

"Fuck this!" Lou growled stalking to them, his hand pulled back and swung, striking the boy so hard red blazed on his cheek before the swing was complete. "Nick! WAKE UP!" he hollered pulling the still overgrown, but now so skeletally thin youth out of Julius' arms and laying him flat.

He spread one of Nick's eyes open with one hand, pinching his lips shut with the other while glaring at Julius, "Jesus Christ shut him up! Shut him up or he's gonna die!"

The soldier scrambled to his pack, tearing through it as the miles slid behind them, drawing them closer to the wall of living dark surrounding the outer wall of the Fierowen. It was a race they might well lose if the sun didn't rise quickly.

"Use your hold!" Julius demanded, unwrapping his first aid kit.

"I can't! Twice in one day was too much… I do it again he could throw a clot and stroke out."

"The Elder can heal that! She cannot wake the dead!" he argued, a huff of relief pouring out of him as he opened a small crystalline container, not unlike the one in which they kept the dried dragon's blood. He drew some of the brown dust onto his fingers and blew it up Nick's nose.

The teen's pinned lips stopped instantly, and he fell still.

"Jesusjesusjesusjesusshit!" Lou cursed pressing two fingers to Nick's carotid and his ear to his chest praying he was hearing the teen's heartbeat and not his own, and feeling breath on his hair instead of his own body shaking.

Around them, their pocket slid to a standstill as the sun finished its arrival over the horizon and the wall of vestiges held their position.

"What the fuck?" Lou huffed, watching, mystified as all around the living dark and its troops, sand rose in a tidal wave just high enough to guard its retreat under the surface of the desert from the rays of the sun.

The bodies of those it had been shielding were left on the sands to pitch tents and shelters, all of them oblivious to the presence of Lou, Nick, Julius, and their horses, less than a dozen feet from the nearest shelter.

"What do we do now?" Lou whispered. Though he was aware they couldn't be heard as long as they stayed in the pocket, their proximity to the enemy forces was still too close for comfort.

Julius shook his head, "We need to get inside the walls."

"You know what the fuck happened? How'd we get here? It was

Nick or Oemir doing it right?"

With a shake of her mane Naiya edged to her charge, her muzzle nudging his head as a soft snort blew a shank of his sweat heavy hair.

"I believe so," Julius slugged hard on a water skin then handed it to the kin of Conchobar who did likewise.

"She is concerned for him too." The captain of the guard noted.

"She sure ain't the only one," Lou smiled gently stroking the mare's cheek even as she lipped the boy's ear, making him snap his head to the side.

"Well that's a good sign," Lou smiled.

"He has always asserted that time and space are the same, though I confess…" he shook his head again, his expression just as mystified as Lou felt his own was.

"Yeah, me neither," he sighed then winced, "eeeww," when the mare slathered her tongue up Nick's cheek.

"Shhhhut up try'na sleep…" Nick groaned, his hand reaching up to stroke Naiya's velvety nose, "s'okay Naiya… just sleepin'."

Meeting eyes with Julius the two men let out matching sighs of relief, "Sorry kid… daylight's here and we gotta get inside the gate… when we get to the tower I promise you can sleep as long as you need."

"Though at this time we will be able to move more quickly with you awake," Julius concurred.

Lou sat him up and motioned to the water skin, holding it at Nick's lips as he came back to them.

His brows furrowed as he looked back and forth between his

companions and the stricken looks on their faces, "I can do it," he swigged from the skin and frowned, "what?"

Lou pursed his lips but blanked his face as did Julius, "Mm mm."

"Dawn already?" Nick asked pushing to his hands and knees, "sorry, didn't mean to sleep so late... gotta pee..." he sat on his knees looking behind them, then turned and looked all around them, "we're in the Fierowen."

"Uh huh."

"Huh," Nick nodded.

"Go pee," Lou muttered, "we gotta get while the gettin's good."

"His eyes!" Julius whispered once he thought Nick might be out of earshot.

"Same thing happened yesterday after his... thing..."

"But they were blue again when he regained consciousness."

Lou ground his teeth, "look what he did..." he swept his arm around, literally not aware of even half of the young man's nocturnal doings.

Julius' face fell with the suddenly cavernous depth of his understanding, "this *will* kill him." He barely even whispered, fighting a layer of moisture over his eyes.

"We got any food?" Nick asked clapping both men on the shoulders as he leaned between them, his black ringed, white eyes on the tower.

Keeping his gaze in front of them, afraid of what Oemir might see if he looked at him, Julius shook his head, "Apologies meleth, we sent most of our supplies with the others, we were supposed to have reached the tower yesterday."

Nick grunted before touching the side of his head to Julius', "S'okay, I'm sure Khazeer's got some rations…"

"S'good to hear you're hungry," Lou wrapped his arm around Nick's shoulders then nuggied his head.

Shooting a grin not meant to be ghoulish at the garage owner, Nick flicked his ear, "dork."

"Let's pack up and get moving," Lou suggested, turning toward their gear as did Julius.

Nick glanced around their pocket, spotting each of the boundary markers before turning his colorless eyes back to the tower, "I wonder which plane it will be easier on," he muttered to himself. He took a deep breath while envisioning their position on the timescape, his hand reaching toward the wall, as if he was about to pull a door open. *"Tempero a celesta, chilith anandemo obieri nin connuluga na nee nana."* He whispered and flung his hand behind him, and as he did, their pocket sped across the sands with all the resistance of a pebble rolling downhill.

Lou and Julius whipped around, horror on their faces as they barked, "NO!"

"Stop!"

--

Catapulted from beneath the sands and into Ula's grotto, Diagas' claws raked across the rock as he skidded, scrambling for purchase. Mindful more of his fragile passengers than himself he landed on his side, "HOLD TIGHT!" he ground, flexing his scales and frills until they stuck out, providing some level of drag to slow them as he slid to a grinding halt with barely a tap to the inner wall.

Even as klaxons sounded within the tower, the three new arrivals each let out a gust of held breath.

"That was fun," Ryan muttered, "...c'we go again?" he asked setting off a flurry of chuckles which soon became full laughter for the three of them.

They were still trying to recover themselves, Areen having helped ease Ryan to his feet while Diagas reached with tongue and claws to re-orient his scales and frills, when the guards arrived.

The six in the lead skidded to a halt, taking quick measure of the situation and the newly arrived trio.

"Danu's mercy is it so?" A six-and-a-half-foot soldier asked before bowing to Areen, "Heru, thank the goddess you're safe!"

The Queen patted him on the shoulder, "It is thanks to Diagas we are arrived safely." She turned to the dragon, motioning to him as well as Ryan who stood leaning heavily on the walking stick, small specks of blood oozing through the blouse they'd dressed him in.

"Ryan, Diagas, this is Leftenant Eggers, Master Wellyn's good left hand." She introduced them then moved to the dragon's ribs where he was having some difficulty righting some of his scales.

"Eggers, Diagas of the Green Flame, and Ryan, Son of Steven, one of the Oemir's guardians."

"The Wee's mate?" he asked bringing a chuckle to Ryan's lips.

"The Wee?" he asked.

"Aye...is that not his..." Eggers began to ask wondering if he'd made a faux pas.

"Oh no, that's his name alright... it's just... '*the* wee'... never heard him referred to like that... I like it," he held out his hand, grinning in spite of his pain as the soldier took it sealing their greeting.

"He will be overjoyed to see you! He has... often has he regaled us with tales of your heroism! It is an honor."

"Really?" Ryan asked.

"Aye Heru," Eggers nodded.

"God I hope you didn't believe half of 'em," Ry smiled good naturedly, "I love him more than life, but the young'uns got stars in his eyes when it comes to folks he loves." He explained.

"I assure you, Heru, he was most earnest in his telling of your good deeds."

Grinning and nodding Ry felt his heart filling, "I bet. It's great to meet you," with his love so close, he felt better than he had in ages. He glanced around the Leftenant, nodding a greeting to the others, several of whom were working their way around the dragon, helping him right himself.

"Hi guys..." his gaze caught several slightly smaller and curvier frames as more soldiers arrived. "...and ladies, nice t'meet ch'all."

"He must be taken to the Elder healer before Wee can know he's here at all. He has been leading through the assaults has he not?"

"Aye Heru, for a mortal human he's done well, we lost none last night, and so far tonight, the wards are continuing to hold... which begs me to ask... how..."

"Dragons are magical beings, there is and always has been much we need to learn from them," she answered, "please, take Ryan to the Elder and be certain Wee does not discover his presence... Is that clear?" she asked of the soldiers present, all of whom acknowledged her order. "And NONE of you are to mention Diagas' presence! You may not even speak of him amongst yourselves." she said and nodded at their acknowledgement once again.

"Diagas, would you care to rest in your old warren?"

The fine emerald scales above the golden eyes arched up, "You kept it?"

"I could not let fear win over hope my old friend," she smiled leaning in to the side of his head and kissing his cheek.

"I would like it very much Areen, and when you can spare a moment, we have dire needs must speak."

"I'll be there before you've settled in," She pointed to one of the other soldiers, "Zara, bring three healthy cows who have not calved in the last two seasons..."

"Two or three who will be headed for the mercy at the end of the season will be enough, the healthy will be needed to feed the people of the Fierowen..." Diagas tilted up a corner of his mouth, "oh...and all the dead pirini you have not yet burned." His lips crinkled and turned up at the side, "...and maybe a few that you have..." he glanced at Areen, "flavor."

"Flavor." They smiled together.

"Heru," Zara bowed before the dragon, "it is an honor and a privilege," she grinned and waved three more guards to go with her to collect Diagas' dinner.

"I am no Heru child..." he sighed.

"If we win, this generation will learn what our dragon kin so ably taught mine."

"Diagas… thanks man," Ryan sighed.

"Nor am I a man…" the dragon smiled.

Ry stopped cold and peered toward the dragon's tail end, "you… are… a guy right? I mean male?"

"This is what has become of humans?" the dragon snickered out the corner of its mouth.

"He's been very nearly dead for quite a long time," Areen explained.

"Sorry," Ryan apologized, "I didn't mean any insult, just thank you."

"No insult perceived human…we shall see each other again soon."

"I shall join you in your warren shortly," she assured.

"Areen…" Diagas spoke softly once all the others were gone and they were alone, "the magic…before we…"

She nodded, "I know… I sensed it as well. Was it him?"

"I do not know, but whoever it was… a pinhole Areen, in the fabric… and we were pushed through it."

She nodded, "I'll be there soon, then we can talk."

She steadied herself to enter the palace while watching her old friend trip the release, opening the way into the tunnels leading to the warrens beneath the tower; and disappearing into the earth.

There were series' of crystalline caves and caverns seemingly born with the planet, well suited with a few alterations, to create a comfortable place for their dragon kin; this is where the last of the green flame clutch took refuge to contemplate things stirring a strange fire in his heart.

--

"Kid you gotta hold off on using your powers okay," Lou breathed as they rested in the shadow of an alcove of the outer wall of the Fierowen.

"Why? It got us here."

Lou shook his head, obviously at a loss for words.

"Heru," Julius took up the explanation, glad the boy's cheeks had filled back out a little, though his normal color was painfully slow in returning both to his skin as well as to his eyes. "Frivolous use of your gifts could leave us without valuable aid at any possible inopportune moment. Your re-emerging gifts must not be squandered needlessly."

"Exactly," Lou huffed, then turned to the Captain of the Guard, "does he have a room in the palace?"

"Of course."

"Do you know where it is?"

"Of course," Julius nodded with a faint smile before turning to the crystalline window to message the interior guard post.

"State your..." a dark brown face with striking golden eyes peered at them and smiled, "Julius! You are alive! Many of us feared you'd fallen on your mission!"

"Syldryl," the Bedowen Captain greeted, "it was, at times, difficult. Have any of the others returned yet?"

"None of whom we are aware, though as you know we are not the only entrance," the guard grinned as a latch clicked and the doors swung open to admit them into the company of two other guards.

"Trindal, Ahrendaria," Julius grinned wrapping each of them into his embrace, one to an arm, "my friends it is good to be back among our kin!"

"Good Goddess!" the one he addressed as Ahrendaria hissed upon taking in Nick's visage, her hand immediately dropping to the pommel of her sword.

Lou stepped forward, nearly shoving Nick behind him, "I know it's probably been centuries since y'all've seen a human," he threw her a rakish smile and respectful bow, greeting her with his most genteel voice, "I am Lou Stewart, son of Conchobar...," then righted himself and jacked his thumb toward his young charge, "this here's Nick of Oemir, one of Howie's kids... he's still here right?"

"It is a pleasure to meet you both Son of Conchobar, and Son of Oemir," she greeted them each with a nod, her expression now more enigmatic than the Mona Lisa, as was Trindal's.

"They'll certainly be returning soon, two with a prisoner of Tur or Semet's forces. Tropus and Sheppard of MacRoich..."

"Boaz," Nick corrected, "he sent Shep and Dylan here," he smiled and motioned to the tower, "They got here yesterday," he shrugged, "though I don't know which entrance they used."

The two guards shared a strange look before returning their attention to the newcomers as Syldryl emerged from the station and joined them, not even a hint of misgiving in his expression.

He'd seen the young human when he made his way into the city before the first assault and knew who he was. Whatever had happened to him since was disconcerting enough for him to leave the guardhouse to make his own assessment.

"How have things been here? How's Wee holding up? I heard Khazeer and Wellyn were injured. Are they recovering?" Nick asked.

Syldryl tilted his head, "they are Heru," he glanced around them again, "if I may ask… where is the Oemir, we had word the soul had chosen the youngest?"

At the thought of Frank, Nick's inner vision immediately focused on him, though to his surprise he wasn't on Earth's timescape, but on Aderyn's. He turned, his eyes closed as he focused and turned again, facing west and south. "The Nahroehn, he went back there…" he smiled at the sight of a small life form moving with his little brother, "Poe's with him…there's something…" Nick cocked his head to the side, a twist of confusion in his expression.

While Nick took a few moments to figure out what was going on with Frank, Syldryl motioned to Ahrendaria to take the horses to the stable for some obviously very well-deserved rest and care.

"…different?" Nick muttered then flicked his head to the side, "…wrong? Almost…maybe…"

"Hey," Lou shouldered the young man out of his reverie, afraid of what could happen if he started doing something unconsciously again, "You said he's with someone?"

"Yeah, Poe… mother's eyes and ears."

"Mother?" Lou asked, "you mean Danu?"

Nick nodded returning fully to the moment, "he'll protect Frank as much as he can."

Dropping a hand on Nick's shoulder Julius met eyes with his old friend and spoke softly, "he needs rest," making sure his meaning couldn't be mistaken. "it is best to keep the number of those who know we've returned to a minimum until we are fit company."

"Will you be in Tropus' suite?" the gatekeeper asked, his brilliant smile a sharp contrast to the deep color of his skin, "or Oemir's?"

"Oemir's. I'll set Lou up with the suite on the left."

"Do you remember the way?" Syldryl asked.

"All the nights we spent sharing our dreams…" Julius shook his head, "think you I could forget?"

The gatekeeper laughed, a warm easy sound, "I'd imagine not my brother. Take our kin, and if you have need…"

"I shall call the kitchen… we need more than drink and revelry for the time." Julius assured with a warm hand to the guard's shoulder and another to Trindal's before leading the others between the siege wall and the inner wall and into the tower.

"C'we hit the kitchen," Nick asked just as his stomach gave a roar and he seemed to turn a little greener than his slow fading bruises.

"I'll see to it Heru," Trindal bowed racing ahead of them into the darkened channel. At the end of it, there was an interior lift, where Nick was less likely to see himself in any reflective surfaces.

Once inside the device, he slid down the wall into a crouch, the exhaustion written in lines on his face slow to go away. "Okay guys, what the fuck?" he asked, resting his elbows on his knees and his head in his hands.

A glint caught Lou's eye when he looked down at the young man's bowed head, "Jesus Christ…" he grunted pointing to a small grouping of silver hairs near a cowlick.

"What?" Nick asked barely glancing up at him.

"You look like hell kid."

"Matched set," Nick muttered, "kinda feel like hell."

The lift opened, allowing Julius to glance around the majority of the level. It took a pair of heartbeats for it to register, but this level, the same as the main library and the majority of the Heru's suites, was fairly covered in dust and chunks of sandstone. Some of the general communication crystals embedded into the walls were even cracked. Many areas of the level were shrouded in shadows, so Lou and Julius looked at each other curiously.

"Probably conserving energy to channel to the lightspear," Nick mumbled, pulling himself up with Lou's help.

Julius led the way just two doors down, "Perhaps we should all stay in the same suite."

"Good idea."

"Good idea." Lou and Nick agreed as the soldier let them into the anteroom, Nick's leaden gait sloughing along the crystalline floor.

Looking around Lou gave a low whistle. The anteroom was modest in size, only about five hundred square feet, but the lavish décor was beyond stunning. The floors of course were of crystal and sandstone but inlaid with jades, jewels, precious metals, and semi-precious stones. In the center, in the shape of a tree of life, its trunk and branches all edged in silver, copper, or gold were outlined DNA helixes as they'd been drawn in the books.

"Holy shit!"

The windows were covered with emerald silk and velvet draperies embroidered with threads of the same precious metals, rose gold, gold, silver, platinum, copper, in forest scenes with stags, satyrs, centaurs, Sidhe and humans, raptors, corvids and all manner of creatures, more than he could spot at first glance. Clearly, each panel was part of an ages long story.

A shiver ran up Lou's spine as another level of comprehension for their situation became clearer.

With barely a glance at the room Nick veered left through a set of wooden doors so highly polished Lou could've sworn they were made of water, and shuffled through as though he knew exactly where he was going. Deep in his guts, Lou knew he did.

"Khazeer's master crafters worked for many a moon to ensure the future Heru would be able to feel at home even when he could not be in the Bedowen."

"It's breathtaking," Lou half whispered.

A hard thud pulled them into the bedroom where Nick was on his hands and knees, struggling to unwind a light rug snared around his feet.

"Tripped over my own feet," he shook his head letting them lift him up. "Thanks guys."

"Enough Heru," a stern tone from Julius took them both by surprise, "to bed. I will wake you when Trindal arrives with food, but you MUST rest, you have spent too much of yourself these past few days."

Wordless, Nick nodded, not moving so much as a hair once they deposited him on the bed then wrapped him in the comforter. He was out almost instantly.

"You Heru…" Julius pointed to a small room on the far side of the armoire they'd found Nick in front of, "bathe, I will find you new garments."

Lou bent his head and sniffed, "Ungh."

Julius raised an eyebrow as half of his mouth cocked, "worse."

Crinkling his nose Lou nodded, "yeah. So where do I get some water?"

Now it was Julius' turn to crinkle his face, "In the bathing room," he shook his head, "come…"

At the doorway Lou's face shone with very happy surprise, "it's a bathroom…"

Pleased but perplexed by his surprise Julius nodded, "yes."

"Like a real bathroom… does the water get hot?" Lou asked moving to the faucets and turning them both, then flipping the lever to close the drain.

"Of course… truly human think you we tend our needs with buckets and pails like in the beginning?"

Biting his lip and scratching his scruff Lou wobbled his head, "well if you're gonna put it like that… it's just… I don't know. How the hell should I know what to expect? You've got elevators, crystal technology, and not a single damn car or plane or even a fuckin' bus I mean how the hell am I supposed to know you have indoor plumbing?!" he fairly railed, though in good humor.

"Who do you think taught your Romulans and Remians about aqueducts, and angles and pressure variances required to keep waters flowing from distant areas? Or pneumatics or hydraulics for pumping that same water or waste?" Julius asked, truly not understanding why it was so strange for Lou.

"Romulans? Like as in…"

"And Remians." Julius nodded.

"Okay not Star Trek…" he frowned, "Romulus and Remus…" Lou thought for a moment before his eyes lit up, "Ah! Aqueducts! Romans! Of course, Romans… right…"

"And piping pressure, and pneumatics and…" Julius started to list things again, but Lou raised his hand and shook his head.

"See that's just it! Hydraulics? Pneumatics? I mean… solar power for shit's sake! And you still ride horses! I mean if you've got crystal tech… what else do you know about? Electricity?"

"Yes."

"Induction?"

"Yes."

"Magnetism?"

"Of course,"

"Then why the fuck do you still ride horses!?" Lou threw his hands up in the air. "Aerodynamics?"

Julius smiled again, "We had to learn how avians fly did we not?"

"Then why the fuck do you still ride horses when a plane can get you across the planet in hours instead of days?"

Julius shook his head, frowning in confusion he reached into a small cabinet for a towel, "I know not what a plane is, other than a tool to shave wood, or a level field. Nor do I know what else to tell you Heru, our ways are our ways, we have always tried to utilize what our world offers with as little disruption to its cycles and systems as possible. We are one with our world and all its creatures."

"Well, it's obvious we could've learned a lot more from your kind before the worlds separated, still not ready to give up my truck, or the jeep. They don't blister my ass," the son of Conchobar muttered taking the offered towel. "Thanks."

"I will find some salve for your..." Julius began with a second arching of his eyebrow.

"My ass'll be fine thanks." The son of Conchobar waved.

"Very well, I shall return shortly with some clothing," Julius pointed to the furthest part of the bedroom, "That suite is where I'll be if you have needs."

Reaching down to feel the water in what amounted to a garden tub, Lou adjusted the temp till it was steaming.

The prospect of sinking into a hot bath at hand he couldn't strip out of his clothes fast enough! A smile of pure bliss brightened his haggard countenance as he sank down letting the water cover him up to his ears, he hoped the sound of his own breathing and heartbeat would soothe the barely contained panic rolling back and forth inside his mind.

12

"But our measures indicate it *should* be morning," Khazeer shook his head while tapping the tabletop as one would a digital watch or a cell screen. Markings illuminated, once again, something else to make Wee's guts kinda crawl with the similarities between worlds.

"I can't read that... but I assume it's a clock?" he asked showing both of them his analog wristwatch which was nearing 11:30.

"Yes." Khazeer nodded.

"And I'm telling you, it's not even midnight yet, or it's not supposed to be, let alone morning. The clouds were racing, you guys were sleeping..."

"You believe the elder son brought on the day?" Khazeer surmised glancing at his best friend who nodded his agreement.

"Unless the dark can do it, and if it could, why would it?" Wee's excitement was almost a tangible thing in the room. Of course he missed Nick, he missed both of his boys, but he hadn't realized how much he missed the elder of his nephews, how worried for him he was.

"Firdur, could not... it can block the light, at its own expense but it cannot alter the passage of time."

"Which is why it fears Oemir, only he, of all our kind can influence the passage of time. No other Sidhe after the first ever had such a gift, such power." Khazeer acknowledged as Tierus entered the chamber carrying a platter of fruits and meats, and a carafe of what Wee learned passed for coffee. It was actually ground root of some kind with the same basic effect, but without the jitters.

"Dagda…" Wellyn said, cocking his head to the side and spocking his eyebrow.

Khazeer nodded, it'd been ages since he thought of the Goddess's first son with her consort Bile'. "Mmm," he hummed, not wanting to speak of Oemir's family with Tierus present. What he and Wellyn knew were details Oemir entrusted to them long ago, and he had no desire to break such trust.

"Dagda! I've not heard that name since I was in napkins," Tierus paused with a smile on his face.

"Just remembering old times Tierus. Are you well this morning?"

The fledgling gave a tiny bow and joined them, "Thank you Heru, yes, just tired. Did any of you see the sky this morning?" he asked setting the platter down.

"I did," Wee nodded.

"I believe your eldest nephew may be nearby," he nodded, pinching a bunch of grapes while collapsing into a chair.

Khazeer and Wellyn shared an amused look.

Noting the silent exchange Tierus leaped to his feet and backed away from the table, "apologies Herus, I forget my place…"

Clapping him on the shoulder, "As our eyes and ears, your place is at the table with us," Wee motioned, sitting beside this young fledgling who was fast becoming something of a squire to the three of them. "What makes you think Nick did it?"

"Well, if he and the young one are both Oemir, then it would be reasonable to believe at least one of them has some of his gifts."

Their silence an invitation to continue, he smiled, "As a child I often dreamed of the first war, and more than once dreamed I saw him in battle.

We were on a great plain. It seemed none of the others could see what I did, they were engaged with the enemy after all. But Oemir, he was being rushed from all sides by Tur and Semet's soldiers, and pirini from above." He sighed, his gaze out the window as if watching the long ago, "he stood still, waiting... it was mesmerizing.

They dove and drove at him full force until they were mere meters away, less than 3.

He closed his eyes and smiled, and everything stopped. They hung in mid stride, mid dive, mid motion as did all the soldiers on the plain, enemy or ally..." he breathed hard, his own eyes closed now, his smile broadening as he recounted the instant, "and he strode out of harm's way." Tierus chuckled as Khazeer and Wellyn shared astounded looks with each other and Wee.

"He turned blades, soldiers, and moved enemies into position to receive blows that would otherwise have missed. And just as he was finding another enemy to battle, it all moved again, at full force and speed. Enemies rending killing blows to their own; arrows, swords, lances, daggers landing them like swatted flies."

The fledgling huffed and smiled again, "it was glorious!"

426

When he opened his eyes and took measure of the expressions around him, he blushed deep red, "apologies...as I said, it is but a dream."

"Do you know what battle that was Tierus?" Wellyn asked, his face almost pure white against the dark beard and moustache he'd been growing for the last few days.

Khazeer kept his face toward Wee though his eyes flicked to his Master of Arms before he chewed his lips for a scant second.

Wee cocked an eyebrow just a hair, knowing something momentous just happened, but neither the king nor his best friend were ready to share it, at least not in front of the fledgling.

Tierus shook his head, again looking sheepish but also curious about the expressions he was seeing, "no Heru, t'was just a dream, always the same, but just..." he stopped, something inside now knowing full well it wasn't, and had never been just a dream.

"It was the battle of Talath o'riches," Wellyn's voice was soft.

"Talath o'riches?" Tierus shook his head, "that's the talath..." he shook his head again, this time looking at Wee, "you call it a plain, a flatland... just this side of Cathbad's Aine Haud, where Tur nearly killed Conchobar..."

"And where later, they *did* kill Oemir." Khazeer finished, then noting the looks around him amended, "well, landed the killing blow."

"We never learned how the battle was won," there was obvious sadness in Wellyn's voice, and in the soldier Wee sensed a well of deep, heartbreaking loss now tinged with something similar to hope.

"I know not what to say," Tierus said into his goblet, unable to meet Khazeer's or Wellyn's eyes. Wee knew the fledgling was hurt

427

by his reputation as the half-mad son of none, but he also knew the youth felt relief since learning the Heru and Master of Arms accepted him. They understood his access to information almost no one else had, and they appreciated both the fledgling's bravery and competence, as well as how his knowledge could benefit the cause of light and life.

"Heru, Master… you both think this means something far stranger than I do, yet you are both aware that I often know things…" Tierus half frowned while glancing from one of them to the other, "what do you think this means?"

Feeling how reluctant they were to speak whatever it was they hadn't come to terms with yet, Wee jumped in to ease the awkwardness of the moment. "I think Tierus, this means you're going to have a very interesting puzzle to solve once we win this war, but until then…" he looked pointedly around the table, "we have current events to worry about. And the King and Master Wellyn need to get some stretching in, so they don't seize up."

They cast a skeptical look at Wee who motioned Tierus toward a wardrobe.

"The Elder brought some light clothes and your swords just before time started racing forward," he explained, "you guys were already zonked…uh, sleeping."

While Khazeer and Wellyn set about stripping from their dressing gowns, Wee laid out extra bandages, salves and leviathan venom provided by Ula, in case either of them opened their wounds.

With both of them standing in the equivalent of their underwear, they submitted to wound inspections by Wee and Tierus before they were allowed to dress for their exercises.

"We'll not be doing battle in our…" Khazeer started but was cut off.

"No armor yet, the Elder wants to make sure it doesn't disturb your wounds." Wee explained.

"There has been a development you both should be advised of, though not a word leaves this room just yet," Khazeer ordered waiting until they all agreed, "the queen has returned with company. We spoke briefly after their arrival, but the time is not right yet to reveal their presence to all. There may well be allies of the firdur among us."

"Yes, I've seen many who no longer have their normal 'presence'. If they cannot be saved, we must purge our ranks of them," Tierus sighed handing Wellyn his blouse before refreshing their brew, "many of the fledglings are too trusting."

"What of your companion Beezle? Is he one you feel is still himself?" Wellyn asked, taking another sip before beginning the slow, precise moves required to warm and lengthen his muscles.

Tierus nodded, "aye Master, he showed me his thumbs last night," he chuckled noting their confused expressions.

"They had him peeling in the kitchen… he is *not* adept," they chuckled, "I sent him to aid the Elder Healer where the worst he can do is poison himself instead of possibly lopping off a finger or two." He looked at Wee, "which is much more difficult to heal."

The three elders chuckled with the fledgling, waiting for him to join them in the first of their warm-up positions.

"How long did you say it would take Fern and Janell to get to the bridge and back?" Wee asked as Wellyn led them through the equivalent of Sidhe Tai-Chi.

"That, kin of Oemir, will now depend on the extent to which

your nephew's acceleration of the night reached. If it was local, which would likely have been catastrophic, they may well be resting still. But if he managed to effect the world," he shrugged, "another day or two before they return depending on where they were when he did it."

"The world?" Wee huffed, a sudden shudder of fear coursing through him. It was followed by a moment of curiosity, wondering what affecting the entire planet could do to the boy who couldn't hold time still much longer than five minutes without getting either a migraine or a giant nosebleed.

"Khazeer, what do either of you know about Oemir's gift?" Wee asked, as Wellyn gathered them to the table to clear the greater part of the room.

With all obstructions out of the way, the king and his Master of Arms greeted their swords, faced one another, bowed, and assumed ready stance.

"He rarely used it," the king replied as Wellyn moved in with a prod at his defenses. "Rarely spoke of it, but when he did, he was often fond of saying, 'the turning of the universes are not for mortals to meddle with.'"

"We tried to urge him to push the firdur back," Wellyn shook his head, defending himself as the king drove him back toward his sickbed.

Wee raised a finger and opened his mouth to warn him but Tierus closed his hand, and lowered it, shaking his head.

"And?" Wee asked, watching, deeply impressed as the two dodged, whirled, struck, feinted, faster, and harder as they warmed up and their bodies got back to work.

"The problem he most often spoke of was that even if he could manage to reverse the universe back to the time before light, there was no way to prevent it coming into existence."

Wee chewed his lower lip while nodding, "certain things are inevitable… there's too much in the universe to control, no one can know where every atom is, or what direction and speed it's going... it's impossible."

"We often talked about maybe moving forward, or kinda sideways, but far as we could tell, that'd just result in a new timeline…" he paused remembering the feeling of being burned to death, undoing itself as Nick pulled star light back through the opening between worlds, "it's just backwards or forwards. How could there be any other directions?" Wee asked shaking his head. This wasn't Oemir this was Nick, a human, and a teenager, not a Sidhe.

As one, Khazeer and Wellyn ceased their sparring, turning to face the young man.

"What I do know," Khazeer sighed, "what Oemir once tried to explain, aside from what we already know of time's nature, is that when universes overlap; as the original thirteen did at their birth, the nature of time is individual according to each universe. Its malleability, he believed was a product of the quantity and types of elements in each."

Wee shook his head, his face squinched in confusion, "types of elements?"

Wellyn's sword sliced the air between the two, but the king parried without so much as a change in his breathing.

"Of course," Tierus smiled, one hand on Wee's shoulder as he placed a short sword into his good hand.

431

"Atoms become molecules which becomes significant mass, which allows for electromagnetism, and often gravity," he nodded inviting Wee to practice with him. He was impressed and unnerved by the level of understanding these kin of theirs had with the workings of the universe. *If we survive all this, I'm gonna have us get some real education, I hope they teach classes.*

His blade angled upward, "Right," he nodded, "right, gravity warps space, which warps time, but the amount of gravity is dependent on the heavier elements created out of the base elements already within that universe…"

"Impressive, we thought most of your kind would have forgotten the basics." Wellyn smiled, fending off a frighteningly strong offense from the king even as he was driven to the farther reaches of the room.

"Do not forget the sympathetic field between universes," Khazeer added, his sword braced crosswise to Wellyn's descending blade, but only for a split second before the king swept the Man At Arm's legs from under him. He grabbed Wellyn's blouse with one hand to arrest his fall, while turning until he was behind him, an arm under his throat and a dagger angled for descent into his chest from above. The perfect place and angle to sever his aorta if he'd been an enemy.

Wee cocked his head to the side, moving slowly through the offense they'd just seen, but winding up on his back with Tierus' counter.

"Sympathetic field? You're talking about something in one universe affecting a similar element or atom in another?"

The king hoisted his best friend onto his feet, as Tierus did Wee, all of them grinning and flushed with the rush of exertion.

"You're still as swift as you were three millennia ago my king."

"When one has been trained by the best of all Sidhe one had best not forget those lessons," Khazeer turned, nodding to Wee, "Yes, very impressive that the knowledge remains among your kind."

Khazeer took up station beside Wee, demonstrating the next "ready" stance, as Wellyn did the same beside Tierus.

His focus on emulating the king Wee smiled, "some people still remember, or at least have rediscovered it... we call it quantum entanglement... or 'spooky actions at a distance'."

Wellyn and Tierus advanced first, slowly enough so Wee could manage with his non-dominant hand to block and counter the incoming blade.

"When the boys came to us we had to study a lot, especially with Nick. We just got all the information we could, or could understand even on a rudimentary level." They returned to their prior positions, repeating the movements several times, each one a little faster and more forcefully.

"I still don't really understand it much, especially the entanglement part, it hurts my head."

Tierus' blade slipped down the length of Wee's, the edge caught only by the guard as Wee's wrist gave way under the increased force. If the fledgling's reflexes had been slower, Wee might have wound up with a split scalp if not skull.

"A blade will hurt far more Oemirkin," Khazeer warned, his voice stern but not unkind.

Wee stopped suddenly as something clicked, "you're not just talking about subatomic particles in one universe being entangled...

433

you're talking about the universes being entangled?"

He looked at the other three, all of whom were nodding in commiseration.

"Yes. What happens in one, effects what happens in the others. Perhaps this is why Oemir chose not to speak much of it," Khazeer nodded, "I often felt it was difficult enough for him to feel at home here, after all, his lineage was often subject to celebrity when out of his Bedowen home."

Wee frowned, "celebrity? Because he could manipulate time?"

The king, disheartened by how quickly he'd grown fatigued, motioned to the table, inviting them to sit and recover for a moment.

Wellyn shook his head with a smile, "no, few ever knew of his talent aside from the Heru's and but a few of the highest officers. In spite of Danu having had many children, he was the first she bore with The Shining One."

"The Shining One? You mean Lugh?" Wee asked, feeling his blood heading toward his feet.

"Yes. Aside from Bile', her consort, she did not favor many gods, she often said she found them too…" he paused, "imperious. Too indifferent to their own offspring. Danu enjoyed nurturing her children, watching them grow and learn."

"Who's Bile'?" Wee asked, sending Tierus into fits of laughter almost causing him to choke some of his root brew.

Wee pounded him on the back, even as he shook his head, "apologies Heru…" the youth chuckled, "truly you do not know?"

"Uh uh," Wee shook his head.

"Bile' is the god of death. Their son Dagda was one of the first

Kings of All Sidhe, Oemir and Dagda were half-brothers." Khazeer explained.

"Ahh, which explains why you were talking about Dagda…" Wee mused then asked, "So what happened to him?"

"He crossed a mound to Terra… your world, to help guide the education and safety of your kind, and in so doing left his younger brother to ascend to the throne when he came of age. We last heard he had become king of a place called Eire as well as their chief Druid. Oemir was proud of his brother and spoke fondly of him and all the knowledge he shared before leaving with the humans."

"Cool," Wee nodded turning to Tierus, "last night you said you found what Khazeer asked you to look for… fill me in?"

With a nod from Khazeer, he and Wellyn rose to resume their practice.

Monitoring their forms as they went through their warm up moves again, Tierus explained, "In the beginning the birth of the triskadecagon caused a spark that scarred the perfect dark. That spark became the great dragon. Her becoming created our star. She shared its life energy and gave birth to the first ones, the Heliosons and the Gloamare." Intent on the king and Wellyn he rose. Wee did too. "Hold! Master Wellyn plant your back foot."

The Master at arms checked his footing and fixed it with a nod.

"Ready stance!" the fledgling commanded before continuing his story, "Together they gathered and combined stray bits meandering close by to create a nest. There they bred, and thus Aderyn was born. My king your left is falling! Again." He commanded.

Wee watched, amazed, learning how to spot what Tierus was seeing.

"Over time the first three bore other life; Heliosons bore the Vetala, who bore the Gargol; the Gloamare bore Felesians and Foenwyn, and Fae. And the great mother bore more of her kind, the dragons, the naga's, gorgons, and the primordial gods; Danu, Bile', Lugh, Morrigan, Camulos, Cernunnos, Eire,…"

Stopping and turning together, the king and Wellyn smiled, "Tierus…" Wellyn's voice indulgent.

Moving to the two of them he continued his story, "Right, right…" the fledgling then looked back to Wee, "you understand."

"Yeah, I get the point," he nodded, "go on."

"Millions of eons passed in every universe. But after so long, there came a day when the great mother found herself nearly spent and lay down to rest for the last time."

The young Sidhe took Wellyn by the hips, tapping his feet to get them into the proper position, checking their alignment before moving up toward his Master's upper body.

"Right, her body became the Dragonbow mountains," Wee nodded.

"Yes. When she lay her head to rest, and the sands of the Fierowen, born of the elements of her very blood, dried, the only thing left to see for hundreds of kilometers was her central horn which rose in a spire." He gave a nudge to Wellyn's shoulders, checking the alignment of them to his hips, then had him raise his sword arm to check how his injury was affecting his balance.

Wee's eyes popped wide, "Are you shittin' me?" he asked looking between the three of them, "This palace? This tower is actually a dragon's horn?"

"It is." Khazeer nodded. "That's what he was confirming

yesterday. He found the vertex of her skull." He smiled, leaning back to view Wellyn's stance from Tierus' perspective. "Very well done!" he praised.

"Heru," Tierus smiled with a bow, motioning the king to stand at ready.

The youngest of the elder Emersons felt his stomach flip, "but the tower's crystal and sandstone... and the mountains are fifteen hundred miles away...that would make the neck alone..."

"Closer to two thousand kilometers away, and the neck with the head almost the same length, which means her tail and hind legs would also be the same length, which explains the Bedowen cliffs at the southernmost border of those lands." Wellyn nodded still holding his position, not so much as a quiver visible in his stance, arm, or blade.

"Wait, wait, wait..." Wee urged and did some quick calculations, "that means her body from nose to tail is like the size of Africa... shit, that's fuckin' huge!" he gasped, "but that can't be, the tower would have shattered by now if it was pure crystal..." Wee shook his head.

Watching Tierus fix his positioning to match Wellyn's, Khazeer explained, "I have the Elder analyzing a sliver. We know the crystals we use for our communications, which come from recovered time separated bones of hers have a very tight lattice structure, but we never needed to explore the true composition of them any further."

"Then why would you need to now?" Wee asked as Tierus stood, backed to Wellyn's side, inspecting the king's repositioning.

"Because if it is what I believe it may be, we may have a way to destroy the firdur or at least force it back, but first we have a hard task before us, only part of which has already been completed." He

437

looked between Tierus and Wee, "This task will require both your special sets of skills."

"Excellent Fledgling," Wellyn complimented nodding to Khazeer.

"Advance Heru." He ordered.

Wee shrugged, "What'cha got in mind?"

"Yes Heru, I too am ready," the fledgling agreed.

Slow enough to stay mindful of the weaknesses left by his wounds, he moved into attack mode, "You both must use your gifts to find no fewer than ninety of our strongest Sidhe to clear the tunnels, and lubricate the machinery. They must ensure that her tears will pass smoothly to each of their perimeter stations, but do not open the portals yet! Surprise must be our most important weapon! The sooner we can get those stones into place, the sooner we can evacuate all but the fewest to the mountains and allow the mages to rest. Once the spells discharge, the firdur and its allies will move in..."

"Holy cow..." Wee whispered, "it'll be like a bazillion search lights all at once!"

Wellyn cocked his head to the side, "I am not certain where a cow, holy or otherwise..."

Wee shook his head, "s'just an expression... like... oh shit! Or wow..."

"Ahh," The Master of arms parried the king, attacking in response, "And with the Oemir, most certainly on his way to us, his gifts will be an immeasurable boon that could once more save both our worlds."

--

Nestled in the crook of the dragon's elbow, the queen of all Sidhe felt a strange sensation deep inside and stretched. Things were always different, her abilities were always a little sharper when she was with Diagas. She attributed it to being one hundred percent safe in the company of him and his family.

In the days of her youth she'd often found herself frightened by the visions her gift brought. It'd been the green flame family who taught her how to focus her way through the fear to learn what she might in order to benefit the majority of life on Aderyn.

This morning, thousands of years later, after what she'd thought were the worst of those fears had passed, she rolled over and gazed into the sun-bright golden eye watching over her.

"He has arrived," she whispered.

"Several of them are here, but them, they arrived moments after he brought mid-morning."

"He what?" she asked rubbing the sleep from her eyes.

"Yes, it should be just past mid night, but he has advanced our world almost ten hours."

"How is that so?" she asked splashing some water on her face.

Diagas shook his head and rolled onto his back, stretching from tail to snout, a satisfied grin on his mouth as his full belly gave quite a rumble.

"After countering the mages spells to allow us passage through the wards last night, then this... there is no doubt, he is far more powerful than he was in the beginning," he stretched his neck and tail, a look of concern on his face, "I fear perhaps even more than a human can withstand."

She strode to the side of his head and stroked his jawbone, "are you comfortable my friend?"

"Mmm very much so, when you are ready so will I be."

Areen's smile brightened the dragon's heart as she leaned in and kissed his cheek, "rest my old friend, it is well deserved."

He watched her leave, closing and locking the door behind herself to keep him safe, then eyed some scraps of pirini in the corner, his tongue slipping out to wrap around a section of spine he savored before belching out a puff of char. Satisfied, he rolled over, and allowed himself to sleep for a time.

--

Frank gasped and clung to the dank rock wall leading to the deepest reaches of the Nahroehn fortress. Features juxtaposed themselves partly from knowledge gleaned from Vahl, and others from some memory deep inside he couldn't remember how he knew. He shook his head breathing the stink of wet mold, it made the back of his throat itch, and his lungs want to seize. So many images, so many moments flitted back and forth in his memory, Oemir's, Vahl's, and his own from those times he'd been in the fortress himself even though they were few and never this far down.

With a grunt, he pushed back, reoriented himself and continued down the dim path, illuminated by only a single band of lightstones of the many woven into his gauntlet. The fewer who knew of his presence here the better. He could easily convince them he was one of the usurped with Vahl's knowledge at his beck and call, but it wasn't worth the risk.

There was also the way the Sidhe was protesting his captivity, it would be best to use the knowledge as quickly as possible then and let the warrior go. Once he had what he needed, Oemir could help him do the rest.

From far below, light began to grow, the faintest throb coupled with a wave of heat for several seconds before the light faded and the warmth retreated, giving him a window in which to move again, to continue his journey deep into the world beneath.

--

Harry sat back, a sigh on his lips as he watched the screen flash, "message sent".

"That'll do for now. Hopefully, they'll get the word out." He pushed up from the chair and headed up the stairs to check on Vahl's body, hoping it was still warm. If it was, there was still hope for him to be returned if Mickey and the boys could find what she needed to cobble together the right spell.

--

The queen's light footfalls coming upon him swiftly, Trindal stopped and turned, "Heru, how are things in the mountain?"

"Well enough," she smiled and motioned to the laden basket over his shoulder, "are they in Tropus' suite or Oemir's?"

The guard smiled shaking his head, "Oemir's m'lady…"

His letting the answer hang between them set alarm bells ringing in Areen.

"What is it?"

He breathed deep, "it's the elder nephew Heru. The others were quick to defend his look, but we were admittedly taken aback."

441

The look she gave bade him continue, "he was pale, near bloodless with almost no color to his eyes... like one of the cursed. Truly Syldryl only admitted him on the word of both Julius and the son of Conchobar. Ahrendaria and I nearly drew on him."

An understanding he wasn't privy to shaped the queen of the Fierowen's face as she nodded. "Syldryl was right to grant them access, the fledglings power is best managed here. Remember also Trindal that both of the sons of Oemir are of men now, not Sidhe, they are neither as long lived nor able to use the forces of their homelands as are we, at least not yet, if they'll be able at all."

The guard nodded, grateful to hear any such assurance from the queen. He didn't mind admitting having been unnerved but the sight of the teen's condition would not go over well among the people of the Fierowen.

As if reading his mind Areen held out her hand, "I'll take the supplies to them, share with ONLY those who know of their arrival the reminder of the fledgling's heritage, and assure them the first son of Danu is and ever shall be the future king of all Sidhe. The nature of the person, be they human or Sidhe, Gargol or Therianthrope is all that matters, and theirs will not be changed."

He handed over the basket but held onto the strap, "you say will not... you did not say cannot." He questioned.

She smiled a knowing twist of the lips, "if it has not after so many millennia, it cannot." She patted him on the shoulder, "rest easy Trindal, and advise the others to do the same."

As assured as he was going to get, he nodded his head parting ways with the queen to do as she asked while she tended the guests.

He felt himself forced under and began to flail, trying to find which way was up.

In his dream he could feel the water flowing into his mouth, threatening to drown him. His hands found the ledges of the tub and his eyes bolted wide as he sat up, gasping. Sweat mixing with the filthy bathwater.

"You are safe," Julius assured from the doorway, his voice soft as he entered handing a towel to the distraught hero while combing his own freshly washed hair.

"Fell asleep," Lou muttered, scrubbing his face as the captain of the guard flipped the drain latch and turned on the water till it was just above body temperature.

Once it was right, he turned a small dial and pulled a central spigot out of its nesting place then handed it to the garage owner.

"Bathing is not much use if one does not wash the dirt away at the end," he smiled perching on a stool.

"Thanks," Lou nodded, taking what amounted to a small shower head, "you mind?" he asked, wondering if the Sidhe was going to watch him, but found himself blushing madly, and more than a little embarrassed when Julius rose.

"Of course Heru," he nodded, taking it back and running the water over Lou's head and backside.

Flustered, Lou grabbed it, "No...that's not what I meant... I meant... can..." he shook his head and chuckled, "fuck it...nevermind." After all, he went to public high school, and at one time had a membership in a gym. "How's Nick?" he asked rinsing himself clean.

"Pink has returned to his face, though I did not open his eyes."

"It's a start," Lou shut off the water, stepped out of the tub and dried himself. For all the times he'd had opportunity in the last couple days to look at the injuries he'd obtained from the vestige he hadn't done it, aside from those few on his belly. He didn't want to see, didn't want to know, and hadn't wanted to think about it. But now, there was no more avoiding it.

He put one foot up on the edge of the tub, starting at the toes and ran his hands up the leg, feeling the indents where the fragment of living dark had driven itself through him to keep him under control. He saw the fronts of his thighs and felt the corresponding divots, these much deeper than the others, where he'd been run through. Those same spots from which Nick said he was at risk of bleeding to death.

Julius' gaze was on Nick, still asleep, while the garage owner inspected his personal bits, wondering how he'd got so lucky as to not have wound up with a finger sized piercing where he never wanted one.

"It felt like it had me pinned to the ground but if that were the case I should've bled out from punctured lungs…" he sort of asked.

"It had you enveloped… it's what it does when it doesn't want to kill its prey… and had you pinned through to the bone."

"Then why through the arms and legs?" he asked.

Julius shrugged, "your limbs could have enabled you to escape if you'd had the will. And they are expendable."

A shiver ran up Lou's back with the simple assessment. "Jesus that's grim."

"Mm," the Sidhe nodded handing handed over a bundle of forest green clothes. "Breeches, blouse and stockings…your boots are still serviceable but if you'd like…"

Lou took the bundle, "No, thanks… they're broken in pretty well… got a pair of shorts in here?"

"Under garments?" Julius asked then shook his head, "no. Apologies."

He shrugged, "Commando it is," he pulled out the breeches and slid into them, surprised at how soft they were, "wow, these are fantastic! What're they made of?"

"Angora goat fur, chamois and doe skin. Soft, absorbent… prevents blistering on long rides," he smiled.

"I knew there had to be a trick," Lou grinned while figuring out the buttons and ties, "so what's buggin' you? You're not sitting here watching me dress cause you can't take your eyes off my hotness."

Julius' lips turned up into a soft smile, "you are quite comely son of Conchobar."

Lou chuckled. "Smooth talker. So, listen, I know what I said the other day, about him being a kid," he shook his head, the buttons fastened though he was having some difficulty with the ties.

Julius motioned him forward and set about tying the legs down to the ankle, "he IS Oemir, yet he claims his brother is the house of the soul."

Lou sighed, "Yeah… when we first got here, he and the kid got poisoned by some of the bad guys, Ilirya said probably Tur or his second."

Julius nodded, "Ne'Min… they have a history."

Lou spocked an eyebrow, "You're gonna hafta tell me about that… I'm gonna need to know as much as I can if I'm gonna keep the kid safe, let alone alive."

With a nod, Julius assured him, "You will not be alone in your task. I will share everything I know… please continue."

"Right, one of 'em took Frank and left Nick. Ilirya took him to Cathbad for healing. Apparently he woke up all the lines in him."

"Which again, begs the question… why does he insist he has no soul?"

Lou shrugged slipping into the blouse once Julius was done securing the ties for him. "Thanks. And I don't know… only thing I can figure is maybe Cathbad did something to make him feel that way? Or maybe 'cause Frank's taken up the mantle he thinks he's not…what… qualified? Worthy… anymore? I don't know man."

"I fear he will sacrifice himself… allow himself to be killed if he cannot see a reason to want to live."

"Yeah… I get the same feeling," Lou admitted, "but there's not much we can do, I mean, this is an all or nothing situation, most folks live, or everybody dies."

"We are a long-lived race." Julius sighed. "Many would say immortal. As such, the passage of time means little to my kind, with one exception."

"Oh yeah? What's that?" Lou asked.

"Anticipation," the Sidhe Captain smiled. "I've awaited his return for over three thousand years. Never have I loved another as much or in the same way I do him.

We were children together, our souls bound and inseparable from the moment of our meeting. In training as fledglings we became lovers and vowed our lifelong union, but before we could

THE END OF THE LINE

wed, he was butchered like a buck…" the Sidhe took a shaky breath, his watery chocolate gaze pleading into Lou's bright green eyes, searching for understanding.

"And now he has returned, no matter the form… I feel him. I felt him in the forest though he was locked within himself, then again in Leanna's suite, and the night he rescued us.

I felt him and he was back, he was mine again, MY Oemir…I feel him inside me," he patted his chest, "our hearts bound, his soul entwined with mine, yet he says it cannot be.

I fear my judgment may be in error, that my wanting may have exacerbated the hurt in him in ways both cruel and selfish."

Lou leaned against the vanity, his heart heavy, "Listen, I know what I said, but I'm not so sure I was right. The things he's done alone, but the way he's carrying himself… you don't know the difference.

We met just a couple weeks ago, your world's time. He was petulant, arrogant, and angry, childishly angry… but when Cathbad did what he did… he seems more tempered. I don't know if I'm saying it right but," he shook his head then continued.

"You've seen him change his age just like I have. But I don't think *he's* actually changing it, at least not consciously… maybe in the beginning sure, but I think his body is trying to keep up with his mind, psyche, soul… whatever it is. Cause seriously if it was me that had two universes on my shoulders? I'd be curled up under the bed and wouldn't come out for all the Jack in Tennessee."

"Your theory, son of Conchobar is similar to what I have also been thinking," Areen's soft voice startled both men as she moved into the doorway, "my apologies for eavesdropping but you were, not quite dressed for company."

She smiled and motioned them out toward the ante-room, "come, Trindal has packed some food and drink."

"Heru," Julius nodded.

"Yes ma'am," Lou agreed wondering just how much she'd heard.

The queen made her way to the bed and lowered herself to Nick's side, her hand gentle as she swept the filthy matted hair from his face. "Nick, come now, you must eat, then you may rest."

He tossed his head to the side, his lips moving before breaking into a smile at the light timbre of the voice in his head.

She smiled as his bright blue eyes opened and latched onto hers, "Areen?" he muttered, "thought you were at the... oh, it wasn't a dream?" he asked pushing himself up onto his elbows.

"No. It was no dream. You managed to get us past the wards while keeping the firdur at bay. All three of us owe you thanks."

He smiled pushing all the way up, "three of you? So it's true? I felt Ry."

She nodded, "he is with the elder healer. She is helping heal him a little more before we tell Wee he's here."

Nick's brows furrowed as he shifted till he was beside her, "he doesn't know?"

"No," she shook her head, "we camouflaged him before leaving the mother... I am surprised you can feel him."

He shrugged and sniffed, "you brought food?"

A brilliant grin lit her face as she guided him to his feet, "yes, come eat and tell me what you've learned so I may relay it to the king."

At the threshold Nick stopped, smiled, and looked from Julius to Lou, "you look good in Bedowen green," he complimented, "you could be one of us."

Lou motioned to Julius, "he found 'em... my clothes are kinda trashed. How're you doin' kid?"

Nick nodded, holding out the chair for the queen before joining them and grabbing a small loaf of bread and hunk of some kind of meat from the basket, "hungry." He mumbled around a mouthful, "you two?"

"Being clean kinda rejuvenates a guy," Lou smiled.

"You Heru are next!" Julius commanded with mock sternness. "Then we will have the elder come to ensure you are well."

Nick shook his head, "I'm fine." He turned to the queen, "Leanna has joined Tur. I saw her in their encampment though something was wrong, it was as if she was wounded, but there was a spell I couldn't penetrate, even on the timescape."

--

Wee frowned waving the next villager forward. There was something gnawing at him, something in the back of his mind he couldn't put his finger on, a sensation of something not quite right.

He shook his head and focused on the golden eyes in front of him. The Sidhe to whom they belonged looked to be about mid-forties though he'd learned during the first siege that Sidhe could be thousands of years old and look younger than middle aged. He'd been amazed by it, and almost wished he could be so lucky.

Over the last few years he'd seen more and more gray creeping and winding into the long curls of his mop, often and in numbers enough to make him wonder if he should cut his hair. Ryan discouraged him, he enjoyed twining his fingers in the rings, almost as much as Wee enjoyed the comforting touch himself.

A twinge burned in his chest at the thought of the love of his life, and he couldn't help but reach out with his senses, hoping the energies here would enable him to find and feel Ry, to know he was still alive and trying to get back to the people who loved him. But he couldn't, and the hurt was almost beyond his ability to tolerate.

"Wee?" Tierus nudged him.

"Right," he nodded and looked up at the next villager, rose and offered his hand, "I'm Howie Emerson."

"I am Rae," she handed him a baseball sized stone, then folded up the satchel from whence it came. "You are the one who has been leading us these last many days. It is a pleasure son of Oemir. A great pleasure."

--

"NO!" Tur ordered a hostile snarl capable of cowing anyone else, aimed at his longtime lover. "We must move as quickly as possible! That... CREATURE," he jabbed his finger toward the newly born child, "notwithstanding... this victory will be ours so long as we do not falter or fall to the machinations of time itself!"

Leanna was just about to contradict him when the offspring standing beside her did so instead, "You have no vision... I AM time and all that may be wrought from it. Your fears stem from the failures of your ages and they will cost us victory yet again!" the youth spat, his face a stern replica of his progenitor when he'd been little more than half a dozen human years old.

To prove his point the child took a moment, his gaze somewhere else until he ran to an area near a chest, at the far tent wall and returned with a scorpion pinched by the tail between his fingers.

He returned to them and set it on the palm of his free hand where it stood, frozen, tail high and stinger extended while he focused on it, pushing its personal time forward on his own vision of the timescape.

Leanna and Tur watched as the arachnid grew larger, darker, and shed multiple layers of exoskeleton into his palm, until it was nearly the size of his hand and black as night.

"Any mage could do the same…" Tur sneered only to be forced to hide his amazement when the creature seemed to be pressed down. Its exoskeleton started to crack, its tail falling, its stinger dulling until it lay on its belly. In seconds its shell cracked like a dish that'd been stepped on, and finally it gave a series of small death throes before its legs curled, its tail flattened out behind it and whatever had been inside the polymer of its outer being was empty, only to be blown away like so much detritus after a scorching summer.

Leanna sat up straight and smug, "and he is less than a day."

Tur swallowed hard and dry, his hateful, mistrustful gaze on the creature she'd brought to being before he wheeled on his heel disappearing into the night.

The child wiped his palm on his pants and moved to his mother's side, a cold, empty smile turning his lips up as she caressed his head and kissed it. "Well done my son, well done." She sighed.

--

Finally having reached the bottom of the kilometer long stony staircase Frank stopped, his breath caught in his throat while sweat burst out over him, sealing his clothes to his body with the heat. He was nearly blinded by the yellowish red light of the magma roiling still another kilometer below him. On his shoulder, Poe nipped his ear.

He shook his head, his brows furrowed, "Why am I here? I knew it just a second ago…" his whisper tapered and was nearly drowned out by the heavy vibration of the molten stone below.

His gaze fell on the slow, hypnotic churning, the brightness and dimness alternating rhythmically, "I never would have believed it if I wasn't looking at it with my own eyes," he stroked the breast of the emissary's eyes and ears.

He drew his gaze away from the stony fires and followed the walls marking what he knew to be the outside of the fortress.

Poe watched carefully, waiting for the boy's attention to fix elsewhere, and when it finally locked on the petroglyphs, he slipped from Frank's shoulder, using the thermals to carry him soundlessly to the far side of the staircase where he could retrieve what would be needed before all things were over.

He rode high on the wave of hot air, and with his gaze split between the boy and the center of the churning life's blood of the planet, he tucked his wings and, as the light faded, dove into the magma.

Taking it all in, the buttresses, the chains of stone and metal securing the base of the fortress to its raft of stone, the fresh rough scratches carved into the walls of the cavern once the fortress had started moving again. It would have been beyond understanding if he hadn't access to Vahl's and Oemir's memories and knowledge. It was a marvel of engineering developed eons ago, millennia before the last war with so many of the Sidhe Heru's working together to create an indestructible safe haven surrounded and protected by Aderyn's own heart.

"I'm going to need help Poe… the dragons maybe? I feel the return of the elders and an ancient, but there will be new clutches hatched in no time. I feel a fire's already burning." He sighed and turned, "Poe?" But the avian was no longer perched on his shoulder. "Where'd ya go Poe?"

Seconds later the raven flew in from the far side of the stairs, a series of chirps seeming to agree with him as he fluffed his feathers, flapping while he threw a stone up into the air and swallowed it, then perched again on the human's shoulder.

"I'm glad you're with me Poe," Frank smiled, starting to walk along the balcony. He needed to memorize the layout of the externa of the structure while trying to find the memories of its creation from either the soul of his progenitor, or his captive whose struggles were growing more feeble the longer his spirit was kept from his body.

As if reading his mind, which may well have been the case, Poe chirped an urgent strain of sound and Frank nodded, "I know. He's strong though, if he would just help me I would let him…" the raven interrupted almost angrily, "I know!" Frank barked, while peering into his inscrutable coffee colored eye. "I will, I promise." He capitulated and motioned forward. After all, in spite of having started out as an enemy combatant, Vahl had become an ally if not friend and Frank was not happy with the idea of being party to his murder.

--

It felt like something was digging under a hang nail in his brain.

The sensation deep and raw enough to awaken him, even through his fevered state. His gaze fell on Shep, snoring lightly across the small, austere room, then rolled out the door and into the hallway.

Fast footsteps shooshed toward their room and he dropped his eyelids to watch from beneath his lashes. The steps were those of the Elder Healer. She was good at what she did, but she was a chatterbox and even worse, one with a knack for knowing when her patients were contemplating going against her direction.

To his relief she didn't so much as glance into their room as she passed by, her kit over her shoulder as she muttered to herself, the sounds concealing the clumsy, herky jerky movements of his rising and lurching toward the doorframe where he watched her disappear into a door, only one word she'd said recognizable to him. "Oemir."

Leaning against the cool crystalline frame, he bent his knees and held on tight, little by little, regaining motion and strength. He had no idea how long he'd been fighting the infection which overtook him, but with Shep still in the room, he got the feeling it hadn't been more than a day, maybe two.

He startled at the sound of the Elder Healer's voice echoing from a distance greater than the door he'd seen her go into. His lips pursed in a frown as he peered out into the hallway, straining his gaze into the distance as a shadow of motion from above caught his attention.

"They *all* have need of your talents Elder," a dulcet, but undeniable voice carried back to him, followed by a masculine mutter he couldn't make out, "yes, the elder first. The fewer who know," the voice was silenced as a door was closed and Dylan felt his blood begin to warm. Nick had obviously returned with several others, and seemed not to be in the best of shape.

If there was a time when he'd be able to best the young man, this could well be the moment. He had to get warm, loose, and strong and be ready to move after the healer and the queen were gone. He didn't want to hurt whoever else might be with Nick but with his little brother's life at stake, anyone else was collateral damage.

Taking advantage of the moment, he slipped out into the hallway, heading to the left to both get his bearings, and find himself a weapon.

"Of course Heru," the Elder nodded, the door latching behind her.

"What happened?" she demanded, her face turning down into a severe frown as she pushed Julius and the son of Conchobar away.

Nick was curled forward in his chair, his hands scrubbing his face while his breath fell heavy and hard.

"We were just eating and catching the queen up on what we found out," Lou started to answer.

"We thought he was choking," Julius added.

"I was," Nick coughed, turning his face up, surprising them all with several new lines etched into his skin, and the stubble over his jaw having become sprinkled with salt as was his hair.

"I have been told you are a child," she frowned, crouching before him, her hand on his forehead as she peered into his eyes.

"I am ancient," he said so softly none but she heard him.

"There's been a shit ton of weird stuff happening to him, but he wasn't doing anything but eating… he wasn't casting or chanting or anything…" Lou explained.

"Weird?" Elder asked.

"I told you I felt something on the timescape… I can't see it though! Whatever it is it has to be tied to time and because of that it's affecting me…" His voice cut off as a thought came to him and left him chilled, Diagas, before disappearing into the dregs of the forest had left them a warning, *'the spawning has come.'*.

Everyone in the room saw what little color there was, drain out of the young man's face.

"What?" Lou asked, "what did you just think of?"

Nick shook his head and licked his lips, his eyes locked onto Lou's, the terror in them unmistakable.

"No, you thought of something…"

Thinkthinkthink don't let 'em know what you're really thinking, AH!, "what if they're trying to tap into my power? Or strip it out of me?"

Lou's eyes bulged, "could they do that?"

"Souls flying around willy nilly, folding a pocket universe like setting up a tent…"

"Motherfucker! The spell on your chest! What if that's how they're doing it? What if it's not Mickey?"

Nick shook his head, "they'd need something I'm con… fuckfuckfuck!"

"You think they may be using Frank?" Areen asked even as Nick shook his head.

"Then what are you…say…ing?" Julius asked, crouching before the young man, Nick knowing he'd just reached the same conclusion he had, after all, Julius knew exactly what happened.

Holding his gaze, Nick shook his head, "I don't know... I need to search their encampment."

"Like hell kid! You're not going..." Lou barked in protest.

"Not physically... scrying the timescape."

"You can't Nick... the shit you've done these last couple days, using your powers is gonna kill you..."

Nick looked up into Lou's jade green eyes, his own crinkled with pain and something Lou would've sworn looked like resignation. "No, it won't... scrying's easy... I know I pushed it a little lately but searching the 'scape's like breathing," he explained, "good to know you care though... thanks."

Lou shook his head, "dumbass," he muttered.

"Takes one to know one," Nick countered with a soft groan.

"Boys and their banter," Elder grunted, grasping Nick by his arm and lifting him out of the chair, "come... I must see this spell," she led him back into his room slamming the door behind them as she ordered him, "out of your clothes."

"Julius, Lou, please, continue, I must be able to tell Khazeer, Wellyn and Wee everything you both have noticed or learned."

Knowing there was nothing else they could do, they returned to the table leaving Nick in the hands of the Elder healer, hoping she could do something to keep him safe if he had to use his powers again.

Nick wriggled out of his t-shirt and down to his boxer briefs as the ancient goddess waved her hand over an area of the wall, making the room painfully bright.

"Ah.. Ahr…" he grimaced as he struggled to bring something forth, their eyes meeting across the room, hers filled with curiosity and suspicion, his with something close to consternation. He frowned, took a breath, and opened his mouth again, this time closing his eyes as he let the sound roll up and out of him, "Ahhrmed," he tilted his head, his eyes still closed so he missed the popping of hers in surprise, "Airmed," he nodded and smiled then looked at her once more, impassive expression. "Airmed, I have stitches…"

"So I see," she snarked, peering close to the burn track around his neck and deep in his chest where his pendant sat, "and my fool brother's handiwork."

"I made him do it," he defended the ancient druid, "but I meant these," he turned, showing her the line of black nylon ties down the right side of his spine.

She hissed, "they've been torn again and again, why did you not use her blood?"

He shook his head, "I don't know." He turned back, showing her the spell carved into him, "can you read this? I feel as if I should be able, but…"

She bent at the waist and ran her hands down either side of his abdomen, leaving the hair colorless in their wake. Her lips pursed as she directed him onto the bed then met eyes with him.

"You are losing yourself to him," she whispered.

"I know," the admission seemed to break something inside, his hands shook, his breath came fast and choked as though trying to swallow sobs, "it didn't… it tried but Frank said there wasn't room, so it went to him. Is it the darkness Airmed? Is it the darkness taking me over? Will I fall to it?" he pleaded.

458

Her normally stern and almost comedic frenetic energy was nowhere to be found as she motioned a chair to come to rest under her backside.

"You should not know my name child, even Cathbad has likely forgotten it…" she soothed with a gentle hand on his forehead.

A soft smile turned up half of Nick's mouth, "you were one of mother's most beloved," his eyes fell closed and his breathing steadied, "ahhhh the tales she would share…"

His voice drifted away, and she set to work, unspooling several lengths of light wax onto his front side, and pressing it firmly to his skin. When his abdomen was covered she sat back, watching as the texture of his hair showed up first, then was replaced by the signs and sigils of the spell.

Once the copying was done, and the wax put back in her bag, she set about removing the stitches and sealing his wounds before churning a crystalline vial between her hands until it was soft and flexible as plastic. She pinched a spiral to the top and stuck it into his vein, filling it with his blood.

Nearly full to the top, she held the oblong bag up to one of the illuminated panels in the room and frowned. There wasn't much she could tell by sight, until she got to her lab and was able to analyze the content properly, but his blood was heavy and though properly red, felt more viscous than the samples she'd taken from Dylan or Shep.

She unwound the spiral and sniffed, the scent was properly metallic. Finally she stuck her finger into it then into her mouth. She was prepared to wince, prepared to spit it out, prepared for something bitter or caustic, but it was just blood, human blood, but just blood. *He asked about the darkness…* she nodded, sealed the end, and set it in her kit where it hardened back to crystal again. Next, she returned her educated gaze to her patient.

With the color erased from the hair on his chest and belly she looked close, frowned, and nodded. By sight alone, there were tens of thousands of tiny divots in his skin, so small very few, if any would think them anything but the texture of him.

"Fffilth!" she cursed, running her hands over the arm closest to her, the scarring there much more prominent. Small cuts made over and over down the paths of his veins as Tur or Ne'Min tried to feed the boy to their firdureen, to breed it within him. She knew the signs. Over the centuries, nay millennia, she'd seen enough corpses subject to their failed experiments.

Humans stolen from their own world by the thousands over the years; men, women, children, infants, fetuses, the aged, the pious, the evil, the sadistic, the holy, the innocent and the damned, none survived but this one. *But has he survived or is his death merely protracted now?* she wondered, then added, *is that what is draining him, or is there something I cannot see?*

As if in answer to her unvoiced questions, Areen entered the room handing a small crystal to the Elder. "He was insistent." She said before leaving.

"Knothead. I have no time for your cryptic…"

"He's dying again yes?"

The Elder gave a curt nod, "he said something might be trying to strip his powers, but he knows not what."

"He knows."

"Do you?" she asked feeling her heart flip with her brother's silent nod. Anything able to keep his acerbic personality from spewing out his mouth, must be dire.

"Well what is it?" she asked.

"He capitulated."

"No," she gasped, her eyes falling closed while hot fear fell into her belly. "For all that is holy…"

"Made unholy by the betrayal spreading its disease through our entire world while laying waste to the last of the Bedowen forests as we speak."

"Does he know?"

"The bitch corrupted an agreement made in sound faith, with an open heart and has unleashed it into our world!" he whispered, exhausted by all he'd done to learn what had caused an almost seismic shift in the level of power over the lands.

"Unleashed?" The Elder frowned.

"I know little more than it was born of firdur, infused with its very beginning… Tur now has what we have long feared. You must find it and kill it… I have seen it draw from him till nothing remains and then nothing will remain of either of our worlds."

"Cathbad," she began to protest, "an infant knows nothing of the purpose others will demand of it. Infants are innocent, I'll not have one butchered in homage to your fear."

"It is NOT SIDHE! Not Nyad, or Dryad or Druid! Nor is it HUMAN! It is OF THE DARK!" he countered, his crystal littered with his sap like spittle.

The Elder wisely bit her mouth closed, let her eyelids fall and nodded her head, "I will arrange a consultation."

"Heed me as you never have before sister! KILL IT, before it kills everything!"

"And if it IS bound to him?"

"We have *other* heroes *and* the younger one… a sacrifice may be required! You do as I say, or I will summon the foen winds…"

"Do not think to threaten me or I'll have you made toothpicks for Ula's sharks!"

"I will give you two days to have the creature slain. Beyond then Khazeer will demand to know why you have not done it, and will do it himself."

He knew better than to threaten his sister, incurring the wrath of the goddess of healing was not to be taken lightly, and Airmed had never taken kindly to her brother's interference in anything affecting her charges.

She fought to control her fury and almost did until the crystal in her palm snapped in two, the harmonic connection to her brother's mound severed.

Her head spinning, her enraged blood barely starting to cool, she finished her examination then woke Nick who apologized for falling asleep.

"Makes my work that much easier. Now, dress and finish eating while I check the others. I shall have all your results by morning. Until then, I want you all to stay away from anyone else. Give yourselves time to recover fully, there is no need to frighten your uncles."

Nick smiled and gave a faint laugh while dressing, "yeah… how's Ry by the way?"

"When I allow him to rejoin Wee, and when he sees you… I am certain his healing will be complete," she assured escorting him into the anteroom as Julius turned Lou by the shoulders and marched him toward the bedroom for his checkup.

"Yeah, yeah, yeah, I'm goin'." He grunted tousling Nick's already knotted hair, then giving him a good-natured shouldering as they traded places.

"How far'd they get?" Nick asked, resuming his place at the table though no longer hungry.

"All we know," Julius admitted, "how you saved the heroes, healed Lou, rescued us. How you saved me and destroyed the firdur, created the pocket universe, drew us here…"

Managed to create a pinhole in the space time of some of the oldest magiks known to even our kind so the three of us were not crushed against the barrier, Areen thought then asked, "Neither of you could cross the bridge?"

"Well, we got in, but," Nick shrugged, "it must've turned us around…" he stopped at the sight of the frown deepening on her face.

"It allows passage, or it does not."

"Seems like turning us around is pretty much not letting us across," Nick frowned filling his mind with memories of the incarnations his soul suffered, but he wouldn't allow her to see beyond them when she pressed her palm gently to his forehead. The ancients already altered Lou's memories, allowing them to unspool at the right time as events may dictate, but Nick had no desire to let anyone else in on the whole of their discussion. He'd tell them what he wanted when the time was right. After all, as the ancients intimated, if there was a possibility of winning this war, it would be through him, but if they knew how, they didn't tell him.

She had no idea what to expect when she sought his experience but the horrors of his incarnations, the despair darkening his soul, drifting through time like filaments of decaying gossamer was more than anyone could have anticipated, though why the first ones would have allowed the bridge to bring this torment to the fore, she could not fathom. Then she wondered if he was aware of them, but only for a split second. *They would have hidden them from him, but there must be a reason… perhaps something in the pains will help with the tasks ahead*, she mused removing her hand.

"What did you see?" Nick asked before Julius could.

Her brows furrowed and she shook her head, "Nothing I have ever seen before… was there anything new to you?"

"No." He patted her hand then cocked his head to the side, "Have you heard from Liri?"

"She has spoken with the Felesians, Jinx has agreed to allow those of her pride to fight alongside us if they will, and Wee, this morning heard from the Therianthropes. They have sent out messengers to collect willing warriors from nearby villages as well. All will be headed here if they are not already on their way."

"And our… other friends?" he asked.

A sly smile crept over the queen's face, "the womb has been set ablaze. Tropus and Boaz will screen all would be attendants with the utmost care."

"Excellent!" He leaned in kissing her cheek before bringing her hand to his lips. "There may yet be reason to hope."

Her smile, wan though it was, brought light to his heart as she rose and headed toward the bedroom, all three of them knowing she was going to see what she could learn from the son of Conchobar.

"Come Heru," Julius smiled with his hand out.

Nick's soft smile both warmed and worried the Sidhe captain's heart as he took his hand and rose, far too many cares racing through his mind.

"Meleth," Julius' finger turned his face so they were eye to eye, the crow's feet that shouldn't be there at all let alone so deep brought pain to his heart, "we know nothing for certain yet, and when we do, we will decide the best course of action. You could never have known..."

Nick shook his head, his eyes glazing as he grasped the warm calloused hand, pressing his lips then cheek into it. "The soul, it knew something... something I no longer recall... that's why it made Frank send me back to Terra," his breath shook, "it was here, but I can't find it..." he tapped the side of his head.

"It was important... the 'why' of it... something they forgot or didn't know... and now I don't remember either," his breath caught in his throat as he grasped the Sidhe's face between his hands pressing their lips together as fear-born tracks ran from his eyes, and oblivion-born desperation drove his heartbeat so hard Julius could taste it.

"What have I done?" he whispered into his lovers' mouth.

"Tell me you believed it to be the right thing?" Julius asked with a caress to his stubbled cheek.

Unable to speak for the lump in his throat, Nick nodded, his eyes closed, his inner world straining not to break apart.

"Look at me," Julius' whisper was a command he couldn't disobey.

Their eyes met and the room spun around them leaving them

sheltered in a warm glade just outside the heart of the Bedowen. They were alone, the sun shining green gold through the umbrella like leaves of the ancient trees. Their uniforms were battered, blood stained and centuries ago broken in as the two sat on a petrified bit of tree trunk.

"Why now?" Julius asked.

Oemir shook his head, "there are many things informed only by instinct until destiny has had the time to determine which way it will move."

The eventual Captain of the Guard smiled, holding his love's hand, "What did you see?"

"Nothing," Oemir answered, and it was both the truth and a lie. He had *seen nothing, the nothing that came after the war.*

"Then there is nothing about which to be concerned," Julius smiled, wrapping his love in his arm. They both knew he was making light, clinging to his ingrained belief in a mutable destiny, if the circumstances were right.

"As always I do appreciate your perspective my love," he smiled in defiance of knowing he would be the one to bring the end to everything. It was for him as it would one day be for one of his descendants, he always knew which visions were unalterable and which were only possibilities. This one, this one would come to pass. The end of all things would come, and he would be the reason.

Nick smiled, his forehead against Julius', his arms around the Sidhe, holding him close enough to synchronize their heart beats.

"Were I capable of it, I would happily tell you all of the universes could not contain my love for you," he murmured with a tender nibble to the Sidhe's lips.

Julius ran his hand to the back of Nick's neck, "Words are ephemeral wisps, you've already told me," he pulled his love close, lips to his ear, "in every way that matters."

Pain marred the elder Emerson's face, "I want to say it, I want you to hear it… you deserve to hear it." He rested his head in the crook of the Sidhe's neck, "how long has it been Julius? How long since I've told you I love you?"

"Far too many an age."

Nick nodded, "you deserve better. Without a soul one can't love, can't hate, can't feel," Nick sighed, wrapping his hand behind the Sidhe's head, bringing him in, holding him tender captive while his other hand snuck under his clothes, caressing his silken skin.

"Then if you could feel those things, what would you say meleth?" His voice smiled while he held Nick close, his cheek against the young man's temple, his hand absently stroking his back.

"What would I say?" Nick asked.

"Mmm hmm."

More than willing to give the Sidhe what he deserved, he answered as truthfully as he could, "If I could feel those things… I'd tell you that never could I love another as I do you. I could not thank all the gods and goddesses enough for bringing our hearts together. And thank you for putting up with me for so long… if I could have chosen a different way, I never would have left you."

"We both have known the pain of what must be done over what one wishes could be," Julius smiled, his eyes closed whether in memory or fantasy, not even he could say with certainty, "though I have longed for ages to hear you tell me again."

The pair stiffened, their attention immediately drawn to the door and down the hall.

"Someone comes," Julius wheeled, shoving Nick behind him, his short sword drawn.

"By the pricking of my thumb'," Nick muttered and checked the timescape, his hand lighting on the Captain's shoulder, "S'okay, s'just D. Probably exploring," he cocked his head to the side watching his uncle's outline seem to stumble along the corridor, "or delirious."

"Shall I retrieve him to his sickbed?"

"No," Nick frowned, "if anyone sees you they're likely to realize we're all back, and I'm not ready for that yet."

Julius nodded locking the suite's main entrance before entering the bedroom to do the same. Areen and Airmed spoke in hushed voices over an unconscious Lou, who lay with a towel over his hips, breathing easy in spite of the occasional shake of the head, moan, or grunt passing his lips.

"He's been through horrors Elder," Nick grimaced, "would you be able to help take the sting out of his trials?"

"He said the same of you both," she remarked as Julius moved into the adjoining suite, locking it too.

At the curious look from the queen, the Sidhe Captain explained, "the eldest of the seniors is prowling the halls, it may not be an accident he is on this level." He turned to Nick, "what are his gifts? Can he see you? Sense you?"

"Not as far as I know," Nick shook his head, "he gets visions, and like my queen," he nodded to Areen, "is able to access the minds of those he touches…" he huffed, his lips tilting up, "though he is nowhere near as adept or kind about it as you are. Where's Wee?"

"Screening the villagers along with Tierus… do you believe he could help?" she asked.

"Yeah," Nick shook his head, "but better to keep him where he is… if we need him he'll know. No other duty would stop him."

"There is an enchantment sublimating his senses," Areen advised then explained, "to ease his fretting over the Son of Steven."

"Ah," Nick nodded, "yeah well, if I need him, no enchantment can stop me reaching him."

"This I believe," Areen whispered, "Nick… I have need to ask…"

The smile that turned his lips was neither sad, nor wry, nor sinister, but somehow something very different, perhaps a kind of wise and almost dark knowing the fourteen-year-old boy she'd met mere days ago, should have had to wait decades if not centuries to earn, "we are all of us… our knowledge is here… poorly organized, but available."

She swallowed hard, a sadness of ages in her eyes as if it was a new thing, "and what of Frank?"

"He is all of us as well."

"That cannot be child!" Airmed hissed rising to her feet and pressing her presence into his personal space, seeking to cow him, but without success.

"It is," Nick nodded.

"Does he know what's going on here?" Areen asked wondering if there should be a binding spell put on the younger, in order to keep him safe from those who might seek to usurp him to determine or somehow undermine their plans.

"He's not allowed." *Yet.* Nick answered, prickling inside over the ease with which the queen simply decided to 'enchant' others, as if she had the right to make unilateral decisions of such delicate nature.

"And what do you know of him and his deeds?"

"Enough to be almost mortally frightened for him." His oblique answer surprised them all.

"Almost?" Areen and the Elder asked.

Nick gave them a single nod, something weighty in his gaze, "almost," he repeated.

13

With light from the outside finally visible from the seemingly never-ending staircase, Frank pressed his back to the wall. His lungs pulling in the crisp, clean air like a bellows while Poe hovered near the entrance, effectively fanning fresh air toward him. For the first time in what felt like far too long, his mind was quiet, and clear. It was like having the house all to himself, and he smiled.

Dirt and sweat streaked his reddened face as he looked down at his shirt, darkened with singe from the heat of being so close to the magma.

"They made it look so easy," he panted, the scene where Frodo and Gollum faced off inside Mount Doom racing through his mind.

Before him, Poe squawked, and he nodded.

"Yeah, but I need a vessel."

The avian squawked again then chirped and trilled, leaving the youngest Emerson eyeing him with deep surprise.

"You sure?" he asked as his old, feathered friend perched back on his shoulder and rubbed its beak against the side of his head. "Okay... it won't hurt you will it?" he asked and received a gentle reprimand in the form of a nip to his ear. "Alright, alright... but you're gonna hafta break Mickey's spell," he explained pulling his shirt off, revealing the carvings she'd made into his chest and belly.

Again the raven broke into a tirade, part of Frank was amazed he could actually understand, and the other part, the one closest to the forefront of his mind didn't think twice about. After all, Oemir had been raised among his mothers' ravens and all the denizens of the forest. He knew their languages as he knew his own as well as the one his most recent incarnations spoke.

"I know it will… but if he can be saved we must, he may not be a friend, but he has been an ally and I'm not a murderer. He did, after all, swear his sword to our cause, and so far has been true."

The raven tilted its head, eyeing him curiously even as he nodded and pressed back against the warm stone; squinching his eyes shut but opening his chest and belly to the razor-sharp talons coming straight for him.

--

In a side room from the Elder Healer's apothecary Julius and Nick worked efficiently, grinding herbs, leaves, and flowers into a paste to be mixed with a gray clay steaming in a head sized cauldron.

Julius grinned as Nick stuck a finger into the clay tasting it while nodding. "Thought so."

"Thought what?" Julius asked, pinching some lavender and borage leaves to add to his increasingly viscous mixture.

"Same clay we got at home, Wee 'n Ry like to put it on their faces and stuff, especially if they're getting zits, or wounds that look dirty and maybe infected."

"Zits?"

"Pimples... spots of nasty that get all red and gross."

"Ah... impurities that come to the surface."

"Yeah," Nick nodded, "much better way to say it. You think this'll help?" he asked.

"Do you not?" the Captain of the Guard asked, amazed by the change in the young man.

Nick shrugged, "I know it's supposed to," he winced, his hand moving to his belly. "When it dries it'll just flake off."

"What is it?" Julius asked, noting the young man's discomfort, "once we add the sap of the rubber tree it will be much more stable."

"Like a wetsuit... neat," Nick acknowledged then winced again, "What the hell man?" He muttered lifting up his fresh blouse only to find a giant "X" over his chest and stomach as if made by two sets of four fingered claws. "FUCK!" he barked scooping out a warm handful of the clay and carefully daubing it over the fresh wounds. "Shit!"

"Avian," Julius noted.

"Yeah, it's Poe... he did it to Frank..."

"For what purpose?" the Sidhe crouched before him, wrapping his torso in clean linen to keep the new wounds sealed.

"Break the spell I think..."

"Such as the one from earlier?"

"It would make sense. Let's just get this finished, there's too much to do still."

"Aye Heru," the Sidhe nodded, his face crinkled with concern as he rose, and they worked to complete their project.

Nick's head was spinning, his stomach rolling back and forth between being alright and needing to throw up.

"Spawning…" he huffed flopping down onto a sack of some kind of grain, "god how could I be so stupid!"

"How could you have known?" Julius asked without missing a beat.

Startling awake Dylan glanced around in the waning light. Dusk was a stone's throw away and for a moment he couldn't remember where he was or why he was here instead of wrapped in his bed, stoned out of his gourd on one of the Elder's potions. Dust motes hovered in the last remnants of day, and voices, however hushed drew his attention down the hall. Then he remembered. Nick. But his nephew's voice wasn't to be heard, the whispers were women's, and the faint snore was too deep to belong to a teenager.

Moving down the corridor he tested each of the doors with the utmost care. The last thing he needed was for anyone to remember him looking for Nick, especially if he wasn't able to conceal or get rid of the body, after all, he was far from healed and there was no way to tell if the teenager would return to his biological age or if he'd stay a physical adult after death.

"If ANYONE should have known it's ME!" He rose, his hands squeezing through his still damp hair, "if we lose its MY FAULT, MY DOING…" he shook his head, "if I could just find what I knew before!"

"No my king… you know as well as I…"

But Nick couldn't or wouldn't hear him. All he could hear was the rage in his head reminding him the end of trillions of trillions of lives in two universes was his doing.

"Frank was right… or the others, they MUST have been…how could I have been so fucking DUMB!"

"You cannot…"

"THEN WHO ELSE JULIUS! You tell me WHO THE FUCK ELSE IS TO BLAME?!" he rounded on the Sidhe.

"Nick," he grasped the young man by the shoulders, forcing their eyes to meet, "there is no one to blame, this has been inevitable since the first spark came into existence, search the first of all your lives, you know the history better than any of us…"

He drew a trembling breath, shaking his head, a twist of his lips betraying some inner conflict he wasn't ready to speak yet, "…that all of life could be undone, if not by me, then by my own flesh and blood… my own… Jesus Christ I have a kid… I'm too old for this," he ran his hands through his hair again, "or is it too young? I don't know anymore."

"As your child, a product of all you are, how can you believe it would end all life? Can you believe a product of your own soul could hate so much, could desire…"

"Soul." Something clicked inside the young man and his expression turned a troubled kind of thoughtful. "Hear me out, when I went to Leanna, it was after Cathbad removed my half of the soul. Later, Frank said it didn't go back to me because there wasn't room. When Ne'Min had me captive, they put dark in me." He winced at Julius' quickly masked horror.

"We figure the dark's why it wouldn't go back. How could that affect a fetus?"

Julius cocked his head to the side, frowning his puzzlement, "Firdur, as far as any of our healers have ever learned, does not alter the makeup of its victim. The emotional and mental state certainly, but it has never been able to change what a person is."

"What about schades? They're not really Sidhe anymore, what changes them if not their allegiance to firdur?"

The Captain's gaze dropped and with it, his expression.

"Julius? What changed them?"

"You did my king."

With a finger under his chin, Nick raised Julius' face and gaze, "Oemir's curse."

"Yes."

"What was it?"

"You swore that the essence of all who gave allegiance to the dark should be eternally naught else but a shade of a Sidhe."

"A shade of.. so more than a spirit, but less than a living being, most likely without a soul, or one so corrupted as to be less than Sidhe."

Julius inclined his head, "Will the curse affect the child?"

Nick flopped back down, "Hopefully not, a baby can't make a choice like that. Look let's assume, at best, it only got genes from me. Whatever else it gets would come from Leanna."

"My love, this is *not* a good thing, any of her remaining soul has fallen to darkness, and through her soul, the child may well be born into it."

476

"The soul's the thing, if the kid has one, there's hope."

"And if they do not?"

"It might not be as bad as we think… I'm functioning just fine, I'm quite practical…even with firdur literally in my veins."

"You always have been practical my king. Let us hope the child is endowed with your nature. Without it, they will have only its mothers hate and malice…"

Nick huffed, "Oy, let's leave the soul out of it for the moment and consider the nature of the people. It does still have access to my nature… if genetic memory's really a thing… if I can tap into that I might be able to balance him or her." He frowned, "though it would mean I'd have to deal with Leanna, see if she can be convinced to let me be part of its life."

Julius's raised eyebrow would've been funny under normal circumstances, but these times were anything but.

"I've got nine months to get on her good side," Nick shrugged, "provided we survive this war."

"What if the child is already drawing from you my king? You are aging in such a way even you cannot control, there is silver in your hair and other marks of a long life full of adventures," Julius smiled in spite of his glassy eyes. "Certainly you noticed after bathing?"

Nick gulped, "let's leave that wolf out the door too huh? We got a war to win first."

The doubt in the Captain of the Guards heart wasn't allowed to touch his enigmatic expression, "You are correct."

With butterflies flitting through his chest Nick nodded, "Of course I am."

He shot an easy smile at Julius then, wrapping his hand behind the Sidhe's neck, his thumb caressing the angle of his ear, he pressed their heads together.

"There is something you should be reminded of when it comes to Sidhe women my king." He motioned to the bench, sliding the bucket of spalls back to Nick.

"This isn't going to be good news."

"No."

--

Leaving the youngest of the junior Emersons in the care of a pair of local wolverines, Poe took wing into the late afternoon sky, veering a hard right toward the caldera of a long dormant volcano, hoping the low vibration rumble he felt while under the fortress indicated the awakening of another old ally.

A strong pull in his breast shifted his attention. He would have to leave the nest alone for the time being. He turned again, taking another look at the unconscious human child and its protectors before gliding effortlessly through the veil into the world of men. Once there, he threaded his way through time and space, until he reached a place smelling of power, the place they were all living, and one lay close to death.

The scent of carrion drew him even closer, bringing joy as he followed it to the back side of the human nest where an adult male was playing with fire and smoke.

Poe dove down and perched on a planter where he squawked, trying to communicate with the human, but this one did not have the children's language skills.

"Well aren't you a big fella," the old human smiled then cut a slice of the raw meat and tossed it to him.

Poe caught it expertly, chirped his thanks, then perched on the human's shoulder.

"Oh boy, you *are* a big fella… just don't peck my eyes out okay?" he asked softly while cutting another slice for the avian.

"Hey Harry…" Mickey stopped short, "Poe…are they okay?" she asked the bird, slipping her hand down its breast until it perched on her hand.

"So that's Poe huh?" Harry asked giving him another slice of raw meat. "Do you know what he's saying?"

She shook her head, "he's not saying…" he swallowed the strip of meat whole then flew to the back door, perching on the handle and knocking on the frame with its beak.

"Well, that's pretty clear…" Mickey spocked her eyebrow and let him in.

"If he shits all over the place you're cleaning it up," Harry warned as they followed him up into the bedroom where Vahl still lay in the bed turning colder and grayer almost before their eyes.

With both Harry and Mickey watching, Poe perched on Vahl's chest and pulled back before letting out a squawk that literally shook the air between them all, his wings beating toward the Sidhe until the vibration swirled its way into the being who took his first deep breath in nearly a full day.

"What the fuck?"

"The boys said you were someone special!" Harry grinned then looked at Mickey, "keep an eye on him, make sure he's okay when he comes around… I'm gonna give this big fella a feast fit for a king!

C'mon Poe, you just saved our asses a shit load of trouble." He held out his hand then set the panting bird on his shoulder, taking him downstairs to give him a good feeding.

--

The door slammed open, sounding like a shotgun blast in the small three-shower section of the truck stop. Charles' heart skipped several beats then rocketed in his chest. He jumped so hard, his vinyl gloves, along with several layers of skin tore from his knuckles on the cement of the stall drain he was unclogging.

"Motherfucker," he hissed turning off his Maglite and stuffing it into his pocket.

"Mr. Brown?" Came a familiar voice.

He craned his gaze around the curtain and sighed, only momentarily glad to see Officer Stern before his spate of relief turned to low-grade fear.

"Officer," he greeted pulling the gloves off and tossing them into the trash before heading for the sink to wash his hands. "What's up?"

"I heard Len got himself a new bus boy who's been doin' him proud," he smiled leaning against the sink.

"Yes sir. A good day's work is good for the soul," he shrugged.

"'Ja get that from the pastor?"

Charles shook his head, "from my momma… pastor only kinda cemented it in." He grabbed some towels from the dispenser, "I don't mean any disrespect Officer Stern, but I got a lot of work to do. Diner's been hoppin' all afternoon, showers and bathrooms are sty's and I need t'get 'em ready for the dinner rush."

Stern nodded, "Sure thing, sure thing…I just need to ask a few more questions."

"Go for it."

"You ever heard of a guy named Ezra?"

Charles couldn't help it, he swallowed hard, he felt his blood drop to his feet, and he watched his face go ashy in the mirror as his mouth ran dry and he nodded.

"Yeah, I know him." Charles swallowed again, "he used to do fund raisers for the church."

"Big benefactor according to Mrs. Everett."

"Yep."

"You said 'used to'?"

Sweat poured down Charles face, "yep, pastor stopped working with him a few months ago, vibe I got was they had a falling out."

"Oh yeah? Do you know what about?"

"Not for sure, why do you ask?"

Officer Stern reached into his pocket and drew out his cell phone.

"Well, see, a colleague got in touch with me about your friend," he fiddled with his phone some more then paused.

"What friend?"

"C'mon son," Stern scoffed, then scrolled some more before turning the screen toward Charles and starting the video.

"Huh," Charles grunted at the vid of Nick, standing in the middle of 6th Street, surrounded by a crowd cheering, and jeering at him, and a cop with his gun trained on the young man, urging him to put down a long, slim, silver blade he had pressed against his own palm.

"Did Nick tell you about this?"

"No sir, wasn't our policy t'ask folk how they got to be where they are in life, especially not when we're evaccing for a flood."

"Yeah, you told me about that… that's when you met."

Charles smiled, "yeah… he had something so… something no other kid I ever knew, ever had…"

"So you said before," Stern nodded, "so… tell me again… how'd you two wind up running away together?"

Glad the cop had finally gotten around to it, Charles nodded and repeated the exact same story he'd told them the other day. The exact same story he and Nick rehearsed over and over for hundreds of miles while on their way home.

What he didn't expect was the next picture on his phone, the shot of Ezra with the words "child trafficker" carved into him.

"Sweet Jesus!" he gasped. Not because the truth of what Nick did was suddenly fresh in his mind, but because it'd obviously taken some time for the body to be found and the picture he was looking at could well have come from any horror movie; purple, black, bloated with the skin having split in several places, most likely due to the heat.

His body spasmed as a cascade of memories came tearing through him. The electrodes in his penis and up his rectum while Ezra forced him to suck him off, then he couldn't see anything but the corpse instead of the living man.

"Oh shit…" he gagged, turning, and vomiting into the drain he'd been working on.

"The carving says…"

"Child trafficker, I saw it…"

"Do you have any idea…" Stern started.

To his chagrin, Charles nodded, "there was a lot of scuttlebutt, lots o'rumor," he spat then turned his eyes to Officer Stern, "it's Texas sir, lots of border kids moving through the state."

"Could that be the reason the pastor broke off with him?"

"Well," Charles swallowed then hocked out a gob of bile before rinsing his mouth, "any man of god worth his salt couldn't let himself do any kind of business with someone who did that kind of thing now could he?"

Letting the non-answer slide for the moment, Stern swiped the photo back to the video of Nick and held it before Charles again, "You see that blade?"

"Uh huh."

"Have you seen it since you've known Nick?"

"Uh uh," he shook his head but broke out into a new layer of sweat, "but officer if you're thinkin' Nick had somethin' t'do with what got done to Ezra, I gotta say… I think you'd be barkin' up the wrong tree."

"What makes you say that? I mean y'only met the boy that night then took off with him the next day… what did you really know about him at all?"

Charles shook his head, "Well, given that picture, there was an awful lot of blood around, kinda all over the place from what I could see, and Nick, well when we picked him up, he was wearing the same clothes as in that vid, and only a few specks on him from his own wounds…"

"You think you woulda noticed…" Stern started.

"All due, yeah, I sure as hell woulda noticed if he had an excess of blood on 'im. We look for it when we pick folks up, see if they been in fights, been injured, rolled, so we can get 'em whatever help they might need, so yeah. I'd'a noticed. Besides…" he paused, blushing deeply, "he was beautiful, I could hardly take my eyes off him at all. So, yeah," he gave a soft smile to the cop, "I'd'a noticed."

--

"They hid it away from him?" Khazeer asked once Areen closed and locked the door behind her.

"If there was interaction at all, they hid it from Lou as well."

"They left nothing?" Wellyn asked.

The queen of the Fierowen shook her head, "The only certainty is that they succeeded in crossing the bridge. As I already said, if there was any interaction with the first ones, it was…" she frowned, "inaccessible to me, so too it must be with them."

"What of their trials? Were you able to glean any of their histories that could be exploited?" Khazeer asked.

"To a point," Areen sighed, "long has it been since I touched a human mind…"

"Which of them do you propose is human?" Khazeer asked softly, then dismissed the question, asking instead, "but why, if they were allowed to cross, would their interactions have been hidden?"

The queen of the Fierowen shook her head, "perhaps with them close to the fore they believed clarity of purpose may be lacking?"

"Or confidence," Wellyn suggested, "he *is* a child, even the most staid of warriors may fall to fear, perhaps the first ones felt they might not rise to the challenge?"

"Perhaps," she mused, "either way, there are several other happenings about which you must be informed."

Khazeer raised an eyebrow, urging her on.

"Cathbad and the Elder, that something is draining the Oemir, a shift in the energies... I overheard Cathbad say. Then last night, Oemir, Nick... what he did," she paused, still barely able to believe the young human man could not only harness, but utilize such power, "... he opened a pinhole in the wards so we could pass through them... I thought they would have been weaker below ground, but they were not. We would have been crushed had it not been for the boy... so much you must... you both must learn. We cannot lose..."

"Do you believe the boy is inadequate to the task?" Khazeer asked.

"And if so, what of the younger one?" Wellyn added.

She shook her head, "for so long we have waited, Ilirya watching, guiding... only to arrive here, at this moment with the first ones..." she shook her head again.

"And they gave no indication of assent or denial of Oemir's request?" Wellyn asked again, before the king could.

Areen circled the table, her lips pursed, her breathing deep and controlled, her response measured, "As far as I am aware, there was no interaction other than the testing of them by the bridge. They survived so we must assume they were at least noticed. Perhaps their purpose was enough to inform the ancients, so no interaction was necessary."

"And from the son of Conchobar?" Khazeer asked.

"His wisdom allowed passage with ease, but still, no interaction." She shook her head, her gaze far away, saddened by the torments she'd been privy to.

"So it is likely they may well have denied the petition for assistance?" Wellyn asked.

"They are the first ones," Areen frowned, "we must act as if they have, but hold to hope they have not."

"That is a fine line to walk Heru," the master at arms frowned.

"Indeed," she acknowledged, trying to shove aside her empathy.

It'd been many an age since the species of man departed this world to claim their own, and just as many since she'd been subject to what humans were capable of doing to suppress, oppress, and repress their own kind. They were fierce and when not equipped to use their ferocity for the benefit of others, they were often driven by craven or cowardly motives to benefit none but themselves.

The few images she'd seen of the boy's most recent incarnations and his tribulations were no fault of his own, they'd been driven by Ne'Min and his quest to destroy Oemir's very soul. But the son of Conchobar's was a different matter.

There was no direct connection to his origin's soul, merely the bloodline, he was just another man born of a continued strand of genes. He had no gifts, no powers, no connection to the universe itself and yet what he'd endured, what he'd survived at the hands of those who were supposed to care for him, confirmed his connection to the first heroes just the same.

"So my queen…" Khazeer brought her back to the moment with a kiss to the back of her hand, "what counsel would you propose given the knowledge you now have?"

"Contact Cathbad, advise him to find the soft spots and send word through the nightbirds with orders for all species to be prepared to escape to Terra if we fail to hold the line here," she took a deep breath, "and pray the goddess sends her emissary to find the half-breed so the human guardians can be marshaled and prepared."

Wellyn and Khazeer shared a look she knew too well, "good, then we are of a similar mind," she nodded then leaned forward between the king and his master of arms, "if whatever is draining Oemir of his power succeeds, we must be prepared to take advantage of the tragedy to keep the races united…"

"And motivated."

"Think you Frank could be…persuaded to take up the mantle?" Khazeer asked.

Areen nodded, "to avenge his brother, the first keeper of the soul, I believe he would accept no other course of action."

"Good, then we have an alternative in case the Oemir himself falls."

"Again." Wellyn added as the others nodded.

--

Far to the north and east, at the horizon, a row of dark gray clouds, as a seemingly unending line of claws crept up, over the rim of the sparsely inhabited terrain. On Aderyn, the ominous creeping of those strange and bone chilling segments slithering their way from the wastelands toward the Dragonbow mountains, any village, town, city, or territory before its approach was in danger of falling not only under its pall, but its spell. On Terra, west of the San Andreas mountains, near the tectonic fault of the same name, an identical formation began to seep upward from a breach in the barrier between worlds. And as the juxtaposed rotations continued their dance, the dark strove to make its way through however many more areas of permeability it could feel and exploit.

--

"How long?" Nick asked, as Julius spread the warm clay mixture up his arm and over the shoulder, not unlike the way he'd soothed the soldier's injuries with the balm only days ago.

"As long as it stays. It will be difficult to say at this point, it may melt, or flake or peel off too easily," the captain of the guard said.

"I should get a little sparring in… see if it holds up yeah?"

Julius nodded, his mind clearly elsewhere as he worked the mixture over Nick's back while Nick slathered it over his chest and belly, "it feels nice, I can see why Ry and Wee get into it." He stopped abruptly, his hands slowing, suddenly distracted as he rubbed the mixture into the fine whiskers over his face.

The faintest whisper of breath caught his attention as Julius turned back toward the storage jar, his gaze fixed on his clay covered hands.

Without warning the soldier turned toward him, his gaze hard, "how many times meleth?" It was less a question and more of a demand to know, but Nick didn't need to ask what he was referring to. Even before learning of his and Frank's shared destiny, death was never far from the forefront of his mind.

"I don't know," he shook his head, "thousands, maybe as many as ten," he shrugged.

"How can you…" he stopped and hung his head, hiding his confusion, fear, and loss from the young half human. "How many have you memories of?" he whispered.

Nick hesitated but found he couldn't lie, at least not to Julius, "some."

The ancient being raised his gaze, "but the queen…"

"There are things no one needs to know. She learned what I allowed her to."

"And me?"

Nick took a deep breath and let it spool out slowly, "you sense too much already… why should I cause you more pain?"

"Why should you bear it all, alone?" Julius' voice was little more than a whisper, his clay coated hand reached up but stopped before touching the young man before him. "The millennia I've spent alone, waiting in hope for your return, even as Ilirya kept watch… at least she could see you, hear you, and in even a small way be with you," he sighed turning to lean back against the workbench..

"I don't know any words deep enough to tell you how sorry I am you went through so much, alone, for so long."

"That you had not even the faintest inkling of my existence at all?" Julius added.

"Or Liri's if that's any consolation."

"It is not."

With nothing he could say, Nick found himself drawn to a small window looking out into the yard and with a swipe of his hand, the crystalline pane went from frosted to clear. "I think maybe I got lost somewhere along the way…" he muttered.

Outside, in the last remnants of daylight, there were Sidhe of the Fierowen milling, sprinting, fencing, fighting, and fitting new and refurbished armor. There was a line in the distance where he could feel Wee doing whatever the king had tasked him with, and he suddenly wanted, more than almost anything else, to see his uncle's familiar face, look into those Emerson eyes and know somewhere, somehow, someone understood why he couldn't speak those things he couldn't. Wee would feel it, and might have the words to explain what Nick could not.

His thoughts were a melancholy maelstrom of possibilities, competing with probabilities, with the few paths he did at least partially recall and with the desperate need to remember what he'd known when he gave in to Leanna.

How long he stood at the window made no difference, in this moment, time itself meant nothing to him. For the first time since he froze Tommy and Bruce while they manhandled Frankie up the side of the dumpster outside Robert Townsend Elementary school, a little more than five earth years ago, he just didn't care anymore.

He knew how this war would end as sure as he knew how almost every one of his previous incarnations had ended. Over and over again he gazed around the yard before him, taking in faces, smiles, frightened eyes, stoic resolve, and fierce determination, as if he could fill himself up with their emotions, knowing he may never see any of it ever again.

"Forgive me meleth," Julius whispered, his warm fingertips feather light on his shoulder.

"What have you done that needs forgiving," he nearly whispered, unable to turn to look to the one person in whose eyes he couldn't bear to see pain.

"Nothing," Julius' hands finally lay atop his shoulders as he leaned back against the Sidhe's warmth.

"Well okay then," he barely breathed as the door was thrown open, startling them both. Julius whirled, keeping himself between Nick and the haggard, almost beastly visage of an illness mad human who could only be Dylan Emerson.

Nick, in spite of startling, barely turned his head. Reflexively he'd scanned the timescape the instant he heard the latch and knew who it was. He also knew something was horribly wrong with the older man.

"Dylan," Julius greeted in spite of his hackles having risen to full alert. He stepped forward, into the man's deep gasps of fevered breath and rattling lungs, "what may I help you with? Water? Food? Help you back to bed?"

"Where is he?" the eldest Emerson grumbled, a glint of light against a short sword in his right hand as he made to push the soldier out of his path.

"You are ill son of Oemir, your kin will need you well," he tried to persuade.

"Where the fuck is that little shitbag!?" he roared sniffling against a head full of congestion while he looked around Julius to peer closely at the other Sidhe in the room.

In spite of his condition he was strong, and half shouldered, half pirouetted around Julius until he stood face to face, blue eyes to blue eyes with Nick. "Where the fuck is he!?" he demanded once again, this time the tip of his blade poking into his nephew's neck, just under his jaw. "D'I know ya'?" came under his breath.

Julius made to subdue the delirious man but a wave from Nick stayed him.

"He is in the desert, searching the corridors of possible futures," Nick's answer and demeanor was so foreign in the moment even Julius couldn't contain his surprise which showed in the arching of his eyebrow and the subtlest upturn of a single corner of his mouth. "What do you want with him?"

Dylan leaned in, peering closely at him, his balance wavering as the stink of sickness rolled off him in viscous waves. "Gonna cut 'is fuckin' heart out…shit thinks he's gonna…" he stopped and shook his head, his gaze sizing this strange Sidhe up, wondering if he could win against him.

"Tell me," Nick urged softly, only to get a heavy shake of sweat soaked greasy hair in return.

"Show me," the younger Emerson smiled, the heel of his hand pressing to Dylan's forehead in exactly the same way Dylan used his gift, and the queen had done to him.

In a heartbeat Dylan fell to the floor, out cold and Nick stood, dumbfounded, and deeply disturbed by what he'd seen and done.

"Meleth?"

"I didn't know I could do that… I'm not supposed to be able to do that, it's his power," his lips trembled and his eyes glazed as he met the Sidhe's curious expression. "Who am I anymore? What am I turning into?"

Julius bent and slung Dylan over his shoulders then stood eye to eye with Nick. "I believe you know the answer."

His brows furrowed, his teeth gnawing at his lower lip, his heartbeat growing heavier in his chest and louder in his head. He wondered if Julius could hear it.

He lurched to the door, opening it, and dashing a little ways up the hall to where they knew the Elder had put both Dylan and Shep to bunk.

"Did you learn what drove him to come kill you?"

"He's delirious with fever and infection."

"It's fortunate he didn't recognize you."

"Yeah," Nick opened the sick room door, happy to see Shep stir with their arrival.

"Hey," he greeted rubbing his hair into an Einsteinian mess as he sat up, "what happened?" he asked watching Julius turn to lay the elder man on his bed.

He no sooner crouched than he felt the human tighten up, wrap an arm around his throat and squirm an instant before something warm stuttered between his ribs.

Nick almost missed it. In an eyeblink Dylan was awake, tightening his grip around Julius' throat with his left arm while his right whipped a second blade out of his back pocket, flipped it open and slammed it into the Captain of the Guard's side.

"NO!" he shouted as the activity in the room froze. "Air..." he started, his inner sight instantly drawn to Elder healer on the timescape.

He saw her turn to learn who was calling for her, but she could see no one, so turned back to what she was doing.

Focused on keeping the people in the room suspended he turned

493

his attention to Dylan, scowling ferociously at the older man, his eyes ablaze with malice. Still, he sent a tendril of will to each of them, drawing or pushing them each backward a scant handful of seconds until they were as they'd been when he opened the door.

Before setting their little group free to move forward again he pulled the blade from Dylan's back pocket, tucking it into a thigh pocket of his breeches.

When they moved forward again and Dylan tried to get the upper hand against Julius, he was rendered almost immediately unconscious, and set gently onto the bed, and though undamaged physically, there was no question he'd been embarrassingly outclassed.

Shep gave a snicker while pushing himself to his feet and approaching the two Sidhe. "What was that about?"

"He is delirious with sickness, his desire was to find Nick and we believe, harm him. Have you any idea why?" Julius asked.

Shep shook his head, "he's been grumblin' and mumblin' on and off, but nothin' I could understand… where is the kid anyway?" he asked finally taking a good long look at the one standing behind the captain of the guard.

He walked straight over, a strange smile on his face as he leaned in, "that you kid?" he asked trying to see behind the clay camouflage to the changes in the young man, "it's the eyes, it IS you isn't it?"

"It is," Nick nodded.

"Whathefuck," the older man breathed reaching a hand up to the jaw he knew had to be a blend of the fine structure of many Sidhe, but the human characteristic of a strong growth of beard and moustache as well. "What the hell's happening t'you? Are you doin' that on purpose? What's that shit all over you… some kind of war paint?"

Nick smiled, "possibly."

"Why's he wanna kill ya?"

Nick gave a half-hearted shrug, "something they did to him while they had him, something in the darkness. I think you'll be safe, or we can get you into another room…"

"I'll hang here, keep a lookout for him till he's right again. He's gonna be right again, right?"

Wordless, the two Sidhe shared a glance before looking at the elder hunter.

"Yeah, alright," Shep nodded, "well, someone's gotta keep him from doin' somethin' he'll regret. I'll take the duty… least for now."

"Thanks Shep. How are you feeling by the way, any murderous impulses?"

"No more than usual," he grinned.

14

"Yeah... it's downloading now," Mickey nodded, the cell cinched between her shoulder and her ear, "ALL of them? Wow, thanks that's gonna be help... and yeah, about the sightings, I heard, in Kansas, town called Lawrence. Rolling waves of darkness."

"Yeah, like what almost got my brother... least that's what he said."

"Either of you see the bodies? They're usually punched full of..."

"Thousands of holes." The younger man finished.

"Yeah, how's he doing by the way, he had some intense bleeders."

"He's alright thanks."

"And you?" She asked closing her eyes against a flash of memory of his chest and back before she'd made his flesh transparent, "You manage to get rid of your... hitchhiker?"

He chuckled, deep and dripping with sarcasm, "Yeah thanks, so my brother said something about bright light to fend off the darkness?"

"Yep, brighter the better…"

"Flashlights'll do?" he asked.

Mickey shook her head as Vahl sat at the table with a cup of coffee warming his hands. "Glad you're back," she nodded to the Sidhe. He nodded but said nothing.

"Sorry," she apologized to the younger brother, "an… ally just walked in. Flashlights may be enough to buy you time to get away, but you're gonna need something order of magnitude… more. Searchlights, spotlights, football stadium lights, none of 'em are really enough."

"But on the website…"

"Did you read the fine print? Any man-made light can't stand up for long against it… it is LIVING, it IS dark… it's goal is to destroy all life, from what we understand, it wants perfection back."

"Perfection?"

"Perfect oblivion, perfect darkness, perfect void, like before the big bang," she grumbled watching as the last of the files finished downloading.

"I don't suppose it has a human form that's killable, you know… like a beautiful woman?" he asked then sputtered, "oh shit…that really didn't come out right."

Mickey felt her lip turn up in a grimace, "I sure as hell hope not. Look, this thing, it's pre-existence, of ANY kind, no planets no man-made gods, no concepts of self-contained emptiness, it's pre-primordial, it's eternal, what came before even the first atom breached the brane, do you get it? 'Cause if you don't there's no way to survive this if it gets into OUR universe. Right now it's taking out all the others and making its way toward us, these bits, and tendrils

497

its sending probing here, it's a claw scratching into the fabric of all existence getting ready to tear a hole so it can get through."

She could almost envision him on the other end of the line running his fingers through that long chocolate hair as comprehension began to dawn, even though it still wasn't enough.

"Got the files thanks... listen, if you guys are gonna head to Kansas to check it out, you gotta know it's a suicide mission."

"Believe me, it's far from our first, besides, we know the area pretty well, and a few of the people, hey you ever heard of Holy Oil?" he asked.

"Yeah, the oil that kept the menorah lit for the full eight days?" She asked as a voice in the background grumbled, "yes that would be it."

"You got someone else on the line?"

"No, he just has... really good hearing," the younger man's voice smiled, something in the timbre of it finally lighting the spark deep inside that she'd been resisting since thinking of him without his shirt on, and the feel of his skin beneath her fingers. It was different than the one his brother had lit, but just as intense. "You think it would do any damage to this 'living dark'?"

"Napalm works so yeah probably, at least to a degree," she nodded fanning some air into her t-shirt as she broke into the same kind of heat she'd felt when they'd met, "Jesus what the fuck is it with you two?" she panted.

"What do you mean?" he asked.

That strange and mildly gruff voice came through the line again, "she's sexually aroused, just as she was with," he paused, "when you first met."

"Oh come on," he grumbled.

"He's right," she sighed, "something about you two… are you from the other side?" she asked.

"Other side of what?"

"The veil, the Sidhe realm?"

"Sidhe realm, no… but we know someone who spent some time there."

"Must've rubbed off on you… anyway fire will eat it away so keep that holy oil handy."

"Napalm? Flamethrowers?" he interrupted.

"Yeah, but if you can't cover the whole thing… look man, until we get some solid intel and a plan, just don't engage, and tell your hunter buddies to just get the fuck out of there if any of you run across it. In the meantime, try to see if any of them have a way to seal this world off from any others. It can't be allowed to take hold here." She snapped herself back to the task at hand.

"We'll find out what we can and get back to you," he agreed, "you'll do the same right?"

"Yeah, just spread the word to anyone and everyone you can, warn them all, this is gonna go global. I promise you, Kansas isn't its first incursion, that's how we almost lost the first time." She exhaled, "Just you guys be safe alright?"

"You all too," he charged before disconnecting the line.

She looked at Vahl, "How do you feel?"

To her surprise his eyes went from yellow to blue to so dark brown they were almost black before settling on a strange dirty

499

yellow again, but he said nothing. Still, Mickey had her own gifts and could sense he was, right now, not capable of… "alive," he whispered into his cup and left it at that.

"What time does Charles get off?" Harry Jr. asked, entering from the living room where he was set up doing his own research while Harry senior, working in the den, leaned back to listen before getting up to stretch. He patted Vahl on the shoulder, "Good to have you back man."

Surprised by the young man's good will, he nodded, "Thank you."

She looked at the clock, "'bout ten minutes, you gonna pick him up?"

"With the dark having been sighted, yeah… I think it might be wise."

"Good, bring lights."

"Lightstones are the best hope any of us will have," Vahl looked up.

"Got any on ya?" junior asked.

"No, there may be some, if they have not been pulverized or incinerated."

"Where?" he asked.

"The other side."

"The other side." Harry senior and Mickey answered together.

Shaking his head Harry Jr. waved them off and left.

"Almost done." Jr. read, drawn to the back of the "rest area" where the long haulers could shower and even catch a nap somewhere that wasn't their truck.

At first he thought it sounded like water sloshing, but a few soft grunts and pants re-framed the rhythm to something all too familiar. With his heart sinking into his stomach he grasped his mini-Maglite in one hand and brass knuckles in the other.

In the narrow crack where the stall wall almost met the floor he saw familiar gym shoes half covered with lowered blue jeans behind bare feet.

The slappy flapping grew faster, whispery, "Yeah, oh god yeah... just a little more...harder son, harder!" brought a deep blush up to his cheeks as he tip-toed back toward the door.

"Oh god, now, now... turn!" the bare feet grunt-panted.

Those familiar gym shoes and bare feet traded places, "over, bend over..."

Then the heels of the shoes were lifted off the floor, and Harry Jr. was out the door, shambling stunned back to his car to wait.

--

"You can snarl and snap as much as you want, but I'm not gonna sit here and do nothing!" Frank argued with the pair of local wolverines keeping watch over him while he cleaned and cooled himself in a slow running streamlet. "Don't you get it? Time is running OUT! It's EVERYWHERE!" He couldn't remember ever having been as tired as he was, but he had to start somewhere, and the low caldera they knew as the roost wasn't far away.

While under the fortress he'd sensed so much, he knew the old allies were gathering and a new generation of hatchlings was about to emerge, but he needed to go North to the roost and find out if anyone still lived or had awakened there.

Night was coming too quickly, and he didn't have the same dark-adapted vision his big brother did to help him where the moonlight couldn't. Frank didn't really understand all the things happening to him recently, especially not while he was swimming in the dark, he was acting on a fidgety need to do SOMETHING, he just hoped whatever it was, would be the right thing.

What he'd felt and seen was still amorphous in his mind, but the feelings were so cold they burned.

The hate bit into his soul and tried to poison him, and he wasn't sure it hadn't succeeded. He could feel Nicky in the tower of the sun, he was empty and kinda dry like a seed husk toward the end of fall and he was angry.

He was angry for having given in to Leanna, angry and not knowing why he'd done it. And he was angry because Dylan wanted to kill him. He believed what the adults called a "fever dream" instead of trusting his big brother's firstborn to do the right thing. And though Frank knew Nick thought he'd sealed himself off from the younger boy, there were some things he'd never be able to hide from Frank, especially now.

Water glazed his eyes while he turned his mind away from the older boy's state. The longer they waited to act, the more certain Nick seemed to become he was going to be killed again, like he was in the first line, and then what would happen to Frank? He'd be left alone to try to resist the plans Khazeer, and his people had for them.

Harry, he thought, *he'll stick with me, he'll help… but what if they're right and Nicky has to die for me to step up so I can save the universes? I don't even have any real power, how can I save anything?* Frustrated by the defeatist thoughts, he turned his attention to the roost and started toward it, wiping the grime from his face with the tail of his shirt, barely missing the golden eyes watching from behind a small gathering of boulders.

She would follow him, it was preferable to going back to the great mother to suffer the company of the others of her kind. But first, she had an errand to run and didn't want to lose sight of the Oemir.

With a slight tilt of her head, she slithered along beside him until the edge of the dead scrub at the border of the Nahroehn and Bedowen forest was almost gone. She pursed her lips and flicked her tongue out, the fork striking the child just behind his right shoulder blade, there she smelled a recent wound where she could leave a drop of toxin without damaging him.

"Ow!" Frank grunted, reaching behind his head to scratch at the sudden stinging itch behind his shoulder. His vision clouded, his feet locking together as he fell to the ground.

From behind, the pair of wolverines approached as she made herself known to them.

In the language of the animals she bade them, "Guard him. My return will come before his."

Ever dutiful, the pair took up station on either side of the boy, one eyes front, the other eyes behind. It was a sacred duty to guard Danu's firstborn.

--

"I will accompany you," Julius nodded.

"No, you won't," Nick dropped a hand onto his shoulder even as the Sidhe soldier started to protest, "I need you to stay here,

Khazeer and Wellyn may be able to spar a bit, but they're not ready to fight yet. Wee's gotta be at his wits end, Ry's not up to peeing by himself from what the Elder said, Lou's still crashed from her sedation, and Dylan's out of his mind." Nick pointed out.

"Heru," Julius leaned in, his teeth clenched, "you are no fool, but you have been irresponsible…you are not yet equipped to use your powers in any…"

"I know," Nick agreed, a look of softness on his face, "I'm camouflaged and there's still some daylight left. They're right outside the wall, I can get myself hidden and under cover before dark falls…"

"No," Julius shook his head, his countenance stern.

"There's no choice. We need to know what they're planning."

"My king…" the Captain of the guard started. He knew well there would be no wiser way to approach the situation.

"That's an order!" Nick's voice was soft but commanding, "our greatest assets are inside this city and inside the tower. If I am gone into the night, every single able body MUST be ready to enact whatever defense Khazeer and Wee have cooked up. NO ONE person can be allowed to jeopardize this position."

Julius cocked an eye at him, "you know what they have planned?"

In his chest, Nick's heart gave two mighty thumps as the part of his mind that accessed Dylan's vision once again showed him the tower cracking and shattering in the darkness.

"No, but *MY* plan requires the tower. Their plans, whatever they are, must not be allowed to endanger it." He cocked his head, "For *me*, you MUST stay, protect all who are left of the Heroes, gather the others and call them to arms… even Tropus, ESPECIALLY Tropus." he urged, and before wasting another second in argument, simply envisioned everything and everyone on the 'scape still as stone. He took and left a kiss with his love, slung his pack over his shoulder and strode out of the city.

He knew he'd pushed limits in the last couple days, but in doing so he'd also been inspired to try other ways to use his growing abilities, hopefully without sacrificing his own essence.

Outside of the gates, his mind's eye focused on the encampment less than a quarter mile away, now bustling with agents of the enemies waiting for night to fall. He envisioned himself on the 'scape, wrapped in a bubble of his own energy, then willed himself to simply, "be there" even as the rest of the area remained still.

It took a few tries to gain more than a few inches of movement, but in spite of the sensation of literally being pulled from what felt like a sticking point, (he likened it to how taffy might feel when it's being pulled in two directions), he started to move.

--

As afternoon angled toward evening, in numbers no greater than two at a time, the citizens of the Fierowen who registered with Wee and Tierus, were assigned among several stations.

Those who passed Wee's senses and the Fledgling's records with flying-colors were assigned into the tunnels of the armory to clean and grease the necessary equipment.

Those whose motives or abilities were uncertain due to age, infirmity or inappropriate skills were sent to gather what means they could and distribute them evenly amongst those who remained at the Tower.

As for those who were skilled, strong and battle ready, they were already at the Dragonbow mountains, training others, and awaiting the signal to return.

Lastly, those whose allegiance was less certain, or clearly lay with either Firdur or the Schades, were assigned to guard the perimeter wall where the Mages would be able to keep an eye on them.

In their recovery room Wellyn girded the King into fresh armor then suffered himself to be aided by his lifelong friend, all before both of them were required to submit to being examined, poked, and prodded by the Elder Healer, to ensure the armor wouldn't add to their wounds.

"Calm yourselves," she grunted checking the fittings and corners, "you're like fledglings at your first tournament."

"Come now, it has been days you've had us lazing about while our citizens face the enemy on their own…" Khazeer began, his tone semi-playful until he was interrupted by something deep and dark in her gaze.

"At least two universes are at risk, are you so eager to see almost nine billion souls fall to the dark?"

Wellyn's jaw dropped at the number and his eyes sought confirmation from his king, who nodded

"I always told you they breed like mice," he shook his head.

"It's just as well our worlds are separating then yes?" the king's grin put his Master at Arms a little more at ease.

The Elder 'harumphed' but said nothing, she'd given voice to her concerns when Ilirya first found the children in their world and

506

knew nothing could change the current course of events. The only way out, as usual, was through.

--

His bubble seemed to sort of skip to a halt a few dozen yards outside the enemy encampment, his body vibrating and feeling a strange kind of weak he'd never felt before. He clenched his fists but felt a deep lack of strength wondering if he could even hold so much as a soda can before things started easing back to normal. In a few more seconds he breathed a sigh of relief and searched out a patch of gray to camouflage in as night came calling.

His position chosen, he settled in and breathed his awareness into the timescape, noting the living, the dead, schades, and the usurped. Vestiges, after having dropped off their hosts, slithered to and through the deeper shadows toward the Tower of the Sun, positioning for yet another siege in the hopes that this time it would succeed and the greatest stronghold on the planet could finally be felled.

The timescape, over the years, had become a natural extension of his inner sight, but never before had he lamented his inability to hear what was going on, as he did in this moment.

Tur and Semet's forces were marching behind a front line of usurped, which were led by an undulating wall of vestiges.

All the tents were of the same relative size so there was no external giveaway as to which one may be housing Tur, but the giveaway was on the inside in the form of the largest Sidhe among all those present.

"Leanna," he breathed, his lips tightening to a fine line.

Tur was easy enough to distinguish, he was almost equal in size

507

to his mistress, but there were guards of much smaller stature as well, and one who seemed almost to radiate the feel of young human.

Frank?! His mind flew to the boy, but he knew better. His little brother was hundreds of miles away, heading toward the wildlands to find whatever wise ones still existed.

A deep, pulsating wave surged through him, bringing with it a nauseating disorientation as he focused on the youth, his fold within the timescape moving closer though he wasn't aware of it. *Who the hell is that?* He shook his head knowing it was no Sidhe, no schade, nor even a human, *not possible! No way in hell could it be possible! No matter how much magic…*

With great effort he shifted his focus to Leanna, wondering if she'd sped up the maturation and birth, could she have extended the spells to it after its arrival, or was it aging at such an accelerated rate because it was born of dark and therefore subject to the curse?

He remembered seeing her form on the timescape, moving as if she were wounded. What exactly those kinds of magiks would cost both her and the child in the end, not even Julius had been able to guess.

The sound of wings flapping behind him went largely unnoticed as the youth inside the tent turned and faced him as if he were standing there. It's crystal clear, golden eyes stared into his, and as a mirror image face came into focus, Nick's heart skipped several beats.

"Father," the boy's voice greeted through a smirk Nick felt curl his own lips far too often in this life, "behind you."

"How?" he whispered as black wings closed on both sides of his head from behind, the longest of the feathers became knobby, taloned fingers driving into his temples and filling his mind with impervious darkness, crushing his consciousness into a deep retreat right into Semet's arms.

"Mmm, too late," the youth smiled as the Heru of the Nahroehn shimmered out of Nick's pocket of the timescape and into the tent with the psyche of his quarry bent over one arm. His face twisted in a sickish disgust, he burped toward Leanna, "That was… worse than eating pirini!"

"No one ever said magic would be palatable," she sighed.

"Still, it was right, he was exactly where it said he was," he confirmed dropping the physical manifestation of the half-human's essence onto the ground at the central tentpole, as if he were something repulsive.

Leanna stepped forward, curling her son into her arm while sneering down at the unconscious half-breed.

She stretched her hand toward the ethereal body, her lips moving in a nearly silent spell as it rose and was bound to the central tentpole with tendrils of her own energy.

"This time there is no one with the power to save him."

"What of the body?" Tur asked.

"When the soul is finally gone, Ne'Min can find and retrieve it. Once it is usurped, we will have the perfect weapon." A depth of cruelty twisted her features, betraying how close she was to completing her transition to becoming a schade. "With the soul severed from its mooring, there will be NO rebirth."

"Finally." The schade king grinned.

--

On the other side of the bridge the three representatives of the great mother's first children watched as Semet's pirini form wrapped the Oemir's consciousness in darkness.

They barely spared a glance from one to the other.

Helioson, its countenance expressionless did flick its gaze to its brother and sister, their reactions visible in his primordial light.

There was tension in the gaze of Gloamare, and hunger turning Vetala's lips, but she was always thirsty.

Thankfully, they didn't have to wait long, before a speck of brightness swirled through the dark within Danu's offspring.

The ancient wizard had torn open the wounds of the soul, exposing the consciousness to the wake of thousands of lifetimes, then the human bade Cathbad to remove the essence of that soul to preserve it for a joining with its other half. It was crude, sinister magic, but Helioson knew it had its purpose, no matter what the human child had intended.

They watched as the spark, born wholly of the human youth, moved through the implanted darkness within its own essence and began to peel away its layers so he could see what Tur had tried to hide.

"I'm not afraid," his Sidhe birthright spoke into this personal void.

And as he spoke, the amorphous layers of darkness retreated in the face of his inner light. He was left standing in the depths of his own existence, ghostly images of those around him on the outside, made visible within. The apparitions around him slowed to a halt, save one who had the look he'd had only days ago when crossing the bridge. "You're mine, my son," he invited as if he hadn't believed in the child's existence.

He extended his hand to the younger version of what seemed to be himself.

"Father."

"Has your mother given you a name?"

"She calls me son too." The child seemed to sigh, "the other one calls me IT and THING…"

Nick's head ducked as he moved to the child and knelt before him, "Often we name our children after ourselves. I'm Nick, as was my father. Would you like to be called Nick too?" he asked.

"You are not alone out there in the world," the child muttered, as he turned up a hand revealing a scorpion on his palm.

Grimacing at the sight of the arachnid Nick shook his head, "No, I'm not. Neither are you. I didn't know you'd be here so soon," he half smiled as he reached out to touch the boy, though he backed away, the scorpion in his palm growing first larger, then smaller as he aged it forward and backward.

Powerful already, Nick thought. "I think I felt you…did you try to push me away? Keep me from coming here?"

The boy nodded, "They want you dead."

Nick shrugged, "Well, I think they want something else, but if they can't get it then dead will have to do."

They both watched as he pushed the scorpion's age forward again as he had before Tur, molting after molting sped up causing the creature to writhe in agony as it seemed to rupture through one exoskeleton after another.

"Stop it, leave it be," Nick whispered.

"It's been dead a while already, I killed it yesterday," he explained as the creature turned to dust as it had in Tur's tent.

"Why?"

"Because I could," he answered with a shrug.

Before he could say or ask anything, Nick's awareness returned to the external world.

Around them, Tur, Leanna, his own Nick Junior, Ne'Min and even Semet, all stood still, eyes on him. For an instant he understood what the scorpion might've felt as something larger than itself tormented it just for fun. It was a state of existence Nick had plenty of experience with.

He opened his mouth to snark out a greeting but realized time was frozen for them. Trouble was, he wasn't doing it.

As if in response to his awareness of the situation, he was free of Leanna's binding energy. He glanced around the tent, his focus split between using his own gifts to make sure time continued to stand still, and noting all the intel he could.

He found himself looming over the table where of course there was a map and what looked like points of incursion where darkness was making its way into this world, or already had.

Moving to grab it, he gasped when the information flowed like water from the tabletop into him, moving from the fingertips of his psyche, up through him until it became a part of his knowledge. Reluctant to trust too much of what was going on, he looked over whatever other documents lay on the table.

One was a closer view of the Tower of the Sun, with what looked like various incursion points along the outer wall.

To the west, at the navel of the continent where the four major territories joined together, it looked as if the darkness had already penetrated there.

Uncertain, his hand trembled as he reached out toward both maps. *Far as I know, this is all in my head, what if it isn't real, what if it is, but it's a trap? What if it's like what they tried to do to me... but if it's real information and I get things wrong...shit!* Wincing his eyes almost closed he touched both of the other documents, absorbing their information as well.

Trap or not, it was potentially too important to leave it behind or get it wrong. Confused and wholly aware of just how out of his depth he was, he turned, looking at everyone present, his gaze lingering on the child, "I'll be back for you Nicky, I promise."

From within a bubble of his own energy on the 'scape, he reached overhead, pulling down the veil between worlds, shielding himself from all of them, except perhaps from his own son, before making his escape.

When he was gone, his namesake smiled but otherwise didn't move until the others were also released.

--

In the womb of the great mother, the refugees of the Fierowen lined up as the last of Diagas' green flames were absorbed by the ancient eggs embedded in the walls. There was the sound of stone cracking, rubble trickling down to the ground as the absorbed heat caused expansion and contraction in the otherwise petrified tissue.

The elders of the Fierowen who remembered times before the last war, when Sidhe and dragon kind honored the traditions laid down by the mothers first son Helios; were the first to come forward as one by one, the eggs began to emerge, each from its follicle.

The two species were bound in a symbiotic relationship honoring life, and the workings of the universe.

The great mothers' knowledge emerged through genetic memory and was disseminated to the Sidhe who passed it forward to the other younger species. In time, there was not a single Sidhe who did not have at least one egg to nurture until its hatching. Those remaining embedded in the walls or still sleeping, were left to await perhaps another age if the world and universes survived for it.

--

Kneeling at the edge of a stream Frank leaned deep over the silty water closer to shore. There was something deep inside, a kind of heaviness he wasn't familiar with until he braced himself on a stone instead of the sandy dirt. The ground was vibrating. His heartbeat picked up and he looked at the wolverine pair escorting him. "I don't suppose either of you speak English do you?" he muttered.

"They do not," a soft feminine voice sort of wafted over him, sending a chill up his spine and into the base of his brain.

He closed his eyes, "whoever you are please tell me you're real and not my imagination."

There was amusement in the voice, "I am real."

He wheeled around, frightened by the emptiness surrounding him, "are you a ghost? Or… something like that?"

"I am not. You need not fear descendant of Oemir." She warned.

A shiver shook him, "oh god you're a ghoul or banshee or something, it's never good when they tell a guy to not be afraid y'know!" he half chuckled half barked as the leaves behind him began to rustle.

When he saw something vibrant red pushing through the greenery, he first thought it was a horse so he looked up to see the rider, but there was none, and there were no forelegs he could see. Though it took a scant extra second he realized it was a snout pushing through the foliage.

"Holy shit…" he gasped backpedaling into the stream, pinwheeling his arms to keep his balance, "fuck… what the…ooop! Wow!"

The mouth turned up as her golden eyes crimped at the corners, "No need for fear son of Oemir, I have been watching over you for quite a while and have not become hungry yet."

"Whathe…" he finally fell back onto his butt before scrambling back to his feet. "You're talking," he breathed then muttered to himself, "I knew they could talk… it's a dragon, they talk, we… they… I thought they…" he raised his head, his eyes meeting hers, "We thought you were all gone, taken by the dark."

"Those who have not succumbed are awakening, we should be there when they gather. They will need to recognize their old ally."

Fully flummoxed, Frank shook his head, "what? Who?"

"Have you your water?" She asked.

Silent he nodded and rose to a crouch, unsure if he was going to need to run or not. After all, he didn't miss the comment about her not being hungry yet.

"Good," she held out a paw, "time grows short, and you are not the bearer of that particular gift, we must move quickly."

"Why?"

"Do you know where you are headed?"

He nodded securing the skin across his chest with a wince as the pressure burned the cuts Poe made, "Wyverns, they're waking, I need to…"

"Exactly, best to get their attention before they are fully awake, lest they adjourn to hunt before the state of things can be relayed. Climb up." She instructed.

While he did so, she turned her attention to the wolverine couple, a series of snarls and yips dismissing them with orders to gather the creatures of the woods and fields and get them moving toward the Tower of the Sun. *"… feel free to feast on any of the enemy you see fit along the way."*

Frank, settling at the base of her neck, between her shoulder blades asked, "What'd you tell them?" as he watched them yipping almost playfully into the underbrush.

"Eat well and join us at the tower when they're through." She smiled. It was close enough, considering she could smell no innocent blood on this one's soul.

He'd barely taken and released a breath of relief when everything blurred around them and she stopped, they were at the base of a slight rise he thought might harbor a geyser, though he somehow knew it was the caldera he'd already been headed for.

"You stay, I will find my cousins." She turned her head as he dismounted, a gleam in her eye which, when fully open was probably close to Ryan's size when he stood up straight.

"What's your name?" he asked.

She smiled, "Your kind call me Garnet."

"I'm Frank, Frank Emerson, it's nice to meet you, and thank you for bringing me here." He couldn't help himself, his best manners came forward though for some reason, all the other Oemirs' voices were silent, leaving his tummy with a strange wiggly feeling he knew better than to ignore.

15

———————

T he queen of the Akirowen cast a quick glance behind her as she

raced toward the lower entrance to her underwater palace. The pool was usually wide open, allowing for whomever of her air breathing subjects to obtain audience as needed. Today she hoped it would hold against the needle thin runnel of dark pursuing her.

Argus, the young giant squid who served not only as the model for the throne in the presentation room, but often as her actual throne and bodyguard raced to the pool's edge, one tentacle in the water, ready to haul her in while the other was poised to strike in her defense.

"Prepare to seal the entrance!" her voice rang in his head.

Never missing a beat, two arms suckered themselves to the crystalline plates on either side of the pool as Ula gave a mighty thrust of her tail, sending herself soaring through the opening.

In midair, her tail split into legs before she landed lightly beside the squid. He closed the way with nary a second to spare before the filament of dark careened into the crystal, rolling into a mass against the obstruction. It felt around the barrier for a possible opening then moved off toward the field of black smokers heating the floes beneath the Nahroehn.

At the rear wall she stroked a series of symbols on the embedded crystal. Around them, the palace began to vibrate, then the hum started, moving up toward the rocky tunnel from the ocean's surface. Once the vibration and hum hit the air, the rocky outcrop would act like the bell of a trumpet, sending the song to radiate outward until a similar siren at the Tower of the Sun responded. All those in the Fierowen would then know the Living Dark has made an incursion to and through the nearest of Aderyn's seas.

Outside the palace the water rippled, carrying the alert to all the marine life it could. Many shoals would head toward various coral reefs for shelter, even the dead ones.

Extremophiles would head either toward the brightness of the icy poles or the molten depths of the black smokers.

Ocean mammals of every stripe would gather in their pods or other family units and head toward sacred areas where their young were nursed for the first experiences of their lives.

The largest cetaceans and leviathans would have to fight their instincts to drop down to the lowest levels in the deepest trenches to hide; but their genetic memory would urge them instead to rise as close to the surface as possible and follow the light as long as possible.

Even with the alarm sounded, Ula's work was only beginning.

There were many seas and oceans on Aderyn, all around the central land mass, and through a myriad of islands; she was obligated to check in with all the subjects of her realm, not just the wildlife, but those air breathing creatures who were not Sidhe and therefore not subject to any of their rulers.

A shiver slithered down her spine as she recalled the Oemir's words coming from the younger of the two as they visited Kieren in the isolation room at the tower. "I remember the part you played in that war…" She was hopeful he hadn't meant it as a warning, but inside, she was certain he had.

She swallowed hard, a faint nod to her head, in the privacy of her own thoughts shame burned her cheeks as she dashed to the armory to meet those of her army not guarding the Fierowen.

It was time to renew ties in an effort of atonement, she could only hope it wasn't too late.

--

When he awoke, it was to a pervasive silence he couldn't remember ever experiencing before. Nothing, from booze to anesthesia to fending off feral were's had ever given him such complete rest.

He slipped back into the Bedowen clothes Julius gave him earlier then started a quiet search of this level, fairly certain everyone else had disbursed, leaving him to recuperate.

Circling the open central core he was able to take in the damage the consistent barrage of sieges had caused. Those few levels above this one appeared dimly lit in spite of the daylight filtering through the crystalline structure leaving him to wonder if they were damaged beyond repair, or just "conserving power", as they'd surmised earlier.

From the levels below though, it was as if he could somehow feel the presence of life energy down there, plenty of it, and the knowledge brought with it a surprisingly strong sense of relief. Now all he had to do was find Julius and get some more of those answers he'd promised the other day.

Instead of taking the lift on the far side of the level, he chose the stairs carved between the balconies, taking them two at a time until he was on the ground level.

To his surprise there was quite a bit of ambient noise down here, *hmm noise dampeners up there? Spells or tech?*

The sounds of struggle were familiar and comforting, but Shep's strained talking made it even more so. He dashed on tip toe toward the familiar voice and found the hunter wrestling with Dylan, trying to get him back to bed while evading the eldest Emerson's hand.

Knowing how debilitating the man's gift could be if you weren't prepared for it, he slunk into the room, looping Dylan's arms into his own, then maneuvering him face first against the wall.

"You gotta calm down man, nobody here's gonna hurtcha, you've been sick since the fortress," he tried to talk some sense into him, but Dylan wasn't having it.

"He's been muttering since we got here, talking about killing Nick, like seriously killing him…"

Lou cocked his head to the side, holding the elder Emerson so tightly he finally stopped struggling.

"Said something about him killing Howie."

"Yeah like that's gonna happen."

"Said something about… 'unmaking' him."

"What the fuck does that mean?" he whipped the suddenly pliant man around, angling him toward a chair before settling him into it.

He grabbed Dylan's face, "What do you mean 'unmaking' him? What did you see? You said something in the forest like you knew

521

this was gonna to happen…"

Slick as snot, D's hand shot out, the heel pressing into Lou's forehead as he rose, pushing the garage owner back toward the opposite wall while this time, instead of pulling information from him, he flooded his mind with the upcoming events haunting him since they arrived in this strange world.

When Shep made to intervene, a single fierce look from his bloodshot eyes and the warning to, "Back off unless you want it too!" stilled the hunter in his tracks.

All three men held their breath until the eldest Emerson pulled his hand from Lou's forehead, letting him off the wall, to stumble forward. Instead of catching him, Dylan turned away to let him stand or fall on his own.

Shaking his head Shep came forward, balancing the stunned garage owner and guiding him to the chair while squeezing his suddenly bleeding nose shut.

Once he was seated they both looked at Dylan, who'd collapsed back onto his bed breathing hard, his own nose even more bloody than Lou's.

"I don't believe it," Lou shook his head with a nod of thanks to Shep.

"What'dja see?" he asked.

"They put dark in him when they had us at the fortress, Nick told me they did the same thing to him when they had him last month."

"Howie told me when he came to check on us, didn't know about the kid though. So… is that what he showed you?"

"No," Lou grimaced, "Howie... flying apart like... soot smoke, Nick somehow making it happen... like you said he said, 'unmaking' him. Down to mist." He turned to Dylan, "do they always come true?"

Still on his back, gasping, his hand on his chest, "I know which ones will. I don't wanna do it, but I'm not gonna let my little brother get turned into smithereens by some... evil little shit."

"He's not evil! He's just a kid!" Lou argued, "what about context? Do you get any of that in those things?"

Struggling to sit up, Dylan shook his head, "don't need it...I felt it, I felt that little fucker tear my brother apart into atoms, what more do I need to know?"

Shep opened his mouth to ask something but a look at Lou's face, made him hold his tongue. The garage owner was looking for something, some kind of reason to disbelieve what he was being told, but he was having a hard time finding it.

After a long moment of silence Lou shook his head, he had to go with his guts, "They put dark in you Dylan. What better way to destroy their enemy than divide and conquer? It's strategy 101.

As for the kid killing Wee? I don't believe it. I CAN'T believe it. The things I've seen him do these last few days outside what he did to save us! I'm not about to believe he's gonna kill his own uncle, whatever's going on in your vision, it's not what you think it is. There's no way it can be."

At this vehement denial Dylan sat up, elbows on his knees, his head turned just enough to sneer at the son of Conchobar, "Fuck you, you don't know shit. Just stay the fuck out of my way."

"Alright that's enough! Both of you! Nobody's killing anybody without a goddamned good reason, least of all family! If what you think is gonna come, we're gonna stop it before it happens, period. Y'get me?!" he demanded.

Lou gave a firm nod, glad to have someone with a little sense to 'em on his side; Dylan's head-cock was far less heartening. For the moment he seemed content to at least bide his time, seeing as how neither of these men was going to let him go out on his own, especially if it seemed he was still bent on murdering his own nephew.

"Now we got that settled… anybody know where he and Julius are?" Lou asked, headed for the door.

"Sorry, or maybe not considering…" Shep nodded toward Dylan, "they left him here a couple hours ago. Haven't seen 'em since."

Stopping at the threshold, Lou turned back to stand towering above the eldest Emerson, he drew the chair over then sat in front of him with his fists entwined in the delirious man's shirt.

"You don't make a move without me, you get it? Not against Nick and sure as hell not against Shep. You don't get to put him in jeopardy just because you got a itch to kill the kid. In your condition you couldn't handle him anyway, he'd chew you up and spit you out. So you keep your eyes on the prize, we got two universes to save before you try to take out anyone on our side with any kind of power that can help keep us all alive.

In between, you got me and Shep t'keep our eyes open and watch for any hinkey shit do you understand me?" he commanded; his voice moderate but undeniable.

Sitting up just a little straighter, his eyes searching Lou's in partial disbelief, Dylan nodded, "Okay… for now."

"I find out you're lyin' t'me when I get back you won't be able to do anything but lay there and breathe… if you're lucky."

Storming across the room, Shep shoved Lou out into the hall, his voice a harsh conspiratorial whisper, "You don't really think Nick…"

"You don't know what he saw," he nodded toward Dylan's creeping shadow, moving closer to the door to listen, "and you don't know what that kid's pulled off over the last couple days," he shook his head. "Nick is a very powerful young man, there has to be more to D's vision, but I'll be damned if I'm going to sit by and let one of the descendants of the first heroes kill one of the guy's who's been raising him for the last four years, and honestly, neither of you are up to the task of stopping him if he does try something."

"So what're you gonna do?" Shep asked.

"Find him and stick to him like glue. Stop him in case he tries to do something stupid."

Lou's eyes shifted to the shadow near the jamb. When Shep's glance saw it too, he nodded his understanding.

"Fair enough," he sighed, "but if you gotta move, don't do it without one of us at your back."

"Let's hope it doesn't go there." He clapped Shep on the shoulder, stepping away and heading toward the entrance. With luck, out in the yard he'd find Julius or one of the others who greeted them when they arrived.

Returning to their room, Shep ushered Dylan to the bathroom, "You need to clean up then get some rest, if we need to get Nick under control you need to be as strong as you can be."

"You really believe him?" D asked.

525

"I believe he's not gonna let anything happen to Howie, and that he doesn't want to see anyone dying for nothing." It was as close as he could come to telling the whole truth.

There was something Lou was hiding, something happened after they split up the other morning, but anything he could say might fan the flames of Dylan's distrust and wasn't going to serve anyone just yet. There'd be time to act when they knew more. Or so he hoped.

--

"The most ancient of our kind have already dispersed to recruit still others of their own generation.

As we make our way to the Tower, others will follow, we will be a moving line in the sand to those who follow the dark and their allies. By the time the last of us arrives at the Fierowen heart, we will be several thousand strong, many with shape shifting abilities." Talmai explained as many of the villagers began moving out into the world, using roads, fields, streams, or sky.

Several of their number looked rather odd with carts harnessed across their chests until they assumed preferred forms, some oxen, some bulls, others; horses, mules, or donkeys. There were even a few of those with a more playful nature, taking forms such as gryphons, manticores, and the odd dinosaur, triceratops or stegosaurus seemed to be favorites.

Eyes bulging in amazement, matching grins on his and Arabelle's faces, Minya couldn't help but ask, "how does conservation of mass work?" for which he received a good-natured swat on the shoulder.

"Can you not simply enjoy the results of all their efforts?"

"What? I'm curious... aren't you?"

Wereiwyn grinned, her arm looped through Wyle's, "that is one of the most difficult aspects of the magiks to master," she leaned close, "the ability to maintain the difference depends on the level of exertion, the form however can be maintained at the size of the individual for quite some time. If you'd like you may begin your practice once we've won this war."

"This world is ripe and flush with life-energy, how much of it is used to buoy the 'shifter?"

Wereiwyn's smile trembled before settling soft on her face, " in our heyday, we could have walked the world as giants of whatever form we could master."

Wyle's smile was sunshine in human form as he pecked his wife's cheek then assumed his lupine form, as she did hers.

"That is so cool!"

"There has been no temperature change that I can sense?" Talmai queried.

"The term is an affect of Minya's, you will likely grow accustomed to it, and him, if given the chance." Arabelle explained, also seeming to glow just a bit with the comfort of companionship stemming from such a dedicated group of allies.

A few hours later, and with several kilometers behind them, a shadow glided through the sunlight, calling Minya's gaze upward, his hand shielding his eyes as a smile perched on his lips. The raven circled down to his shoulder, it rubbed the chipped side of its beak against his ear, trilling and chirping softly for a moment before he launched into the sky, calling its blessings to the caravan as he continued on his way.

Arabelle shot a side eye to the strange Sidhe, "So, you congress with the emissary of the Emissary... you are not so derelict as you pretend."

"Careful there, you might find something to like about me."

She turned her head away, nose a little higher as she gave a haughty but playful sniff, "Not without a bath first."

"Flatterer," he muttered, holding back a smile.

A moment later she stopped, hands on her hips, head cocked to the side, "Well?"

Taking a peek around at all the other curious faces at the head of the grouping he chuckled, "He said the Oemir has gone to rouse allies of the West. And, most of the citizens of the wild are making their way toward the tower as well. We are not to fear them if we cross paths on the way."

"Is that all?"

"He said there is a surprise awaiting our arrival but didn't say what." The strange Sidhe finished with a shrug.

"I'm not often fond of surprises."

"I wouldn't have guessed." Minya sighed, "can't blame you."

--

Striding toward the tower's foyer, trying to decide which way to go, the ring of swords clashing to the right, drew Lou toward it.

There was no combative urgency to the familiar song, merely the steady strike and counter of practice.

He veered to the closed room, part of him wanting to throw the twelve-foot doors wide, make a powerful entrance fit to stun the very king of all Sidhe. His heart, beat hard enough to feel the pounding in his throat. Whatever was going to happen, he needed to be smart. Dylan was a wild card, and after what he'd been shown, Lou couldn't be sure he'd wait to hear reason, or learn the circumstances of what Nick would do to Wee and why. If it was one of those things the eldest Emerson knew would come to pass, Lou had to find out why.

From what he'd seen the last few days of Nick's growing gifts, what he saw him do to the vestige, let alone helping purge them all of the darkness… he just couldn't believe he'd turn his powers on Howie.

He pushed down on the door handle while rapping three times and entered to find Khazeer and Wellyn, sheathing their swords.

"Son of Conchobar, we heard you were returned, along with a few others." The king welcomed him, motioning to the table where the remains of their morning brew and breakfast sat.

"No thank you, have either of you seen Julius or Nick?"

The two shared a look, their brows furrowed, their expressions almost as if they were twins.

"We have not, we heard they were recuperating as were the elder and the son of MacRoich." Khazeer explained.

"What troubles you?" Wellyn asked, but Lou waved his hand to dismiss the question, frustration twisting and flushing his face. He knew how he WANTED to react, he knew how it was his nature to react but something deep inside was exerting an influence he'd only ever felt on a small number of occasions, each of which alone was a unique reason he was still alive.

As if his turmoil were speaking aloud, the king and his Master of Arms remained still, time was all it would take.

He wheeled releasing a great rush of held breath. His mouth

opened and closed a few times. He wasn't used to having others with power or influence actually possibly on his side. But here he was.

"I think Dylan should be… I don't wanna say 'locked away' but…"

"Sequestered?" Wellyn offered.

Lou's head twitched and his eyebrow shot up, "Oooh, hair splitting… but yeah. His sickness makes him a danger, especially to Wee."

Their heads cocked to the side, just another betrayal of their similarities.

"But they are brothers."

"Well, D thinks Nick is a danger to Wee, and if he goes after Nick then Wee is sure to get in the way and wind up getting hurt or dead, which… given what's going on with Nick… could wind up getting D killed…and if that happens… everybody loses, and I'm pretty sure Nick couldn't live with himself if…"

He paced a circuit around the warriors, his thumb nail between his teeth as he measured how much he could, or should trust these two. After all, they had an entire universe to protect, and the life or death of three humans would likely be considered nothing more than collateral damage to them.

He stopped, his gaze narrowing on them as if he could somehow see the intents of their hearts, when his life-saving instinct took advantage of his stillness and spoke again. *Trust them enough.*

Nodding with the knowledge he really had no choice, he drew and exhaled another deep breath, "Look, I need information but if you're gonna stand there and blow smoke up my ass just tell me now and I'll walk outta here and figure it out myself."

"What information do you seek?" Khazeer asked.

Shaking his head, Lou paced before them, then to the table and back to the Fierowen leaders, then back to the table where he poured a mug of root brew.

"Everything, Julius, Nick or Oemir, the extent of his powers, the history between him and Ne'Min, Semet and Tur... their powers.

Why the curse? Why would they side with something that wants to destroy all life?" he swilled hard on the brew.

"Is there anyone who can just... download the history of it all into my head? I mean if you all have powers then there has to be some kind of way to just put it all in here..." his fingers tapped his temple.

Once more his frustration gushed forth in a harsh breath, his features, so similar to his progenitor, twisted in a level of emotional agony neither of these virtually immortal beings had felt since they were fledglings themselves.

"How do we defeat darkness? It's half the daily celestial cycle, it's natural, it's normal, it's one half of the whole... granted this dark is conscious... but without its other half, without light, its own existence becomes just as meaningless as light without it..." he grunted, leaned hard against the table, and rubbed his temples. "Gives me a frikkin' headache."

He turned, his gaze over his shoulder at the two leaders. "I think Nick is gonna sacrifice himself, I think he almost wants to."

Again, they shared their twin-ish look as Lou straightened up and turned until he was facing them full on.

"Hey, you asked." He shrugged, his relief at finally getting his trepidations out in the open, fully palpable.

Motioning to a chair, Khazeer and Wellyn sat with the surprisingly perceptive young hero.

--

With a break in the line of those who were being assigned their stations and tasks, Wee sat back, cleansing himself with a deep round of box breathing. With his eyes closed he envisioned himself and Ryan moving through Umatilla, just life-watching and enjoying each other's company.

Beside him, Tierus sat, his gaze scanning the villagers from the Fierowen as well as others from the surrounding settlements or those who'd come from the Dragonbow mountains.

He didn't have Wee's gift to call upon to determine who wished to be of service, or who was here to exploit weaknesses in the name of sabotage. He hadn't expected their assigned task to be as trying as it had been. He'd never had reason to suspect true treachery from his fellow Sidhe and found it exhausting. It was obvious the son of Oemir did too.

Wee nodded, addressing his concerns as if he'd spoken them aloud.

"It's definitely exhausting, I haven't felt anything like this in… years. At least since the boys came to us and I had to get used to both of their minds in the house too. 'Specially Nicky, being a teenager is hard enough but with all the crap he had buzzing around in his head, it was… like… trying to tread water in a never-ending hurricane."

He shook his head and waved his hand at the surrounding kingdom, "then to find out there's this whole 'nother world we needed to deal with, to help protect… with all these *beings,* and *creatures,* and everything we thought was mythology was really real and still exists, just in a whole different universe that used to overlap with ours… and it's like does it explain entanglement? Is *this* what quantum entanglement is or is that a whole different kind of otherworldly shit with its own insanity we still haven't discovered or learned to understand…"

"Breathe son of Oemir, your senses are raw, overused and long overtaxed with the unexpected burden of leading the defense of the Fierowen… all to avoid the fears you harbor on behalf of those you love…" the grinning fledgling sighed patting him on the shoulder.

"You have done well thus far by maintaining focus on each moment as it comes. To succumb to the full wash of concerns at this early stage of things will only be a disservice to those waiting to rejoin you."

A sudden flush of tears seemed to almost fly from his eyes as he sniffed, scrubbing his haggard and scruffy face with his hands, "You're right, of course you're right… miles to go before we sleep and all," he turned his forlorn gaze to the youth, "I miss my husband. I don't even know if he's alive or…" he hiccoughed, "…not."

Tierus' expression softened despite his stony, searching gaze roving over the milling villagers, "be assured, if he were to pass beyond, you would have known whether by informant or heartbreak."

Wee nodded, his hand falling to the lightstone he'd been given. "We're gonna need as many of these as we can come up with before the next night falls." He turned his gaze toward the tower, the areas from which huge blocks of sandstone had fallen from the "framework" of the structure during the nightly sieges would have terrified him if he hadn't been brought up to speed by the king and Wellyn. Still, using the enemy to do work that would've taken all the residents of the Fierowen at least twice as long, had inherent risks,

533

such as the potential for irreparably damaging the tower, in case life and light survived this war.

"How many more assaults do you think it'll take?" he asked.

Tierus glanced at the tower, "Another night or two should suffice. What we need is to speak with either your elder nephew or the Oemir himself, if Nick is the keeper of time and its passage, he may well be the fulcrum on which victory or defeat will turn."

Breath caught in Wee's throat, as he recalled the fledgling relating his memories of the battle of the Talath o'Riches, during which Oemir held combatants in his thrall long enough to turn the tide to their advantage before he was slain. His windpipe snapped closed so quickly he choked on a gag as an amorphous multitude of probabilities swam through his existence to careen with the weight of molten foundry slag into his belly. The sensation making him grasp at the table for stability, the color gone from his suddenly waxen face.

"That's why they want him, or want him dead." He slapped his hand over his mouth, his eyes wide as platters as he pushed to his feet, tearing at full speed back to the tower. He had to know!

--

At the gate Julius stood beside Syldryl, his eyes the only part of him moving as he scanned the horizon, searching the shadows for any signs of Oemir's return.

From within the guardhouse Ahrendaria emerged, "Tropus and Boaz have entered via the Northern horn, they bring word of the enemy's progress near the mountain, and apparently, a captive."

"I will go." Syldryl offered but Julius stayed him with a hand on the shoulder.

"The Heru bade me keep the others safe, it is my duty," he nodded moving like a wisp of the wind back to the tower, entrusting his old friend to watch for his love.

--

The sensation of weight returned as Nick's consciousness settled back into his body. His gaze roved through his personal pocket of the 'scape and the first thing he wondered was how safe he could really be if Semet had been able to find him and steal him from himself so easily.

It took a few moments of contemplation before he nodded, realizing the possibility the Nahroehn Heru only found his consciousness and not his body. After all, didn't he hear them mention something about going to find his body after they destroyed his soul?

"Joke's on you fuckers," he sighed, "no soul, nothing to kill but a body." *And that's worked so well for you all over the last few millennia hasn't it?* He allowed himself a moment of relief before turning his attention to his son, "I have to rescue him." In his minds' eye, the war maps he'd seen, whose information he'd somehow managed to absorb, aligned themselves as if he were looking at them as they'd been spread on the table.

What if they're a trick? Who's side is he on? He tried to keep me away… or did he? My guts, he stilled his racing thoughts for a moment before frowning, *not talkin'… I know, I know… give it time. Now that's irony.* With the weight of all of existence on his shoulders, he didn't bother rising to his feet before envisioning, as he'd done earlier, the timescape moving around him, so very like a magician's tablecloth being yanked without disturbing the dishes. To quiet his mind, he took in as much information as possible while passing the enemy forces on his way back to the tower.

535

On the 'scape, outside the wall, his attention was drawn to something strange about the Sidhe who appeared to have been posted as guards. Curious, he veered closer. His blood turned cold at the sight of those insubstantial outlines indicating Schades, but there was something different in these, a strange feel of superimposition; like a bit of paper tucked into an envelope too large for it, and held up to the light. The looks of them just didn't *feel* right.

His mind went back by what was now somewhere around ten days, at least on Terra. The day he'd seen Tommy's mom Lizzy on the 'scape, the day the schade riding her had sliced him partway down the back, trying to make a meatsuit of him. *God it seems so long ago.*

His initial reaction was to take one of them, see if it was a schade riding the Sidhe or if it was darkness inhabiting it, but two things kept him from doing it; first, they were outside the wall, second, almost all of them seemed to have the same…affliction. *I don't believe in coincidences.*

As he dwelt on what to do, he noted three of these "guards", all of whose presence on the 'scape appeared normal, were distributing lightstones to everyone, and wondered at it. A sly smile came to his features and hung around. If these were possessed, either by schades or darkness, and they were to activate the stones, the light itself may save the 'host'. *Interesting.*

Deciding to leave the situation as it was for the time being, he moved to the front gate, and in an alcove of shadow, slipped out from his pocket and back to the shared world.

--

In the main entranceway of the tower Wee skidded to a halt, a sharp, melodic 'ping' hit his ears. He patted himself down, pulled his phone and turned it on, his expression confused. There were no messages, no calls, notifications, nothing. Then it came again, followed by another a few seconds later.

Light flashed at varying points in the walls down the hall, then traveled up the spire with fine bands of light rising as if along a Jacob's ladder.

"What the fudgebar?" he muttered heading toward one of the flickering panels as the door to Khazeer and Wellyn's suite opened, the two Sidhe, with Lou at their side, emerging at a jog and morphing into a strident run deep into the heart of the spire.

"What is it?" Wee asked joining them.

"The Akirowen siren! Ula's song of distress!" the king answered.

"Darkness has infiltrated her central sea, near her palace." Wellyn explained as the siren grew in volume, pitch, and intensity to the point where the tower itself began to vibrate.

"The first warning of firdur openly on the move." Khazeer added as a chunk of sandstone fell from well above them, directly into his path. He barely altered a step as it crashed to the floor, shattering exactly where he'd been a microsecond before.

"Sheesh!" Wee gulped finally recognizing Lou. "How ya' doin'?" he asked.

"Freaked the fuck out... you?"

"Same."

They followed Khazeer and Wellyn into the lift, taking it to the highest point in the tower, just above which the light-spear sat gathering sunlight on its mobile platform.

"You alone?" Wee panted as the car began its rise.

"Nuh, Shep's watching over D, he took some pretty bad hurt, got an infection too."

"Nick? Frank?"

"Dunno, Nick seemed to think Frank was gathering allies or something."

"Alone?" Wee frowned.

Lou shrugged, unsure of how much to tell this young man, it was clear in the weariness of his expression the last few days had been deeply taxing.

"C'mon man…"

"About Frank? I don't know, he went off with some of the other Fierowen soldiers after the group he was leading came to rescue me and D from the fortress. He left us with Shep and a few soldiers, they got drawn away, left us some horses, but we couldn't get away in time and got captured and held prisoner. Next thing we know, we're drowning in dark until we're not. It was inside us, then suddenly there was Nick, and some kid named Torn, and a dragon, Dia…something."

"Diagas?" Khazeer offered.

"Yeah him…"

"But Nick, you saw Nicky? Is he okay?" relief and worry fought for space on the young man's face.

Lou gave kind of a half-shrug, "seems to be so far… goin' through some changes though… learning to use his powers a bit more, so, that's something."

"What aren't you telling me?" Wee asked, a stony edge to his voice.

"Just stuff I don't know." He turned to the king and his man at arms, "Either of you seen Julius lately?"

"We have not," Khazeer shook his head.

Wee touched the king on the forearm, "The battle of Talath o'Riches...do you think what he did back then could be why they've been working so hard to ruin him? I mean his soul?"

The two Sidhe met eyes, impressed with the line of thought, "Considering the torments my daughter has witnessed through the last ages, and given him comfort through, it is in fact, very likely they have been working to corrupt his will and make him useless."

"And what the Elder mentioned when she examined him," Wellyn added.

"What? What'd she mention?" Wee asked.

"There was evidence Tur and Ne'Min may have attempted to force firdureen into him to grow, it would darken his every thought, every action, feeding the firdureen until it was powerful enough to overtake him, making him the perfect weapon to use against those who have so long awaited his return."

The memory of darkness moving through the boys' veins, up the sides of his neck flashed in Lou's mind, and though he shook his head, he wisely held his tongue. This was not the time yet, though if they'd succeeded, it would go much further to validating D's vision.

The lift slowed, the rear door opening to admit them to the command center. From up here they were able to observe the whole of the Fierowen embraced within the walls, as well as several villages at the furthest reaches of the outer perimeter.

"Damn man, this is like the observation deck on the Sears Tower! You can see for miles... good god, even where her paws came to rest on the flatland. Where is everyone?" Lou asked.

Wellyn slipped off to a different area while Khazeer met eyes with Wee. It took a second for his questioning gaze to prompt the youngest of the elder Emerson's to use his talent to ensure it was safe to speak around the son of Conchobar.

"Yeah, he's fine," Wee assured.

"Many of our people have been disbursed to secondary or tertiary locations. Those who remain within the city walls are providing the appearance of a greater number than are currently here."

Lou nodded, "got it, giving cover while others get to safety."

"Ish." Wee nodded as the siren song built around them, traveling up the crystalline walls right behind the light which dropped them off.

Looking down, Lou noticed it seemed to be raining sandstone from the lower levels.

"This place is going to shake apart," he muttered surprised by a broad grin on the king's face.

"She will hold," he promised.

--

"Do you know where he's gone?" Nick asked as the ground itself seemed to vibrate.

"Tropus and Boaz have returned from the mountain, it is our understanding Julius went to meet them near Heru Ula's entrance."

"What is this?" Ahrendaria asked touching the surprisingly durable rubberized paint.

540

"A test," he smiled focusing for a moment on his first finger which was still well coated.

To the surprise of both of his old friends, the digit lit up with the power of a small flashlight, clearly surprising the two warriors.

"The hard part is keeping your focus, so you don't light up at the wrong time," he smiled.

"It seems similar to the protective paint Lugh often wore in his travels, we have heard it was one of the reasons they called him 'the shining one.'" Syldryl smiled.

Beneath their feet, the vibration grew in intensity, coming to them as if from a great distance. The Sidhe warriors exchanged looks Nick knew weren't normal.

His belly gave a twist as the vibration grew stronger and a block of sandstone fell out of the wall beside them, revealing a crystalline foundation beneath.

His mouth dropped open in a surprised 'o' as he grinned, "Well, I'll be damned..." as the puzzle pieces swirling in his mind finally started to form a picture. Another wave of vibration came, drawing his attention out of his thoughts, "I know this..." he breathed, "this is bad."

Syldryl nodded, "Yes Heru, it IS."

A golden shaft of setting sun drew his gaze, making a connection between the sound and what it meant, after all, he'd been slated to become king one day.

"Ula's entrance," he breathed dashing straight into the palace. He would get there much faster if he simply cut North from the center of the tower than going all the way around.

--

At the ports along the coastlines, moored ships weighed anchor whether or not their supplies were done being on or off loaded. Those who had leviathan escorts moved first, bottlenecks between piers and slips were common, though navigated with scant few mishaps thanks to the giant sea creatures. Those who were not affiliated with leviathan escorts were made to wait or try to squeeze between other, larger ships, which frequently caused damage whose effects would not be known until later when they were under some kind of pressure.

Thousands of kilometers away from any dry land mass of any size; a tremor, in the depths of the sea, momentarily juxtaposed with a place on its sister world, called the Mariana Trench, a tentacle slipped through the interworldly fistula. Sea creatures from both worlds, in the midst of their daily activities found themselves the first witnesses to a destructive power unknown for so long, it might as well have been new.

Gripped, held, and annihilated by the questing tendrils of living dark, the blood of creatures from both worlds mingled, stabilizing the alien bridge, and locking the fates of the worlds together, as living dark widened the breach, and quested forward.

--

"Thanks for waiting, sorry I'm late there was..." Charles began, pulling the seatbelt on and locking the door.

"Don't lie about it." Jr. asked, his voice soft.

The two met eyes, Harry's sad, Charles' turning red and glassing up.

"Why?"

Charles shrugged, "Extra bills, thinkin' 'bout hittin' the road when this is over."

"Extra bills…" the slightly older teen nodded pulling his wallet from his back pocket. He ripped the Velcro open, pulling out the few bills he had one at a time and throwing them at the boy, "A few extra bills… here, here's a ten, eleven, twelve, thirteen, thirty-three, sorry man s'all I got right now… I can hit the ATM if you let me…" he stopped, slamming the wallet into the glove box as Charles's head dropped down.

"I thought you love him. And I thought you hated what the pastor did to you, now you're doin' it t'yerself!? What the fuck is that?"

"At least *he* wants me." The teen muttered nodding toward the truck stop, collecting, organizing, and straightening the bills between them.

"He wants you?"

"When he passes through yeah. Gets lonely on the road."

"What about Nick? Were you planning on talking with him or just buggin' out?"

Charles shook his head, "He doesn't want me. Nobody does."

"Oh poooooor baby! Nobody wants you? That's why he asked you to come across the country with him, right? Jesus Christ man…"

"Emilio KILLED HISSELF so he didn't have to deal with being who he was or coming back to me! My own parents disowned me, they'd rather throw away their own kid than accept me! At least I brought in money for the church! And the one person I give my heart to, who gave me hope that god put *someone* out there for me claims doesn't even have a *soul*, so he's incapable of love! What the fuck is wrong with me!? What did I ever do so bad nobody can love me?" he hitched through the tears and snot sniffles, handing the bills and wallet back to Harry, who traded them for a smashed box of tissues from his door pocket.

"Tell you what," he started.

"I'm not takin' this to pops, please don't you either! My life, what I do with my body's nobody's business, and I swear if you…"

Harry pressed a hand against his mouth, "This is you and me talkin' nobody else." He grimaced as another flow of tears and a nose bubble popped over his hand, "Dude…" he wiped it on Charles' jeans.

"Sorry."

"Whaddya wanna do with your life man? You wanna let other people tell you what you're worth for the next what seventy years?"

Charles opened his mouth to crack wise, but Harry's expression stopped him.

"Yeah, don't even…point is, if we manage to keep the world from gettin' wiped out, school starts in about six weeks. You don't wanna live with Nick and the fam, you come stay with me 'n mom till graduation. Meantime, maybe get yourself something p.t. for what mom calls 'pin' money. There's all kinds of 'wanted' and 'loved', seems you just haven't experienced much variety in that department."

Charles sat stunned silent.

"You're gonna hafta do chores though. You get the dishes, I hate doin' dishes. Make my fingers all pruney n'dry." Jr. added, pulling a handful of tissues and playfully poofing them against Charles' wet cheeks till the teen took them from him.

"Just think about it."

Charles nodded.

"Meantime, we got work t'do."

Later, in the living room, gathered around the flatscreen; Harry's senior and junior, Mickey and Vahl leaned forward, reading an article about a sudden patch of unidentifiable dark material in the Sargasso Sea.

"Says the sea is named after a kind of algae, maybe a bunch of it died? I mean… global warming right? If we got whole coral reefs going bleach dead…" Mickey started.

"Says it's unidentifiable, algae would be identifiable…" Harry junior pointed out.

"Hang on, that's not all…" Charles' fingers flew over the keyboard popping up half a dozen more news articles from around the world, centering on patches of unexplainable darkness in or around various towns. Towns with electricity cut, with streetlights exploded then turned to sand; and the last one, a transformer station near a small town in Kansas where every piece of equipment seemed to have been punctured, as if by an aerator, the metal on the edges of each of the holes rusted to crumbling.

"That's the one our hunter friend and his brother checked out, said they found two bodies inside the fence, holey-d straight to hell." Mickey explained.

Harry senior leaned back, a woosh of air from his previously held breath, "vestiges…"

"Or straight up dark itself right?" junior added remembering the night he met Nick and dropped him off at the end of the street. They'd just pulled over to see if the cops were at the house yet when a column of black punched the car, trying to get in. It was his first encounter with living dark.

Then there were the aftereffects of a vestige getting itself around the older hunter of the two they'd met at Silas Templar's house. The way it appeared to have driven long fine spikes through almost every part of him. No. He didn't like these things at all.

"Charles, make a folder and post it on every hunter, wiccan, cryptozoology, alien, and paranormal board you can find in the history." Harry senior instructed.

"Make sure you put it out on every social media…" Mickey began to add.

"Yeah, already did that… you want me to get onto the Oemir website 'n make it downloadable there?"

"You can do that?" Harry asked.

Charles chuckled, "it's a Squarespace site, same kind we used at the church, and they stay logged in, the password's saved… piece of cake."

"If you're in, make sure you send it out to all the email addys in their list then." Harry junior added.

Charles nodded, his fingers flying over the keyboard, as the files he'd put up on the tv stayed there.

"I believed the city itself to be amazing, but this is…" Vahl shook his head, "to think your species has come so far."

"Well, our days are about a third longer than yours, so…" Harry senior explained, "you back to normal?"

His expression more aged than he'd been the day before, Vahl gave a curt nod, "I was born and raised to hate your kind. I am begun to understand why."

Mickey's head snapped to look sharply at him, "share with the class?"

"Why does anyone hold hate in their heart for another?"

"Jealousy?" Harry junior guessed.

"Fear," Charles answered, "but why fear us? You're immortal and have magic, and powers. You have basically forever to do anything you want…we're so tiny in comparison."

"So are killer bees," senior muttered.

Vahl sipped at the cran/raspberry sparkling water he'd taken a liking to. *But I am no longer a fledgling…*

"The Nahroehn, my homeland has a nature that challenges those born there to survive by any means. It forged and tempered our Heru Semet from the moment of their birth."

"Their?" junior asked.

"The Heru embodies the greatest powers of both the masculine and the feminine. When you are one of their chosen, no task is too great or onerous to appease them. When they are the feminine, they are as a great mother herself. When they are the masculine, they are as the great father himself. Any dutiful child will do or be anyone they ask merely for a look of favor." He'd been carefully watching their expressions and knew the question they were each asking within their own heads. So he answered them, "Yes, even I."

--

Racing quietly, his ears straining to hear the sounds of voices as

547

he turned to the north, sprinting the corridor to Ula's entrance, he set his feet and slid down the ramp into her grotto, his head turning this way and that, to see if Tropus and Boaz were here.

The familiar scent of the sea filled him, hitting him with a pang of longing to be tenting at Secret Camp RV Park just on the back side of Otter Point State Park, or even dealing with the summer crowds at Gold Beach, just anywhere he and Frank could be splashing around, racing up the coast while Wee and Ry played their own weird version of Pacific Football in waist-high water. From what Nick could tell, it was more about just chasing each other, getting cardio and resistance workouts they couldn't really get in the neighborhood.

He was struck by a sudden desire to strip down and just dive into the little bay of sea water maintained for Ula's ship when she arrived.

"Tropus?" he shook his head. There was business to be tended to, recreation would have to wait. "Boaz?" he reflexively scanned the 'scape, but he couldn't see either of them here, Tropus's stature alone would've been a giveaway.

Frowning he pulled his vision out a bit to see if he'd maybe passed a room where they might've been, but there was nothing.

There was a sandy, gentle, kind of shooshing sound toward the rear of the grotto, with a hint of movement showing on the 'scape.

"Hello?" he crept toward what looked like a trap door in the floor.

A second later, what appeared to be a very large slab, rose just enough to catch his attention. This was followed by something large, and red, with two prongs at the end flicking out and retreating an instant later.

His lips turned up as the corners of his eyes turned down with good humor, "Diagas? Is that you?" he asked, moving with great care toward the slab, just in case it wasn't. "I can't see you on the 'scape, are you in there?"

The enormous, split tongue flicked again, waving up and down in such a way Nick couldn't help but think of an excited child. He crept another step closer, his gaze intense on the slight opening beneath the stone.

In another instant, a flash of gold, with a slim vertical pupil brought him to a stand-still.

In complete opposition to the caution his brain was calling for, he allowed himself to fall forward, onto his forearms and toes, his body plank-straight as he moved closer to the opening.

"Are Tropus and Boaz in there with you?"

A serpentine hissing whisper responded, "Come down and sssseeee for yourssssself." The invitation sending shivers down his spine while making his innards squeeze.

Still, he inched forward, the stone rising higher by inches until the single eye almost entirely filled the space.

He drew a deep breath, barely acknowledging the human part of him dealing with a terror so deep he thought he might turn into a puddle.

It's fine, it's Diagas. He assured the now tiny part as he slipped into the dragon's warren, the Sidhe part of him delighted with the relaxed demeanor of the great creature.

"You're playful, you must've eaten," he surmised, noting how down here Ula's siren was little more than maybe music from a house down the street on a windy summer day. He was glad of it, the sound played his nerves like over-tightened instrument strings.

The giant creature rolled onto his side, flashing a well-rounded belly while one of his talons loosened some of the bones and gore from between his teeth.

"Two sleeping cows ready for the mercy, and more than a dozen pirini! I haven't eaten this well in millennia," he sighed.

From the shadows behind their old ally, Tropus and Boaz came forward, each barely showing an egg they'd been charged with nurturing while in the mountain.

"So it's true?" Nick grinned, well aware of the inert, perhaps unconscious form deeper in the shadows.

"Indeed," Tropus smiled, a shadow of his former self finally coming to the fore.

"What of your guest?" Nick asked with a nod toward the shadow, "have you learned anything yet?"

"Quite a bit in fact," Tropus nodded, "There is much to bring to Khazeer."

"Have you filled in Areen?" He asked, a fist close to his mouth, the forefinger absently flicking his lips as he struggled with the whirlwind of thoughts threatening to overwhelm him. There was an image in his mind, a place in a canyon, near dusk. It seemed there was a tornado just waiting to devour him. But it was no place he could recall ever having been.

"Not yet."

He turned to Diagas, "Where is she?" then before the dragon could answer he gave a dismissive wave. "It doesn't matter."

He wheeled to face Tropus, "Can I trust you?" His brows were furrowed deep, "I don't know if I can, I don't really think I can… or do."

Next he turned to Diagas, "You I trust, but you weren't there as far as I know…" He lunged toward Tropus, his fingers outstretched toward his head, "I have so much already, but what you have…I want to rip it out of your mind," he ground through clenched teeth as a heavy sweat began to seep out of the cracks in the paint.

"I was there," Boaz finally stepped forward. "You speak of the feast, not the last feast, but the one before the kin of the Nahroehn split between Tur and Semet yes?"

Nick didn't miss Tropus' mouth open, as if to protest, then close it without so much as a whisper. He knew he would never tell this human youth everything he should know, even were they to win this war and the Oemir within him become king of all Sidhe, and then were he ordered to, even on pain of death, he would not. But Boaz had no such compunction.

"S'what I thought," Nick muttered though without malice, or anger of any kind yet. It was brewing though, deep inside, it was brewing quickly.

Boaz stepped forward. Kneeling before Nick he bowed his head, "I may not have all the answers you seek Heru, but you may search as you will through my recollections."

A shudder ran through Diagas, fluffing his scales and frills at this change in the half human. When they met in the forest he knew there was far more to this one than met the eye, and it was all teetering on the verge of a collapse which may destroy the youth.

"What is it you seek?" the dragon asked.

Nick shook his head and shrugged his shoulders, "Order.

There's a, a jumble. To start at the beginning? The why, the how…
all of it." His breath caught in his throat as dark, hot anger
blossomed in the center of his chest, racing to grow to rage.

"I wanna know why my little brother's heading into a den of
wyverns, why HE ventured into the magma chamber beneath the
Nahroehn fortress…. Why did we build it? Why does it move? What
does the darkness really want? Was it really here first or was it…"
He stopped nearly choking on something he couldn't give form or
voice to just yet, "how did we let it happen!"

His voice grew louder, his rage threatening to take him over as
firdur grew, spreading through him, darkening his veins even
beneath the paint, so deep they could be seen coloring his neck
toward his face, camouflaged more by the beard than the covering.

"Calm yourself child!" Tropus warned and still took a step back
as the youth shot him a murderous look.

Tropus, Diagas, and Boaz all cocked their heads as something
strange seemed to roll over him, surging, as a wave through the blue-
gray seal over his skin. As it moved it carried a strange type of
illumination, that among the natives, only Diagas had ever seen
before.

But Nick, he'd seen it in every Halloween "haunted" house or
party he'd ever been to outside of the ones in school, when they'd
gone to school. It made the phosphorescent paint on his bedroom
ceiling glow, and every bit of lint on a black outfit too. Black light.

The curious thing was the spalls crushed into dust for the paint
they'd made were from the tears of the great mother, just like every
lightstone they'd ever known of. If he was going to give off light,
just as he'd demonstrated at the gate, it was supposed to be whole,
white light. His breath caught again, *UV is part of the whole… it's me.*

My frequency changed.

Bidding Boaz rise with a hand on his elbow, he stopped, his head cocked toward Diagas, "You have genetic memory."

The quizzical look of a single eyebrow shooting upward on the dragon's face brought a faint rush of comfort to Nick as he asked, "that which came from the great mother?"

Nick nodded.

"We do."

"What was that?" Tropus asked, his uncertainty written plainly on his face.

"I need to know Diagas, not just the lessons you…"

"Zu is the most ancient left of us, he will have a better…"

"Nuh uh," he shook his head. "You and I have worked together before. I trust you, and right now, there are only two others I feel the same way about, and none among the Herus."

Understanding what Nick was saying, and more importantly where his sentiments were coming from, the last of the Green Flame Clutch gave a respectful bow, "What information do you seek?"

"Three things, first, when firdur became aware. Then, why did some Sidhe side with it? And of course, what caused the enmity toward me, toward Oemir…" he paused then shrugged, "Okay, a fourth… what did they hope to gain by tormenting me through so many thousands of years? If you have any insights about that. If not," a dark look crossed his features as another wave of the strange illumination passed over him, "I'll have to ask them myself." Watching the waves pass over his forearm, he wiggled his fingers, met the dragon's gaze, and together they shared a knowing smile.

He wheeled to face Tropus, "I get what Leanna wanted when she stopped you from killing me, but how could you be okay with the idea of your daughter wanting an offspring of Oemir's line just so she could have a tool to help destroy all life? And knowing she could be capable of such a thing, how could you not understand why it was impossible for me to love her?" he asked then continued.

"Instead of leading as a king should, you allowed her to dragon-nap, to capture, incarcerate, and feed YOUR lands on the lifeblood of the children of the great mother herself! It's no wonder the bridge sought to swallow you up. Your guard should have let it." He spat, a hint of the depth of fury the Bedowen king couldn't have guessed this human child would have the temerity to divulge here and now.

"So many millennia and you are still a self-righteous, arrogant…"

Tropus began but was cut off as Nick strode to stand before him, almost three feet shorter, but with the kind of stony resolve no one would have expected from a half human. Again, Diagas found himself impressed with this youth.

"This from you? Born to be king of your own realm, resentful of the birthright of another slated to become King of All Sidhe for no other reason than it wasn't you! Or was it resentful of me because I loved Illirya and not your daughter?"

The challenges erupting from this new Oemir, the truths, he'd held cloaked in secrecy for millennia, held in a heart darkened with envy, resentment, and thousands of years of denied cravings now spoken so boldly were as a slap in the face.

They brought to the fore the shames Tropus had been feeling since he allowed Fetik to beat the child nearly to death, then added his own insult to the injuries meted out by the corrupt Sidhe. He tried to tell himself it was because the wrath of his daughter's wounded pride had poisoned him. But it was, at least in part, a lie. Any further, he was still not ready to admit, even to himself.

"For every life stolen before its time, for every innocent lost fighting an enemy you gave refuge, you deserve a thousand times each of the thousands of tortures my soul has endured through the millennia. Death is too easy for what you have enabled!" He turned away, reading the stricken glance on Boaz's face, then the enigmatic expression on Diagas'.

He wheeled once more, "Even as the first son of Danu and Lugh as the deliverer of laws, your fate is not mine to dictate." *Would that it were.* He thought as a third pulsing of that strange dark wave moved over him, this time extending out to crackle the air around him.

"They kinda looked like they were getting high from the uv one." The memory of Frank's voice, full of excitement, warmed him.

As it did so, neither Diagas, nor Boaz missed what happened when that strange crackle surrounded Tropus, illuminating him and his corruption in a way at least Boaz had never seen before.

Nick caught a glimpse of it as well before waves of dizziness tried to expose his sudden weakness. But he was accustomed to the occasional assault of his being through starvation, dehydration, or over-exertion, this too would pass.

Tropus loomed over him, his teeth grinding, his eyes blazing hatred as he wondered how he could have ever had the slightest charitable thought toward this human *thing*.

"I could snap you as a twig..." he threatened.

Nick stood tall, his body filling out just a bit more though he could never reach the giant king's stature, "Maybe, but I'm sure with your "moral fortitude" you wouldn't live long enough to enjoy having done it. Why don't you go find Khazeer, we have worlds to save." He turned his attention back to Diagas, having noted Boaz's expression of pure shock before literally turning his back on Tropus, wondering if he would indeed try to snap him like a twig, and whether or not Boaz or Diagas would allow it.

Rebuked, the Bedowen King turned to leave the warren, Nick couldn't help but wonder if part of him was doing so only because he believed none would survive what was coming. If so, Nick wondered the same thing.

16

"There are literally tens of thousands of points where they cross!" Charles protested.

"Most likely more," Harry nodded.

"We don't need to join them all, we just need to get portals set at each chakra point so our world can use the living energy of their world to build and fortify wards that can protect us *both* if we can. If we can't then there are going to be places where we'll lose contact during the rotations, it's going to have to be enough." Mickey explained.

"Earth watch satellite's already picked up encroaching darkness coming up from the Mariana trench," Charles explained.

"They can't see down there, it's the deepest place on earth," Harry Jr. protested.

"Yeah," Charles nodded. "And it's already risen to the surface." He pointed to the report he'd just pulled up, "They're sending ships out there to see if it's oil or not."

"How do we know it's not oil? You're makin' a pretty big leap here kid," one of the others on the internet call contested.

"Oil doesn't move like that," Charles clicked the "play" arrow on the video which showed approximately ten seconds of darkness turning and moving like a dog does to find the right spot to drop its load.

"Shoal of fish?" another suggested weakly as almost everyone either shrugged or shook their heads.

On the T.V., dozens of sets of eyes rolled, heads shook, scowls grew, and a few threw pencils in the air or simply tuned out.

"Hey! You ass clowns wanna live or you wanna die!?" the older brother, of their new friends shouted, "All we're askin' for is you go set up a portal at your nearest chakram…"

"Chakra," his brother corrected.

"Whatever," he snarled back.

There were a few jokes about some "Warrior Princess" among some of the older guys, and a few lewd comments from both some of the guys and girls present, before Harry Sr. leaned into the camera on his laptop.

"C'mon y'all, if we can get some fortification going here, it can roll over the other world and at least give it some measure of protection. Might even give us a means to coordinate with 'em, they use crystal tech, not too different from ours."

"Why should we care?" One of the women asked, her feet up on her desk as she sipped from a mug.

"Yeah, it's a whole other world, who gives a shit, we got enough crap to worry about here…" Another added.

"This living dark shit is tearing people apart, and we've even run across some of the hunters, healers and shaman's that got ate up by those vestige things, we gotta help ourselves before we can help anyone else." Yet another interjected.

The scowl on the older brother's face grew hard and angry and he leaned into his own camera, "Just a couple years ago more than half of you helped us saved THIS WORLD from literally dozens of legions of demons about to be unleashed from devil's gates all over this planet! It ain't that different!" he reminded them all.

"That really happened?" a few of them asked, "I thought it was just one of your bullshit stories."

Those who'd been there confirmed the truth of what the older brother was saying.

Indignant, he rose and started peeling off his outer shirts, "I'll show you bullshit, I got the scars to prove it! Thousands of 'em! EVERYWHERE!"

"Don't... just..." the younger one shook his head with his eyes closed, "keep your clothes on... please."

Deflated, he shrugged back into his shirt and swigged from a whiskey bottle, "Scars or not I'm still damn pretty!"

"This is like herding feral cats," Harry Sr. rolled his head, cracked open a beer, and sat back, his actions mirrored by at least half a dozen of the hunters, mages, and shaman in the meeting.

After another ten to fifteen minutes of grumbling, arguing, name calling and various side jokes and conversations, the group settled down and got to business in earnest.

--

From the far side of the control room Wellyn called Khazeer to the outer deck.

559

It seemed from every direction, billows of dust spoke of travelers headed toward the Tower of the Sun, though distance was hard to gauge at this height, it was clear there were many people of the remaining lands on their way. The question was, of them, how many were coming to defend against the darkness, and how many were working with it.

"Ilirya comes from East of the mountain, with, it appears, the Felesians, and whoever else they have been able to muster," the smile in Areen's voice was unmistakable as she joined them from the lift.

Her tone began to darken as she continued, "there is no sign of the Cyclopes, no word from Steropes or Gregaria," she wrapped her arm around her husband's waist, "and as we feared, the Gargol are also no more. Poe brought word from Minya and Arabelle's foray into their village."

Tears flowed from her eyes as they glanced from one to the next of those present. "Other than a single head, no more than dust was found."

Lou felt his brows furrow, his questioning gaze turned to Wellyn, "They were light brought to life from the stone flesh of the first ones."

"No more than dust... literally made of lightstone, they were obliterated," Lou translated to himself as the others nodded. "Living dark, or could vestiges have done it?" he asked.

"Even Tur or Semet's people could have with firdureen at their side," Wellyn explained through the horror on his face.

Once again the lift opened, unleashing Tropus, Boaz, Julius, Shep and Dylan onto the platform.

Lou looked at Wee, "The gang's all here… almost. Look, just remember Dylan's been pretty delirious for days."

The youngest of the senior Emerson's brows furrowed, but his guts made him give a faint nod he hoped D didn't see as they joined the group.

"S'nice up here… Anyone seen Nick?" He asked scanning the platform.

The other heads shook.

"Your tower is falling apart Khazeer," Tropus noted, his expression curious as the king and queen smiled at one another.

"So it is."

"I thought you were gonna go stick to him like glue?" D half snarled with a slap to Lou's chest.

"I got side-tracked. Y'know…the alarm."

Sharing an almost instantaneous look with Julius, he gave the faintest quiver of his head, "He may not have returned yet. He bade me watch over the Herus until his return. But when the alarm sounded…"

"You got anything?" D asked his baby brother.

Wee assumed a familiar posture, as though listening to something far-away, then shook his head, "Nada."

"You said 'returned'," the apparently murderous Emerson turned to Julius, "Where'd he go?"

"My Heru commanded I stay to guard the others, he need not divulge his plans to me."

Those present noted D's deep scowl, all of them recognizing he was still possessed of whatever sickness his captivity had caused.

Julius gave a non-committal nod to Lou, the corner of whose mouth stretched just enough to betray his approval.

"We got other stuff t'talk about D, take a look around, all that kicked up dust out there? It's folks coming this way. We don't know who's coming to help or blow the world apart, we'll worry about Nick later."

The dark shape of Danu's emissary caught Areen's attention before passing overhead, but not emerging from the far side of the platform. He would, as always, share what was necessary with those who needed to know.

"Come," Khazeer motioned them inside where every approaching group could be watched while they caught each other up on what they knew and planned for the upcoming, and possibly final assaults.

A great distance away, even further north than the tower itself, a faint puff of yellow followed by a strand of dark one might have thought to be smoke from a good campfire, brought suppressed smiles to the faces of the Sidhe around them. Allies they hadn't known to have survived, it now seemed, had arisen once again, and with them, hope.

--

"How could you lose him!" Tur railed, towering over Semet, his fury a literal force vibrating through the tent, much the way their anger did on Terra. It even caused nosebleeds in those present.

Semet's gaze fixed on the child standing beside his mother, his hand in hers, a look of curiosity on his face, as the Heru of the Nahroehn raised their crooked, talon-like finger, pointing to the boy.

"It must have far more power than we could have imagined." Semet's persona was a perfect blend of both of their facets, but Tur was well accustomed to their wiles.

Leanna straightened, her air, haughty, and righteous with an aura of danger pulsing around her. "You would place blame for your own short-sightedness on a newborn. Beyond despicable Semet, your credibility is beyond repair."

"He was HERE!" Semet raged, "consciousness constrained! Separated from the body! Who else could have known let alone would have the power to set it free!"

The child looked up into his mother's face, wonder and curiosity easily read on his features, a reminiscence of hope in the combination.

"It may be an assumption Semet, but perhaps HE would have." She snarled.

"There is no way a HUMAN would have the knowledge…"

Stepping away from her son, leaving him out of reach of the treacherous Nahroehn Heru, she towered over them, her teeth not quite splintering under the force of her grinding, "He was born ONE OF US! And no matter where or in what species the soul returned, never forget he is the first son of Danu and Lugh! EVERYTHING his first life knew is at his disposal, as is every talent brought about by every successive life he has lived! You are not, and never have been a FRACTION of what he is!"

Semet's face twisted with disdain, "You are still besotted! Enamored as a fledgling with its first arousal!"

She rose up straight, her face impassive, "Think you I would waste the energy of my love on someone who did not return it? If so you are a far greater fool than I've previously thought. I have everything I desire from him." She returned to her son's side, taking his hand in hers. Looking from the child to her millennia long paramour, her smile flared hot, "Here, is where those who hold my heart live. I pity the one who has never known such joy as I am able to both share and still call my own."

Semet's glare shot to Tur, whose lips tilted, saying all he needed. The princess required no one to defend any aspect of her life after all.

"Perhaps cousin, you should take wing to the tower, learn what you are able about the state of things." Tur suggested after another moment.

A dark and bitter smile crossed Semet's features, "Indeed, a wise idea cousin." They nodded before shifting shape and taking wing.

--

Beneath his feet the vibration he'd begun to feel just a few minutes ago turned to something deeper. The first vibrations felt like a hum moving through the air happening to jiggle the ground a little too, but this, this was something coming from near this world's very core.

Considering he was standing fewer than a dozen yards from the subterranean edge of a two mile diameter caldera, and what he was certain was about to happen, it was not at all surprising. Utterly terrifying, yes. Surprising, no.

In the distance, about what he presumed was the mid-point, Garnet's front claws sliced into the hard baked earth, little by little creating a fissure between the outside and the inner sanctuary of the largest Wyvern nest one could ever imagine.

It's like slicing into a pie crust. He thought, while dancing from foot to foot before looking around and noting a nearby shrub. She took a glance back at him, noticing his movement, then smiled to herself when he dashed behind the greenery, the scent of his relief bringing a smile of humor to her lips while she scratched at the Wyverns' door.

--

Sitting cross-legged, his gaze fixed deep into Diagas' golden eye, one hand on the side of the being's head, his once nearly black hair now heavily salted with silver, Nick blinked and took a deep breath. *All that time, that frustration, the rage...*

His gaze shifted, taking in the warren as if he hadn't seen it in years.

"Diagas," he sighed, something both lost and resigned in the sound.

"It is only a sliver," the dragon agreed, "but still, it IS hope."

Stiffer than he should be before the passage of several decades, Nick pushed to his feet, stretched the kinks out and headed toward the stone entry, his hand on a lever, "and you will go to Zu and the others?"

"I will."

"And will they listen?"

"They will know the truth, and do what must be done so revenge may be had later."

Nick nodded at the captive. "And him?"

The dragon's lips pulled back, his fearsome rows of teeth glistening as his gaze narrowed on the servant of darkness, "...a snack before I leave."

Nick smiled, "enjoy. We'll meet again soon." He pulled the lever and headed up.

"Oemir," Diagas stopped him, the forks of his tongue trembling.

He turned.

"Your leg… it will buzz soon."

Pursing his lips Nick felt his breeches, his eyes lighting up as his hand landed on his phone, which seemed to awaken at his touch.

His smile seemed to light up the room, "They found a way…" he swept the green button, dashing out of the warren, "Hey, hold on," he turned to the dragon, "Diagas, thank you."

Dashing down the tunnel toward the center of the spire, he winced as the sound of a scream cut short, and the crunch of a body's worth of bones was left behind.

"Who is this?" he asked dashing into the lift and sweeping the panel until it showed the command deck, his hand somehow granting him access to the literal pinnacle of Aderyn's planetary power.

"It's me kiddo," Harry's deep soothing voice was the greatest sound he'd heard in what felt like years!

"It's Us!" the others shouted, as in the background what sounded like a stadium of people cheered.

"Oh my god, how long is this going to last?" he asked as the lift began its rise.

"Long as the chakra's are aligned with a cell tower," Mickey explained. "We haven't got satellite positions locked in yet."

"Gimme a minute girly!" A sharp voice snarked, "Can't rush the computers, the genius is already done."

"So a few minutes…how the hell did you guys manage this?!" he half demanded, amazed, but then shook his head, "Who the hell, nevermind, you can tell me later. When's the next time we'll be able to talk after the line goes dead?"

"This time of day," Charles could be heard in the background, "we're kinda at an equatorial crossing, so probably an hour or so once we lose contact. Are you alright?"

"So much better now! Look I'm about to go into a strategy session…"

"Nick, where's Frankie? We can't get hold of him?" the worry in Harry's voice was unmistakable.

"He's on the other side of the continent, about to marshal the wyverns, he's a little worse for the wear, but he's okay. If we win this he's gonna deserve a summer vacation like you can't imagine."

"You got it kiddo," Harry acknowledged over all the other voices demanding attention.

"Did he say wyverns?"

"Did you say wyverns?" two of several could be heard asking over the line.

"What the hell's a wyvern?"

"S'a kind of dragon dumbass."

"Are there dragons there?" others asked.

"Give me an hour, then see if you can give us a facetime or zoom, I miss you guys so much! I knew you'd think of something!"

"We're working on it from our end, but we got a bandwidth problem when it comes to vid." Charles, Harry jr. and a couple hunters from their call chimed in.

"You can do it! One hour!" he grinned, his heart racing with joy as he ended the call and returned the device to his pocket, at the same time the door opened.

With half his vision on the 'scape, Nick easily recognized each of the people who'd gathered to await his arrival. First were Lou and Julius with swords drawn. Tropus, Wee, Shep and Areen as the next line of defense, Boaz, Khazeer and Wellyn as the last line of defense.

Holding back and hoping to blend into a shadow in the corner stood Dylan, trying to digest this fully grown, weathered warrior was his nephew, and wondering how he was going to have to modify his plan in order to save his little brother from what was coming for him.

With the door fully opened, he held them all still for a moment. He returned Julius and Lou's swords to their sheaths, then resumed his place before them, and allowed time to move forward.

His hands closed on Julius's face, his smile, and grinning bright blue eyes unmistakable as he pressed his lips to the Captain of the Guard's then pressed their foreheads together.

"Meleth," he sighed then turned, grasping Lou's hand, and clapping him on the shoulder.

"Maps?" he craned a look at a large table in the center of the enclosed room. "Ah good! We have very little time and far too much for you to catch up on."

Ignoring their questions he led them inside and began to re-organize the strategic model they'd been working with.

"Diagas will be heading back to the rest of the dragons when he finishes his snack. Frank, Garnet, and Poe are marshaling and leading the wyvern forces... Wee, get Tierus up here," he tapped his ear, indicating the buds they all wore now, even as Julius slid one into his ear as well.

"Nicky? Is it really you?" Wee couldn't stop himself from asking as he fingered gray streaks his nephew was far too young for.

"Yeah."

"What happened to you?"

A strange kind of smile broke on his face as he realized they all wanted an answer.

"I've been, uhm... traveling. Now, we have a sliver of a window available to us, but a lot of things have to be timed just right, on both of our worlds. The bitch of it is, when it comes to the timing, if I try to interfere with it on any level, we are one hundred percent fucked. So pay attention like our universes depend on it and save your questions for later. If we win."

Wee flicked the tail of his bud, "Tierus, c'mon up to the command deck."

"On my way." The fledgling responded, having grown accustomed to many of Wee's verbal expressions.

"What is that all over you?" Wee asked, a tentative finger prodding his covering.

He looked at Julius, "How much is left?"

"Kind of a war-paint the kid says." Shep answered.

"It has lasted well. Enough for a full coat or half for two?"

"It's an experiment Julius came up with, a damned good one too!" Nick nodded, "I'll need it all."

Khazeer looked to Wellyn, "it appears very like the paint Lugh often wore."

"Syldryl said the same thing," Nick grinned, "or maybe it was Ahrendaria, let me show you," he motioned them around the table so everyone could see as he held his hand forward, and with a smile, lit it up until the hand itself had the glow of a good-sized lantern.

Startled by the brightness he was able to muster, all of them, including Wellyn, Khazeer and Areen winced, averting their eyes, "Almost identical to Lugh." Wellyn nodded.

"So that's why he was called 'the shining one'." Wee nodded his appreciation.

Slowly Dylan leaned forward, though did not approach the others just yet.

"Well now hang on kid don't you think the rest of us…" Lou began.

"No."

"But if we make enough.." Shep joined in.

"No."

"There are not enough…" Julius tried to explain.

"Now just hold on, I'm the one who's the most direct…"

Nick crossed his arms, his hip cocked, his eyebrow spocked and a cocky smile on his face, "Oh really? And NO."

"Whatever you're plannin' Nicky, we're not gonna let you do it alone," Wee added.

When he had enough, the elder Oemir shook his head and allowed his entire upper torso to flare and hold until they were all silent and shielding their eyes.

Lou's hand came to rest on his forearm, "I think you made your point kid."

"There are NO ARGUMENTS, if we stray from the path by even a whisper, it's OVER. Do you understand!" he demanded not unkindly.

"Just where exactly did you go traveling to?" Shep asked.

His gaze snapped to the seasoned hunter, "Before the birth of the universe." *And the end of all things.*

For a long moment, with his soft declaration, the gathering turned their gazes to him, stunned into silence for only a few, but very poignant heartbeats before a throat cleared.

"Can any of you imagine an entire battlefield lit up so brightly? It may keep the vestiges and firdur away, but it will not solve the problem or put an end to this threat." Khazeer advised, catching the surprised attention of all those other than Wellyn, Wee, Areen and Nick, getting them back on track.

"Why can't you use your power? It's kinda the only real weapon we got, aside from the tower," Shep asked.

It was a fair question, and Nick had the necessary answer, "It's not a weapon, it's a tool. Firdur is connected to time. It's infiltrated both worlds far enough that if I manipulate so much as a nanosecond once tonight's attacks begin in earnest, it will KNOW we're wise to it, and will destroy *everything* in one move. It must be made to believe we see tonight as just another series of futile actions. It must believe we are defending and cowering rather than lying in

571

wait."

Tropus, his tone relaxed and strong met eyes with the boy who now looked more like Oemir than he had up to this point. "You doubtless learned much from Diagas."

With Tierus joining them, they turned their attention back to the table as Nick craned his head to meet the Bedowen king's gaze, all heat gone from his own, "I got my answers."

He smiled then began to lay out the necessary scenarios. "Like I said, there's a sliver of a chance, a tiny window of opportunity..."

"Are you sure Nicky? I mean you have this gift for a reason..."

"Dude you killed a vestige." Lou divulged drawing an amazed look from Wee and a horrified one from D.

Squeezing his fingers about a centimeter apart he replied, "Vestige, small part of the whole," he let the inference hang, Lou, and Julius well aware of how much it'd taxed him.

"So, from the great mother's own memories, given to her children, and shared with me... this is how it has to go..."

--

Leftenant Eggers skidded to a halt on the deck of Ula's grotto, his gaze fixed on Diagas, who, despite his sphinxlike posture appeared anything but enigmatic.

"Leftenant," the dragon greeted and received a deep, respectful bow in return.

"Diagas of the green flame, how may I serve you?" he asked without a hint of waver in his voice.

"I have a task for you." He invited with an extended claw. "Have you ever met a wyvern?"

Climbing up until he was perched between Diagas' shoulder blades the leftenant shook his head, "I have not."

A bright smile turned up the corners of the dragon's mouth, "Then this shall be interesting. Hold tight now." He instructed before lurching through a break one of the mages was holding open in the wards at the far side of the entrance.

Behind the departing pair, three of those able bodied and chosen, moved into the tunnel, draining the water from it as they, like the others, began the task of cleaning and greasing the way for use later into the night.

--

17

Deep in one of the lower chambers, shrouded in cool and soothing darkness, a door opened, bringing with it a soft billow of breeze stinging like razor blades as Ryan's gimping shadow laid long against the slant of light.

A wet snort and hoof clop greeted him as a series of small lightstones embedded into the walls began to glow the further he moved into the room.

"That you Raziel?" he asked and received another clop and snort. "Kieren you in here too?" he asked as the warrior stepped from behind a dressing curtain garbed in soft fabrics of Fierowen blue.

"Yes."

"The elder healer told me to get you guys out of here and into the stable if your skin is healed, is your skin healed?"

A faint smile twitched the corners of the ex-Nahroehn's lips, "it has, though we are still... more sensitive than we are accustomed." He cocked his head to the side, "You have also been injured."

Slow to move his arms away from his torso, Ry concentrated on breathing through the stretch, handing Kieren a cloak, and moving toward Raziel with the other.

"Got your hair back eh fellah?" he muttered using the horse's body to walk his hands up toward its back even as he snorted and nodded his head wildly.

"He was nearly insane with itching for several days," Kieren smiled from the other side as he helped right the cloak over Ilirya's most cherished and beloved friend.

"I could not be sure he would not try to use me as a brush," the warrior smiled then rested his forehead against the stallion's neck. It was clear the two had formed a bond during their convalescence.

"So, what happened to you?" Ry asked, part of him wanting to hate this being in spite of the fact he wasn't the one who'd tormented and sliced at Wee and Tommy, but simply because he came from the same land as the one who had.

"Semet, the Heru of my homeland was not pleased I survived Owain and Petrouk, the one your half-breed…"

"Yeah I remember."

"In their displeasure Semet presented firdureen with a… feast."

"Oh my god… and it left you alive?"

"A fate far worse than death. Still, the emissary's emissary led one of Heru Khazeer's messengers to me."

The grimace of sympathy and pain crossing Ryan's face left little doubt in his mind whatever else he may have to face before all this was over, one way or the other, he was currently in a place and among people he would die to protect.

"And you?" he asked as the two cleaned up the room, pushing beds and equipment off to the sides, along the walls to make room for whatever it was they needed the tunnel for.

"Cathbad's mound collapsed while we were under it… popped me like a bug," he ground as he used muscles he hadn't in what felt like ages.

"Oooh!" Kieren's look of horror and distress actually brought a chuckle to the hunter.

"Yeah." With the room largely cleared, he smoothed the cloak over Raziel, gently scratching wherever he felt the horse twitch in the way he would if he were beset with biting flies. He leaned toward the fluff covered ear, his eye meeting the beautiful brown of the horse's, "You protected my boys, there isn't thanks enough," as tears slipped in slim threads down his face, he rested his head gently against the warm jawbone then kissed and stroked its cheek.

Unashamed he met Kieren's curious expression.

"She won't let me see my husband yet. I get why, but…" he stopped, sniffing back his hurt.

"It hurts your heart." The soldier nodded. "I have never been fortunate enough to have loved or been loved so deeply."

"Be grateful," he gulped then pointed to a small side tunnel. "They said this one will take us outside. We take a left once we're between the walls…"

Raziel nodded, nudging the burly blonde then took the lead, to bring the men literally out of the cool and soothing darkness, and into the last full hour of daylight, where they were to rejoin the world.

--

Frank stood, numb with amazement as wave after full-spectrum rainbow wave came rushing out of the slice Garnet had carved into the plain, until the whole of the caldera's surface was cramped with nearly a thousand wyverns of varying ages, statuses, skills, and sizes, all gathered to get a glimpse of the reborn Oemir and serve to protect their world as they had millennia ago.

"They are far wiser and more knowledgeable than most are aware. They are just as able to understand your kind, both with language, and your gifts. Fear not Oemir, they have much to offer and are eager to do so, for the continued existence of all."

"Yeah, getting to stay alive's a pretty good motivator," Frank nodded, though he still couldn't stop his legs from shaking as he stood atop Garnet's head before a vast sea of two legged, winged, ancient terrors called wyverns.

"How come Leanna napped you guys but didn't get them?" he asked quietly.

"Even beings as long lived, and often well-tempered as Sidhe, have biases. The Bedowen Princess, being both ill-tempered and deeply biased always underestimated the Wyvern community."

"I guess in the end that was a good thing."

"Indeed, now, keep the images of our needs in your mind and there will be no mistaking what must be done." She assured.

At first the images came in a frenzy, the molten cavern beneath the Nahroehn tower and its stone platform with its chains, the tower of the sun with vestiges and walls of dark rolling over it, destroying everything. A fear in the form of movie battles he'd seen where the heroes were nearly overwhelmed.

The reptilian ocean before him began to undulate, the citizens looking to one another for clarification, growing restless in his projected uncertainty.

He sniffed hard, tears of desperation, and fear of failure rolling down his face, his body trembling so hard he thought he might just fall over.

"You got this shrimp-o, just breathe."

"Breathe young Oemir," Nick and Garnet whispered.

She raised her head, a series of chuffs and calls emanated to calm the suddenly uncertain family members.

"I told them you are gathering your thoughts."

He nodded and scrubbed his face, "Thanks," as the small form of a familiar sight flew into view from the direction of the tower.

"Poe," he sighed, feeling his legs begin to steady as the emissary of the Goddess flew above the ocean of waiting beings, chirping, and cawing over and over again as he performed a spellbinding aerobatic dance to capture and hold the attention of the entire congregation. His 'speech' also strengthened the heart of the little boy inside the fledgling Sidhe Frank had become. He finished with a flourish, cartwheeling through the sky to perch on the littlest Emerson's shoulder, all eyes followed him, then held on Frank, whose legs stopped shaking, and breath steadied.

"That was better than even Aragorn!" he whispered, stroking the proud avian's breast with a gentle finger. "Thanks, a loooooht!"

Poe, while having no idea who or what an Aragorn might be, understood all too well he'd impressed the youth down to his very heart. He fluffed with pride, giving a cursory preen to his upper wing, before doing the same to the half human child while quickly filling him and Garnet in on their part of the plan; the instructions he'd got from those at the tower were so clear and simple Frank's mind filled with visuals easily read by the entirety of the assembly.

In mere moments, the sea of wyverns separated into three groups. The largest, of roughly two thirds the population would accompany Frank to the area surrounding the Tower of the Sun, and wait in camouflage until the dragons arrived and they were signaled to move.

In his mind, Frank saw a 'Poe's eye view' of the Fierowen city. There, it appeared the sandstone within the honeycomb structure had mostly fallen away, leaving the gleaming almost ivory colored foundation and structure visible causing a raucous cheer to go up among the crowd, many of whom flapped, jumped, and swooped low in celebration, all of them, as one envisioning the entirety of the Fierowen city bursting to a brilliance to rival the sun.

Almost instantly, and despite some uncertainty, with their projected visual in his mind, Frank, grinning with their excitement pressed his finger across his lips, asking them not to draw attention to themselves. They did, but murmurs, flaps and tiny blows of celebratory sparks still peppered the group.

Sensing his confusion Poe gave a quiet set of croaks and clicks.

"Part of the plan huh? If you say so." Frank nodded, as from this grouping, a large, fully mature, copper colored female took wing to land beside Garnet, accepting the role of protector of the Oemir.

Turning to face one of the obvious leaders of the wyvern family, Frank gave a deep bow, "You have my gratitude…" he cocked his head to the side, "do you have a name?"

With what he would swear was an indulgent smile, a series of gurgles emerged into the air while an image of this female standing guard over her portion of the resting flock seemed to waft into his mind.

He pursed his lips for a moment, "I can't pronounce that. We have a guy among our kind who holds the weight of the world on his shoulders, kinda like you do for your kind. Can I call you Atlas?" he offered projecting an image of the famous Titan into her head.

Her smile split into an enormous, terrifying grin as she gave a series of long nods and shot a fine spray of what appeared to be molten liquid into the air where it quickly cooled and rained down as ash, eliciting another cacophony of roars and wing-flap cheers.

"Your version of fireworks, cool."

And so the next segment gathered, this grouping of a few dozen, larger than average, almost bull-dozer looking wyverns, gathered around Garnet, led by a blue-green male with the kind of expression etched into his face indicating he "brooked no guff", as Harry Sr. would have said. He craned his neck, his eye coming uncomfortably close to Frank as the corner of his lip rose up and he seemed to whisper something sounding like one of Ry's beer burps but with a vastly different smell.

"Oh!" Frank's eyes lit up as an image of one of the most well-known giants of human lore popped into mind, "Goliath...s'that okay?" he asked as the impressive being dipped his head in a bow, just as Frank gave the same respect.

"Thank you." This time, the image he shared was of the platform the Nahroehn tower floated on, and its chains of stone being destroyed by this group of wyvern "roughnecks".

Frank's hands flew to his ears, and he crouched quickly at what he thought was an explosion. He realized it was a roar of excitement as they veered toward the leaning finger of rock which protected Tur and his corrupted schades for far too long. As one, they shimmered into a state of camouflage, disappearing in silence making it clear they'd been waiting a long time for a chance like this.

Lastly came the youths, those who'd only hatched within the last century or so and had no practical experience fighting for anything other than a place in the pecking order of the nest.

"And the future for all," Frank muttered as a canary yellow set of twins approached. They stood about twice Frank's Sidhe height, but each about half as broad as Garnet's head.

Frank bowed deep for the third time, his head cocked to the side as the male squawked and the female trilled. The littlest Emerson couldn't help but grin as a scene of a famous set of twins fighting each other on the floor while they turned old came to mind. "That's Fred and George... they're the cleverest in the wizarding world..." and before he could finish his request the pair were squawking together, pecking, and preening one another with their expressions open and radiating excitement.

Frank and Garnet shared a chuckle as a blur of opalescent emerald green came to a stop before the group of youths.

"Diagas," Frank sighed as more than a dozen Fierowen elders and Leftenant Eggers climbed down, their outer garments heavily laden in various places.

"Fred and George," Diagas smiled.

"Well in the movie they're both boys but...they seem to like the names as they are."

The electrical charge of excitement rolling off the youths was unmistakable, they were really just glad to be part of saving the universe, and getting a chance to meet real dragons, even if they weren't born yet.

The Fierowen elders lined up as the wyverns approached,

sniffing them to find the eggs with which they'd be most compatible to stand guard over.

An image burst into Frank's mind, George asking if they were to guard the eggs here at the nest, or if there was somewhere else they had in mind.

"Oh no," Frank shook his head, sharing with them the image of the magma flowing free through the Nahroehn without the fortress to obstruct its movement. He showed them being led by Poe and diving into the stream with their charges, filling the flow as it moved through the heart of the land, the brightest, and hottest place in this world. There they would nurture the eggs and wait. At the top of the stairs, Goliath and his team would stand guard over them, and outside, Poe would keep a discreet eye on the site. It was certain the catastrophic collapse of the fortress would, at least, bring pirini to investigate.

"When the time is right, you'll know what to do."

The air of excitement thickened all around as members of each of the groups broke toward their assignments shimmering into camouflage, leaving the plain to appear as barren as it looked when they first arrived.

Atlas tilted her head so Frank could ride back with her.

"Thank you Garnet," he bowed his head, "stay safe?"

"We will meet again sooner than you know young Oemir. Atlas will care for you as none other could."

"I know," he smiled then looked to Diagas as Leftenant Eggers helped the last couple of the Fierowen elders back up before climbing back up himself. "You'll be with the others after you drop them off then?"

The last of the green flame clutch angled his head, "I have my position. We shall meet again soon if all goes well."

"And if it doesn't, there'll be nothing left to know," Frank sighed.

Sensing the young Oemir's sudden sadness, Atlas, with an image of clouds flowing beneath them, asked if he'd like a flight to lift his spirits.

A small wave of nausea slithered through his belly as he remembered the feeling of being jostled about by the pirini who'd snatched and poisoned him before Poe and his clutch-mates came to his rescue.

"No thank you. Maybe when we win… if…" he paused, *stay positive,* "If the offer still stands." He forced a smile then wrapped his arms around a cluster of frills and leaned in close to her neck, closing his eyes and trying to hide his sudden overwhelming fear from both of them.

--

Comfortable with how the meeting and division of assignments among the wyverns went, Poe noticed a large obsidian form flapping into view from the Northwest then angling toward the Fierowen tower.

Through a spatial slip, he returned to the command center where the Heru's and Heroes continued to work out the finer details of their plan for this battle-front. Landing quickly on Areen's shoulder he told her of the Nahroehn Heru's flight in this direction, then slipped away, returning to observe the fortress and watch for the pirini to arrive, he had a surprise for them.

"Focus on your personal losses, they'll feast on your grief." Nick reminded

his human family as Lou and Shep nodded, "Show time."

They leaned studiously over the duplicate of the map Nick had absorbed. With no one certain whether it was a decoy or not, they'd decided to use it to provide disinformation. They were certain Semet would be the spy sent to learn their plans, given their therianthropic nature.

"What about Ula? That siren was her ocean under attack, wasn't it?" Shep asked, almost demanding.

On the 'scape, Nick watched Semet's avian form perch bat-like on the outer wall, just above the western threshold. With a pointed glance at each of them he nodded then indicated where they were.

Khazeer nodded, "The Akirowen Heru and her oceans will be well protected…"

"How? Just being under water doesn't mean she's safe, this stuff, this dark moves through air, water, vacuum as far as we know, s'what you said b'fore right Nick?"

"Yeah, it does, but she has many worthy warrior subjects on islands, and atolls, most of whom are capable not only on land, but in the water as well. She has her mariners, krakens, leviathans, deep-water subjects, cetaceans, cephalopods and even more important, extremophiles. She is well protected. The warning was for us."

"Extremophiles? What like those water bug things? How the hell can that help?!" he demanded

"Bears," Dylan corrected.

"I know what they are!" The smitten hunter bit, drawing a quiet smirk from Lou, and a surprised smile from Dylan and Wee both.

"As it did the first time, the dark will attempt to smother the land before it begins to wring the life out of the seas." Khazeer assured.

"Only this time she gave us warning." Nick explained, the hint of bitterness in his voice took them all by surprise.

"The point is," Areen interjected, "the queen is quite capable of defending her territories, we have our own concerns to address. Many of the surrounding towns have, or are evacuating. Our numbers have not recovered since the first war. Tur and his accursed, along with their firdur and firdureen, I fear, have cost us many of our allies before we were even aware they were in danger."

As Semet crept closer, an eye peering in, via a half-hidden corner, the Herus and heroes kept their thoughts on the plans they needed relayed to Tur and his forces while the first part of their own plans and forces crept into place.

"Exactly," Nick tapped the map, "these are the areas it appeared they were going to disburse their forces from, if we send small teams to reconnoiter…"

Semet's smile turned sharp and their eyes cruel, proud they'd been forward thinking enough to leave an opening through which they could be privy to what was foremost in this new Oemir's mind.

--

A sharp trill brought the group to an almost instant stand-still. Minya pressed his finger across his lips as he dashed behind a tree, slipping out from the camouflage spell covering their growing numbers. Dashing like a streak, a few hundred yards, barely able to be seen even by those most experienced with traversing the forests, he scoured the trees, the brush, and intersecting paths.

No sooner had he caught a familiar scent than he was

accompanied by a wolf on either side, the three of them crouching in wait as the scents grew stronger.

Above them, a falcon lit on a branch, facing the same direction the scent was coming from. It hopped twice then gave two sharp calls before taking off and returning back to the cover of the camouflage.

"Wait here," he whispered, zipping to a tree near the two women, before crossing his arms over his chest and clearing his throat.

With their swords drawn and pointed a hairs' breadth from his chest, he grinned, "Hello ladies, care for some company?"

"Identify yourself!" The taller of the two demanded.

He stuck his right hand out, but only turned up the palm of his left to show he was hiding no weapons.

The shorter one leaned in, whispering into the taller one's ear, though he did hear a single word, "…Wee…"

His smile grew to exceptional proportions, "You may call me Minya. You were sent by the kin of Oemir."

"Yes," the shorter one breathed seemingly amazed, "I am Janelle of the…"

The taller one's cautionary elbow stopped her talking.

Smiling, his well-honed senses certain these two Sidhe were in earnest, he explained, "We are headed to the Fierowen to save our universes."

"We?" the stauncher woman questioned just before the two wolves emerged from the brush and began to sniff them, their inherent respect and caution regarding wolves held them still while they were assessed.

As Wyle and Wereiwyn assumed their bipedal forms, the two ladies couldn't stop their grins of delight.

"Therianthropes!" Janelle exclaimed, reaching out and taking their hands, pressing them to her forehead while the other waited her turn. "Truly it is a joy to see you!"

"We thought you were lost either in time or the first war. I am Fern." She introduced; a sly but genuine smile aimed at Minya.

"He was right!" Janelle half-whispered excitedly as the camouflage was extended over them at a signal from Talmai, who came forward and introduced himself.

An ibis headed woman and jackal headed man came forward, offering water and dried meat to share with the women who stood marveling at the wondrous sight surrounding them.

"Which one?" Minya asked.

"The Wee," she answered bowing her thanks to those who made them welcome. "He told us that even if…" she shook her head, "that there were bound to be others who would come and fight."

A chuckle-snort popped out of him, "*The* Wee. I am eager to meet him. Can you tell us, how…"

Fern pulled her crystal, "They have been informing more this day than the last two, but…"

"It seems we are on the threshold of destiny once again." Talmai nodded, holding his own crystal up.

Fern's expression turned contemplative, "Only this time, there are no partial measures."

Minya dropped a gentle hand to her forearm, "then we must win, there is no alternative."

"You scoffed when I told you of the Wee…?"

"Not scoffed, amused. I never heard him referred to as "the" Wee. From what I've learned of all he's done, it fits very well."

She scrutinized him closely, "Humph."

"Were you able to reach the first ones?" he asked as their eyes popped wide with surprise.

"You shall grow accustomed to him if time permits. We saw the 'crossing lights' just after we left Fauxston." Arabelle emerged from behind the women who once more showed their delight, this time, at the sight of a familiar face while they traded hugs and other greetings.

"We met with them…" Janelle nodded, her eyes betraying the depth of fear she'd had while facing the most ancient of living beings in this or any world they knew of.

"They were aware of the situation," Fern sighed.

"But?"

"They spoke only of their awareness."

"So," Minya nodded, "we continue as if they will not intervene."

"So we too surmised." Janelle nodded.

The news was shared among the crystal holders as the group moved forward, spread out over kilometers so their passage was less conspicuous the closer they came to the outer edges of the Fierowen. All too soon, many of the groupings came upon the first of several details of schades with firdur guarding them.

--

Looking out from a checkerboard of faces, or looking down from a circle of them, disbelief and amazement was the common expression. The Heru's and heroes were amazed by what Harry's team and the hunters managed to pull off. And likewise, those on the terra side were having a hard time believing they weren't being played for fools.

Tropus, Areen, Khazeer, and Julius each held active crystals angling down so the first wave of defenders, could see and transmit the sequence of necessary events to the defenders on the edge of the Fierowen territory, those who were waiting to close the trap on the agents of the dark.

"We got kind of a genius over here," one of the hunters pointed to himself, "with this information I can get the timing's down to atomic clock level, but it's gonna be up to the magic users to make it happen. How many we got Bev?" he asked of middle-aged woman playing cat's cradle in one of the squares.

She sat up straight shuffling some papers while the cat's cradle continued to play by itself, "With misssidhe100," she motioned to Mickey who grinned with pride, "we got fifteen, two for each chakra depending on how long this goes on."

"And considering our planet and sun are larger than Aderyn, that makes the coverage area significantly larger too."

"Which is exactly what we were hoping for," Lou nodded with Shep at his side.

Nick blew out his held breath, "Way I figured, we need these chakra's rolling open for at least twenty-four hours, to get as much overlap as possible. The days here are right around sixteen hours each. If we could do a solid thirty-two there it'd be optimal." He glanced at Khazeer who nodded his head.

"And considering we're pretty sure the first one's aren't gonna show…" Lou added.

"You'd think they'd give a fuck if the entire goddamned universe was gonna get off'd," Dylan groused quietly.

"They have access to many dimensions the darkness may not," Areen tried to explain.

"That's not an excuse." Wee admitted, fighting a loose, electrical sensation in his low belly.

"No, but it is a reason they may be less… attached to life here." Wellyn noted.

"This is truly astonishing Oemir," the king of all Sidhe breathed, it'd been millennia since his heart beat with this much excitement, enough to bring small dots of perspiration to his forehead and upper lip.

"I can't believe were talking to a whole 'nother fuckin' world!"

"It explains so much!" another nodded.

"All the lore… so much…" a third whispered.

"You guys made this possible, far as I'm concerned, YOU are the real heroes, no matter what happens." Nick reminded them, as the rest nodded in firm agreement.

"We win this, we're gonna have one helluva shindig!" Shep offered with a smile, his heart aching. He didn't have to imagine Tommy's excitement over what'd been accomplished here, he could see his nephew's bright cornflower eyes shining, his face flushed and his uncontainable grin just like he'd seen it since the day the kid was born.

"Y'all better beat this darkness down," one of the more grizzled hunters brought the conversation back on track, "so far, we've tallied up, on a global scale more than a hundred fifty small towns and villages disappeared, like *Roanoke* type disappeared, except nothin' but aerator marks 'n rust instead of a word where this dark shit's come through, and satellites show it moving toward high population centers."

"And before you ask, no cops, no military, no jets deter it. At least in the states."

The younger of the brother hunters added, "we did drop an anonymous tip that fire seems to have an effect."

"Yeah," the same grizzled man butted in, "then we hear a shit load of folks and villages, not to mention military going in and setting fire to wherever it was headed, whether or not the people were evacuated! Fuckin' brilliant!"

"Collateral damage."

"Collateral damage."

"Collateral damage." Almost every human chimed in, most with air quotes.

Around the table there wasn't a face without a grimace or wince at the idea of such vicious action.

"Okay, so, everyone's checked in, the external teams are in place and under camouflage," Nick gazed in earnest into his phone's screen, "the barrier spell will," he air-quoted, "'fail', when the walls are fully exposed. That's when the usurped, and smaller vestiges will enter."

"And you'll be at the vertex waiting for them all to get inside." Tropus nodded.

591

"Exactly."

"If all goes well here, it is likely the only vestiges Terra will be forced to contend with are those stranded there once the sun-cycles have finished." Boaz nodded.

"Nicky? What about Frank?" Harry Sr. asked.

"We're still in contact," he tapped the side of his head, "he knows what I know and is relaying it to Poe and the wyverns."

"Just checkin'."

"Good."

"Alright everyone, from this point out, it's catastrophic contact to the other side ONLY!" Harry urged.

From both sides of the veil, "Good luck."

"Godspeed."

And, "Kick some ass!" Were cheered as lines of communication were closed.

Nick met eyes with each of the Heru's then turned to the Sidhe he loved, "Julius, Tierus will help you make sure everyone can handle whatever weapons they choose," He turned to Lou and shook his head, "and no we don't have any mini-guns, and you can't handle a claymore, but we do have something special you might like."

The Herus smiled in such a way Lou couldn't help but blush, wondering, "Can all of you read minds?"

"We prefer not to, but we are a long-lived people, and mortals, are more apt to see the world with newer eyes that often betray the thoughts behind them." Areen explained.

"So in other words we're like children to you?" Dylan's petulant response was all the proof required to validate her tactful evaluation.

"You have an exuberance and passion we often find refreshing."

Nick tapped Lou on the chest, "Come to the armory with me, I have an assignment for you." He turned to Julius, "it'll only take a minute then he'll meet up with you for weapons check before heading out. Shep, D, stick close to Wee, you guys watch each other's backs."

Lou opened his mouth to protest but closed it a second later, after all, if Dylan was with Wee, Lou would always know where he was.

"Nick," Wee began, "are you sure you can do this?"

"Technically, I'm the only one who can." He wrapped his arms around his uncle, one of the few unrestrained hugs he'd given anyone not Frank in the last four years, "Look, one way or the other, these parts we have to play in this... I've seen all the variations... we each gotta do what we gotta do, it's kinda that simple." His gaze flicked to Julius.

"You like him huh?"

"I've loved him since we were fledglings, and will until the end of all things."

"Whenever that may be?"

The only reply necessary was an easy smile bringing the paint over his face to a soft glow for all to see.

Lou motioned to the horizon, "Let's get on with this, sun's going down."

--

Under cover of the last rays of day, Goliath and his team glided down the tunnel to the platform on which the tower balanced as it inched along the magma flow.

As Frank saw when he and Poe were down here, this was the place they'd created to serve as a refuge and strategic center for the Herus, and leaders of all races to gather and plan their fight to stop the advancement of the dark. It was also the place where Tur's betrayal sealed the fate of this world, and the last one entangled with it.

Nine teams of four flew through the enormous cavern, enjoying the lift from the magma thermals before assuming their positions at the base of each of the chains.

At the top of the staircase, Garnet lay between the wall of the entrance and the ground, camouflaged as she watched and waited for the first domino to fall.

Nearly a mile away she could see the ripple of the wyvern youths' camouflage as they waited for her signal.

It began very quickly. Once the teams chose their chains, all Goliath had to do was give them the order.

Thirty-six acting as one, they spit their fires, acids, ices, lightning, and all their caustic agents at the bottom half link carved from the platform. They followed with claws and jaws, breaking the stone, and repeating the process layer by layer, until, as one, they stopped with the last cracks forming.

Together they flocked to the far side of the tower, from the highest point they could reach inside the cavern, halfway down the tower, they gathered, pushing, beating their wings, straining their prowess in contests of strength and endurance against one another, competing to see which of them could be the first to make the icon of schade betrayal shift its weight.

All around them, the cavern roared with encouragement, taunts, and other sounds of the wyvern language chanting a rhythm in time with their concerted efforts.

A thunderous crack, the sound not different from that of a cliff wall falling, brought another roar and another push, and another, and another, as on the surface, what few schades remained in the fortress dove into the nearest shadows, to escape the tremulous shattering of their home.

From their safe and hidden vantage, many of the youths watched in amazement as the rounded top of the tower moved, degree by degree, cutting faster through the upper crust than it had in the movement of all its millennia combined. Many of them held their eggs up and spoke to the dragons within of the miracle of the pillar of betrayal being destroyed by the strength and will of their wyvern cousins.

Her head craning up, her body inching away from her waiting position, Garnet couldn't help herself when the first schade emerged into the open. From behind it, her tongue slithered out, wrapping around the head of the surprised being. In a whip-like motion she flung it into the camouflaged area where a lucky youth caught it, snapping it in half so another of its nest mates could also have a bite.

Over and over again Garnet fed the youths on those emerging schades until beneath them the ground began to quake as if the great mother herself was rising back to life!

The tilt went from inches, to feet, to yards in a matter of seconds once Goliath and his crew managed to nudge it past the tipping point. A row of thirty-six, very self-satisfied wyverns hovered where the top of the fortress used to be.

--

Near the western gate, a tidal wave of darkness thrashed, rising up and crashing over the wall, curling like a claw, trying to tear and shred.

Almost instantly the ground began to shake. Tur, Leanna and Ne'Min felt their hearts lift for the first time in millennia. When the wave of darkness withdrew leaving the white crystalline substrate intact behind a cascade of broken orange sandstone, their joy became confusion.

Another song of joy surged through the assailing forces as another wave of rumbling vibration rippled around the outer wall, the coordinated attacks near each of the primary gates appeared to have done nothing more than expose the foundation.

"Find out where it broke!" Tur demanded, waving his hand to dismiss a quartet of pirini to scout the area.

In seconds they returned, the leader bowing on its knee in front of him, "Heru, it is not the wall but something in the forest, near your fortress." It explained.

"Go bring me word!" Tur ordered as out from around the tower itself another cascade of layers of sandstone, literally vibrated out of the honeycomb structure, rained down into the city streets.

Above them, electrical charges zipped in starburst formations through the whole of the protective field as it shrank, and finally crackled out of existence.

"Forward! Now! First wave! TAKE THE CITY!" Tur ordered as the usurped and their vestige handlers charged the gates, encountering the first line of Fierowen defense.

Lightstones and gauntlets of lightstone lit up in fits and starts.

From its new rocker platform, the light spear fired sporadic and weak bolts of illumination that frequently missed their marks, as they were supposed to.

In the armory Nick, at his actual age and physical stature, sat on the apex of the great dragon's skull. From his hair to his toes, wearing only his boxer briefs, and all but a few handfuls of the rest of the paint. His focus remained steady on the timescape, watching for the right moment. When he told them earlier if he messed with any aspect of time, in any way, he'd been more serious than any of them realized. There were three parts to his job, but he and Diagas were the only ones who knew it.

He frowned, as on the Aderyn 'scape, strange "pops" of light winked into and out of existence with a strange kind of wiggly appearance to them. *That's the mages...* he wondered looking closer.

"Uh nuh," he grunted when one of them, holding a lightstone, activated it, only to release a blast of energy very similar to the appearance of a schade inside a human meatsuit. He swallowed hard watching as it possessed the holder of the stone.

Fuck, what the fuck? A schade ghost? It's possessing them! Shit... He pulled his gaze back to where he could see as much of the landscape as possible. Stunned almost to disbelief he stroked the tail of the bud in his ear. "There are DARKSTONES, repeat, someone created DARKSTONES, schade energy inside. They gave them to the mages it's possession by schade! Be careful!"

In the background he heard voices questioning what he said and what it could mean but he broke the resonance frequency and returned to his observation, suddenly sweating buckets beneath the paint. Terrified by how this could change things.

Working hard to keep his focus, with shaking fingers he scratched a break in the seal above his lip, another on each side of the back of his neck, one at each elbow and another behind each knee. He'd never be able to do what he had to if he sweated the covering off.

He wanted to check what time it was but was afraid of doing something spontaneously or subconsciously. He knew this was not the time to test his luck. Every insecurity he had about his ability to concentrate, to control his own mind, to dare to hope there might be a future for all, came crashing through all the knowledge he'd gained from Diagas.

The confidence he'd had only a few hours ago was gone, just like his Sidhe body was gone. Once again he was just a kid, *just a screwed up little fourteen-year-old kid who doesn't know shit from shineola,* "STOP IT!" he ground between clenched teeth. "I know what I have to do, I know HOW to do it, I AM ENOUGH."

He drew a steadying breath, shoving those doubts into the same lock box under the stairs in the back of his brain where all his nightmares stayed tucked away. There was work to do, and if he was lucky, just this once... he blew the breath out and sat up straight, with his hands at his sides on the skull. He crossed his legs and let his vision encapsulate as much of the local geography as possible, he drew another breath then released it slowly, "Not yet, think bright, not yet, but bright!" and waited.

"You got this Nicky, you're okay, you can do it easy peasy." Frank's voice was a balm to the rawness left by his burst of fear.

"Miss you shrimp-o, you good now?"

"Yeah, Poe's going after pirini at the fortress, I'll remember it for you."

"Good, give 'em hell Frank! For every single one of us!"

His focus shifting back to the city within the walls, he watched as the first defense team retreated slowly, coaxing the encroaching forces toward the tower, filling every bit of space possible without letting them into the spire just yet.

Outside of the wall, between the defensive teams waiting to close the trap, the level of darkness shifted. There were fewer usurped, fewer schades, pirini, and corporeal sympathizers.

The next wave consisted of Foenwyn and dark Fae, as well as pixies, imps, and brownies, all waiting for the first wave to thin ranks on both sides before they would risk moving in. But they didn't know about Talmai and his therianthrope kin nearby. After all, most avians seemed to enjoy pixies, imps, and brownies. Foenwyn and Fae were more of an acquired taste.

Toward the Western gate, a lone shape with a small tube in his fist moved stealthily around the combatants, using a map Nick pressed into his mind, from cover to cover until he reached the backside of Tur's tent.

--

18

Between the wall and the outer tower, the most hale of the Fierowen warriors, as well trained and adept as they were, were having a surprising degree of difficulty against the schades and usurped. None of them could have foreseen the mages being possessed by schade spirits transported by corrupted lightstones, the result would mean a terrible tragedy if they managed to fight back the firdur and its allies again.

Anyone who hadn't had their lightstone in their possession since the arrival of "the" Wee, was relegated to sole use of their gauntlets. Many hearts faltered momentarily when they heard Jullius call out over their receivers, "Take him! Do NOT KILL HIM! Do not kill ANY of them! The Wee is possessed! I repeat WEE IS POSSESSED!" Those nearby froze as he grabbed Dylan by the throat of his armor, wheeling him to his younger brother who stood dazed, but struggling against Tierus' very solid hold.

"Tierus, take them to a prison cell, prepare all the cells to contain the possessed!" He ordered, then made sure he had Dylan's full attention, "Stay with him! Do Not listen to anything he says, do not let him out of your sight!" He pointed to Tierus commanding, "Nor you, either of them!"

In the few seconds it took to wrestle control of Wee from Tierus, he fought furiously, breaking Julius' nose, and nearly gouging out an eye before he was wrapped into the Captain's elbow, struggling so hard he almost took them both to the ground before succumbing to the effect of the sleeper hold Lou showed him.

He tossed the youngest of the senior Emerson's back to his fledgling guard, "Faster than ever before!" he commanded as the fledgling left Dylan struggling to keep up as he raced through the tower, down through angled corridor after angled corridor until they reached a windowless cell.

Wee, and the thing inside struggled and squirmed, nearly breaking free of Tierus' grip just as they entered the room.

"I apologize my friend," Tierus grunted and literally threw the young man into a wall, giving himself time to get out into the hallway and lock him in.

Panting hard, leaning against the wall, Dylan's eyes wide with fear he breathed, "can it get out? If it leaves him can it get out? Get somebody else?"

Tierus shook his head, "never before has this been seen. I have no way of knowing son of Oemir. We will find a way to save him. Our Elder will find a way to save them all."

"Where'd they get the damned things?" Shep's voice came over the bud.

"Tierus!" Wellyn called, "Do you recall where or who…?" He asked, through sword, spear, and shield clangs.

From nearby a growl grew more fierce as Shep was beset by several schades at once. "C'mon yousonofabitch!" He challenged with an intense and explosive volley of grunts, expletives and

601

definitive clangs which finally gave him a moment to catch his breath.

"God I love this thing!" he gasped pulling the finest sword he'd ever wielded from the three schades he'd run through, with a minimum of fuss.

With a nod, and pinching a runnel of blood from his broken nose, Julius shot him a grin before dashing off, chasing another grouping of enemy combatants.

"Damn these guys are fast," Shep grunted.

"Maybe you're just gettin' old," Dylan teased through the bud as loud, dull thumps crashed repeatedly against the cell door. "Get 'em Shep."

"Focus!" Boaz barked, his eyes drawn up along the wall of the tower where a schade was running, in all defiance of gravity, toward the front entrance.

"What the fuck?" Shep breathed, "Can these sons of bitches fly?!" he demanded.

"Almost never," Wellyn answered from his post beside the king near the main entrance to the tower, "only the most powerful may be able to rise on their own, most can only counter a small amount of what you call gravity," he was cut off with a series of blows sounding suspiciously like flesh on flesh.

"Softer landings, longer leaps." Khazeer finished just before he apparently joined his Master at arms.

"Well it's headed your way, from above!"

"What about the mage's magiks? Can they…" Shep started to ask before his breath was cut short and replaced with struggling wheezes and weak defensive sounds.

"Where are you?" Boaz called.

"Head West!" Julius ordered over the sounds of his own conflict.

When he found Shep, the older hunter was crumpled on his knees, a severed lower arm on the ground beside the severed head of a mage.

"It was poised to kill him. It had me held at bay, I had no choice." A kind faced fledgling explained as his eyes filled with tears.

"Beezle, did you see the schade leave him?" Julius asked as the youth shook his head.

Boaz helped Shep to his feet, then gave a spin to his sword slicing the head off a schade slinking through the melee toward them.

"Still as precise as ever." Julius beamed with pride.

"I had an exemplary master," tipping a sprinkle of Her blood into his palm he turned Shep, grasping his bleeding stump. "Apologies MacRoich."

"Ahfuck!" the hunter cursed, drawing a deep breath, gritting his teeth, and squeezing his eyes shut as the healing powder hit his nerves, driving his consciousness back, but not completely away.

"Take him," Julius directed Beezle, who grabbed the severed arm and the human. "It is nearly time!"

"It IS time," Khazeer's voice came over the buds, "lead them in. If you have one of the possessed bring them to the prison level!"

Foot by foot, those who had gauntlets held firdur and firdureen at bay while those with prisoners brought them inside, and the more adept warriors kept them covered as they retreated, almost ready to begin phase two.

--

"You revile his existence yet demand he constrain a battlefield ranging the entirety of the Fierowen?!" Leanna spat.

"I only wish him to hold fast Khazeer and his people, allow firdur to move as it must to destroy both the weapon and the symbol! Darkness itself will finish the rest." He turned his gaze to the child.

"Are you able to perform such a simple task or are you not?" He asked peering almost directly down into Nick Jr.'s craning face.

He didn't know what to say, he'd heard what his father told the others about touching time, that it would be the end of all things, and he knew someone was coming for him.

Tur blew out a harsh breath, "What of the battlefield does it know?" he demanded of Leanna.

Her disgruntled sneer was an expression he wasn't often subject to, "Why do you not ask HIM?"

Tur's hand leaped into the air, as if to strike her, but halted as Ne'Min rushed between them, his face flustered and filled with fear.

"What is it!?" Tur demanded.

"The fortress has fallen!" he gushed, "And something does battle with the pirini!" He turned pointing toward a blank spot in the sky where the peak of the Nahroehn fortress no longer stood above the treetops.

"What!" Tur thundered as a flash of light caught his eye, his vision finally able to make out subtle differences in shades of darkness engaged in furious aerobatics. The pirini were easy to spot for their size alone, but the other avian could not be so readily identified. It could be a night bird, an owl or something else, there was no telling.

A strand of fire whipped from the smaller avian, wrapping around one of the pirini who lost control as it's feathers burst into flame, erupting into a brilliant fireball as it spiraled out of the air then disappeared, before it hit the ground.

"What is it?" he demanded with furrowed brows and a furious scowl directed at Leanna, "I thought you said they were extinct!" his voice rose.

"They ARE, have you not seen the Bedowen?! There is little if anything left alive in my homeland! They are NO MORE!" she railed in return.

"Nicky can you hear me?"

The boy looked between the adults then fixed his gaze on the drama in the distance. *"You are not my father. You are the Oemir."*

"I am, you may be one day too."

"If mother and her consort accomplish their goal, there will be nothing and no one."

A sad sigh came before he spoke again, "I'm so sorry you already know so much."

"I am the son of my father born of the will of my mother with the knowledge of firdur, this frightens her beloved."

"Does it frighten you?" Frank asked.

"I have not lived long enough to fear no longer existing."

"Can I share something with you?"

"Yes."

"Has your mother held you?"

"Yes."

"Show me?" So he did. Sending the memory and the sensation of being held in Leanna's arms, either to be fed in those first hours of his life, or to ensure no one thought to move against him. But there was something missing even in those moments of nurture and protection. He was a prize, something to give his mother status over her concubine and Ne'Min, and the worst part about it was the knowledge of being nothing more to her.

There was a flash of something kept secret in the boy's experience, a few seconds he held deep inside, like a precious gem he feared losing if he shared it. A flash of an instant, Nick bent on one knee in front of him, and a wave of warm radiating to encompass him, making him feel something he had no experience of, but found comfortable and desirable like a blanket or resting on a soft cushion.

"That feeling…we call it belonging. Being wanted just for being you, not for what you can do." Frank explained then opened some of his own experience to the child.

Nine tiny, human years of nurturing and protection from so many people in his life left tears of sadness running down his face. The idea this young boy might never experience such feelings threatened to break his heart.

"There's a man, a human of Lugh coming for you." He breathed, focusing on what he wanted his nephew to feel. All the warmth, love and care amassed in those nine years, from all the people who'd

shared their hearts with him in so short a time.

"No matter what happens Nicky, you deserve to know that this is for you too."

Silently choking on a sensation he could not know yet as heartache, but warmed with possibility, Nicky crept backward, stealthy.

He didn't move to wipe the tears from his face, he didn't sniffle. He made no move to draw attention to himself as he lowered to all fours, crawling backward, under the tent wall where a pair of warm arms scooped him up, a gentle hand over his mouth.

"I'm here to take you to your father…" he whispered with a glint of light shooting off the coating of blue gray on his face.

The boy pointed, "They may not allow it."

In his free hand, the metal tube snicked into extension, a four foot long, dual pointed spear, almost as light as a feather twirled in the moonlight dispatching the two guards who stumbled upon them before they realized what they were seeing.

"Whatever happens, no powers okay?" Lou warned swinging the child up onto his back.

"I know."

--

Borrowing Atlas' excellent vision, Frank leaned on her shoulder, watching as Poe toyed with the pirini sent to investigate the destruction of the fortress. The Emissary's emissary was putting on an incredible show, both aerobatics and fireworks.

When they were down in the area of the magma flow, inspecting the base of the fortress, Poe hadn't appeared to be bothered by the heat at all, and here he was breathing fire! Frank couldn't help but wonder what else their magnificent friend could do, as if interdimensional travel and fire breathing weren't enough.

Taking a look around from his vantage point, Frank marveled at the stealth the therianthropes were exhibiting as, using mostly their avian forms, they joined with the owls and nightbirds, picking off nearby allies of the dark lying in wait for more of the Fierowen defenders to fall.

He smiled when, just before sunset, Atlas showed him a group approaching the eastern gate, though it appeared only Ilirya was arriving, the wyvern guardian's vision, as acute as any hawk or eagle, with the spectral range of most reptiles, including its dragon cousins, could see hundreds of small predators moving through knee high grasses. There was something familiar about how they moved, but Frank couldn't put his finger on it. He hoped he'd eventually see what they were.

As if reading his thoughts, which was undoubtedly the case, a vast array of images were shared with him, of cats. Some with spears and shields, some with elements of clothing on, but most of them "au natural" as Ry would say.

"Just like the leopard lady in the painting!" he recalled then winced as the enthusiastic youths shouted and cheered the young leader.

Looking to the east, Atlas chuffed and nodded toward the Akirowen, once more her vision serving to supplement Frank's human limitations. His heart leaped to a hard gallop and smile that felt bigger than his whole body lit up his face.

"Sunlight's coming!, it's lighting Ula's territory and heading this way!"

"Perfect! Thanks baby boy, how long till it gets here?"

"Couple hours looks like. It's almost time Nicky, can you see 'em?"

"Yep, just a little closer."

"Don't worry about stragglers, that's why we're here! You do what you gotta do."

Sitting otherwise still as a stone, working to keep every part of his mind in check, Nick allowed a small smile to break on his face, *"We're gonna get confused if you call both of us Nicky y'know."*

There was a good natured 'huff' followed by, *"Focus!"* before radio silence fell between them again.

"Focus," Nick sighed.

"Fuck Focus! Light it up kid! Light it all up!" Lou shouted, sprinting through the gate with Nicky on his back, a few lagging schades following.

He set the boy down, "Get to the tower, remember NO POWERS!" then pulled a pair of slitted eye covers to his forehead while he fought the incoming schades, his spear, glinting and fluttering as he thinned the herd coming toward him.

When the bulk of them were near enough he lowered the covers and focused on lighting the paint over his face, neck, and arms. The sudden burst of brilliance stopping the schades in their tracks, scorching them in what appeared to be agonizing slowness.

"Finally," Nick sighed dropping his own glasses over his eyes. He used memories of the same warmth and love Frank had projected to Nicky, filling himself up with all those moments he too had been gifted, even when he'd been too afraid to accept them.

It was like throwing a light switch. Behind the covers, he closed his over-sensitive eyes, but the world around him was still blinding even through his lids.

Impossibly, the brightness began to grow until his eyes rolled back into his skull and there was nothing but white all around him. Even in his imagination, there was nothing else he could see.

--

Minya gasped, clutching his heart, his face a mask of crushed wonder and bittersweet satisfaction. At his side Arabelle grasped his chin, "What is it?"

"I never got to know…" he sniffed as a wave of tears ruptured forth, streaking down his face and into her hand.

Righting himself, he held up the lightstone Wereiwyn gave him, "Lights up now!" he shouted as their camouflage fell and a line of light, at least a kilometer abreast on the wooded edge of the Fierowen, burned white, an instant before the first wave of white ran up the walls of the tower of the sun. Each wave was followed by another, and another, each coming faster and thicker until the wall and the spire were pure white, its radiance reaching out in every direction, making contact with the circle of defenders as they pushed forward, herding the second wave of firdur toward the outer wall.

Inside the tower, the first waves of Nick's light brought smiles to those fighting back-to-back in the center as the outer doors were opened and great billows of firdureen tried to escape into the structure.

By the time they descended on the heroes, Herus, and all the warriors; attempting to feast on their flesh, it was too late. The light was constant and growing brighter.

A sound echoing the first wail of awareness, cascaded through the crystalline structure, it began to vibrate with primordial cries of terror until the first of the mosquito sized creatures seized then popped, leaving a leaflet of what looked like ash to float to the floor.

"Here we go!" Lou called, dashing, blood and goop covered, to the group of warriors, scooping the child into his arms and tucking his eyes hard against him while covering his head.

As the light grew stronger throughout the tower, it crept into every corner and crevice.

From the vertex of her skull where Nick sat, feeding his light into the structure, through every tunnel and corridor the intensity grew. At the nine exterior tunnels, sealed at the outer edge of the outer wall by the great dragon's largest tears, the light filled and rose through there as well, shining for dozens of kilometers in every direction, chasing what Dark hadn't been trapped within the Fierowen, away from the tower and into retreat, where eventually it would meet with the sunlight either native to this world or borrowed from Terra.

From the remounted lightspear at the top of the tower, its radiance exploded in every direction, blazing pure brilliant white light further than any eye could see.

This is when the dragons went to work with the roaring cheers of thousands who'd thought they were gone, urging them on. They found the greatest body of Darkness and used their variety of fires, lightnings and a few of them, glows of their own, to finish driving the trapped bulk of the dark toward the tower.

--

In the center of her throne room, lit from above by the light of another sun, Ula swept tears of joy from her face. Not only was it filtering down where there should have been none, but somehow, from the very depths of her ocean, white light, the same kind as

Khazeer's tower at night, crept and pulsed through the deep, illuminating her palace, driving the encroaching dark away while her bioluminescent subjects drove it toward the aqueduct she often used to reach the Fierowen tower.

"They found a way."

--

"What you're seeing behind me is the city of Athens Greece. It's two a.m. here and this part of the world is lit up like high noon!"

On the web call and in Buck Forrester's "anti-evil fortress" raucous cheers exploded, hugs, high-fives, real and virtual cascaded in rounds as toasts were made and tears were shed.

"Earlier this evening, late yesterday depending on where you are, Athens was in the midst of a literal "black out". That same darkness that's been showing up in so many places all over the globe was here too. So impervious even the lights of the Parthenon couldn't be seen from our helicopters... but no more than ten minutes ago, it seems a new, second sun has risen on the historic city, and the darkness that enveloped it is withering!"

"Ohmygodohmygodohmygod, it worked, it fucking WORKED, it worked, It WOOOORRRRKKKKED!" Mickey shrieked leaping into Harry Sr.'s arms, then junior's then Charles' before turning to the computer screen, "Cypher you ARE A FUCKING GENIUS!" she screamed then kissed the screen and even turned to give Vahl the biggest and possibly only other hug he'd ever received in his life.

"Trading daytime man, theirs for ours and back again..." Harry jr. leaned into the screen, "she's right man, you ARE a fuckin' genius!"

On the screen, the older of the hunter brothers raised a toast,

"I'm thinking even a particular MIT Badass we knew would agree man. Two worlds saved by math, who knew huh?"

"Universes."

"Whatever."

The younger of the two fingered moisture from the corners of his eyes, returning the toast. "To Cypher, two worlds!"

"Universes."

"Whatever."

Everyone joined in, whether on the computer or in the house, toasts were raised and World War Win level cheers could be heard out on the street all day and into the night, each time another news story told of the mysterious rise of what appeared to be a second sun managed to burn away the mysterious, invasive darkness all over the world.

--

"Do it Nicky, it's starting to fight back." Frank urged as out of a glowing river of orange-yellow where the schade fortress once stood, what looked like a fountain erupted into the air, at first tiny glowing bits flew into the air, or raced, waddling across the land. Those in the sky began spinning with uncertainty until their wyvern guardians rose high above, catching their attention with calls of encouragement.

They circled the area shooting their specialties, fire, electricity, poisons, acids and whatever was in their makeup. Teaching through example as the newly hatched dragons, each no bigger than a medium sized dog, got control of their wings, or for those without wings, their legs. They also began to puff, and to huff, some sputtering, some sparking, but all of them exuding a palpable joy as

613

they learned what it felt like to be alive.

"It's beautiful Nicky, I'll save it for both of you."

At the Fierowen lands, the blinding brilliance of the entire tower and wall, lit up and radiating an intensity of light to make the sun look weak, began to sputter. The cycles of radiance slowed back down to bands.

Converging on the Fierowen from every direction, dragons, new hatchlings, and every wyvern descended on the vestiges, leaving the Dark itself alone. It was the intelligence behind the birth of the vestiges and firdureen, this was what wanted to destroy all life. And there was no way to destroy it.

Outside the wall, the Dark stopped trying to retreat, in fact its attention swung toward the tower. The dragons and wyverns who'd been working to keep it close slowly started to back off as they too grew mesmerized by this brand-new sight.

With the struggles against the dark waning, those defenders outside the wall cast questioning glances at one another.

Several Felesians trotted through the ranks telling everyone they could to, "Shift if you can!"

"That cat just talked," Minya whispered out the side of his mouth to Janelle.

"She is a Felesians, many of them live between worlds and can speak several languages of your kind."

"Note to self, feed the stray cats." He nodded then asked, "Why shift? Can't you see blacklight? How the hell is he doing that?" he then wondered, grinning as those who couldn't see the UV light, but only its effects, marveled at how everything seemed to glow in a way few of them had ever seen so prominently.

"Look at the dark." Fern elbowed him.

A moment later, he not only noticed the dark, but many of the others, particularly those who were able to see the UV and not just its effects, seemed to be enthralled by it. Many of them rocking as if in time to a song or rhythm only they could see or hear.

Inside the city, the fighting stopped. Just as the ground was outside, the inside floor was covered in a dusting of firdureen ash. The last of the dark were the vestiges, if any of them remained outside, and the Dark itself.

"What're you doin' kid?" Lou muttered looking at Shep who shrugged.

A memory burst to the forefront of his mind, the day after he met the kids and Harry, when they went back, the day they helped him save Rose. Frank led them into the woods, a flashlight in one hand and a few slips of colored plastic in the other, Frank pointing the colored light at the schades they saw, without their knowing.

"Light filters," he sighed, "I'll be goddamned! Fucking LIGHT filters!"

Shep's brows furrowed, "look around kid, it's black...light..." he stammered as it dawned on him too.

"The dark," Lou bit his lips as he remembered it climbing through the veins of Nick's arms, and up the sides of his neck when he killed the vestige that nearly, well technically, had killed Julius. "it's in him...oh sweet Jesus what the hell's he gonna do?" he gasped as if he'd just run a five-minute mile.

"He will do what he must," Julius dropped his good hand on their companion's shoulder, before offering it with a smile, to the child.

615

"Did you know about this?" Lou barked.

Julius' smile trembled, "The king need not explain his plans to me."

Reading the look of desperation on the garage owner's face all too easily, Shep grasped his forearm. "You can't. WE can't. Whatever he's doing, it has to be done."

"You gonna quote Spock me t'me now?" Lou groused.

"If you're askin' I'm guessin' I don't need to." He looked around to Khazeer, Areen and Wellyn, "What do we do now? Do you know what he's planning? What he's gonna do?"

The shakes of their heads were reluctant, "He helped us to make our plans, never revealing he had his own." Areen explained.

--

In memory, Julius' voice comforted him, "this has been inevitable since the first spark came into existence, search the first of all your lives, you know the history better than any of us…"

"So wise my love," he breathed, turning his memory then to the journey through which Diagas guided him to the answers he required.

"What is the first law of magic?" the dragon asked after Tropus and Boaz left the warren.

"The law of names. To know the name of something is the first step in understanding if not mastering it."

The dragon's smile was indulgent, "look into the memory of the great mother, daughter of Nyx, and learn what we know of the first consciousness in existence."

Just as he'd channeled all the love he'd ever felt through this life earlier, now, he let his uncertainties, fears, and the suppressed rage of three thousand years of ruined lifetimes loose. The dark Ne'Min and his cronies had spent so much time trying to infuse into him while he was their captive was about to serve a purpose far from whatever they'd intended.

"Erebus," he breathed, "join me." He envisioned a swath of this primordial being wrapping around the tower and following the UV rings down to their origin until it met him at the vertex of the great mother's skull.

From outside the wall, those who were not devouring or destroying the vestiges, watched in fearful amazement as a mass of dark did exactly what Nick envisioned.

At the vertex, the first primordial god emerged, slowly, almost tentative, it twined itself around the alluring, dark glowing boy. It sensed the similarity of its own essence. He knew dark, and maybe even understood it.

"It's okay," he whispered, "you know me, you're part of me."

When enough of itself filled the room, it finished wrapping around him. "Come into me," he invited. And it did.

19

All was void.

T here was nothing in existence. Nothing to move or to take up space. There was no breath because there was no air because there was nothing to require it. There was no color, there was no light, there was nothing to reflect or refract the light which did not exist.

It didn't know if it awoke, there was no sleep for it to awaken from.

It only knew that, it noticed, and it noticed that it noticed.

It continued this way for what temporary things would eventually call eons.

It accepted noticing as all there was, it was all it had ever known, but whether it was a thought, or the happening that happened first, it didn't know.

In a language some creatures would eventually speak, the word attached to the idea that seemed to 'pop' into its awareness was, "Else?" Then there it was.

In the presence of this tiny, new thing, barely able to be

recognized as "different". It, became First. There was an "else" now, and it too was aware.

Eventually, this new thing began to be different. It grew, and as it grew, so did First.

Through uncountable eons it was Else and First, they grew, they changed, they danced becoming one before returning to themselves, and in time, they shared a new idea, this one, "other?"

And suddenly there was.

More eons passed with First and Else wondering what "other" wonders they could bring into existence. There was light, and with light came new things neither of them knew could happen. Their creation had created something of its own. It created ripples in what was once Void, those ripples might have wondered "what if?" before becoming tiny self-contained packets of energy.

Before long, their creations were creating their own creations, with First and Else marveling together at what they brought about.

With the filling of void, with growth and change, First and Else created a way to mark these new things, it started as "before" and "after", but eventually became called Time.

During their travels through the seemingly endless expanse, watching lights, atoms, molecules, and all manner of energy creating their own, First and Else came upon something that stopped them. It held them mystified as they watched, in a tiny, distant corner of all there was, something great was born from one of their creations' creations.

Something had learned to create universes.

In those rapidly expanding universes came tiny creatures, over and over and over again until some of them stayed, at least longer than most of the others.

It was these creatures who were born with the knowledge of the beginning of all things, and they who taught their own offspring of the need to honor First, which they named Erebus, the primordial god of darkness, and his sister Else who they named Nyx, the goddess of night.

--

Nick gasped, choking as if he'd been without breath for those eons of shared knowledge. There was a sensation running through him, reminding him of, not quite gratitude, but something similar, as if Erebus was glad someone understood its beginning.

Then, the God of Darkness took over, unaware, and some would argue, uncaring of the fragility of its host.

Maybe it was relieved, maybe it was vengeful, maybe it was both, but there was another sensation under all the conflict and chaos Nick sensed but almost couldn't believe he was reading right. It was almost a kind of loneliness.

There was a deeper part of him, the deepest part, understanding to the most miniscule degree, what it might mean to be the first consciousness in existence where there was nothing other than it. The idea itself was almost beyond fathoming. Except he'd felt it. There was acceptance because acceptance was all there could be, but after Erebus brought Nyx into existence and learned what it meant to have "Else", everything changed. Neither of them knew it, or understood as they created the structures of existence, but they created another thing too, they created fear, they just didn't know it right away.

As far as Nick was aware, Erebus was the only one who felt it, who felt lost without his other half. It was alone, even amidst all the lives, universes, and worlds they'd wrought, the eons of creations, could not replace the loss of what Erebus knew to be its other half. She was the only 'other' who knew Void, who knew a time when there was only the three of them, and the only other "thing" to exist at all, would eventually be called "potential".

Existence, their creation had become so big, so full, that Nyx, always before at his side, a part of him, was now often gone, to some place, he knew not where. His fear became rage and hatred for all the things drawing her away and keeping her from him, and he would not stop until he had his Nyx and Void back. Nothing else mattered. And so, in rage and despair, he began to shatter creation wherever he found it.

Captive of Erebus, raging through the universes existing inside his mind because they existed outside his mind, Nick began to wonder if he'd done the right thing. Nebulae were destroyed, obliterated out of existence, stars of every kind, smothered out of existence, planets with the building blocks of life winked out of existence, the destruction of even the subatomic energy signals that once defined them, gone. All that was left in the wake of each piece of destruction was void. But it wasn't.

Unbeknownst to Erebus, the creation they'd wrought became self-perpetuating, every time he crushed something out of existence, the void left in its wake became fertile ground for something new to come into existence. *An eternal game of whack-a-mole,* Nick thought. He had to get Erebus' attention back.

He tried to stop it, to slow it down, to cool the heat of its despair, but it had hold of him, it flung him, racing him back through the building of the universes, straining against the will of all other existing things, to continue.

"Stop!" Nick gasped as he got the first inkling there might be something wrong with his body.

--

"It's been four days! How is he even still alive?" Lou breathed, back to working on the hangnail he couldn't seem to get rid of. He waved his hand toward the barely living mummy on the bed, "how does anyone survive that?"

Shep thrust a sharp elbow into his side motioning to Nicky who sat playing on a phone.

"He knows." Lou groused a little more subdued.

Without looking up, Nicky nodded but oddly said nothing, aloud.

Minya stepped forward ruffing the little one's hair then dropped a light hand on Lou's shoulder, "how did I survive their slab for eighteen years?" he looked at the grinning, happy, different version of his little brother Harry made possible, "Took Frank to set me free."

"Not to mention getting pureed in a friggin' interdimensional vortex." Harry Sr. added. "Dumbass."

"Aw shut up man, the way had to be cleared and you know it."

"Mm, damned 20/20 hindsight." Harry turned to Frank, "any idea what's goin' on in there?"

Frank and Nicky jr. exchanged looks, "eternity?"

"Eternity." They said together.

The click of the door latch rang like a shot through the room as Dylan craned his head in.

"Hey, how's the Wee?" Minya asked, waving him in with a smile as Arabelle elbowed him smiling with good humor despite the protein synthesis covering her neck and half her face.

"Resting, Ry's helping him through it." He squatted in front of Nicky Jr, his hands on his knees, gazing into the gold/amber eyes that were the most different thing between his father and him. Everything else proved he was undoubtedly born of his father's soul. The one he hadn't been aware of having at the time. "Did I thank you for saving my brother?"

The enigmatic boy tilted a shy smile at the man. Given what he knew the older man had seen happening to his little brother, and the vantage from which he'd seen it happen, Nicky couldn't find it within himself to hold a grudge. After all, Lou and Julius protected him as he drew schade essence from his great-uncle once the dragons and wyverns signaled the completeness of Dark's disappearance from the outside world.

"I'm sorry about your mother," D offered, his hand hovering halfway toward the boy, wanting to give comfort, but not comfortable even offering it let alone giving it.

The boy's head dropped down, his gaze at the floor. "Her crimes were unforgivable." He raised his eyes to look from Dylan to Frank who wrapped his arm around his nephew, "I hurt without her."

Frank dropped his forehead to the boy's temple, "We all know how that feels, way too well." He shook his head in answer to his nephew's unspoken question, "no, not really, you just kinda get used to it."

Ilirya knelt before him, a gentle stroke to his cheek, "We are kin, we are all your family, though I am grateful Zu spared your grandfather."

"I heard Diagas stood up for him?" Shep asked, his good arm

around Ula's waist, the other, with its reattached forearm still wrapped tight and held in a sling.

"There was no evidence he took part or even knew of what she'd done to maintain the verdant pretense of the landscape."

"Nicky must've," Frank started then smiled at the youth, "Nick, must've sensed it after he caught me. That must've been why he brought us back to Terra to take me to the hospital." He craned his head to look into Ilirya's eyes, "Speaking of hospital, how are Raziel and Kieren?"

"I am pleased to say their injuries were minimal." She smiled, "What of your half-breed? Will she be in attendance? We heard her gifts were instrumental to the days of the twin suns."

"Truly, it has been millennia since we had so many humans on Aderyn, it brings to memory so many times of our youth." Julius sighed, laying his heavily bandaged hand atop Nick's head before leaning down to kiss his unresponsive lips. "Come back to me meleth, like you promised."

Ilirya dropped her hand to his shoulder, "If he is at all able, he will."

"I think Mickey said she and her mom were gonna come once her mom got off work." Shep answered.

"Her MOM!?" Lou goggled.

"From what I heard," Harry Sr. piped up, "she wants to go to some town called Sedalia to learn how to grow her powers. The place is a magnet for supernatural f-uppery, one of the witches who helped stabilize the portals is like some big wig in the wiccan world."

"Say that ten times fast," Dylan snarked, grinning as both Nicky and Frank started to do just that.

"I thought she was all Nick, all the time?" Shep asked.

"Now don't quote me on this, but I'm pretty sure I heard her tellin' Harry junior maybe it was time to take a new direction instead of repeating the past again."

"There does seem to be quite a bit of that amongst the survivors," Ilirya smiled, "even among the other species, there is a feeling of new beginnings, as if a long curse has been lifted."

"Kinda has don't cha think?" Frank nodded as did the others.

--

"It WILL NOT WORK!" Nick strained, pitting his will against that of the primordial god. "What you un-do, will only come to be again, as it MUST!"

The amorphous being slammed into him, filling his mind with its experience of the timescape, pushing backward, back to the beginning it craved.

"Erebus! SEE WHAT I SEE!" he demanded, forcing the greatest piece of knowledge Diagas gave him into his mind. On the 'scape, he envisioned a place, it didn't matter where they might currently be.

"Look around! SEE WHAT I SEE!" he demanded again pulling the 'scape under and behind them, ensuring the being knew which direction time was moving.

All around them, little by little, space sprawled out, the distance between creations grew greater and greater, the spaces between them swirled with the same dark energy Nick used to attract its attention. He nodded, "look…" he waved his hand, slowing their movement forward.

"Time is *my* gift," he began and felt himself being squeezed by the furious swirling energy as it cut off his air. "YOU CREATED IT!" he choked, gasping as it loosened its grip just enough for him to continue. "You and Nyx, you created the before and after because you were losing track of your creations, from those two points YOU created the measures of TIME! It started from two points, the moment you were in, to the next moment to come, YOUR PERCEPTION made the rules! You CAN'T GO BACK to the beginning! You can't because you didn't make it so you could. But there *is* another way."

It released him, its attention focused on the 'scape around them as he pushed it forward, eon by eon, creating more space between the universes and everything within them.

"Nothing can last forever. Not even you, not Nyx, not your creations, eternity only exists because there's nothing yet to mark the end. Your pain, your grief, your loneliness FEELS like eternity because you know when it began but don't know when it's going to end! But I have been to the end of all things! I know where she is along the way and can take you to her, and I can return you to a new Void." He dangled the carrot, pushing the 'scape even further, until the very last thing of all their creations slipped from sight.

Every direction they looked, was the primordial god's precious Void. Its rage flared, grasping, and squeezing until Nick was almost certain he was about to be crushed out of existence.

"She... will... come..." he gasped, "she must..." he flicked his gaze to a swirling mass of slightly different darkness, "she is part of us." He knew the sparklers going off were inside his mind because when he opened his mind's eye, there was only Erebus, Void, and finally Nyx, racing toward her other half, swirling around him, wrapping him to her and twirling through the emptiness that was

626

once again all theirs.

An elegant swirling dance of devotion and joyful wholeness, in the ballroom of eternity, returned to existence just for them.

Knowing he would've been feeling a smile to stretch his entire face, he swam in relief, and leaving the pair to themselves, let go.

--

"Awake my son."

"Mmom?" he cracked his eyes open, "mm had the dream again." The curtains billowed with a breeze, sunlight aiming right at his eyes.

"Which one?" she asked, the bed dipping as she sat, her hand cool on his sleep-hot forehead.

"Flying through the stars," he smiled rolling his head deeper into her hand.

"Oooh the good one!" her voice returned his smile. "Ah Well, it may not be through the stars, but if you awake now, perhaps one of the dragons or wyverns will take you for a flight."

His eyes burst wide open to a magnificent storm of riotous burgundy curls half hiding an enigmatic smile. A squawk at the foot of the bed drew his attention just before the raven launched to him, landed on his outstretched legs, and cocked its head at him as if to say, "Well?"

"Poe?" he ran his finger down the bird's breast, "Mother, Danu."

She cocked her head to the side, the single eyebrow he could see arched deep into the tumult of her waves

"Am I dead? Did I die? I mean finally *really* die?" he asked as Poe hopped to his shoulder and he swung his feet off the bed, pushing up to go to the window. "I almost expected to hear a lawn mower, god it's a beautiful day! It's… perfect. Too perfect to be real?"

She moved to his side, sweeping him into her embrace, squeezing him gently against her curves, "No love. Not dead, merely… as the mortals say, 'sleeping in'."

In the distance, as if from far down the street he could hear the first calls of a pulsing siren.

"You see the glory of the day out there?"

"Uh huh?" he nodded as she sat once more on the edge of the bed, drawing him to stand before her.

"This day is for you, a 'special order'."

"Whaddya mean? Why?" his lips pursed and eyes squinched with suspicion.

"What does each day bring?" she asked, Poe hopping from his shoulder to hers.

"Another…" he stopped as it dawned in his mind, "a new beginning." He nodded.

"Exactly, and you my son have helped ensure countless new beginnings for all living things."

His shoulders slumped and head bowed down, his voice soft with a hint of defeat. "But I've been to the end of all things…"

"Yes," she gave a tender stroke to his cheek, "all things must end, but even when fate itself decreed they must, they did not. And that is largely because of you. One day, all things will end, but that day is NOT today. You have fulfilled your oath to avenge our sister worlds and all those who suffered or died in the grip of madness.

Today, is made to welcome you to YOUR life, it is yours to make of it what you will, a precious thing delayed for too long."

She rose to stand before him, her finger under his chin, "Go live it with all the trials and triumphs you've been awaiting."

As her lips touched his forehead he closed his eyes and felt his body take a breath. The first, it seemed, in several millennia.

--

2 Months Later – Terra

Keeping his rump firmly pressed to the brick and cement community entrance marker, Nick leaned forward, his smile bright and welcoming despite his frail appearance.

"Well, I'm happy you're keeping the case open, but I'm sorry we couldn't give you anything else about the guy who did it. If we run across him, we'll call you ASAP."

"Good man." Both detectives waved and nodded before pulling away from the curb.

Already worn out, the older boy, locked into looking nearly twenty until his actual time caught up, leaned back as Frank hopped to the top ledge, kicking his feet against the bricks while Nick tried to recover.

"S'a good thing Mickey got that "satisfaction" spell from Bev." Frank grinned.

"Yeah, how did she say it worked?"

"She said, if there's evidence pointing to a reasonable conclusion, they'd be satisfied. Sure seems like it worked."

Nick patted his little brother on the knee. "Yeah, what day is it?"

Frank looked at the wristwatch he'd taken to wearing, "You made it almost fifteen minutes this time."

"At least I know what century it is."

"Can you find what year it is?"

Nick cast a sly side eye, "I'll tell you when we get back and I can look at the calendar."

With a chuckle Frank nodded, "It's Thursday. What happens on Thursdays?"

Nick closed his eyes, his lips lemon puckered as he tried to remember. "Tuesday and Thursday, Shep manages Lou's shop while he trains with Wellyn. When he's done, he goes over...for... for...therapy when Lou comes back."

"Good, what else?"

"Ry... Ry goes across too; he's almost done though."

"Well, he doesn't have re-learn how to use a reattached arm." Frank smiled.

A moment later, after fully catching his breath Nick met Frank's eyes, "Is it just me or does getting back to "normal" feel really weird?"

Wise beyond his years Frank cocked an eyebrow, dropping a hand on his big brother's shoulder, "Nick, we haven't had anything resembling any kind of 'normal' since before dad was killed. That's almost seven years. Literally half your life and..." he frowned trying to do some math in his head.

"Just say seven ninths, it's easier."

"Seven ninths of mine! Definitely easier, thanks." He hopped down. "You ready?"

Nick gave a nod, pushing off the brick and taking a steadying breath. He looked up the gentle grade leading to their street and shook his head.

"Besides," Frank started, "Harry's got a girlfriend! How is THAT normal?"

"Junior's back in school."

"So's senior... Miss Robinson..."

"Coo coo kachoo," Nick added.

"Yeah, what does that mean anyway?"

"I think it means he REEEAAALLLY likes her," he snarked. "Well, at least it's not grammar school. Still, goin' for a degree man, who'da thunk it?"

Frank's head was bobbing, "In social work, it's not like it isn't what he's been doing for almost twenty years anyway."

"Yeah, but now he can get paid for it." Nick sighed, stopped, and bent over, clutching his knees while he caught his breath. "I'm glad Charles decided to take the pre-req's for community college. You know where he wants to get into?" he asked.

"School wise? Nuh uh." Frank patted him on the back and lent his shoulder as Nick pushed himself straight up again.

"I don't know about school, but he wants to get into The Center for Missing and Exploited Children, how awesome would that be for him?"

"And for kids! With his eye for detail," he leaned in close to Nick's ear, "I heard 'em tell Harry that guy Ezra's place was cleaned so good there wasn't any but his own skin cells there!"

He grabbed Nick's hands and started urging him up the rest of the rise. "Come on, we gotta get stuff ready."

"Who's coming through?"

"Wellyn, Julius and Lou of course, maybe Ilirya too, she wasn't sure."

"Cool. What're we showing 'em?"

"What do you think? You OWE me a marathon, and until our books get here... Ry ordered 'em yesterday by the way, so we get the weekend at least, we gotta enjoy what time we're gettin'."

"And you're not tired of magic?"

Frank stopped, cocking his head to the side, "it's in our blood, how can we get tired of it?"

"Fair point," he smiled and with a small burst of energy lurched a few steps further until he reached the crosswalk, stopping when he saw Harry senior's "new" used car in the driveway. Grinning he grasped the street sign, holding onto it for just a moment as Frank raced past, then stopped in mid stride, "Hey! No powers!" then was released with a smile. At the front door he waved Nick forward, "C'mon let's go see what they got for Nicky!"

Cut a guy some slack, I've been to the end of all things... he thought with a chuckle as Frank turned back, "Yeah, but that's not today!"

End.

Thank you for taking time to join us on this adventure.

Reviews are the lifeblood of any author's existence. If you found anything worth reviewing in this series, I would deeply appreciate hearing from you either on Amazon, or wherever you leave reviews.

Remember 10% of all book sales go to The Trevor Project and ItGetsBetter.org.

Now, in the words of Danu, "Today, is made to welcome you to YOUR life, it is yours to make of it what you will, a precious thing…"

GRATITUDE

First gratitude goes to you, the reader, the traveler who joined us on this adventure. You have my deepest thanks.

Amanda Martin, and our publishing and promotions team, such a dedicated group of talented allies I only ever dreamed of having before. Thank you for all you've all done to make Nick and Frankie's odyssey finish coming into existence.

Barbara Lee Carlton, who started my love of reading, leading by example. I miss you mom.

Jodi Gil... I don't have the words other than Thank You, and I'll always be older than you. You've made my life so wonderful in more ways than you'll ever know.

Kat W Svendsen – You keep me as sane as I am, and you've always got positive and pragmatic input! Definitely always needed and appreciated!

And of course, tremendous thanks to my SPN FANily.

Last but not least, Krip, Kast, and Krew... Boys...Sam and Dean, the living embodiments of perseverance. Carry on you wayward sons.

TikTok: @jacarltonauthor

Instagram: Instagram.com/jilla.carlton

Twitter/X: twitter.com/jillacarlton

YouTube: @jacarltonauthor

Contact: info@authorjacarlton.com

Made in United States
North Haven, CT
29 December 2025

83859958R00349